10/10

The
Vanishing
of
Katharina Linden

The Vanishing of Katharina Linden

A NOVEL

HELEN GRANT

DELACORTE PRESS

NEW YORK

Published in the United States by Delacorte Press, an imprint of The Random House Publishing Group, a division of Random House, Inc., New York.

DELACORTE PRESS is a registered trademark of Random House, Inc., and the colophon is a trademark of Random House, Inc.

Originally published in hardcover in the United Kingdom by Penguin Books, an imprint of the Penguin Group, a division of Penguin Books Ltd., London, in 2009.

Library of Congress Cataloging-in-Publication Data

Grant, Helen
The vanishing of Katharina Linden: a novel / Helen Grant.
p. cm.
ISBN 978-0-385-34417-3
eBook ISBN 978-0-440-33961-8
1. Missing children—Fiction. 2. Missing persons—Investigation—Fiction.
I. Title.
PR6107.R368V36 2010
823'.92—dc22
2010003415

Printed in the United States of America on acid-free paper

www.bantamdell.com

2 4 6 8 9 7 5 3 1

First Edition

Book design by Caroline Cunningham

For Gordon

The
Vanishing
of
Katharina Linden

Chapter One

My life might have been so different, had I not been known as the girl whose grandmother exploded. And had I not been born in Bad Münstereifel. If we had lived in the city—well, I'm not saying the event would have gone unnoticed, but the fuss would probably only have lasted a week before public interest moved elsewhere. Besides, in a city you are anonymous; the chances of being picked out as Kristel Kolvenbach's granddaughter would be virtually zero. But in a small town—well, small towns everywhere are rife with gossip, but in Germany they raise it to an art form.

I remember my hometown as a place with a powerful sense of community, which was sometimes comforting and sometimes stifling. The passing of the seasons was marked by festivals that the whole town attended: Karneval in February, the cherry fair in the summer, the St. Martin's Day procession in November. At each one I saw the same faces: our neighbors from the Heisterbacher Strasse, the parents who gathered at the school gate every lunchtime, the ladies who served in the local bakery. If my family went out to dinner in the evening we were quite likely to be served by the woman my mother had chatted to in the post office that morning, and at the next table would be the family from across the street. It would take real ingenuity to keep anything secret in a place like that—or so everyone thought.

Looking back on that year, those were innocent days; a time when my mother cheerfully allowed me at the tender age of ten to roam the town unsupervised—a time when parents let their children out to play without once entertaining the horrific notion that they might not return home again.

That came later, of course. My own problems began with my grandmother's death. A sensation at the time, it should by rights have been forgotten when the true horrors of the following year unfolded. But when it became clear that some malevolent force was at work in the town, public opinion looked back and marked Oma Kristel's death as the harbinger of doom. A Sign.

What was really unfair about the whole thing was that Oma Kristel hadn't so much exploded as spontaneously combusted. But Gossip is Baron Münchhausen's little sister, and never lets the truth get in the way of a good story. To hear the tale retold on the streets of Bad Münstereifel, and especially in the playground of the *Grundschule,* which I was attending at the time, you would have thought my grandmother went off like a blaze in a Chinese fireworks factory, filling the air with cracks and pops and dazzling flares of colored light. But I was there; I saw it happen with my own eyes.

Chapter Two

I t was Sunday, December 20, 1998, a date that will be forever marked in my mental history. The last Sunday before Christmas, the day we were to light the last candle on the Advent crown, the last day of my grandmother's life, and, as it turned out, the last time the Kolvenbach family would ever celebrate Advent.

My mother, who at that time was one of only three British citizens living in Bad Münstereifel, had never quite come to grips with German Christmas customs. She usually forgot about the Advent crown until the first Sunday was upon us and the only ones left were tatty lopsided efforts stacked up outside the supermarket on the edge of town. This year's crown was a sad-looking affair with four improbable blue candles squatting uncomfortably on a ring of artificial greenery. Oma Kristel took one look and marched off to get a proper one.

The one she bought was a beauty: a big coronet of dark green foliage interwoven with crimson and gold ribbons and decorated with tiny Christmas baubles. Oma Kristel carried it into our dining room as ceremoniously as though it had been a jar of frankincense for the infant Jesus Himself, and set it down in the middle of the table. My mother's crown, with the unseasonal blue candles, was relegated to the sideboard and eventually, still unlit, to the trash. If my mother had any opinion about this, she did not express it other than by a slight tightening of the upper lip.

That Sunday a special dinner was being planned. As well as Oma Kristel, we were also expecting my father's brother Onkel Thomas, Tante Britta, and my cousins Michel and Simon, who had all traveled down from Hannover. My mother, who normally had a robust attitude toward German housekeeping, had worked herself up into a state of frenzy over the cooking and cleaning. Our house was one of those old traditional Eifel houses, constructed of a kind of half-timbering called *fachwerk;* wildly picturesque to look at, such buildings are low and dark inside, with tiny windows that admit only the stingiest amount of daylight and make the cleanest rooms look dingy.

The menu proved to be an equal source of stress; Onkel Thomas was a man of very plain tastes and would as soon have thought of eating witchetty grubs as something non-German. My mother tormented my father a little beforehand with threats to serve up curry and chips, but in the end the prospect of Onkel Thomas pushing the dinner around the plate with a fork like a pathologist investigating a stool sample was simply too much. She determined to make *Gänsebraten,* roast goose with a stuffing of *Leberwurst,* muttering, "Anything with *Leberwurst* in it is sure to be a hit with Thomas and Britta."

While my mother was putting the finishing touches to the goose, and my father was uncorking the wine, Onkel Thomas and his family arrived. Onkel Thomas almost blotted out the light as he came through the front door, his shoulders filling the frame. Tante Britta, a tiny woman with sticklike limbs and a birdlike swiftness in her manner, followed him, and behind her came Michel and Simon.

In Germany, it is considered proper that a child should go and shake hands when meeting someone; I hated doing this, and hung back, but Oma Kristel pushed me forward with a well-timed poke in the back. Reluctantly, I held out my hand to Onkel Thomas, who enfolded it in his enormous fleshy paw.

"Hallo, Pia."

"Hallo, Onkel Thomas," I replied dutifully, willing him to let go of my hand so I could wipe my fingers surreptitiously on the leg of my trousers; Onkel Thomas always had clammy hands.

"You've got bigger," he commented in his hearty way.

"Um-hmm," I murmured, then with sudden inspiration, "I must go and help Mama in the kitchen."

With some relief I escaped into the kitchen, where condensation was running down the tiny windowpanes and my mother was moving about frantically through the steam with rather the effect of someone stoking the boiler in the engine room of a steamship. She fixed me with a steely gaze.

"Out," was all she said.

"Mama, Onkel Thomas and Tante Britta are here."

"Oh, God," was my mother's encouraging remark. She shooed me out of the kitchen and back into the living room, where I discovered Michel eating the last of the chocolates that St. Nicholas had brought me on December 6. The ensuing rumpus lasted until dinner was ready, and my mother emerged from the kitchen with a harried expression to tell us that we could take our places at the table. She regarded Michel's red face, blotchy with crying, and her upper lip tightened again, but she said nothing. Discretion is the better part of valor; she went back into the kitchen and finished carving the goose.

The moment my mother announced that dinner would be imminently on the table, everyone rushed to the bathroom, Oma Kristel included. Managing without a last-minute cosmetic repair job was simply not an option with Oma Kristel, whose one overriding vice was vanity. None of us had ever seen Oma Kristel without makeup, or with her hair au naturel; the latter was always set and sprayed into a sort of glistening silver helmet.

Today the hairdo had wilted slightly because Oma Kristel had been into the kitchen several times to dispense advice about the making of glazed peaches to go with the roast. She therefore took an enormous can of hairspray like some sort of torpedo into the bathroom with her, as well as her bulging bag filled with expensive lipsticks and industrial-strength wrinkle removers.

Oma Kristel looked good that day, as my father, Wolfgang, and his brother Thomas lugubriously agreed at the funeral. Always careful with her diet, she had retained an elegant figure right into her old age, with slim legs encased in sheer stockings and fashionable little black leather shoes with high insteps and pointy toes. She wore a skirt of some velvety black material, unsuitably tight and undeniably chic, and a shocking pink mohair sweater cinched at the waist with a thin black belt. To her bosom, which still had a jutting appearance reminiscent of a wartime pinup, she had attached a large diamanté brooch like a medal pinned to a uniform. I like to think that, as she took her final look at herself in the big bathroom mirror, she was satisfied with what she saw.

At any rate, she spent some time touching up her makeup, so that my mother was actually putting the plates on the table before Oma Kristel got to the hairspraying bit.

"Oma Kristel!" my mother called in a tentative voice, not liking to adopt too strident a tone toward her strong-minded mother-in-law.

"Mama!" bellowed Onkel Thomas, who was less sensitive on such topics, and who was no doubt looking forward to gorging himself on the goose and *Leberwurst*.

Oma Kristel patted her hair into place, and then sprayed it with the dedication of a car mechanic giving a BMW a paint job. She managed to frost her bosom and shoulders with the stuff too, until the pink mohair was glistening with tiny droplets and there was a fog of hairspray hanging over her. Then she put the can back into her bag and marched straight to the table.

The main lights were out and my father was standing ready with the box of matches poised to light the Advent crown. Oma Kristel just shot him a look that said "Who's in charge here?" and stretched out her hand for the matches. She slid open the box, extracted a match, and struck it with a flourish.

The flame flared up in the gloom of the unlit room, a tiny golden beacon. For a moment Oma Kristel held it aloft, then the unthinkable happened. The match slipped out of her fingers and fell straight onto her pink mohair bosom. With a *whooomph!* like the sound of a gas furnace firing up, the hairspray with which Oma Kristel had doused herself ignited, obliterating her in a column of flames.

For one ghastly and endless second there was silence, and then all hell broke loose. Tante Britta let out a full-blooded horror-film scream, pressing her hands to her face. There was a crash as my father floundered around in a tangle of chairs, trying to lay hands on something that would douse the flames. Onkel Thomas, struggling to take off his jacket to wrap around the blazing figure, was swearing mindlessly, his eyes round with horror. Both Michel and Simon were howling with terror. I think I was in the same state myself; for days afterward my throat was hoarse with screeching. My mother, who had just come through from the kitchen with the roast goose in her oven-gloved hands, dropped the whole thing on the quarry-tiled floor, where it exploded on impact.

Only Sebastian in his high chair remained unmoved by the whole thing, apparently under the impression that this was part of the normal Advent entertainment. The rest of us panicked. And then at last with a horrid finality Oma Kristel pitched forward onto the dinner table in an explosion of shattered wineglasses and broken crockery.

My father and Onkel Thomas finally sprang into action; my father upended a jug of mineral water over Oma Kristel's smoking remains, and Onkel Thomas spread over the whole mess the jacket he had finally managed to remove. It was too late for Oma Kristel, however; she was *mouse-dead,* as the Germans say. The shock had stopped her heart with the finesse of a sledgehammer smashing a carriage clock. Her still elegantly shod legs akimbo, she looked like a shopwindow mannequin, and not like Oma Kristel at all. In the silence that followed, Sebastian at last began to cry.

Chapter Three

I think that's what attracted me to the story of Unshockable Hans, the intrepid miller who was supposed to have lived in the Eschweiler Tal, the valley to the north of the town. If you believed all the local legends, that valley had to be the most haunted place on earth—it was simply chock-full of ghosts—and Hans was the only one who dared live there. That—and his singular name—made Hans a far more real character to me than any of the local historical figures such as Abbot Markward, about whom we completed endless dreary projects at school.

The idea of a person who could face down witches and ghosts without turning a hair was inordinately attractive to someone who was dragging a lurid family history around with them like a ball and chain. Now that I am nearly old enough to be considered an adult myself, perhaps I could face the gossip and the teasing more easily; at ten, being the girl whose grandmother exploded felt like the worst thing in the world, and the loneliest.

Unshockable Hans wouldn't turn a hair if every single member of my extended family had exploded, of that I was sure. I imagined him as a big, deep-chested man, dressed in the traditional woodsman's jacket, leaf green with horn buttons. He would have a broad, pleasant face, a bushy beard with streaks of gray in it, and twinkling blue eyes. He would have heard the story of my grandmother's demise, of course, like everyone else within a ten-kilometer radius. Still, he would greet me in a friendly but grave manner, not referring to the incendiary finale of my aged relative.

If anyone mentioned it, any of those old harridans who haunted the streets of the town like vampires looking for unprotected throats, he would simply look at me with those twinkling eyes, ruffle my hair, and say, *"Ach, Kind,"* as though it were merely some childish piece of tom-foolery that was under discussion. As though it were not the hottest topic in the town for the last fifty years, and the social equivalent of a leper's bell for me.

I didn't go back to school on the Monday and Tuesday after Oma Kris-tel's accident. The school didn't bother to telephone when I failed to appear; Frau Müller, who worked in the school office, occupied the house opposite ours, and had been out in the street with her antennae twitch-ing the moment the ambulance siren was heard.

As is usual in these situations, a classmate was delegated to bring the homework to me. Perhaps I should have smelled a rat when it was Thilo Koch who brought it on Monday, and Daniella Brandt on Tuesday. Nei-ther of them were friends of mine.

Thilo was one of the oldest children in our class, having started school at seven; he was tall for his age, already carrying a large belly, and with savagely short hair and eyes sunk into the flesh of his chubby face like buttons on an overstuffed sofa cushion. Generally I kept away from Thilo, as you do from a bad-tempered animal.

Daniella Brandt was not as openly imposing as Thilo, but she could be just as dangerous in her way. She had a sharp-boned pale face and a thin, pointed nose like a beak, as though she wanted literally to peck at other people's weak spots. Neither Thilo nor Daniella had ever shown the slightest inclination to do anything to help anyone else, nor were they the obvious choices for such an errand; Marla Frisch, who lived three houses down from us, would normally have dropped off my home-work, as she did when I had chicken pox in the first grade.

Thilo didn't actually get into the house, as it was my father who opened the door. Thilo was that stereotypical creature, the bully with a broad streak of yellow; he took one look at my father, who was red-eyed but still imposing, and decided not to argue the toss, although he did thrust his close-cropped head as far around the doorframe as he dared, hoping perhaps for a glimpse of sooty ceiling or blackened tablecloth. My father took the homework papers out of Thilo's chubby hands, pushed him gently out, and closed the door.

The following day Daniella Brandt turned up and actually managed to get in. My mother, who answered the door, assumed she was a school friend. I was sitting in the living room, curled up in my father's favorite armchair with a book I was unable to read owing to the memories that kept running through my head like a short video clip on an endless loop.

The door opened and my mother appeared. Daniella was behind her, her pointed face a white triangle in the gloom.

"Look who's here," my mother said in a vague-sounding voice. Her gaze seemed to trickle over me, then slide away. She was still numb. My father had been able to cry, but my mother had still not taken in Oma Kristel's death; for days afterward she wandered around like someone in a dream, carrying the same Christmas ornaments between rooms as though preoccupied. She brushed her hands against her apron and disappeared in the direction of the kitchen.

Daniella slipped into the room with the speed of a weasel. Where my mother's gaze lingered distractedly, Daniella's seemed to stab the air. Her eyes were everywhere; I could have sworn her long thin nose was twitching too.

"I've brought your homework, Pia," she told me, but her eyes did not meet mine; she was glancing at every corner of the room with barely concealed curiosity.

"Thanks," I said tersely. I did not put the book down; pointedly I waited for her to go.

There was a long pause.

"I'm sorry about . . . you know," she said eventually.

"About what?" I said sharply. I turned one of the pages so brusquely that it tore.

Daniella gave a little laugh, like the short bark of a vixen. "About your grandmother," she said in her best *what, are-you-stupid?* voice. She drew a line along the floorboards with the toe of her shoe, then shook back her mousy hair from her face. "Everyone's talking about it," she informed me. "We just couldn't believe it, you know?" She lowered her voice conspiratorially, with a glance toward the door in case my mother was within earshot. "Was it here that it happened, in this room?"

I did not look up. "Go away or I'll scream," I said.

"Don't be silly," said Daniella in an offended tone. She breathed a heavy sigh, as though talking to the terminally stupid. In my place she would have been lapping up the attention, that was for sure; it would have been worth losing both grandmothers and perhaps an aunt or two as well, just to be center stage for once. "Come on, Pia . . ."

"Go away or I'll scream," I repeated.

She gave that little affected laugh again. "There's no need to be—"

She didn't get any further because I suddenly put my head back and *did* scream, repeatedly, at the top of my lungs. Before Daniella had time to react, the door crashed back on its hinges as my mother charged into the room like a rhinoceros defending its young. Incongruously, she still had a blue-and-white-checked oven mitt on one hand.

"My God, Pia! What's happened?!"

I shut my mouth abruptly and regarded Daniella balefully. My chest was heaving with exertion. My mother looked from me to Daniella and back to me again. Then, very gently, she took Daniella by the shoulder and started to steer her out of the room.

"I think you'll have to go, dear. Pia's rather upset," she told the stunned girl as she opened the front door with the gloved hand. "Thank you for bringing the homework," she added. "It was very kind of you."

A moment later she drifted back into the living room; her sudden burst of energy appeared to have dissipated, and she looked distracted again. She came over and knelt down in front of me, as though I were a toddler.

"Did your friend say something that upset you?" She might as well have said *your little friend.*

"She's not my friend," I announced.

"Well, it was nice of her to bring your homework," said my mother.

"It wasn't nice at all," I told her, feeling as though another scream might well up at any moment. "She wanted to know if this was the room where Oma Kristel . . . you know."

"Oh," said my mother. There was a very long pause while she

considered. At last she patted me on the shoulder. "Never mind, Pia. It'll be a nine days' wonder. They'll soon get sick of talking about it."

My mother was right about a lot of things, but on one topic she was spectacularly wrong, and that was the fascination with Oma Kristel's death. Even now, so much later, and after all that happened that terrible year, I am quite convinced that if you mentioned the name of Kristel Kolvenbach to anyone in Bad Münstereifel, they would instantly say, "Wasn't she the woman who exploded at her own Advent dinner?" A nine days' wonder it most certainly was not.

Chapter Four

❧

The *Grundschule* opened again in the first week of January. I usually walked to school with Marla Frisch. However, as I was packing my *Ranzen,* the capacious satchel that allows the German schoolchild to carry backbreaking amounts of schoolbooks, I was surprised to see Marla pass by our front windows without stopping, her light-brown pigtails bouncing. By the time I had shrugged on my winter coat and opened the front door, she had disappeared around the corner. I looked after her, puzzled. Well. Perhaps she thought I wasn't coming back to school yet.

I hoisted my *Ranzen* onto my back, called goodbye to my mother, and stepped out into the cobbled street, closing the door behind me. It was still not quite light, and the sky was leaden. Tiny flakes of snow whirled through the air and my breath came out in little puffs. The few people who passed me pulled their coats tight about themselves, wincing against the cold.

As I reached the school gate I looked at my watch. It was twelve minutes past eight; the bell would ring in three minutes exactly. I hurried inside, took the stairs to the first floor two at a time, and shrugged the *Ranzen* off my shoulders. As I hung my coat on a peg, I looked up and saw the sharp-boned face of Daniella Brandt peering around the doorframe of the classroom, a second before it whisked back inside like a rat vanishing into its hole.

I stood there by my peg for a moment, wondering whether it was just my imagination, or could I hear a sudden outbreak of excited whispers from the classroom?

"Frau Koch says her grandmother really did explode!"

"Went off like a bomb—"

"Burnt to a cinder—"

"They could only tell who it was by her teeth, my Tante Silvia says."

Suddenly I didn't want to go in. A chilling premonition broke over me. It would be no use screaming now; Frau Eichen would never stand for it and, furthermore, against a class of twenty-two ten-year-olds it would be worse than useless—it would only serve to make me an even more irresistible target of curiosity.

Nobody cared about Oma Kristel, about the way she had tried to keep herself attractive long after Youth had packed its bags and moved out of the aging tenement, about the way she always had some little gift for me, a sample bottle of unsuitable scent or a brooch made of sparkly paste. Her love of cherry liqueur.

None of it meant anything to them; no—what they wanted to know was whether she had *really* gone off like a Catherine wheel, throwing off sparks in all directions. Was it true that every hair on her head had been burned off? Did they really have to identify her by her rings? Was it true that Tante Britta had had an epileptic fit when she saw it happening? Was it true that—?

The whispers stopped the moment I rounded the doorframe and entered the classroom. Twenty-two pairs of eyes, wide with curiosity, were fixed on me as I made my unwilling progress into the room and pulled the chair out from under the table where I usually sat. Frau Eichen had not yet arrived; she had to drive down from Bonn and quite frequently turned up only just before the bell rang.

As I slid into my seat, the silence about me was palpable, the other children standing and staring at me like cattle, keeping a safe distance. When I pulled a library book out of my bag and banged it down on the tabletop, you could feel them flinch away. I noticed then that nobody else had put their things down on my table. Someone had left a *Ranzen* patterned with pink flowers on the chair opposite me; with a sudden dash, Marla Frisch retrieved it and retreated again.

Before I could think how to react, the bell was ringing and Frau Eichen came into the classroom, looking slightly harassed, her chestnut hair escaping from its silver barrette, and her cardigan sliding off one shoulder.

"Sit down, class," she barked at us, trying to cover up her own lateness with a touch of acerbity. There was a sudden flurry of movement. I looked down at my hands, not wanting to catch my classmates' eyes, but all the same I was aware that no one was taking their seat at my table. Space seemed to yawn endlessly on all sides of me.

There was a slight altercation at another table as Thilo Koch and another boy both tried to sit on one chair at the same time. Frau Eichen, who until then had been preoccupied with unloading her armful of files and books onto her desk, suddenly looked up and found that the entire class except for me was trying to fit at four of the five tables, and that I—Pia Kolvenbach—was sitting in solitary state at the remaining table, with my head down and the back of my neck crimson with embarrassment. As she took this in, there was a loud *thump* as Thilo Koch finally managed to shove the other boy off the chair and onto the floor. Then there was a moment's silence.

"What," asked Frau Eichen in a voice that positively crackled with frost, "is the meaning of this?"

Absolute silence reigned as Frau Eichen looked in exasperation from one face to another.

"Who normally sits at Pia's table?" she demanded. This was met with some nudging and whispering, but it seemed no one was prepared to own up. Frau Eichen picked out a face from the gaggle squashed up together at the table by the window.

"Maximilian Klein."

But Maximilian showed no signs of moving; he seemed to shrink back into his place crushed between two other children, looking anywhere but at Frau Eichen or myself.

"Marla Frisch."

At that I raised my head; Marla and I were supposed to be friends. I caught her eye and shot her a pleading glance. She looked away.

Frau Eichen was becoming a little pink in the face; she was unused to such flagrant disobedience.

"Will someone kindly explain what is going on?" she demanded. "Why is Pia sitting on her own?"

Eventually it was Daniella Brandt who spoke, never one to resist an opportunity of getting into the limelight.

"Please, Frau Eichen, we don't think we should have to sit with her."

"What do you mean, you don't think you should have to sit with her?" snapped Frau Eichen.

"In case it's catching, Frau Eichen," said Daniella with a smirk. One of the other girls let out a stifled giggle. Frau Eichen's eyes flickered over me momentarily, as though trying to discern symptoms of some unpleasant affliction. Then she gave a heavy sigh.

"In case *what* is catching?" she asked in a weary tone.

"The exploding," said Daniella, and let out a little shriek like a hyena laughing.

That was enough; the class erupted. Some of the girls were making a play of trying to move their chairs a little farther back, out of range of Pia Kolvenbach, the Potentially Explosive Schoolgirl, but mostly they all just clutched their sides and howled with laughter. Just as the first wave of mirth had broken, Thilo Koch made an exploding gesture with his arms, accompanied by a ripe farting sound, and they were all off again, red in the face and hanging on to each other as though they might literally be swept away on a tide of merriment.

I looked at Frau Eichen mutely for help. To my dismay, I could see from the congested expression on her face and the tight pursing of her lips that she, too, was fighting against a rising wave of laughter. Then she saw me looking at her and, with a force of will that can only be described as titanic, she composed herself and banged hard on the table with a book, with a sound that cut through the laughing like a gunshot.

"Be quiet!" she bellowed. After several seconds of choking and coughing there was more or less order in the classroom.

"Resume your places!"

No one moved. There was a very long silence, punctuated only by the creaking of chairs and the uncomfortable shuffling of tightly packed bodies jockeying for position. After what seemed like an eternity, I heard the sound of a chair scraping back, and someone stood up.

Oh, no. StinkStefan. He wasn't even at my table to begin with. What was he doing? Twenty-one other pairs of eyes were fixed on him as he made his way purposefully over, swinging his scruffy *Ranzen* by one hand and carrying his chair with the other. He set the chair down next to me, sat down, and folded his arms as though waiting for something. At that point, I really could have sunk through the floor.

StinkStefan, the most unpopular boy in the class. If I needed *him* for an ally, then it really was all over for me. I ducked my head again, determined not to catch his eye. He needn't think I was going to be grateful for his support. Still, for all that his gesture was unwelcome, it did the trick; a moment later, two other children were on their feet, lugging chairs and bags back to the table. Finally, Marla Frisch came too, though she looked as if she were being marched to her own execution, and she sat as far away from me as she possibly could.

When the bell rang at the end of the morning, it was a blessed relief, and I took care to spend so long packing my bag that the others had all gone before I crept out of the classroom. All gone, that is, except StinkStefan. He was standing on the other side of the heavy fire door, by the head of the staircase, waiting for me.

I shouldered my *Ranzen,* pushed open the door, and marched resolutely past him without saying a word. As I went down the stairs I thought I heard him say something, and without intending to I half turned and glanced back at him. Our eyes met. For a moment we regarded each other, then with a toss of my head I was running down the staircase, down the corridor, out of the school doors, anywhere, away. But it was no use: StinkStefan and I were already a pair.

Chapter Five

❧

There was no snow the day StinkStefan met Herr Schiller, but the weather was diamond bright and bitingly cold. Huddled in the depths of a down jacket, I was stalking swiftly down the Kölner Strasse, the wide street that leads north out of the town, when I realized that Stefan was at my heels. I kept up my pace, ostensibly to keep warm; but there was also a certain satisfaction in trying to outpace Stefan.

In my haste I nearly barreled into someone on the corner by the bridge.

"Fräulein Pia."

My eyes were level with a smart old-fashioned greatcoat with a red carnation, bright as a splash of paint, in the buttonhole. I looked up and saw a craggy face looking down at me, bushy eyebrows raised above startlingly blue eyes.

"Herr Schiller."

My heart instantly sank. At any other time I would have been delighted to see Herr Schiller; now I saw his eyes move to the shadow behind me and I knew I'd have to introduce him to Stefan. I glanced about me as though seeking escape, but it was too late.

"Is this a friend of yours?" asked Herr Schiller, his voice faintly amused.

"Um . . ." While I dithered, Stefan had slipped his right glove off and was extending his hand.

"Hello, I'm Stefan Breuer."

"Heinrich Schiller," said Herr Schiller gravely, grasping the proffered hand. He turned to me. "And where are you going in this inclement weather, Fräulein Pia?" Herr Schiller always spoke like that; he never tried to talk down to me simply because I was a child.

"To the park in the Schleidtal."

"I see," said Herr Schiller. He pushed back the sleeve of his coat and looked at his watch, a great silver antique. "Well, should you wish to drop by later on when you are both thoroughly frozen to the bone, I should be delighted to offer you some hot coffee—or chocolate, should you prefer."

I looked at Stefan. "Well, actually . . ." I hesitated. "I'm not really doing anything now."

"Nor am I," cut in Stefan, with a challenging glance at me.

"And it is quite cold," I said, doing my best to ignore him.

Herr Schiller gave a dry, creaking laugh like a pair of old bellows. "Then please, come with me. We can stop at the Café am Fluss for cakes. You may choose the cakes, Fräulein, and Herr Breuer can carry the box."

Obediently, we fell into step beside him. In spite of his age—he was in his eighties—Herr Schiller was surprisingly sprightly. He never used a cane, even when the ground was slick with frost; now he forged ahead. At the big gate, the Werther Tor, Herr Schiller disappeared into the to-bacconist's; Stefan and I waited outside.

"How do you know *him*?" said Stefan out of the corner of his mouth, glancing round to check that Herr Schiller was out of earshot.

I sighed. "I used to go and see him with my *Oma.*"

"The one that—?"

"Yes." I fixed my eyes on the cobblestones and waited for the in-evitable questions to follow, but Stefan said nothing. I shot him a side-ways glance; he appeared to be engrossed reading a poster taped to the shopwindow, advertising an over-thirties party in the spa hotel. I re-lented.

"He's old but he's cool," I said. "He tells me all this stuff—well, he used to, when I went round there with Oma Kristel. Things about the town in the olden days."

Stefan looked at me dubiously. "History?"

"No, *interesting* stuff," I said. "Like—well, Herr Schiller says there used to be this ghost of a white dog, and anyone who saw it—"

Herr Schiller emerged at the top of the steps outside the shop, and I stopped abruptly. But Herr Schiller was not looking at me, nor had he heard me saying his name. He was staring at someone on the other side of the street, and his face was set, although with anger or dislike I could not tell. I followed his gaze and saw a figure I recognized.

"Herr Düster," said Stefan under his breath. He had recognized that meager form too, in spite of the battered-looking hat that was pulled low over the eyes.

Herr Schiller descended the steps. As he passed me, his elbow thumped my shoulder, but I swear he didn't notice. He approached Herr Düster like a man backing a dangerous animal into a corner, squaring his shoulders as though he wanted to herd Herr Düster away from us.

"*Guten Morgen,*" I heard him say, and although his words were polite his tone was accusatory.

Herr Düster raised his chin a little, so that his eyes glinted darkly under the brim of his hat. His gaze danced from Herr Schiller to us and back again. There was something threatening in it, yet at the same time wary, as though he were a feral animal driven by extreme hunger to consider attacking human beings. He growled something unintelligible, then very deliberately turned his back and slunk away. He had a curious gait, faintly furtive; he made me think of a crab creeping across the seabed. He slid past the front of the post office and disappeared around the corner.

"Come," said Herr Schiller sharply, and we trotted after him.

I dared not ask him about Herr Düster. The old man was a legend among the schoolkids, rather like Herr Koch's evil German shepherd, Troll, which would fling itself against the garden fence barking and snapping wildly if you passed by. Seeing Herr Schiller's reaction somehow made Herr Düster more sinister. At that time, having to speak to Herr Düster, or meeting Troll when there was no fence between you, seemed liked the scariest things that could happen to you. Until, that is, Katharina Linden disappeared.

Chapter Six

Oddly enough, I have a very clear memory of seeing Katharina Linden that Sunday. I hardly knew her—she was in another class, with the other children from the outlying villages of Eicherscheid and Schönau, and I don't think I had ever even spoken to her, but I knew her by sight.

I saw her standing by the fountain in front of the photographer's shop. The fountain is a curious gunmetal gray creation with a statue of King Zwentibold of Oberlothringen gazing benevolently down from the top. Although it was February, and uncomfortably chilly, the sun was shining and Katharina was bathed in its cold pale glow. The memory is so sharp that sometimes I doubt myself—did my mind create this image because I *wanted* to see her, or was she really there?

She was dressed as Snow White—an instantly recognizable outfit because it had been based on the Disney costume: blue bodice, yellow ankle-length skirt, red cloak, a high collar, and a little red bow in her dark hair. I think that was why she or her mother had chosen that costume—Katharina had thick wavy hair that was almost jet-black, so she was the perfect Snow White, with her rather pale skin and dark eyes. When she vanished, it almost seemed like something from a fairy tale, as though she were one of Grimms' twelve dancing princesses, who somehow got out of a locked bedroom every night and came home in the morning with their shoes worn to flinders. But Katharina never came home at all.

I don't know who first realized something was wrong. The procession started—as is traditional—at eleven minutes past two. All the Karneval floats were lined up in the road outside the Orchheimer Tor, the great gate at the southern end of the town. Full-volume Karneval music crackled through enormous speakers, competing with the shouts and cheers of the crowd.

As the first float passed under the Tor, Stefan and I with a dozen other children darted forward to gather up handfuls of the sweets and little trinkets being thrown out. The haul was always good and we were well prepared, with canvas shopping bags to carry our loot in. The actual floats themselves were of less interest than the gathering of the booty, but I remember there were several very impressive ones that year—a pirate ship with real cannons belching forth dry ice, and an undersea scene with fish and octopuses, surmounted by Neptune on his throne, attended by bare-shouldered mermaids shivering in the February air.

Nearly everyone was in costume: Marla Frisch passed by, dressed as Red Riding Hood, studiously failing to notice me. Thilo Koch appeared as an overweight pirate, his potbelly straining at the satin of his shirt. Much as I hated him, I could not help feeling envious: at least his mother had *bought* him a costume, a proper one.

My mother had never quite grasped the Karneval concept. She seemed to think that some kind of extra merit points would be awarded to parents who made their children's costumes. Buying was cheating, in her book. She didn't see how much I longed to be like Lena or Eva from my class, dressed up in a Barbie Princess costume or a fairy dress from Kaufhof.

This year she had dressed the family up as characters from the Wizard of Oz: she was the Tin Man, my father was the Scarecrow, and Sebastian was the Cowardly Lion (though you might have mistaken him for Toto, so vague was my mother's representation of leonine anatomy). I was Dorothy, dragooned into a blue-and-white-checked pinafore dress with a frilly white blouse underneath and a pair of old pumps painted red and peppered with sequins. After Daniella Brandt had stopped, her head on one side, and asked me whether we were supposed to be the

Von Trapp family, my cup of bitterness overflowed and I resolved that next year I would *buy* a costume, even if I had to save up my entire pocket money between now and then.

Stefan was slightly better off; he had a clearly recognizable Spider-Man costume complete with face mask. We made an odd pair, Dorothy and Spider-Man, scuttling through the cobbled streets with our bags stuffed with candy, popcorn, and plastic toys. Still—Karneval is a time for strange sights, when sour-faced neighbors turn jolly for the day, and straitlaced old ladies dress up as vampires or French maids. It was also, as it turned out, the ideal time for someone—or something—else to stalk the streets, someone whose strangeness and inhuman intent went unnoticed in the general mayhem.

As the procession moved through the town, Stefan and I followed it, threading our way through the crowds together. I remember seeing Katharina Linden at the fountain as we reached the junction in the center of town. It must have been at about a quarter to three.

A little farther on I remember seeing Frau Linden, who was dressed as a clown in a kind of multicolored romper suit and a green curly wig. She was holding Nils—the younger of Katharina's two brothers—by the hand. Nils was dressed as a ladybug, and looked thoroughly disgusted at the whole proceedings; he was swinging on her arm and complaining vociferously about something.

Perhaps that is why Frau Linden failed to notice her daughter's disappearance at first; she was preoccupied with the much younger Nils. And, after all, Bad Münstereifel was a small town—everyone knew one another, and even during Karneval there were enough friendly faces around that you needn't worry about your children. Or so everyone thought.

When the procession had reached the Werther Tor, we wandered back to the fountain where we'd passed Katharina Linden, and sat on the edge of the stone basin, full of candy and feeling contented in a slightly queasy way. The crowds were dispersing, and the floats had been replaced with a squat street-cleaning machine that growled over the cobblestones like an oversized vacuum cleaner, followed by a team of bored-looking men dressed in orange overalls and armed with trash bags.

I looked away, up toward the archway leading into the St. Michael

Gymnasium, and saw a flicker of color as someone dressed in a clown suit came hurrying out. It was Frau Linden, minus Nils. She moved quickly across the Salzmarkt and out of my line of vision. I didn't think anything of it at the time, but I was a little surprised when several minutes later she appeared from the alley at the side of the *Rathaus,* and came hurrying down the street toward us. I dug Stefan in the ribs with my elbow to make him look up.

"What?"

I nodded in the direction of Frau Linden, who was now making a beeline for us. I was formulating some silly remark when I saw her expression. Her face, normally warm and kindly, had a frigid, set look to it that sat oddly with her emerald-green wig. Instinctively sensing that something was wrong, I got to my feet as she came up to us.

"Have you seen Katharina?"

Her voice was taut, vibrating as though it would suddenly break and shatter her composure. I looked at her uncertainly.

"We saw her earlier on," I told her.

"Where?" There was an unstable urgency in her voice. I found myself leaning backward, thinking that she might take me by the shoulders and shake me; she had that sort of look.

"Here," I said. "By the fountain." From her face I could see this was not the answer she wanted; I suddenly felt hot all over, as though I had told her a lie.

"Did you see where she went?" snapped Frau Linden.

"No," said Stefan, and Frau Linden shot him a look, as if she had only just noticed him.

"No, sorry," I said, echoing Stefan. We looked at each other uncomfortably.

Frau Linden suddenly seemed to sag a little, as though the energy that had drawn her toward us had drained out of her. Now she did reach out with one hand and touch my shoulder.

"Are you *sure?*" she asked me. "Are you really *sure* you didn't see where she went?"

"No," I said, then, realizing that this sounded ambiguous: "No, I didn't see where she went."

"She's probably gone around to Marla's or something," suggested Stefan, trying to be helpful.

"She hasn't," stated Frau Linden bluntly. She looked about her in a preoccupied manner, as though she had left Katharina somewhere like a forgotten bag of shopping.

Then her arm dropped to her side, she turned and hurried back up the Marktstrasse, without even bothering to say goodbye. Stefan and I exchanged glances. This was odd behavior from an adult.

"*Komisch,*" observed Stefan.

"Yes," I agreed, shrugging.

It was getting chilly standing there in my gingham dress, and the curt exchange with Frau Linden had dissipated my holiday mood.

"I'm going home," I said, and after a pause, "Do you want to come?"

Stefan just nodded. We picked up our bags of loot and set off for my house. I was sliding my key into the lock when my mother opened the door from the other side.

Typically for my mother, she did not waste time greeting Stefan and asking him all those mundane adult questions such as *How is school going?* or *How is your mother?* She launched straight in with "Has either of you seen Katharina Linden?"

We looked at each other. Had all the adults gone mad?

"No," we both said in unison.

"Are you quite sure?"

"We saw her at the fountain earlier on, but she's gone now," I said. "We told Frau Linden that." I looked at my mother doubtfully. "Why is everyone looking for her, anyway? What's she done?"

"She hasn't done anything," said my mother. "She's just disappeared." She eyed me and Stefan dubiously, obviously reluctant to say anything that would alarm us. "Well, she's probably just gone home with a friend," she said eventually. "I'm sure she'll turn up."

"Frau Linden said she'd already tried Marla Frisch's house," I pointed out. There was a silence. "Where's Papa?" I asked.

"He's out," said my mother. She sighed. "He's helping the Lindens look for Katharina."

"We can help too," suggested Stefan. He pulled the Spider-Man balaclava off his head to reveal sandy hair sticking up every which way in untidy clumps. His face looked eager; I wondered if he was letting the Spider-Man outfit go to his head. "We can look for her. We know loads of places, don't we, Pia?"

My mother shook her head. "I think it would be better if you both stayed in now," she said. "Let the grown-ups look for Katharina." Her voice was mild, but the tone was unmistakably firm. Abruptly, as though changing the subject, she said, "Do you two want some hot chocolate?"

Five minutes later, Stefan and I were contentedly enthroned on the long bench behind the kitchen table, our mouths ringed with chocolate. For the time being, Katharina Linden was forgotten.

Chapter Seven

*I*t was fully dark when my father finally came home. He was still in his Scarecrow outfit, although his brown face paint was all smeared, as though he had been wiping the back of his hand across his face like a little child. As he stood stamping his feet on the doormat, my mother came out of the kitchen, drying her hands on a tea towel.

"And?" was all she said.

My father shook his head. "Not a sign of her anywhere." He bent to unlace his shoes, breathing heavily. When he straightened up, he said, "Someone thought they saw her up near the Orchheimer Tor, but it was another child in a similar costume. Dieter Linden's still out looking, but I don't think he'll find much now it's dark."

I was listening to this from the kitchen table, where I was working my way through my supper: gray bread, a slice of cheese, and a smear of *Leberwurst.* My father's choice of words struck me as odd even at this stage: he didn't think Herr Linden would *find much,* as though he were not looking for a person but a thing, or worse, pieces of a thing.

"I wonder what—" my mother began, then glanced back into the kitchen to where I was sitting and hastily added, "I expect she's gone home with one of her friends and forgotten to call her mother." Then she and my father went through into the living room and closed the door.

Their voices resumed, but at such a low level that I couldn't have made sense of any of it unless I had pressed my ear to the door, which would have been far too risky. I looked down at my piece of *Leberwurst*-coated bread, with a neat semicircle bitten out of it in the shape of my .teeth. I wondered whether Katharina Linden really *was* at a friend's house. If not, where was she? It didn't make sense. *People don't just disappear,* I thought.

The next morning being Rosenmontag, there was no school. My parents had half promised to take Sebastian and me to another parade some kilometers away, but when I got up at half past nine it was to discover that my father had already gone out. My mother was in the living room, dusting the furniture with a grim expression. I didn't need to ask whether our excursion was off. My mother was attacking the cleaning with the zeal of someone gritting their teeth and undergoing some particularly unpleasant therapy.

"Where's Papa?" I asked.

"Out," said my mother tersely. She straightened up, rubbing the small of her back. "He's gone to help someone with something."

"Oh." I wondered whether he was going to look for Katharina Linden again. "I think I might go around to Stefan's after breakfast and see if he can come out. Is that OK?"

My mother paused for a moment. "How about you stay here today, Pia?"

"But, Mama . . ." I was dismayed.

"Pia, I really think it would be best if you stayed home." My mother sounded weary but firm. "If you can't think of anything to do, you can help me with the cleaning."

"I've got homework," I informed her hastily, and beat a retreat to the kitchen before she could rope me into anything.

The day dragged by horribly slowly. I wondered what Stefan was up to. Was he outdoors somewhere, or had his parents also imposed a curfew on him? I wondered if it had anything to do with the Katharina Linden thing that seemed to be sending all the adults temporarily weird.

At five o'clock, when it was dark, my father came home and almost instantly disappeared into the living room again with my mother. They were in there for about half an hour, after which my father went upstairs for a shower and my mother came looking for me, with a serious expression on her face. I recognized this as her *here-comes-a-little-talk* look. I was sitting on the living-room floor with a magazine; she came in, sat down carefully on the sofa, and patted the cushion next to her. With an inward sigh, I got up and went to sit next to her.

"What?" I said.

"Don't say 'what?'" said my mother automatically.

"Sorry," I said, equally automatically; it was an exchange we had had a thousand times. "Is it about Katharina Linden?" I asked immediately.

My mother cocked her head on one side. "Yes. I'm telling you about this because you're bound to hear about it when you get back to school," she began.

"They haven't found her, have they?" I said.

"Well, no, they haven't, not *yet*," said my mother, laying emphasis on the last word as though to imply perfect confidence that Katharina would be found at any moment. "But I hope they *will* find her, very soon." She sighed. "There may be a perfectly innocent explanation. Perhaps she went home with a friend and didn't tell anyone."

She stayed overnight and still didn't tell anyone? I thought skeptically.

"All the same," my mother was going on, "we should all be just a little . . . careful for a while. We don't really know what's happened." She reached out and rubbed my arm almost absently. "I'm sorry we even need to have this conversation," she said. "But you never know . . . Pia, you must promise me not to go anywhere with anyone without telling me first. You remember that book you had in the second grade?"

"Ich kenn dich nicht, ich geh nicht mit," I quoted, then looked a little askance at my mother. "Do you think someone's taken Katharina, then, like in the book?"

"I hope not," said my mother. She seemed momentarily at a loss how to proceed. "Just be careful," she said at last. "And if you see anything odd, Pia, you come and tell me or Papa, understand?"

"Hmmm," I said noncommittally. I was not sure what she meant by *odd*. "Sebastian's crying," I pointed out, tuning in to a muffled wailing from upstairs.

My mother got to her feet. "All right, I'll go and see to him. Just re-member, won't you?"

"Yes, Mama." I watched her leave the room and start up the staircase. I didn't move from the sofa, but sat there swinging my legs against the front of it and thinking over what she had said. *Anything odd.*

Now that I'm older, I can see what my mother meant by *odd.* Adults think something is odd if it doesn't fit the normal routine. The person who puts down a package on a railway platform and walks away from it. The car that's still behind the lone woman driver even when she's made four or five turns and maybe even doubled back on herself. Things that don't fit the usual pattern. Danger signs.

But to me, when I was ten, *odd,* or the word my mother actually used, *seltsam,* which means "odd, peculiar, strange, weird," could sig-nify a great many less tangible things. It could mean, for example, the deserted locked-up house by the Werkbrücke, which the schoolchildren always scurried past at top speed, deliciously afraid of seeing some un-speakable face pressed against the dusty window glass.

It seemed to me—if not to the adults—that Katharina Linden's disappearance could be attributed to some supernatural agency. How otherwise could she have been spirited away from under the very noses of her family, in broad daylight too, in a town where everyone knew everyone else? I did not know—I did not know *yet,* I told myself, for I was determined to find out—who or what it was that had taken Katha-rina. Still I was now convinced, correctly as it turned out, that she would never be seen alive again.

Chapter Eight

That icy February, when Katharina Linden vanished, the entire town was in a state of shock, and yet nobody thought it would happen again. During Karneval, Bad Münstereifel was full of people from goodness-knew-where, and there was so much mayhem going on that anything might happen. Once Karneval was over, and the town was quiet again, nobody really expected another child to disappear. All the same, my mother began to take rather more interest in my comings and goings than was comfortable. There was to be no more roaming around the town on my own, and she was reluctant to let me go off to the playground in the Schleidtal, even if Stefan came as well. Going to Stefan's house was out too, since it meant being smoked like a herring in the fumes of his mother's chain-smoking. It was a relief for me and Stefan to be able to escape to the more agreeable environment of Herr Schiller's house, where nobody asked about homework and we could beg him to tell us old stories of the town. That was how he came to recount the tale of Unshockable Hans.

"Unshockable Hans?" said Stefan. "What kind of name is that?"

He and I were sitting on the overstuffed sofa in Herr Schiller's living room, sipping coffee so strong that it almost took the enamel off your teeth.

"They called him that because he wasn't afraid of anything or anyone," answered Herr Schiller, his tone very faintly reproving. "He lived in a mill in the Eschweiler Tal, long ago, before your grandparents' parents were born."

"The Eschweiler Tal. We've been there with the school," said Stefan.

"Then you will know, young man, that it is a very quiet place. Lonely even, especially in winter," said Herr Schiller. "Now, that mill had a bad reputation. A ghost mill, they called it, infested with all sorts of witches, phantoms, and monsters. It was as though the very timbers of the mill had soaked up the unearthly forces that seethed and thronged in the valley, like the wood of a wine barrel takes up the stain and scent of the wine."

Stefan shot me a glance at this extravagant piece of narrative. I ignored him.

"No one had ever succeeded in staying in the mill for any length of time—not, that is, until Hans moved in. Previous inhabitants had been chased out; hardworking, unimaginative men who had invested most of their life's savings in the mill had fled from it like frightened children, their faces as white as milk. It was not that Hans was too insensitive to feel or see the things that swarmed around the mill; it was simply that he did not fear any of them. He could walk through the mill at night, when the building was full of furtive scratching noises, and malevolent eyes glinted redly in the darkest corners, and he would be as relaxed as a visitor wandering through a greenhouse full of tropical butterflies. And perhaps because he was so totally unafraid, it seemed that none of these creatures could touch him."

"Cool," said Stefan.

Shut up, I telegraphed at him with a furious glare.

"The phantoms waited eagerly for Hans to flee like the others," went on Herr Schiller. "When he didn't, they redoubled their efforts. Things with far too many spindly limbs and leathery wings articulated like the spokes of an umbrella would dive upon him as he strolled through the mill after sunset, and tangle in his flour-dusted hair; grotesque faces would leer up at him out of the water butt outside, or from the corner cupboard where he kept his knife and plate. At night the creaking of the mill's timbers mingled with groaning and wailing that would have made anyone else's hair stand on end. Hans endured it all unmoved.

"Well, at last the things that infested the mill grew angry. At night the creaking of the beams sharpened to shrieks, and by day the great cogs of the machine seemed to move more slowly, as though working against some unseen resistance. If Hans cared about these things, he gave no sign.

"However, one day late in April he left the mill and walked into the town. When he returned he had a little package in the pocket of his breeches, carefully done up in a clean handkerchief. Intrepid as he was, Hans knew that in two nights it would be Walpurgis, the eve of May Day, when the witches gather for their Sabbath. The unseen foes with whom he was struggling for possession of the mill were certain to make some kind of attack.

"The last day of April was cloudy and overcast, and a chill wind was blowing. Night came in early and inside the mill it was dark, the light from Hans's one little lantern hardly penetrating the deep shadows. Hans ate his solitary dinner of rough bread and cheese, said his prayers like the good Catholic he was, then put out the lantern and lay down on the pallet that served as his bed. Hans always slept well, caring nothing for little scuffling footsteps on the floor of the mill, or tiny clawed feet running across his blanket in the night. Tonight he slept on his back, his face turned boldly up to the ceiling and his beard quivering gently to the rhythm of his snores.

"For several hours his sleep was undisturbed. The oppressive atmosphere that had haunted the mill for days seemed to have lifted. The wind outside had dropped, the clouds had parted and the full moon shining through the little window above Hans's rough bed outlined the few sticks of homely wooden furniture and the parts of the mill machinery in glowing silver.

"Perhaps it was the light that woke Hans up. At any rate, he opened his eyes and looked about him. Was it his imagination, or had he seen two twin lights, hot and red like the glowing embers of a fire, winking at him from a corner? Yes; there it was again—*blink-blink,* as if something were watching him, but shutting its eyes lazily for long seconds. Hans coughed gently, as though to show his unconcern, and was about to turn over and pull his blankets around him, when he saw a second pair of lights glowing from the top of a cupboard. Again they seemed to glint for a moment and then blink out.

"Hans considered for a moment, then he pulled the blankets around his shoulders and closed his eyes. Hans being Hans, he would actually have managed to fall asleep again, but just as he was drifting into slumber there came the sound of velvet feet padding softly across the earthen floor of the mill.

"This time, since Hans was lying on his side, he had only to open his eyes to see the source of the sounds. A large cat was strolling across the room, a cat with inky-black fur that shimmered like taffeta, and great green eyes that glowed phosphorescently in the darkness. Abruptly it stopped, settled itself on its hindquarters, tail curled elegantly about its haunches, and regarded the miller with its luminous eyes.

"For several seconds Hans and the cat stared at each other. Then Hans said, '*Ach,* pussycat—I've no milk for you.' And he turned his back, pulling the blanket with him. Then there came a hissing, like an intake of breath, and another cat came padding out of the darkness, and then another. They wound their way through the patch of silver moonlight on the floor; they weaved in and out of the legs of Hans's solitary chair; they sprang onto the sacks of grain and perched on the stout timbers of the mill. They slipped like quicksilver through the chinks between the planks of the door and slid knifelike between the stones of the walls. They oozed like viscous honey from the cracks about the window frames.

"If Hans had opened his eyes, he would have seen some of them come right *through* the walls, stretching as they did so, pulling their hindquarters after them. But Hans did not need to see this to know what they were; they took the form of cats, but his nocturnal visitors were *witches,* assembling for their great Walpurgis Night meeting in the place where they always met, and determined to turn this audacious mortal out.

"At last, when the whole floor was packed with furry bodies, the cats began to cry. They howled and screeched together in an unearthly chorus. At first Hans put his fingers in his ears, but it was no use: the sound that the cats made was not heard only by the *ears,* you understand; it could also be heard by the *soul.* It was a song of damnation, evoking the milling pit of lava into which the tainted soul must fall and shrivel to a crisp, but stay eternally and exquisitely conscious, ever burning, an immortal ember in the sluggish lake of fire. I think if you or I had heard it, we would have lain right down and died."

I shivered. "That's horrible."

Herr Schiller continued, unperturbed. "But Unshockable Hans was made of sterner stuff. Since the diabolical song could not be ignored, up he sat and looked boldly about him, as though the sounds were nothing more than the normal yowling of a queen cat come into heat. *'Himmel!'* he exclaimed. 'How is a man supposed to sleep with a racket like that going on? Be quiet, the lot of you, or you'll go out, even if I have to take each and every one of you by the scruff to do it.' And so saying, he lay down again.

"For one second there was silence. Then there began a screaming that was like tortured metal, as though all the fiends of Tartarus were bursting through its iron gates and streaming forth, devouring everything in their fiery path. Then with a screech that overtopped them all, the largest and wildest cat, an enormous tom muscled like a bull, with fur the color of jet and blazing yellow eyes, made a mighty spring onto Hans's chest, and sat there like the demon Nightmare, snarling into his face with its wicked fangs.

"Up sprang Hans at once, grasping the creature with both hands so that he felt the terrible strength of its sinews and bunched muscles under his fingers, and flung it from him, as far as he could. Then he reached under his pillow and drew out the little package that he had brought back with him from the town. Tearing off the wrappings, he revealed a rosary—a plain wooden rosary with polished brown beads, which Hans had received from the hands of the holy Fathers.

"With a great cry, he threw the rosary straight at the snarling creature that had attacked him. 'By the name of all that is holy,' he cried at the top of his voice, 'I order you to leave—*now!*' And as the last word fell from his lips, every one of those diabolical cats vanished and he found himself standing alone, breathing hard, in the dark and silent mill. He had won. The pests had been routed, and the mill belonged to him. Then at last Hans lay down and slept the sleep of the righteous until morning came."

Chapter Nine

✦

*H*err Schiller fell silent. The hand that had mimed the casting of the rosary at the demonic cats dropped to the arm of his chair, patted it lightly, then moved to his pocket, fumbling for his pipe. There was a long silence while he lit it, puffing gently, little wisps of white floating up like smoke signals.

"Well, I don't think that was very scary," said Stefan eventually. I shot him a furious glance; if his chair had been closer to mine I would have aimed a furtive kick at his legs.

"You don't think it was scary?" repeated Herr Schiller. I was thankful to notice that he did not sound annoyed—more amused. If Stefan had offended him, it might have been the last visit to Herr Schiller, in which case I would never have forgiven Stefan. Our newfound alliance would be dissolved, even if I spent the remainder of my schooldays playing and working all on my own.

"No," said Stefan, quite casually. When Herr Schiller said nothing, but his bushy white eyebrows went up, Stefan was encouraged to continue: "I don't think there's anything frightening about a bunch of cats."

"But these were not really cats, were they?" probed Herr Schiller in a conversational tone. "They were witches." He smiled faintly. "You should never judge by appearances, young man." There was a hint of reproach in his voice.

"Well, I thought it was a brilliant story," I cut in defensively, trying to signal my annoyance at Stefan. Who did he think he was, criticizing like that?

But Herr Schiller appeared not to have heard my comment. He raised a hand in the air in an admonitory fashion, his piercingly blue eyes still fixed on Stefan. "Of course," he conceded, "there *is* nothing very alarming about an ordinary pussycat, lounging in the sunshine or washing itself on a windowsill. But imagine what it would have been like several hundred years ago, when the night was unbroken by electric light, and outside the little circle of your candle flame everything was endless black. And then if suddenly you were to see a pair of eyes glinting at you, where a moment before there had been nothing . . . and if you knew that this was not really a cat, but something much, *much* worse, which had assumed this innocent domestic form so it might slip unnoticed into your house while you slept . . ." Herr Schiller's voice had sunk almost to a whisper, so that both Stefan and I involuntarily leaned toward him. "A thing so horrible, *so horrible*—"

"*Aaaahhhhh!*" screamed Stefan suddenly, so loudly and unexpectedly that I almost jumped out of my skin. Stefan had gone the sickly color of feta cheese, his face almost blue in its whiteness. He seemed to be attempting simultaneously to climb over the back of the leather armchair he had been sitting in and to point over Herr Schiller's shoulder at something that was just coming into view.

"*Scheisse!*" I squealed, forgetting for once that I was in the presence of one of my elders.

Herr Schiller's house was a traditional Eifel house, dark and gloomy even in broad daylight. It was now early evening, and the corners of the room were sunk in darkness. Out of one of these pockets of blackness there appeared first the silken head and then the sinuous body of an enormous tomcat, blacker than the shadows, and with great yellow eyes like headlights.

I realized later that the creature must have been sitting on the sideboard behind Herr Schiller's armchair, but at the time it was like some uncanny materialization. My heart thumped wildly, and it was several moments before my eyes connected with my brain and I realized what I was seeing.

"You dope, it's Pluto," I almost shouted at Stefan. "Sit down, you idiot—it's Pluto!"

Herr Schiller, who had been arrested midsentence by Stefan's scream, pipe frozen between hand and lips, now jumped as though someone had touched him with a cattle prod. He was on his feet faster than I remember seeing anyone of his age ever move before. His face was a mask of horror.

"Out, *out*!" he was shouting, gesticulating at the cat, which spat derisively, its back a jagged arch. But the street door was closed; there was nowhere for the cat to bolt even if it wanted to. With considerably greater daring than I could have shown, Herr Schiller reached over and grasped the creature by the scruff, hauled it swinging and scratching to the front door, and cast it out into the street. The slam he gave the door afterward must have rattled that old house down to its foundations.

As the sound died away, we all stood there, panting like racehorses. Stefan looked as though he was going to be sick. Poor Herr Schiller looked almost as bad; the sudden rush of adrenaline that had fueled his assault upon the cat had passed like a flash flood, leaving wreckage in its wake. I was afraid he might collapse and so I offered him my arm. He looked at me for a moment, his expression unreadable, then took my arm and allowed me to lead him back to his armchair.

"You are an idiot, Stefan," I snapped, not adding, as I might have, *You nearly gave the old man a heart attack.* "It was only Pluto."

Pluto was a well-known fixture in Bad Münstereifel, at least among those who lived in the old part of the town. A large, foul-tempered, and unsterilized inky-black tomcat, he had once made it onto the front page of the local free newspaper (admittedly during a quiet week as regards other news) after a resident of the town accused him of making an unprovoked attack on her pet dachshund. Describing him as "only Pluto" was rather like describing Baron Münchhausen as a bit of a fibber.

Still, I was annoyed with Stefan, not least because I was afraid that this piece of high drama really *would* spell the end of my visits to Herr Schiller. That evening my suspicions seemed to be confirmed, since Herr Schiller seemed suddenly tired and quite relieved to see us go.

Normally he would stand on his doorstep watching me as I went off up the street, but this evening Stefan and I were scarcely on the cobblestones before we heard the door quietly click closed behind us.

I set off up the street at a fast pace, half wanting to leave Stefan behind. *StinkStefan.* I might have known he would mess it all up. I considered just running home at top speed without speaking to him, but as I reached the bridge over the Erft I heard him coming up behind me, panting with exertion, and I relented. Still, I was not going to make things easy for him. I stood on the bridge looking down into the shallow but fast-flowing waters of the river, and waited for Stefan to speak first.

"Why did you run off like that?"

Typical StinkStefan question. Like all those others: *Why won't you let me play with you? Why can't I be on your team? Why won't you be friends with me?* This was not a good start.

"Because you nearly blew it. In fact you may have blown it. He's never sent me off like that before."

"I couldn't help it," said Stefan, brushing a strand of dirty blond hair out of his eyes. "That monster cat gave me the fright of my life."

"It's only Pluto," I pointed out frostily. "You've seen him hundreds of times."

"He made me jump, creeping out of the dark like that. And, anyway," Stefan went on, "didn't you think it was a bit weird, the way he appeared just as Herr Schiller was telling us about Unshockable Hans and the witches' cats?"

"Not particularly," I lied. "Pluto gets into everything. Frau Nett said she found him in the kitchen of the bakery once, eating a bit of *Apfelstreusel.*"

Stefan's face fell a little. "Well, all the same . . ." he said lamely. "I think it was creepy." He looked down at the muddy waters below, thinking. "He certainly gave Herr Schiller a shock," he said eventually. "Don't you think that's a bit strange?"

"Well, Pluto's not his cat," I pointed out. "He probably wasn't expecting to see the old fleabag practically sitting on his shoulder."

"Hmmmm . . ." I looked at Stefan sideways and could see a familiar expression on his face, one that meant wheels were turning. "Pluto belongs to Herr Düster, doesn't he?" he said.

"Ye-e-es," I conceded suspiciously.

"Well, don't you think it's odd that—"

"Oh, come *on!*" I snapped, cutting him off midsentence. "What do you think, that Herr Düster *set* Pluto on him or something?"

"I don't know," said Stefan, but you could see the idea had appeal. "I mean, those two hate each other, don't they? Maybe Pluto didn't get in there by himself. Maybe Herr Düster put him in through the window or something, to give Herr Schiller a fright. Maybe he was hoping it would give him a heart attack."

"Nice idea," I said untruthfully. "But who's going to leave a window open in *this* weather?"

Stefan shook his head, as though he were an inspirational leader frustrated at the inability of his followers to see the bigger picture.

"It didn't have to be the window. Maybe he put him in through that old chute where they used to put coal and stuff in the cellar."

"*Quatsch,*" I said rudely. "That's absolute *Quatsch.* And, anyway, how was Herr Düster to know we had been talking about Unshockable Hans and the cats? You think he's psychic or something?"

The thought seemed to strike Stefan. "Maybe he is." He pushed himself away from the parapet of the bridge and began to walk slowly toward the Marktstrasse. This time it was my turn to tag along after him. It was almost dark now, and as we passed the red *Rathaus* the first few flakes of falling snow were dancing in the air.

"Stefan, I have to get home. My mother will go nuts—it's already dark."

"I know. It's all right."

Stefan didn't need to make any remark about his own mother. I remember thinking that Frau Breuer probably wouldn't notice if Stefan didn't come home at all, a thought that seems horribly callous in the light of what came afterward, when other children really did fail to come home.

We stopped for a moment by the old pillory in front of the *Rathaus.* Stefan kicked it idly with the scuffed toe of his sneaker as we stood there, awkwardly saying our goodbyes. Eventually I said, "See you tomorrow, then," and turned to walk away.

I had hardly taken three steps when I found there was someone blocking my path. I looked up, snowflakes whirling into my face, and found myself looking up into the gargoyle features of Herr Düster. In his dark coat he looked like an undertaker. His expression was hostile. Heart thumping, I froze.

Herr Düster's eyes slid over me and then his gaze seemed to snag on Stefan, half visible in the colonnade behind me. With a snarl he pushed past me and disappeared into the Fibergasse, the alley at the side of the *Rathaus*.

"What did he say?" said Stefan, coming back up to me.

I shook my head. "He said, *go home.*"

"Go home?" Stefan shrugged. "That's all? He looked like he was swearing at you."

"No, that's all," I said, and shivered.

Stefan looked at me. "You want me to walk you back to your house?"

I glanced at him. StinkStefan, my knight in shining armor.

"Yes," I said, and meant it.

Chapter Ten

⁂

I remember once, when I was quite little, asking my mother about Herr Schiller and Herr Düster. I was puzzled about them because someone had told me they were brothers, but they didn't look at all alike, and they had different names.

Herr Schiller was a tall, broad-shouldered man, with a large-featured, benevolent face. His startlingly blue eyes were overhung with bushy white eyebrows that would not have disgraced St. Nicholas. His hair, which was dead white, was still abundant and always neatly groomed. His mouth was wide and amiable, although when he smiled he rarely opened his lips, perhaps being self-conscious about his teeth, which were stained yellow from decades of smoking.

Herr Schiller was always immaculately turned out. Sometimes he wore an ordinary dark suit with a crisp white shirt and a silk tie, and at other times he wore a traditional costume, a dark green woolen jacket with pale horn buttons, matching breeches, and woolen socks. He was considered something of a local character—not an eccentric, something still frowned upon in German society, but a gentleman of the old school, the sort you no longer see anymore, with perfect manners and a dash of gallantry. *Not,* as Oma Kristel used to observe in a tone of frigid disapproval, *like that Herr Düster.*

Were it not for the uncertain notion that he and Herr Schiller were brothers, I would never have taken them for blood relatives. Although Herr Schiller was tall, Herr Düster was of medium height and had a skinny, paltry look about him, as though he had never eaten well in his life. In fact Pluto looked glossier and better fed than he did.

Only in his eyes could one discern any point of similarity with the urbane Herr Schiller—they were the same bright cornflower blue. But they were overhung with iron-gray brows that gave Herr Düster a surly expression, as though he were permanently glowering at someone, which in actual fact he very often was.

The popular legend among the local children (and probably their parents, too, when they were schoolchildren) was that Herr Düster had been a member of the National Socialist German Workers' Party, who'd somehow managed to escape justice. He had been having an affair with the Bürgermeister's fiercely ugly daughter, and she had somehow got him off the hook; or he had been certified temporarily insane by a doctor he was blackmailing; or he had spent three years after the war hiding out in the ruins of the old castle on the Quecken hill, creeping out at night to steal chickens to eat raw: all these were cited as genuine reasons why Herr Düster had never been brought to justice.

As for the dislike between himself and Herr Schiller, for a long time I just took it for granted. It was after seeing them pass each other in the Werther Strasse one afternoon, Herr Schiller inclining his head with frosty civility and Herr Düster slouching past as though he hadn't noticed, that I asked my mother about their relationship.

"Are Herr Schiller and Herr Düster brothers, or aren't they?" I wanted to know.

My mother looked up with mild interest.

"Yes, they are brothers." She thought about it. "Not very close brothers, though. Your Oma Kristel is always saying that Herr Düster must be a terrible trial to poor Heinrich"—that was Herr Schiller's Christian name.

"So why have they got different last names, then?" I asked, still not having got to the bottom of the matter.

"Funny," said my mother, "I once asked Oma Kristel that."

"What did she say?" I asked.

"She sniffed, and said some people *had* to change their names after the war, and that it didn't stop those who were around at the time remembering who was who and what was what. I suppose she meant people who belonged to the Nazi party," she mused. "The older people in the town must remember who some of them were."

"So *was* Herr Düster one?" I persisted. "Is that why Herr Schiller doesn't like him?"

"I don't think so," said my mother. "I had the impression it was something more personal than that, a family feud or something." She eyed me suspiciously. "We don't know any of this for a fact," she said. "I don't want you going around telling people Herr Düster is a war criminal or something, Pia. Understand?"

"Yes," I said impatiently. "But if it was a family feud, what was it about?"

My mother put down her work and looked at me askance. "What is this, twenty questions or something?" She shook her head. "It's no use asking me. Oma Kristel's the expert on Bad Münstereifel gossip."

I never did ask Oma Kristel about it. I couldn't imagine asking my grandmother prurient questions about "poor Heinrich's" past. Besides, Oma Kristel did not like to talk about the war and the postwar period; it was too painful a topic. Evidently other adults felt the same, because the page on the town's history in the annual tourist brochure mentioned such interesting events as the building of the B51 highway in 1841 but leaped neatly from the 1920s to the 1950s without one reference to the horrors in between.

Truthfully, it was hard for me to imagine anything as awful as the Second World War touching the town; looking at the half-timbered buildings and cobblestones you would think the twentieth century had bypassed it altogether. It was strange to think that so many of the old town houses had been bombed flat. It was a miracle really that the medieval walls, the old red *Rathaus,* and the church survived.

After the war there was a time of terrible hardship and the nuns of the local convent set up a sort of soup kitchen to feed schoolchildren who would otherwise have been too famished to apply themselves to learning. This was not a topic that was covered in my fourth-grade project about the history of the school. It was my mother who told me about it, rather to my father's disgust—the British tendency to put "Germany" and "the war" in the same sentence had not escaped him, and he suspected her of making a sly dig at her adopted country. Photographs of the postwar period showed children of my age dressed in ill-assorted and tatty clothing: saggy sweaters made from wool unraveled from older items, and hand-me-downs too big for their recipients. Apart from anything else, it was all horribly dowdy. I could see why Oma Kristel spent the rest of her life in an eternal quest for Glamour.

Quite often she went to Herr Schiller's house looking like some sort of movie star, even affecting a little fur collar that looked like a real animal, with jeweled eyes and a tail hanging down at one end. She wore heels so high that they were a positive endangerment to a woman of her age; she could so easily have broken an ankle. But Oma Kristel refused to believe in osteoporosis. She continued to mince about with her heels clacking on the cobblestones and the tail of the dead fox swinging from her shoulder, looking like Marlene Dietrich.

She first took me along to Herr Schiller's dimly lit old house when I was too young to put up a fight about being dragged out to visit one of Oma's ancient friends, and later on I was quite happy to go with her anyway. Herr Schiller's house was fascinating, full of strange old items, such as a sepia funeral photograph from about 1900, showing someone lying in their coffin surrounded by flowers, and a miniature ship in a bottle, tacking eternally across a sea of frozen blue putty.

Herr Schiller himself was an absolute mine of weird and interesting information. I don't remember how he first fell into the role of storyteller; perhaps Oma Kristel had marched off to the kitchen to take charge of coffee-making, and he had felt obliged to amuse me somehow. At any rate, it soon became a regular thing of ours, that I would demand that he tell me "a scary story" and he would bring out some nugget of local history or some gruesome snippet of Eifel legend.

The story of Unshockable Hans and the cats, told to Stefan and me after Katharina Linden's disappearance, was his most lavishly embellished so far. He set out to thrill us, to take us with him into a world of darkness and spirits, a realm of ghosts, witches, and monsters, where danger lurks but a stout heart and a strong faith will always conquer, where Good wins and Evil can be vanquished with a flourish of a rosary. And for a while it worked and we were comforted. That is, until later, when the next child vanished.

Chapter Eleven

❧

In some far-off, terminally optimistic part of my mind I had thought that the disappearance of Katharina Linden, which was naturally the talk of the town, would have superseded the sorry tale of Oma Kristel's combustion. If this sounds callous, I can only say that at that time none of us as yet *really* believed in her disappearance. Bad Münstereifel was, after all, the town where Pluto's attack on an overfed dachshund was front-page news.

I hoped in vain, as was evident from events on the first morning back at school after Karneval. It did not make anything better—if anything, it made things worse.

The headmistress, Frau Redemann, had called a meeting in the school hall for all classes. A good deal of elbowing and whispering went on while we waited for Frau Redemann. Even the first grade knew what had happened, though I doubt their parents would have been edified to hear the loving and entirely fictitious description Thilo Koch poured into their waiting ears, of how Katharina Linden's corpse had been found in the Erft, *chopped into such tiny pieces her own mother didn't know her.* By the time Frau Redemann appeared we had worked ourselves up into a fever pitch of anticipation.

"Good morning, everyone," she began. "I am sure you all know why you are here this morning. Katharina Linden, from fourth grade, has been missing since the Karneval parade on Sunday. We are, of course, hopeful that Katharina will be found in the near future, safe and well."

She paused, and some of the smaller children turned around to look at Thilo Koch rather dubiously. Thilo smiled smugly, like an odious policeman who has been first to discover the corpse.

"Obviously, this is an extremely worrying time for the Linden family. Daniel Linden is not attending school today. However, when he does return I do *not* want any of you mentioning Katharina's disappearance in front of him. In particular, I do not wish to hear repeated any of the unpleasant and lurid stories that I have already heard being circulated in the school this morning." At this, Thilo's smile wavered a little. "I would also urge anyone who thinks they may have any *genuine* information about Katharina's whereabouts to come and see me in the school office.

"I would like to add that until we know exactly what has happened, we should all take a little more care than usual." *Take care of what?* I wondered. *That Thilo Koch's mad axeman doesn't sneak up on us?*

"I also ask all of you to remember: Never go with anyone you don't know. Go straight home after school. Keep your parents informed of where you are going. And if you see anything that seems *strange* in any way, come and talk to me or to your teacher."

Again that word *seltsam*. As we all trooped out of the hall, I wondered what Frau Redemann would say if I told her about Pluto's sudden and sinister appearance, which now seemed like some sort of omen, a sign that something malevolent was afoot. However, I was not able to pursue this train of thought for very long before my own woes overtook me again.

"Look, it's *her,*" said a voice from behind me that I recognized instantly as Thilo Koch's. "The exploding girl."

"The walking bomb," said another voice, that of Thilo's arch-ally Matthias Esch, a boy who was almost as tubby and malicious as Thilo himself.

I feigned deafness, but knew the reddening of the back of my neck would show them that I had taken in every word. I put my head down doggedly and began to mount the stairs to my classroom.

"The walking bomb," repeated Thilo's repellent voice from close behind me. There was a scuffle on the staircase as he jostled Matthias. "Hey, maybe that's what happened to Katharina Linden. Maybe she just got too close to the exploding girl here, and she caught it."

"Caught what?" Matthias Esch was as dim as he was nasty.

"The exploding, stupid." Thilo's voice was ecstatic; he had tapped into a new vein of spite and it proved to be a rich one. "Maybe that's why they can't find her. She just exploded—went off like a tonne of dynamite, and blew herself into such little bits you wouldn't know it was her."

"*Klasse,*" said Matthias, overcome with admiration for the concept so neatly described.

"We *definitely* shouldn't have to sit next to her," continued Thilo in a voice that probably traveled the length of the school. "It might be one of us next."

"Yeah, sure," cut in a voice. "It probably *will* be one of you two. Eat one more *Wurst* and you most definitely *will* explode, you *Fettsack.*"

It was Stefan; StinkStefan to the rescue. My heart sank further; it seemed it was still me and StinkStefan against the World.

The days ran on, and before you knew it we were at the end of a week and Katharina Linden had still not been found. As far as the adults' conversations went, the gloves were now off, and her disappearance was being freely discussed on every street corner and in every boutique as an "abduction."

Those of us who were still walking to school, as opposed to being driven by anxious parents, were treated to a gauntlet of photographs of our former schoolmate on the newsstands and the police posters scattered about the town. There was even a blurry one of Katharina in her Snow White costume under the terrible headline *Who Gave Her the Poisoned Apple?*

Green-and-white police cars appeared at every corner or cruised slowly past the school bus stops, and on Friday morning Herr Wachtmeister Tondorf, one of the local policemen, came to give us a talk at the school. His usually jolly face was sober as he went over the by-now familiar ground of not getting into anyone's car and not talking to strangers.

Looking back, I don't think at that stage anyone expected another child to disappear. The police cars, the escort to the school buses, the serious talks were all meant to make the local community think that something was being done. Even assuming that something sinister had happened in the first place and Katharina hadn't fallen down a manhole or something, no one believed that anything else would happen.

My mother still allowed me to walk the short distance to school, but on the second or third morning, when I happened to glance back, I caught her hanging out of the front doorway to keep me in view until I had come safely to the corner of the street and within sight of the school gates.

School itself was dismal. Thanks to Thilo Koch I was even more of a leper than before. Home was little better, since my mother was reluctant to let me go out alone. I sometimes thought that were it not for the diversion of Stefan and my visits to Herr Schiller's house to hear his gruesome tales, I would have died of boredom. As it was, though, I nearly wrecked my chances of going there again.

Chapter Twelve

ell us another story, Herr Schiller." This was from Stefan, who was sitting on the edge of a claw-footed and overstuffed armchair that looked as though it had been made for Herr Schiller's grandmother.

"*Bitte,*" I corrected him in a disapproving tone that Oma Kristel would have been proud of. Not that I was such a stickler for manners— but I knew people of Herr Schiller's generation were.

"*Please.*" Stefan corrected himself. "The one about the cats was cool."

Herr Schiller raised one eyebrow and regarded Stefan quizzically over the top of his spectacles. "I seem to remember that at the time you told me it was not scary at all, young man." His expression was stern but his voice was cheerful.

Stefan looked down, temporarily at a loss, but when his head came up again he was smiling, rather shyly. He and Herr Schiller regarded each other in silence for several moments, and then I was surprised to see Herr Schiller's craggy face break into a smile, too.

A little flush of annoyance ran through me, like a tiny electrical charge traveling along a wire. Sometimes the two of them made me feel like an unwelcome third. And besides (said a mean little voice at the back of my mind), who did Stefan think he was, anyway? He was still StinkStefan, the most unpopular boy in the class, if not the entire school.

"I don't want to hear a story today, *actually,*" I cut in, and instantly felt self-conscious at the edge in my voice. Still, it worked; both their heads had turned my way and they were now looking at me, Stefan with a look of irritation at the interruption and Herr Schiller with a smooth expression that betrayed no recognition of my rudeness.

"I wanted to ask Herr Schiller something," I declared.

Stefan sighed. "Go on, then." The suffix *dummy* hung unspoken in the air.

"Well . . ." Now that I had center stage I was not at all sure I wanted to deliver my soliloquy. But I saw one of Herr Schiller's bushy white eyebrows starting to lift as though being drawn up his forehead by an invisible string, and so I plunged ahead.

"I wanted to ask you about . . . well, about the things that have been happening."

"The things?"

"Yes, well, you see, my mother said we should look out for anything that was *seltsam,* and then I started to think about all the stuff you told me about, about the cats and everything, and how they just went through the walls, and how Pluto did it too. I don't think it's right—I think there's something strange going on, Herr Schiller, and since you know so much about all that kind of thing I thought maybe you might know who or what did it, and where we should start looking."

This was a relatively long speech for me, and I had got to the end before I realized that Herr Schiller was looking at me with an expression of total and bemused noncomprehension.

"Start looking for what?"

"Katharina Linden," I said, as though it were self-evident.

There was a long silence.

"I don't understand what you're asking," said Herr Schiller at last.

"You know," I persisted uncomfortably. "The girl from my school who disappeared."

Embarrassment loosened my tongue and I found myself running on uncontrollably. "The thing is, she was there by the fountain, we all saw her, and then she wasn't there anymore and Frau Linden said she couldn't find her and had we seen her? And no one just vanishes into thin air, so it's obvious it must have been . . ."

My voice trailed off and I fell silent without finishing the sentence.

"It must have been . . . ?" prompted Herr Schiller, but I was unable to complete the phrase. I had been going to say *magic,* but I now realized how stupid that sounded.

"It just didn't seem right," I finished in a small voice.

Herr Schiller regarded me for a very long moment. His lips were tight shut but I could see a little muscle in his jaw working, as though words were struggling to get out. Looking at him with my cheeks reddening, I was suddenly struck by how ancient he looked. The lines in his face looked as though they had been carved there, the bright-blue eyes sunken into shadowy hollows.

Then he turned to Stefan and made an odd little movement like a bow. "Young man," he said, in a tone that had joviality smeared all over the stiffness underneath like greasepaint. He turned back to me. "Fräulein Kolvenbach." He sighed. "Forgive the rudeness of a very old man. I am very tired and I'm afraid I must ask you to leave."

I gaped at him. Behind Herr Schiller I could see Stefan making *you idiot* faces at me.

I was not sure what I had done, but I had evidently put my foot in it to a cataclysmic extent. "I'm really sorry," I stammered. "I didn't mean to—"

"Please don't apologize," said Herr Schiller in a weary voice. "I am simply tired, my dear. I *am* over eighty, you know." At that precise moment he looked more like a hundred and ten. "Go now, but come and see me again soon, won't you?"

Stefan and I got to our feet, and before we knew it we were once again out in the frigid air, with cobblestones under our feet and a firmly closed door at our backs.

"Nice one, Pia," said Stefan with heavy irony.

"I didn't do anything," I said defensively.

"You must have," Stefan pointed out. "You must have offended him really badly or he wouldn't have asked us to leave." He looked at me speculatively. "What were you trying to ask him, anyway?"

Now that I had to put it into words again, it really sounded stupid.

"Well, since he's an expert on all that sort of stuff, I thought he might know something about people disappearing."

"All that stuff? You think a witch got Katharina or something?" he said incredulously.

"Shut up," I told him helpfully. I glanced around me, as though looking for someone more interesting to talk to. "I don't want to talk about it. I'm going home now, anyway."

Stefan shrugged. "All right. See you tomorrow."

I didn't reply; I didn't want to give him the satisfaction of knowing that I would be hanging around with him for yet another day of social leprosy, even though we both very well knew I would be. In defiance of my mother's instructions to stay together, I walked off, once again leaving him standing alone.

"You're home early," said my mother as I let myself into the house.

"Hmm," I said discouragingly. Of course, my hangdog looks and low state of mind did not pass unnoticed under the maternal radar. My mother was out of the kitchen, wiping her hands on a tea towel and ready for action, before I had made it to the foot of the stairs.

"What's up?" Her tone was brisk. I sighed and shrugged my shoulders.

"Nothing, really. I just . . . Herr Schiller . . ." My voice tailed off. There was no way to explain without my mother reaching the inescapable conclusion that I had somehow been rude to the old man.

"Herr Schiller what?"

"Oh . . ." I shuffled my feet uncomfortably on the wooden floorboards. "We had to leave, that's all. He said he wasn't feeling well."

I must have sounded unconvincing because my mother cocked her head and said, "Have you two been making a nuisance of yourselves?" I did not reply. "Herr Schiller is over eighty, you know," she went on. "I'm not sure he can cope with two youngsters for hours on end."

"It wasn't that," I said defensively, and then instantly realized that I had dropped myself in it.

"So what was it?" was my mother's immediate riposte.

I gave a deep sigh. "I think I—I think he was upset about something I said." I looked at her earnestly. Her lips were pursed. "I didn't mean to upset him. I mean, I'm still not sure what was wrong." By this time my mother's mouth was drawn so far to one side of her face by skepticism that she looked as though she had been painted by Picasso.

"Pia." The word was heavily loaded with reproach. "What did you say? Tell me exactly what you said."

"Mama . . ."

"Pia, what did you say?"

"Well, I didn't say anything rude. Honestly, I didn't. I just asked him about the stuff that's been happening in the town. You know, about Katharina Linden."

"Oh, Pia." Now her lips relaxed but her brows were knitted and her chin drawn back, as though she were seeing something shockingly sad. Then she sighed very heavily and reached out a hand to touch my shoulder. "Well, I suppose you couldn't have known." She shook her head. "Come into the kitchen for a minute."

Mystified, I followed her, wondering what I had done. Were Katharina Linden and Herr Schiller somehow related?

"Sit," said my mother, indicating the bench seat by the table. Obediently I sat, as she settled herself on the other side. So it was clearly going to be another little talk; two in one week was a record even for me.

"Look, Pia, perhaps I should have told you this before, but I didn't think it would be helpful. I'm not surprised Herr Schiller was upset when you asked him about Katharina Linden's disappearance. Did you know that he had a daughter who disappeared?"

"No." I was genuinely shocked.

"Well, he did, so obviously it's not the best topic to discuss with him. That's partly the reason I didn't mention it before. I was afraid you might be curious and ask him about it."

I was indignant at this—how could she think I would do such a thing?—but to be honest, if I had known about it, I *would* have been consumed with curiosity. It might have been difficult to stay right off the topic, and a ten-year-old's attempts to approach the subject in a subtle, roundabout way would have been picked up a mile off by someone as sharp as Herr Schiller. Still, the cat was out of the bag now; I might as well ask my mother all the questions that were seething to the surface of my mind.

"Is Herr Schiller married?"

"He's a widower," explained my mother.

"When did his wife die?" I wanted to know.

"Oh, I'm not sure . . ." A funny look passed across my mother's face; I'm almost sure she was about to say, *You'll have to ask Oma Kristel,* and stopped herself just in time. "I think it was during the war."

"How old was the little girl?"

"Oh, Pia. I really don't know that. I only know what Oma Kristel told me a long time ago. I think the little girl disappeared *after* her mother died, but I don't know what age she was."

"Did they ever find her?"

"No," said my mother. She seemed lost in thought for a moment.

"What happened to her?" I persisted.

"Nobody knows," my mother said. "She just . . . vanished. It was wartime, you know. All sorts of awful things happened. Your granny"—by this she meant her own mother in England, Granny Warner—"told me a house in her street was hit by a bomb and they never found a body at all. It must have been vaporized." She glanced at me. "This is rather a gruesome topic, isn't it? Shall we change the subject?"

But I wasn't finished yet. "Was she in a house that got bombed?"

"No, she wasn't. It wouldn't be a disappearance if they knew what had happened, would it?" said my mother. She sounded a little impatient. "Why don't you ask—no, listen, Pia, this was precisely the reason I didn't tell you about it in the first place. You can't start asking questions about it. You'll hurt Herr Schiller terribly." She shook her head again. "It sounds as though you have already offended him by asking about Katharina Linden."

"I didn't mean to . . ."

"I know you didn't, but I think you have offended him. Perhaps I should call him and apologize . . ."

In fact she *did* try to telephone him later that evening, but although she let the phone ring twenty times there was no reply. At length she decided to leave well enough alone; after all, what could she say to apologize that would not include mentioning the taboo topic? And I—I sat upstairs in my room with a book I was not really reading and a cup of cocoa that went cold on the top of my bedside table, staring out the window at the dark and mourning the sure end of a friendship.

Chapter Thirteen

"This town!" my mother was shouting. "This town! That's what the problem is!"

Sebastian and I, at the kitchen table, stared at each other and listened in silence to the argument. Sebastian's eyes were round with astonishment. He was used to my mother's occasional explosive outbursts of temper when they were directed at one of us children—when we had done something particularly annoying, such as the time Sebastian emptied a full pot of honey into the kettle to "make hot honey for Teddy." To hear it directed at our father was quite different, and somehow chilling, like the first icy gust of wind that signals the end of summer. I looked at Sebastian and saw from his expression that his infant mind was also groping about, trying to imagine what Papa might have done that was so *böse*.

"This bloody town!" added my mother in English for good measure. She regarded my father balefully, a formidable sight in her plasticized apron, a stainless-steel frying fork brandished in her right hand for emphasis.

"*Ach*, this again," retorted my father in disgust. I marveled at his courage; my mother looked as though she might beat him around the head with the frying fork.

"What do you mean, *this again*?" my mother demanded.

My father regarded her stolidly. "Everything is better in England," he said.

"Well—" began my mother, but then obviously changed her mind, thinking that even for a raging Anglophile the riposte *Well, it* is *better* was overstating the case.

After the briefest of pauses she went on, "I know it isn't perfect"— in tones that implied she knew the exact opposite—"but at least where I grew up kids didn't get spirited away off the streets while their parents were two meters away." This exaggeration was typical of my mother, and always infuriated my father, who like many Germans was completely oblivious to irony. The exaggeration was not what caught my attention about her little speech, though; it was the word *weggezaubert,* which literally means to be made to *disappear by magic.*

But before I had time to digest this notion, my mother was ranting on. "I don't even want to let Pia out anymore. Wolfgang, when we moved here I thought we were at least doing the right thing for the children. A small town, everyone knows each other, countryside all around. Now it seems like we're living in the middle of *A Nightmare on* bloody *Elm Street*!" She was back into English again, as she always was when she got really angry.

"You can't blame the town for that," protested my father. "These things happen everywhere."

"Not everywhere," snapped my mother. "And, anyway, this thing happened *here,* didn't it? And haven't you noticed what's happening to Pia in your *friendly* little town?"

My father swung his not inconsiderable bulk around and regarded me briefly. "What is happening to Pia?"

"All her so-called friends are avoiding her. Well, all except Stefan Breuer, and he hasn't exactly had an easy time here either, has he?"

"That's hardly surprising when his father is drunk on the streets at lunchtime," retorted my father.

"That's what I mean!" rejoined my mother. "Always gossiping, and everyone judging everyone else."

"I am not judging, I am telling the truth," said my father. "He *is* drunk at lunchtime. It is not gossip; I have seen him myself."

"Ooooh!" screeched my mother. "Why do you have to be so bloody *German*?"

My father regarded her expressionlessly. Then he said quietly, "And why do you have to be so bloody English?"

For a moment they looked at each other in silence. Then my mother opened her mouth to say something, but what it was going to be I do not know because at that precise instant we heard someone knocking loudly on the front door.

Now, when I finally come to tell the story of that strange pre-millennium year, I am years older, almost an adult myself. Even so, people often do things that I struggle to understand. Their motives are hard to fathom.

When I was ten, adult behavior seemed completely incomprehensible. You could say something apparently quite innocent, or repeat something that you had heard adults saying, and find that you had caused horrible offense. You could have something hammered into you by one set of adults and find another set apparently propagating the exact opposite.

Adults: they were so unpredictable that nothing they did should have been able to surprise me anymore. Still, that morning something did.

The knocking was Herr Schiller. My mother, still flushed from the argument, and still clutching the frying fork, opened the door and found Herr Schiller standing on the doorstep, as always looking as though he had been dressed by a personal valet.

"*Guten Morgen,* Frau Kolvenbach," said Herr Schiller, making a very slight bow. He lifted his hat and extended a hand to my mother.

"Herr Schiller," said my mother, sounding surprised, but remembering to take the hand and shake it politely.

Still sitting at the kitchen table, I heard the exchange of greetings and my heart sank. This could mean only one thing: I was in trouble. Herr Schiller must have come to make a complaint to my mother about my offensive behavior. I felt hot with guilt and embarrassment, and also a little indignation: after all, I hadn't *meant* to upset him. If my mother had told me about his daughter beforehand, I wouldn't have asked him about Katharina Linden.

At that moment I almost felt I hated him; it was so unfair, and so typically adult. I slipped down from the bench seat and was brushing crumbs from my trousers when my mother came back into the kitchen.

"Herr Schiller is here to see you," she announced.

I was incredulous. To see *me*? I wondered whether this was some sly introduction to the inevitable scene. Did he want to make sure that the complaint was made in front of me? Unwillingly, I followed her into the living room.

Herr Schiller had been sitting in my father's favorite armchair, but as we entered the room he stood up. As he did so, I noticed with surprise that he was carrying a little posy of spring flowers. For a second, the idea floated through my head that my mother had given them to him as some sort of reconciliatory gesture. Then I saw that he was holding out the flowers to me.

"Fräulein Pia, these are for you," he said, and smiled. Behind me, my mother quietly slipped out of the room and went to investigate Sebastian's progress with his breakfast. I merely stood and stared at my visitor, unsure how to react.

"Please, take them," said Herr Schiller. He took a step toward me and there was nothing to do but accept the flowers. I stood there, bewildered, burying my nose in the soft petals, more to hide my embarrassment than to smell their delicate scent.

"I'm sorry," I blurted out at last, not quite daring to raise my eyes to his face. "I didn't mean to . . ." My voice trailed off; I was not sure how I could complete the apology without straying onto forbidden ground. *I'm sorry I mentioned disappearances . . . I didn't know your daughter disappeared . . . I didn't mean to upset you by talking about people disappearing . . .* In the end I said nothing, but Herr Schiller came to my rescue.

"Please don't apologize, Pia." His voice was kindly. "It is I who should apologize, for asking you to leave so abruptly."

I did look at him then, as it was so unexpected, an adult apologizing to a child like that, especially when the adult had reached such a respectably old age, whereas I was only ten years old and the school pariah to boot. Herr Schiller was smiling at me, the map of wrinkles on his ancient face all seeming to turn upward so that they looked like the tributaries of a spreading delta.

"I'm really sorry, I didn't mean to say anything wrong," I ventured at last. "I didn't know . . ."

The words sounded lame to me; in Bad Münstereifel everyone knew everyone else's business, so ignorance was no defense.

"Of course not," said Herr Schiller, a little sadly, it seemed to me. "You are a good child, Pia, a kind child."

A little encouraged, I tried to explain myself: "I only asked you about—you know—because you know so much about the town . . . and about all the funny stuff that's happened here in the past."

"The past?" repeated Herr Schiller. He frowned slightly, and my heart seemed to lurch—did he think I was referring to his own past again?

"The miller and the cats . . . and the treasure in the well . . . and the one about the huntsman—all the strange things like that. So I thought you might have some clues . . ."

Herr Schiller stared at me for several seconds. Then, very carefully, he lowered himself back into my father's armchair, his hands clutching the armrests for support. When he had settled himself, he said, "So, Fräulein Pia, you think that the witches took the little girl away, or something like that?"

I eyed him; it did not look as though he was making fun of me, as a lot of adults would have. It looked as though he was taking me seriously, actually considering the idea as a real possibility. Still, I replied rather carefully, "I don't know."

"But you think . . . maybe . . . ?"

"Well, everyone—I mean, all the grown-ups—keeps saying to look out for anything *seltsam*," I told him.

"*Etwas seltsam*," he repeated thoughtfully, tapping the fingers of one hand on the arm of the chair. Then he fell silent again, as though drifting away on a tide of his own thoughts.

"Herr Schiller?" I said tentatively.

"Yes, Pia?"

"You're not angry with me anymore?"

Herr Schiller made a noise that was something between a snort and a chuckle. "Of course I'm not angry with you, my dear. And you have some very interesting ideas."

"Really?" I was both flattered and astounded.

"Yes, really," said Herr Schiller. "You see patterns where other people see nothing."

I was not sure what to say to this. If I had seen a connection between the disappearance of a little girl and the stories of hidden secrets, terrible fates, and eternal hauntings that Herr Schiller poured into my fascinated ears, it was not a pattern that any adult other than Herr Schiller was likely to take seriously. I was not even sure it made sense myself; and my mother would treat it as the domestic equivalent of wasting police time.

"Herr Schiller? Are there really any such things as ghosts?"

The old man did not even show surprise at the question. He heaved a sigh. "Yes, Pia, there are. But never the ones you expect."

I pondered this. He had the answer down pat; but did it really mean anything? I had heard my mother with my own ears telling Sebastian that St. Nicholas was going to fill his shoes with presents on December 6, and up until fairly recently she had still maintained the pretense of the tooth fairy. I was reluctant to categorize my old friend with the mendacious majority of adults, but was he just humoring me?

"No, I mean *really*?" I persisted.

Herr Schiller smiled. "Pia, have you ever seen a ghost?"

"No . . ."

"Does that mean there aren't any?"

"I don't know . . ."

"*Na,* have you ever seen the great pyramid of Cheops?"

"No," I said.

"And does that mean there isn't one?"

"Of course not."

"Well then." Herr Schiller sat back in my father's armchair with the look of one who has proved his case.

"I don't think my parents believe in them," I pointed out.

"Probably not," agreed Herr Schiller equably.

"I just thought . . ." I paused. Would I be putting my foot in it again if I mentioned Katharina Linden? "I really want to help find Katharina," I ventured.

Herr Schiller followed this somewhat crooked line of logic perfectly. "And you think, Fräulein Pia, that there is something unholy going on? And that is why the little girl disappeared?"

"She was *weggezaubert*," I said; *spirited away.*

"*Ach, so,*" said Herr Schiller thoughtfully. He didn't laugh at me, or tell me to stop talking nonsense.

Emboldened, I went on: "I want to see if I can find out what happened, that's why I wanted to ask you about the weird things that have happened in the town, in case there was a clue."

We looked at each other.

"What do you think?" I asked him cautiously.

"I think, Fräulein Pia, that you have discovered an angle that the police will not be covering in their investigation," said Herr Schiller drily.

"Do you think so?" I asked eagerly.

"Yes, I think so."

"Then will you help me?"

Herr Schiller studied me for a few moments; his expression was unreadable, but his eyes twinkled. Then he lifted his gnarled hands. "I am a very old man, Pia. Too old for running all over this town looking for clues—or ghosts."

"Oh, *you* needn't do any of that," I assured him enthusiastically. "I'll do that—and Stefan," I added as an afterthought.

"Then how can I help you?" inquired Herr Schiller.

"Well, can you keep telling us the old stories?"

"*Sicher.*"

"And we'll come and tell you what we find, and you can help us work it out."

"I should be delighted."

There was no time for further dialogue because my mother put her head around the living-room door, and said, "I'm terribly sorry, Herr Schiller, would you like a cup of coffee?"

"No, thank you, Frau Kolvenbach," said Herr Schiller. He rose from the armchair and stood there for a moment, his hat in his hand, beaming down at me. "And thank *you*, Fräulein Pia."

My mother looked at him quizzically; what was there to thank me for? She was somewhat mollified on the subject of the offense I had given Herr Schiller, since he had obviously come to offer an olive branch, but she was still not convinced that I was not "bothering that poor old man." In the end she settled for, "I hope you thanked Herr Schiller for the flowers, Pia."

"Thank you, Herr Schiller," I parroted obediently.

Herr Schiller extended one wrinkled hand toward me, and for once in my life I was happy to shake hands with an adult: it was not like being nagged into it by Oma Kristel; it felt more like we were co-conspirators.

"*Auf Wiedersehen,* Pia."

"*Wiedersehen,* Herr Schiller."

Chapter Fourteen

❧

The end of the spring term that year was a relief; three whole months of being the class pariah and unwilling consort of StinkStefan had worn me down. As March turned into April, the parental curfews slackened a little, and we were allowed to go off to the big park in the Schleidtal, or to the swimming pool, or even to take a train and go to the cinema in Euskirchen. In between, we went to Herr Schiller's.

We listened to his tales with a renewed interest, now that the town seemed to have passed into a story all of its own—the story of the little girl dressed as Snow White, who stepped out of her life and into nothingness right in the middle of a Karneval parade. I puzzled over the details of what Herr Schiller told us, trying to fit the events of the past few months into the pattern, as though I were trying to complete a huge and complicated jigsaw puzzle without being able to see the picture on the lid of the box. Judging by Herr Schiller's stories, Bad Münstereifel had to be one of the most haunted places in Germany, if not the whole world; monsters and ghosts and skeletons seemed to pop up in every corner.

Stefan, whose parents did not police his television viewing as strictly as mine did, had seen numerous horror films, and not just the ancient version of *Nosferatu* that periodically appeared on television; he had even seen *Poltergeist* and *The Shining*. As a result, his views on the subject were more developed than mine; he thought there was some evil influence working out its purpose in the town. He postulated all sorts of theories: the Lindens' house was built on an old graveyard where the bodies of plague victims had been buried; Katharina had meddled with occult powers she did not understand, and had been carried off by them; the Linden family were under some sort of terrible curse, which led to the early demise of the eldest child in every generation.

"Herr Linden is an oldest child," I pointed out when Stefan expounded the last of those theories. "He's the oldest of two; Frau Holzheim is his sister. So how come *he* didn't disappear when he was a kid?"

"Maybe the curse skips a generation," suggested Stefan, undaunted.

I was not convinced, and appealed to Herr Schiller on our next visit.

"Are there any stories about curses on people?"

Herr Schiller pondered this, taking slow sips of coffee from a delicate-looking cup with yellow and gray roses on it.

"There was the knight who lived in the Alte Burg on the Quecken hill," he suggested eventually.

"I've heard that one," I said, disappointed.

"I haven't," Stefan pointed out. He looked eagerly at Herr Schiller; really, for someone who seemed to make himself so objectionable to his classmates, he could look wonderfully appealing to adults. Herr Schiller could not help but retell the story, in spite of my discontented expression.

"The old castle on the Quecken hill was built before the castle in the town, over one thousand years ago," began Herr Schiller. "In the castle there lived a knight, with his wife and only son. The old knight was an avid hunter and his son shared his love of hunting; there was nothing he loved more than to ride with his hounds through the woods.

"In due course the old knight died, and without his father's guidance the young man began to neglect his other duties in order to indulge his lust for the chase. Every day he rode forth from the castle, mounted on a fine black stallion, with his hounds baying as they streamed through the gates, and spent many hours hunting. At last, he even usurped the Lord's Day for his pursuits.

"His mother, the old knight's Lady, was a devout woman, and her son's behavior wounded her very deeply. At first she tried to remonstrate with him, pointing out that if he would only fulfill his duty to God first by attending church on Sunday morning, there would still be plenty of time left for hunting afterward. But her prayers fell on deaf ears.

"At last, one Sunday morning the mother could contain herself no longer. As soon as the sun was up, her son was out in the castle courtyard preparing for the hunt. A young squire was holding on to the reins of the black stallion, who pawed the ground and blew out hard through his nose, with almost as much eagerness for the chase as his master. The hunting dogs were already baying and straining at the iron chains that held them. The young man was stalking about the courtyard impatiently, berating his servants for their tardiness.

"As he did so, a window opened above him, and his mother leaned out, to beg her son one more time to come to church. 'The day is long enough for hunting afterward,' she cried. But once again her son refused to listen. Swinging himself into the saddle of his great black horse, he signaled to the gatekeeper to open the gates. The hounds were loosed, and with a cacophony of howls and the strident note of a hunting horn the hunt sallied forth. The Lady, her heart overflowing with the bitterest pain, cried out after him, '*I wish you may hunt forever!*'

"The day passed, evening came, and at last night fell, and there was neither sight nor sound of the young man, nor of his great stallion and his pack of savage hunting dogs. A week passed, then a month, and at last a year had turned around, and still the young man did not come back.

"When the old mother died, the castle fell into ruins, and in the course of time it became as it is now, a heap of moss-covered stones, overgrown with weeds, with trees thrusting up through its former courts and halls. But the huntsman's soul knew no rest; it was condemned to roam forevermore in the woods and chases where it rode to hounds in life."

Herr Schiller leaned a little closer. "They say that he still rides out of the old castle on moonlit nights. Poor tattered soul, not knowing or remembering why he is there or what he seeks, restlessly roaming the forests—forever—"

"He's still there?" interrupted Stefan. "Has anyone seen him?"

"In some of those lonely houses at the edge of the forest, people have lain in bed at night shivering, listening to the sound of hoofbeats and the howling of dogs as the hunt passes by," said Herr Schiller. "But none would dare go out to meet him."

"They didn't look?" interrupted Stefan. He shook his head. "*Angsthasen.* I would've looked."

I could see what he was thinking, and what my mother would have to say about it: *No, you may* not *sit up until midnight on the Quecken hill; what are you thinking of, when we still don't know what happened to poor Katharina Linden? And you'd be fit for nothing in the morning . . .*

With a sigh I picked up my cup and took a sip of cold coffee. The spectral huntsman was cursed to roam the woods for all eternity; it seemed I was cursed to be haunted by StinkStefan for at least as long. And much though I enjoyed Herr Schiller's storytelling, it did not seem as though we were getting any closer to the truth about Katharina's disappearance.

I looked at Stefan and Herr Schiller, who were deep in a discussion about the likely route the eternal huntsman would have taken, Stefan drawing it out on the coffee table with his finger. They seemed to have temporarily forgotten me, which only added to the sum of my woes. Summer seemed a long, long time away.

Chapter Fifteen

Of course, it was Stefan who broached the idea of going up to the Quecken hill at night; knowing my mother's probable response, I would as soon have thought of asking to ride the train into Köln to go nightclubbing.

I thought it might be possible to visit the castle ruins in the daytime; we might even tell my mother it was for a school project. But Stefan was adamant that there would be no point in going up there if we couldn't go at night.

"You know," he said suddenly, "we should go up there on Walpurgis eve."

"Stefan . . ." I began reluctantly; the entire concept was so unrealistic as to be not worth considering. But he was already caught up on a wave of his own enthusiasm.

"No, really. We must." His eyes were shining; a lock of his dirty blond hair fell over his face and he brushed it back impatiently. "It's the witches' night, right? If there's anything to see, it has to happen then."

This made sense to me, but still did not get over the fact that it would take some genuine magic to get me out of the house and up the Quecken hill at night.

"My mother is *never* going to let me go up there after dark," I pointed out.

"Can't you make up some excuse?"

"Like what?" I could not think of any possible circumstances under which it would be allowed.

"We'll—we'll say we're going to put up a *Maibaum*."

"A *Maibaum*?" I had to admit this was a stroke of genius.

A *Maibaum*—or May tree—was a tree, usually a young silver birch, chopped off at the base, the branches decorated with long streamers of colored crêpe paper. Every village in the Eifel had one on May Day, but it was also a tradition that young men would put a *Maibaum* up outside the house of their girlfriend on the night before May Day, so that she would see it when she got up in the morning. This meant that the last night of April had to be the only night of the year when half the youth of the town could be creeping about in the small hours with legitimate cause. All the same . . .

"Who would we be putting a *Maibaum* up for?" I asked. "And, anyway, girls don't usually put them up at all."

"Easy," said Stefan, who was obviously developing the plan at breakneck pace. "We'll say we're helping my cousin Boris."

"Hmmm." I still had my doubts.

Boris was a hulking monster of an eighteen-year-old, with long hair that looked as though it had been styled with motor oil, and mean little eyes so deep-set that they seemed to be peering at you through slits in a helmet. As far as I knew he had no girlfriend and, even if he had, he did not give the impression that he would be the sort who offers flowers and opens doors and puts up May trees. Certainly, I couldn't imagine him asking two ten-year-olds to accompany him on a romantic mission of that kind. Still, in the absence of any more inspired idea, I agreed to suggest the plan to my mother.

"*Schön,*" said Stefan airily, as though it were already fixed. He got to his feet. "Come on, let's go and ask her now."

"Absolutely not," said my mother, predictably. Both Stefan and I stood before her in the kitchen, like two kindergarten kids getting a tickingoff from the teacher. My mother had been in the process of frying some meat for a casserole, and the neglected pan sizzled alarmingly behind her as she faced us.

"But, Frau Kolvenbach," said Stefan in the polite voice he used with such good effect upon susceptible adults, "we'd be going with my cousin Boris."

His efforts were wasted, however; my mother was flint-hearted. "I don't care, Stefan. Pia isn't going out God-knows-where after dark."

"Boris is—" began Stefan, but my mother cut him off.

"Boris is going to have to put up his May tree by himself," she retorted. She eyed Stefan skeptically. "Is Boris that tall boy from the *Hauptschule,* the one with the long hair and the biker jacket?"

"Yes, but—" began Stefan again, but in vain.

"Then he looks quite big and hefty enough to carry his own *Maibaum,*" said my mother with finality. I opened my mouth to say something, but she raised her hand warningly. "No, Pia. The answer is no. Now, I don't want to discuss it anymore," she added, turning back to the stove. She prodded the meat with a frying fork, shaking her head. "I'm surprised your mother is letting *you* go out after dark, even with your cousin, Stefan."

"Um," said Stefan noncommittally. He looked at me; it was time to make our escape.

Up in my room, we regarded each other gloomily.

"I told you," I snapped.

He shrugged. "It was worth trying." For a while we just pondered.

"What now?" I said in the end, in a somewhat listless voice.

Stefan looked up. "I'm going on my own, of course."

"Really?"

"Well, your mother's never going to change her mind, is she? I can tell you all about it afterward," said Stefan. And I had to make do with that.

As it happened, the last day of April 1999 was a Friday, which lent an advantage to Stefan's plan; should his mother choose that day to shift a little within the haze of smoke and alcohol in which she was always enveloped, and inquire into her son's proposed excursion, at least she couldn't complain that he had school the next day. I made Stefan promise to come over as early as possible on May morning to tell me what he had seen. The plan finalized, we clattered downstairs.

"Can Stefan come over tomorrow morning?" I asked my mother.

"If he comes at a civilized hour," she replied.

"Seven o'clock?" I said hopefully.

"Ten o'clock," said my mother firmly, and disappeared back into the kitchen.

Stefan did not come over at ten o'clock that morning, nor did he come at half past ten, eleven o'clock, or noon. I sat by the window in the living room, nursing a comic book and peering out into the damp street, hoping to see him come running up through the rain.

The day wore on, and eventually I was persuaded to go finish my homework; my mother promised to call me the instant Stefan arrived. By the time I had finished the last page and was slipping the folder back into my overstuffed *Ranzen,* it was half past three, and still no Stefan. I went downstairs and found my mother energetically mopping the kitchen floor; Sebastian was perched out of harm's way in his high chair, looking a little like a tennis umpire as he watched the mop head whisking back and forth across the tiles.

"Did Stefan come?" I asked in a slightly accusatory tone. Maybe he had turned up and been sent away again because I was doing my homework.

"No," said my mother, pausing in her metronomic motion. She rubbed the back of her hand across her chin and glanced at me. "Perhaps he can't come today, Pia."

"He *promised* he would," I said stubbornly.

"You'll see him on Monday at school. What's so important about today anyway?"

"Nothing," I said, biting my lip.

"Well—" She was starting to sound exasperated. "Can't you call him?"

"Mmmm." The thought of getting Frau Breuer's irritable, smoke-roughened voice at the other end of the phone was daunting.

"Out from under my feet, anyway," said my mother, and the discussion was closed.

I wandered through to the living room and looked at the telephone extension as though it might bite me. It was now three thirty. Time seemed to have slowed down. Monday morning was an eternity away. Where on earth was Stefan? Had he completely *disappeared?*

As the thought occurred to me, it sent a shiver through me like a tiny electric shock. Perhaps he *had* disappeared—just like Katharina Linden. *No. Don't be so stupid.* But the idea grew on me, the more I tried to convince myself that it was utter rubbish. Supposing he had gone up to the Quecken hill, and whatever it was that had got Katharina had got him, too, while he sat up there in the dark, waiting and watching?

I imagined him sitting there on one of the broken and mossy chunks of masonry, hugging his knees, shivering a little and peering into the dark. Had something crept up on him? Had it taken him with it, carried him off on its endless sweep through the darkened woods? An image of the spectral hunt formed in my mind's eye, only instead of a knight it was Stefan who clung to the horse's mane, his face like a pale moon and his eyes pits of darkness.

At last, even I could see that there was nothing for it; I'd have to telephone the Breuers. I hoped that Stefan would answer, so that I could bawl him out for not showing up, and then pump him for information. If not Stefan, then Frau Breuer was the lesser of two evils; she was bad-tempered but at least she was comprehensible: you could tell exactly how rude she was being to you.

Stefan's father, Jano, on the other hand, had such a strong Slovakian accent that I could hardly understand his German. To converse with him was to pick your way through a thicket of stunted phrases and mangled vowels in the sure knowledge that if you said, *"Wie, bitte?"* once too often he would lose his temper. So as I dialed Stefan's number I was praying that it would not be Jano who answered.

The phone rang eight times, and then suddenly it was picked up.

"Breuer," barked a voice in my ear.

"Frau Breuer?" I quavered. "It's Pia Kolvenbach."

There was a short pause at the other end, during which I could hear Frau Breuer breathing heavily into the receiver, a sound reminiscent of a Rottweiler panting.

"You can't speak to Stefan," she eventually informed me.

"But—" I frantically tried to summon up the right words, afraid that she would hang up on me. "But—is he *there?*"

She snorted in disgust. *"Doch,* he's here. But you can't speak to him."

Chapter Sixteen

❧

The following morning dawned gray and uninviting. I looked out at the damp street, the cobblestones gleaming wetly, and my heart sank. Sunday seemed to stretch out before me like some uncrossable wasteland; Monday was a million years away, and I was going to spend every one of them shut indoors with no one but Sebastian to play with.

I looked into the living room, but my father was in there, reading a newspaper. He said nothing, but the slight raising of his eyebrows signaled that I was surplus to requirements, so I shut the door. Then I hung about on the staircase for a while, swinging on the newel post and scuffing my feet on the stairs. My mother, hearing these irritating noises, stuck her head around the kitchen door to remonstrate with me, but before she had time to fire off a remark, there was a loud knock at the front door.

Stefan! was my first thought as I sprang down from the stairs and headed for the door; the second was the surprising realization that I was actually *looking forward* to seeing him—to seeing *StinkStefan.*

"Pia, your hair—" began my mother in an irritated voice; she also made for the door, but I was too quick for her. I pulled down the heavy handle and swung it open.

The smile died on my face. It was not Stefan.

"Oh," was all I could find to say as I stood there in my scruffy jeans with my unbrushed hair hanging around my face in tangled hanks.

"*Guten Morgen,* Frau Kessel," said my mother, with more presence of mind; she elbowed her way past me, wiping her hands on a tea towel, and held out her hand, which Frau Kessel shook, somewhat gingerly.

"*Guten Morgen,* Frau Kolvenbach," replied Frau Kessel with aplomb. She was a small woman in her seventies, comfortably compact, with a bosom almost as intimidating as Oma Kristel's had been. She always dressed very neatly, but in a slightly old-fashioned style; today she was wearing a moss-green wool suit with a large and ugly Edelweiss brooch pinned to the front of it. She had a mass of pure white hair that had become as thin and gauzy as cotton candy; she habitually wore it piled on top of her head. Today it had been back-combed and stacked up so high that she had rather a Marie-Antoinette effect.

Underneath this improbable confection beamed her chubby face, with its twin flash of well-polished spectacles and expensive false teeth. She looked like an adorable old *Oma;* in fact she was the most vicious gossip in the whole of Bad Münstereifel.

"Won't you come in, Frau Kessel?" said my mother, not betraying the effort it must have cost her to utter those fateful words. My mother could have cleaned and scrubbed for a week, and presented two charming children with neatly brushed hair and matching outfits (me in a dress, of course), and still Frau Kessel's beady old eyes would have found something to complain about to the next person she visited.

"Thank you," said Frau Kessel, stepping carefully into the house, looking around her with avid-eyed interest.

"Please, do come into the living room," said my mother in a bright voice, and opened the door. My father got to his feet, folding the newspaper he had been reading, and extended his hand.

"I didn't see you in church this morning, Wolfgang," was the first thing Frau Kessel said to him once the greetings were out of the way. She spoke in an arch tone.

"No," answered my father, refusing to be drawn; Frau Kessel knew perfectly well that my father went to church only when absolutely necessary—for family weddings and funerals, for example—and that my mother being Protestant, *evangelisch* as it is called in Germany, she was not likely to see the rest of us in Sts. Chrysostom and Daria at all.

Still, she was never one to pass up an opportunity to needle someone; she kept the hundred-candle power smile going for half a minute as the silence stretched out between them, before finally conceding defeat and saying, "I do *so* miss seeing dear Kristel there every week."

"Yes," said my father, and sighed.

"Would you like some coffee, Frau Kessel?" interposed my mother, before the old woman could advance further on the topic of Oma Kristel's churchgoing habits. "*Freshly ground* coffee," she added, seeing Frau Kessel hesitate.

"Thank you, I will," said Frau Kessel with the gracious air of one granting a favor.

She took the seat my father offered her, and settled herself in it with some care, like an elderly hen preparing to lay.

My mother departed for the kitchen, still smiling tautly—she couldn't stand Frau Kessel—and my father and I looked at the old lady expectantly. We were under no illusion that this was a purely social visit. Frau Kessel had come over because she had Something to Say.

"*Nun,* it has been an exciting week for the town, don't you think, Wolfgang?" was her opening sally. I looked at my father, puzzled. What was so exciting? My father also looked blank. Frau Kessel looked from my father to me, and then back to my father again. Her eyebrows lifted a little, and she cocked her head to one side, as though considering; could it *really* be that we were the only people in Bad Münstereifel not to have *heard*?

"An exciting week?" repeated my father eventually. There was something inevitable about conversation with Frau Kessel; she would throw out the bait, and then wait until the victim couldn't bear not to bite. Now she sat back in her armchair, as though to express astonishment, folding her hands together in her green woolen lap.

"Where there's smoke, there's also fire," she said in a voice loaded with meaning.

"Did something catch fire?" I asked.

"No, *Schätzchen,*" said Frau Kessel, giving me a soulful *oh-you-poor-child* look.

"Then why—" I began, but she cut me off.

"I really think you can't have heard," she announced in tones of artificially heightened surprise; her eyebrows were now so far up her forehead that they looked as though they might scurry into the towering thicket of white hair. She looked at my father reproachfully. "Of course, if you had been in church this morning, you would have heard Pfarrer Arnold mentioning it."

She put up a hand and patted her hair. "That is to say," she went on, "he didn't mention it *directly,* but we all knew what he was *referring* to, and there were those who thought that it was in rather doubtful taste to be launching straight into a sermon of *forgiveness.*" She sniffed. "I mean, it isn't as though they've found the *child,* is it?"

Frau Kessel, whose confidences were always labyrinthine, had now lost me completely. I looked at my father again; he appeared mystified too.

"Found the child?" repeated my father ponderously.

"*Doch,* the little Linden girl."

My father considered for a moment, then gave in. "Frau Kessel, what are you trying to tell us?"

Frau Kessel looked slightly affronted. "About Herr Düster, *natürlich.*"

"What about Herr Düster?" asked my father patiently.

"Why, they've arrested him," said Frau Kessel with relish. "Yesterday morning, at eight."

"They've *arrested* him?"

Frau Kessel made a little moue of impatience; she was clearly tired of my father repeating everything she said, and wanted to get to the meat.

"Yes, they came yesterday morning and took him away in a police car." Frau Kessel spread out one hand and studied her immaculately manicured fingernails, as cool as the expert witness in a murder trial.

"Did you see it?" I asked with interest.

"Not *personally,*" said Frau Kessel, in tones that implied this fact was of no consequence; she had her spies everywhere. "Hilde—that is to say, Frau Koch—saw it, with her own eyes. She was watering her flowers at the time."

Frau Koch was Thilo Koch's grandmother, and almost as toxic a personality as her grandson. Of course, the flower watering was a pleasantry;

Hilde Koch was very likely up at dawn spying on her neighbors, and at the first sign of anything as interesting as a police car she would have been out of doors with all sensors on red alert.

"What happened?" asked my father.

"Well," said Frau Kessel, "Hilde said that they came at eight o'clock, two of them, in a police car. She thinks they came early in order not to be seen. Of course," she continued conspiratorially, "not everyone would feel happy about living next door to someone who . . . well, you know. So perhaps it was as well. She said she knew Herr Düster was at home; he'd already been out once, to take the paper in or something. When they knocked, he opened up straightaway, and they all went inside. They were in there for quite a time; Hilde said she had watered all the flowers twice before they came out again, but she couldn't go inside; she said she was transfixed.

"Anyway, eventually they came out and Herr Düster got into the back of the police car and off they drove; Hilde said he was sitting there as rigid as a figure on a meerschaum pipe, didn't show any sign of emotion at all. She said it made her feel quite ill."

"Well," said my father, at a loss for any other remark. Then he looked up thankfully; my mother was in the doorway, carrying a tray laden with coffee cups, a pot of coffee, and a stack of cookies, the standard offering to placate visiting demons. He rose to help her.

"It's all right, I can manage," she began when Frau Kessel's voice rose above hers.

"I was just telling Wolfgang—Herr Düster has been arrested."

"Really? What for?"

Frau Kessel flashed her glittering false teeth. "The little Linden girl—what else?"

My mother set down the tray on the coffee table, her face serious. "That's terrible. Are you sure?"

Frau Kessel gave her a look that should by rights have curdled the cream in the milk jug. She hated her nuggets of gossip to be questioned. "Hilde Koch saw him being driven away by the police." She accepted a cup of coffee with a large quantity of cream and spiked with two lumps of sugar. "Of course," she added, after taking a cautious sip, "it did not come as a surprise to those of us who have lived in the town as long as *I* have."

A wrinkled hand embossed all over with rings hovered for a moment over the cookies, and then retreated without selecting one.

"Once you have seen Evil in Action, you never forget it." You could hear the capital letters in that portentous voice; Frau Kessel's delivery was nothing if not dramatic.

I reflected that if she wanted to see Evil in Action she had only to look in the mirror every morning, but wisely I kept this to myself.

"Well, he is a little—er—*unfriendly*," suggested my mother cautiously.

"Unfriendly!" Frau Kessel was outraged at this understatement. Then she collected herself, leaned forward, and patted my mother on the knee.

"Of course, you could not be expected to know."

She managed to make the remark sound insulting; my mother could not be expected to know anything because she was a foreigner, probably with a comically poor grasp of German. Seeing my mother heating up for a tart retort, my father stepped in and rescued her.

"I don't know either, Frau Kessel."

"*Ach,* Wolfgang!" Frau Kessel shook her head. "And when Kristel was so close to poor Heinrich—Heinrich Schiller, I mean. We always thought it was so charming that she took Pia to visit him—since he lost his own daughter, of course." She heaved a theatrical sigh, and then, perhaps noticing that her whole audience was still looking unsatisfactorily bewildered, she decided to put her cards on the table. "We all knew Herr Düster was responsible."

"You mean for . . . ?" began my father, his brows furrowed.

"For taking Gertrud," finished Frau Kessel. She shook her head. "I don't know why he wasn't put away then. That poor little thing—no older than Pia, and such a beautiful child. Poor Heinrich was never the same afterward—and how should he be? With Herr Düster living a few meters away, and nobody doing anything about it."

"That's a terrible accusation." My mother sounded shocked.

Frau Kessel shot her a narrow glance; had she overreached?

"I'm not making an accusation," she retorted, tossing her head. "I'm repeating what is common knowledge in the town. Ask anyone."

"How did they know it was him?" I asked.

Frau Kessel looked suddenly uncomfortable, as though she had only just remembered that I was there. She reached out one of her jewel-encrusted claws and would have patted me on the head like a small dog if I had not ducked out of her way.

"Never mind, *Schätzchen,*" she told me. "Just remember that you should never, *ever* go anywhere with a stranger."

I remembered something. "But isn't Herr Düster Herr Schiller's brother? Then he wasn't a stranger, was he? He was her uncle. It's OK to go with someone if they're your *family.*"

"*Doch,*" said Frau Kessel curtly, irritated at being contradicted. "But how poor Heinrich came to have a brother like that, I cannot imagine." She sniffed. "No wonder he changed his name."

So it was *Herr Schiller* who had changed his name? I was opening my mouth to ask another question when my mother cut me off. "I don't think this is a suitable topic for Pia," she said firmly. Before I could protest, she said, "Can you go into the kitchen and make sure Sebastian is all right, please, Pia?"

I slouched off reluctantly to find that Sebastian had got into one of the food cupboards and torn open a packet of asparagus soup; he was now sitting in the middle of a little snowdrift of the stuff, drawing squiggles in it with a wet finger, which he occasionally inserted into his mouth. By the time I had extricated him I could hear my mother talking to Frau Kessel in the hall, and then the front door closed firmly behind the old woman.

"Thank God for that," said my mother with a sigh. I was disappointed, however. There was so much more I would have liked to ask Frau Kessel, but now she had sailed off like a little ship laden with Pandora's boxes of other people's secrets. My mother saw me looking wistfully at the door.

"Pia," she said sternly, "I don't want to hear you repeating any of that to anyone, understand?"

"Why not?"

"Because we don't know if any of it is true."

"Do you think Frau Kessel was lying?" I asked doubtfully.

"Not exactly," said my mother, and I had to be content with that.

Chapter Seventeen

❧

On Monday morning I was up before the alarm sounded. Ignoring my father's suggestion that I eat more slowly and with my mouth closed, I bolted breakfast, slung my *Ranzen* onto my back, and by eight o'clock sharp I was outside the school gate. I was not disappointed; at two minutes past, Stefan appeared. He looked a little pale, but otherwise perfectly all right.

"Where *were* you? Did you go up to the Quecken hill? Why didn't you come over on Saturday like you promised?" Impatiently, I bombarded him with questions.

"I was sick." He shook his head. "We can't talk about it here."

He was right; little groups of children were starting to flow through the entrance to the school courtyard. We adjourned to the girls' bathroom on the ground floor; Stefan said the boys' was a better bet, as it was much less often visited, but I absolutely refused to go in there.

Barricaded into a cubicle in the girls', I immediately demanded, "So? Did you go? Did you *see* anything?"

Stefan nodded, his face sober.

"Well, *what* did you see? Was it the huntsman?" In my eagerness to know what had happened, I was almost jumping up and down.

"I'll tell you," said Stefan slowly. "But when I've told you, I don't want to talk about it anymore. OK?"

Why not? I nearly blurted out, but with an effort I restrained myself. "All right."

There was a pause that stretched out for such a long time I started to think Stefan was never going to utter a word. Then suddenly he said, "It was dark up there, very dark." He folded his arms, rubbing them as though he were chilly. "And cold."

He looked at me, and I had the eerie sensation that he was not seeing me at all, but looking right through me into another time and place.

"There was *something* up there, but I don't know what it was. I went up to the castle just after half past eleven—I know it was then because I heard the bell in the church clock strike twice as I went up the track through the woods.

"The moon was out, so I could just about see where I was going. I didn't want to put my flashlight on unless I really had to, in case someone saw it. I didn't see anybody, though. It was dead quiet.

"When I got to that bit where you have to leave the track and go up through the bushes, I did switch the light on. I wanted to go up to the turret because it's the highest bit, but I was afraid of falling in."

I knew the place he meant. The turret was the only thing that looked in any way like a proper castle, but even so what was left of it was sunk *into* the ground, rather than standing out of it, forming a circular pit about four meters deep. I understood Stefan's cautiousness; if you fell into it you would never get out on your own, not to mention the fact that you would be at the mercy of whoever—or whatever—came along.

"It was horrible going through the bushes—the brambles kept sticking to me like little claws and there was all sorts of stuff underfoot that I couldn't see, squashy things and dry, hard sticks. It was like walking over a carpet of bones. I could feel them snapping under my feet. I started thinking that maybe it was the bones of the knight who lived there, him and his hounds, and when the clock struck midnight they would somehow gather themselves up in the dark, and make themselves back into the shapes they'd been when they were alive.

"I kept looking around, afraid that I would see the knight suddenly stand up in the undergrowth, with the moonlight shining on his armor, and a clicking sound from all the little pieces knitting together, and underneath the helmet nothing but a skull."

He shuddered. "Well, I got to where the turret is, and I had to go up that bit on my hands and knees. The mud was all slippery. I got to the top somehow and sat down behind the little tree that grows there, and then the first thing I did was switch the flashlight off. I heard the church clock strike a quarter to midnight. I thought I'd wait until it struck twelve and then I'd come down again.

"I sat there for what seemed like ages. It was cold, and once some stupid bird hooted up in a tree and I nearly jumped out of my skin. But after a while it wasn't so scary anymore. I didn't think anything was going to happen.

"Then all of a sudden I heard this noise, a little crackling noise, and I thought my heart was going to leap out of my chest. I had this really clear picture in my head, just as clear as if I'd really seen it, of the bones of a hand lying on the ground among the weeds, and then gathering themselves up, just like someone pulling on the strings of a puppet."

Stefan stretched out a hand toward me, palm upward, and slowly curled it into a fist. Involuntarily I stepped back.

"I just stayed where I was. I wanted to get down, to run, but I didn't dare. So I just sat there, with my arm tight around the trunk of the tree, and—and waited."

Stefan's voice broke slightly on the last word; with a shock I realized he was close to tears.

"It wasn't long before I saw them. I think there were four of them, coming up into the old castle ruins the same way I had. I couldn't see much, just dark shapes moving through the bushes. I'm not even sure they were all *standing up,* like people. One of them just seemed to be crashing around in the undergrowth like an animal.

"They came *really* close. I thought they were going to come right up to the turret, where I was sitting. Maybe the one crawling in the undergrowth was tracking me. Perhaps he could *smell* me, like a hound. But it wasn't a dog crashing around in there, it was something much bigger. I didn't want to think what would happen to me if it found me."

Stefan put his hands over his face, as though trying to shut out the sight. He said something muffled; it sounded like *Gott.*

"Stefan—"

I was not sure what to do, whether to try to put an arm around him.

"What if they'd found me?" he blurted out suddenly. He thrust out an arm toward me. "Look! Just *look*! I dug my fingers so hard into the tree trunk, they're still covered in green stuff—I can't get it out. I shut my eyes—I thought it was the end. I just knew that whatever it was lumbering about in the bushes would find me.

"After a minute or two I thought the noise was not so loud, so I opened my eyes again and the dark shapes had moved farther away. I suppose they hadn't smelled me at all."

I said nothing. The thought of sitting up there in the dark, praying that I would not be discovered—or smelled out—was too horrible to contemplate.

Stefan raked a hand through his dirty blond hair and then went on. "I think they went downhill a bit. I could hear a crackling sound—but I couldn't see much. I didn't dare come down from the turret in case they heard me. And then—then I heard voices. I think they were whispering." He turned a pale face to me. "Maybe that's the sound someone makes when they talk if—if they're just a—a skeleton."

Quatsch, I wanted to say, but nothing came out. My mouth was dry.

"It seemed to go on forever. I couldn't hear what they were saying. I didn't *want* to hear it. I stuck my fingers in my ears—but then I took them out again, because I thought, *Supposing they come up here and I don't hear them coming?*

"And then—then I saw a light. It was little at first, then it got bigger—or else it was coming closer, I don't know. It was yellow. I always thought the light around the huntsman would be green and glowing, but . . ."

Stefan's voice trailed off.

"But what?" I prompted him impatiently.

He shook his head. "I don't *know* what I was seeing. I felt strange—sort of dizzy, and I had this horrible feeling in my stomach, the way you feel if you look out the top window in a very high building. I kept looking at this light, getting bigger and bigger, and thinking that if I didn't get away soon I never would, and the whole town would be looking for *me* next.

"In the end I crawled down the bank at the side of the turret, and crept off through the bushes, as quietly as I could. It seemed to take forever, and I cut my hands to pieces because I was on my hands and knees most of the time, and the ground is covered in sticks and stones and brambles."

Instinctively I glanced at Stefan's hands and saw that they were covered in half-healed scabs and scratches.

"The whole time there was still this whispering. It sounded—sort of like it was something *important*. Something—I don't know—*urgent*.

"I nearly got back to the path, and then I put my knee on something, a piece of tree bark I think, and it made a really loud snap. I thought I was going to die. *Now they have to have heard me,* I thought. Any minute the one who had been floundering around in the bushes would come crashing toward me. I wondered what the last thing I saw would be. I kept thinking of something with hair and teeth, like a hound, but not a hound.

"I just went on staring into the dark, straining my eyes, trying to see if anything was coming for me. After what seemed like ages, I realized they hadn't heard me at all. The voices were going on just the same as before, and that light was flickering among the trees.

"I couldn't stand it there a second longer, so I risked it and stood up, and just ran for the track. Somehow I didn't bump into anything or fall over. Once I was on the track, I just ran and ran until I was at the bottom of the hill. I didn't even look around.

"But, Pia, that's not all. Just as I was standing up to run for the track, I heard something else. Not whispering. I can't say what it was exactly. It was a kind of—a *beating* sound."

I stared at him. *"O Gott,"* I breathed with a sudden cold flash of realization.

"What?" said Stefan, his face puckered with alarm.

"You know what it was?" I said, and the rising feeling of dread within me curdled into horror. "It was *hoofbeats*."

There was no more time for discussion. The bell had rung several minutes before; we were already late for the first class. We slunk upstairs to be greeted with a telling-off from Frau Eichen, and then had to sit through two periods of math before we could talk any more. I sneaked a few sidelong glances at Stefan. He still looked pale; I wondered if he was ill.

As soon as the bell rang for the *Pause,* I leaned over and said, "So why didn't you come over on Saturday?"

Stefan waited for the others to pack up their things and leave the table, then he said very quietly, without looking at me, "I was sick."

"Sick?"

"Doch." He sounded almost angry.

"Well, what was the matter with you?"

"I ran all the way down from the Quecken hill, and when I got home I was really ill. That's why I couldn't come over."

"What, you ran so much that you were sick?"

"No," said Stefan. This time he did look up, and his eyes were full of anger. "I was *scared,* all right? I was scared."

I looked at him for a long time, while various responses to this ran through my head. *How could you be so scared that you were sick? Were you really and truly sick?—did you throw up? What did your mother say when you came back so late?* But in the end what I said was: "You've got to go back up there with me."

"No way," said Stefan. "Absolutely no way."

Chapter Eighteen

Of course, he *did* go back there with me, though it took two whole days of persuading, nagging, and flagrant bribery—*I'll give you my pocket money for the next three weeks*—before he agreed to do it. Even then it was only on the condition that we went in broad daylight. Stefan was not going to risk being caught up there at night again.

As luck would have it, Wednesday was always a light day for homework, so we were able to meet relatively early in the afternoon. I told my mother that we were going to the Schleidtal to play mini-golf; Stefan merely told his mother he was going out.

As we toiled up the footpath that led to the castle, I tried questioning Stefan about Walpurgis Night again, but he was not forthcoming. He had been so frightened by what he saw, and he had thrashed himself so hard running down the hill afterward, that he had simply been ill. That was all the explanation he could give.

"Maybe it was shock," I suggested as we left the footpath and started up onto the uneven ground that had once been a defensive castle. A mulch of last year's leaves squelched underfoot, but new green shoots were everywhere.

Stefan wasn't listening. He had paused, and was looking from side to side as though trying to orient himself. Then he pointed.

"Let's go up to the turret. Then I can work out which way the light was coming from."

We scrambled up the steep bank to the edge of the ruined turret. Stefan went around the side and squatted on the mossy hump that had once been part of the battlements. I scrambled up and sat beside him, and for a while we sat there in silence like a pair of owls on a branch.

"That way," said Stefan eventually, pointing. He got up and started following the line of the wall. I trailed behind, picking my way over the broken chunks of masonry that stuck up from the earth like a ragged line of teeth.

Glancing around, it was hard to imagine what the castle must have been like when its battlements and turrets were still intact. All that could be seen now were the crumbling traces of walls, worn almost down to ground level, the stones picked out in vivid green moss.

It was a scene not only of desolation but of desolation wreaked long ago. It was impossible to imagine the castle ever having been inhabited. Even the ghost of the eternal huntsman should have worn away to nothingness after ten centuries.

We came to the vague outline of a corner and stopped. "Around here somewhere," said Stefan, looking about him. We climbed down onto the mulchy ground. I glanced at him expectantly. I wondered if he would suddenly be struck with a strong sense of an uncanny presence, whether he would go horribly pale or sick or faint.

Disappointingly, he actually looked relaxed, relieved even; daylight seemed to have vanquished his fears. He kicked his way through the tangle of undergrowth with apparent nonchalance, and I followed dispiritedly behind him. I wished I had been allowed out the night Stefan had kept watch at the turret; I wished *I* had seen the mysterious light and heard the insistent whispering. It would have been good to be the girl who helped solve the Katharina Linden case, instead of the girl whose grandmother had exploded at the family Advent dinner. I wasn't greedy; it needn't have been Katharina's actual corpse that we found; a severed hand—a finger—or even a piece of her clothing would have been enough; the little red bow from her hair, perhaps.

I imagined being thanked by the police; receiving some sort of prize from Herr Wachtmeister Tondorf; Frau Redemann calling the whole school together and telling them that Pia Kolvenbach (with some assistance from Stefan Breuer, I conceded generously) had been instrumental in solving the mystery; Thilo Koch nearly dying of jealousy because it wasn't him who did it; me retelling the story to an enthralled circle of my classmates while Thilo jumped up and down at the back, trying in vain to hear what I was saying. It was a pleasing image. So pleasing, in fact, that when Stefan stopped short I ran straight into the back of him.

"Look."

I looked, and at first I was not sure what I was seeing. Chunks of masonry, just like all the other ones littering the site. But then the shattered stones coalesced into a shape, and I realized that I was looking at a circle. A perfect ring of stones, arranged with precise order and neatness.

We approached it carefully and stood looking down at the stones.

"*Na, und?*" I said. "It's just a circle. It's probably the bottom of another turret, or maybe it was a fireplace or something."

"No, it wasn't," said Stefan with conviction. "Look: there's no moss on any of the stones." He was right; there wasn't. "If it had been there since who knows when, there would be moss all over it, right?"

"Right," I conceded, impressed with his deductive skills. I moved to step into the circle, but he put out an arm to stop me.

"I don't think we should go in."

"Why not?"

"It might be—you know, black magic."

I stepped back hastily. "What's that thing in the middle?" I asked. We both craned forward, trying to look more closely without actually entering the circle. It was a little pile of stones, with a larger, flat stone balanced on top of them. On top of the flat stone was a little heap of something burned.

"Hair," I said, shuddering with disgust.

"It's not hair," said Stefan. "Look, it's sort of crumbly. It looks like herbs or something. Maybe tobacco—or other stuff."

"Other stuff?"

"You know." Stefan rolled his eyes at me; why did I have to be such an innocent? "Stuff like Boris smokes."

"Oh." We looked at each other. Suddenly I couldn't stop myself; a giggle came bubbling up inside me. "Do you think the eternal huntsman smoked it?"

"Idiot," said Stefan, but he was laughing too. He mimed someone taking a long drag at a joint, then intoned, "*Mensch,* when I smoke this stuff I feel like I could ride forever." We clutched our sides and shrieked with laughter.

"Do the hounds smoke it too?"

"*Sicher,* and the horse as well."

We laughed ourselves hoarse. At last, when I was beginning to think I would actually be sick from laughing, Stefan suddenly said, "It was a black mass."

I stopped giggling. "That's not funny."

"I wasn't *trying* to be funny." He pointed at the little heap of burned stuff. "That would be the—you know, the table, like in church."

"The altar," I supplied.

"Yes, and the stuff on it, that's the offering."

"The offering?"

"The sacrifice."

I didn't like the sound of that; it made me think of religion classes with Frau Eichen, and bearded patriarchs dragging their sons up hills to slaughter them because God told them to do it. And everyone else thinking it showed what wonderful trust in God the old man had, and not thinking how the little boy might have viewed the situation, Daddy waving a carving knife around and only just deciding at the last minute to kill a ram instead.

"That's creepy," I said, ever the mistress of understatement.

"That's what I saw," said Stefan, thinking aloud. "It wasn't the huntsman and his men, it was a black mass. The light was the fire when they burned the stuff, whatever it was." He turned to look at me, his face serious. "The voices . . . that was them saying the black mass."

"And the hoofbeats?" I asked.

Stefan looked at me, and I could almost see his mind working as he ran through the possibilities. Then his eyes widened and his lips parted; I could actually *see* it, the moment that the idea dawned on him.

"Cloven hooves," he said.

We stared at each other. "Let's get out of here," I said hastily. Stefan did not need to be told twice; we both turned and set off over the uneven ground, clambering over the tumbled mounds of earth and broken stones, with as much haste as we could manage without breaking into an undignified scramble for safety. We reached the path and set off downhill without looking back once. Stefan was striding so fast that I had to trot to keep up.

"Are we going to tell anyone?" I asked him, panting with exertion.

"No way."

"Not even Herr Schiller?"

"Well, maybe him." We both knew Herr Schiller was different; he was a grown-up, but he wouldn't assume that we were making it all up; and he would know what to do. If, that is, there was anything we *could* do. Perhaps, like stepping into the stone circle, it was a thing best left undone.

I left Stefan near the cemetery at the foot of the Quecken hill and hurried home, my mind fizzing like a wasps' nest with toxic thoughts: whispers at midnight and unseen presences calling up the Devil, and burned sacrifices. Little girls who vanished without trace. Witches and spectral huntsmen and cats who were not really cats.

When I let myself into the house my thoughts were so saturated with these eldritch horrors that it was hardly a surprise to see my mother looking as white and shocked as I did myself. It was not until she threw her arms around me and began hugging and shaking me in turns that I realized anything was wrong.

"Where have you *been*? I've been *sick* with worry."

My father came out of the kitchen, and as I registered the fact that he was home from work early I saw that his face, too, was pale and drawn. I looked from one to the other in confusion. What on earth was going on? It was several minutes before I worked out what must have happened.

Another child had vanished.

Chapter Nineteen

❧

That Wednesday, when it happened, it was clear and bright; not hot, but sunny. It was the middle of the day, a time when the town was relatively full, with little knots of schoolchildren wending their way to the bus stop, staff from the shops popping in and out of the bakeries for lunch, working mothers hurrying home to be there when their children arrived. Little groups of those powerful German citizens known as *Senioren* stood about putting the world to rights. An ordinary, cheerful weekday.

Of course, even at busy times of day there were dark and quiet parts of the town; the little backstreets where the overhanging houses leaned toward each other overhead, and the high walls threw deep, damp shadows. But even in these quiet places, you would not have felt particularly threatened. Aside from a brief moment of excitement in 1940 when Hitler used a bunker in nearby Rodert, the last big event had been the flood of 1416. Nothing ever happened here—and *nothing* is precisely what seemed to have happened to Marion Voss. In fact, *nothing* is what she vanished into, what she became.

A few people remembered seeing a little figure, *Ranzen* on back, pigtails bobbing as it progressed down the street that day; but was it her? She was of average height, she had light brown hair, she was carrying the same galloping-horse-patterned *Ranzen* as thirty other little girls her age. Herr Wachtmeister Tondorf helped someone who might have been her to cross the road on the way to the Klosterplatz, where the school buses were parked. Frau Nett from the Café am Fluss saw a child who might have been her stumble outside the bakery and be helped up by an older girl. Hilde Koch claimed to have seen a little girl who was *certainly* her outside the kiosk at the Orchheimer Tor, clutching a bag of candy. But no one saw where she went.

It seemed that somewhere along her way through the town she had stepped off her path, turned up an alley or gone into a building, and vanished into thin air, dissolved into the ether. It was like one of those magic tricks where you see the magician put something into a box, and then he opens it, and you can see that it is empty. One moment she was there, skipping along the street, and the next she had gone. All that remained were glimpses, fragmentary memories that hung on the air reproachfully, like the echo of a cry. Marion Voss had become—nothing.

To me, the vanished child, Marion Voss, was even more of an unknown quantity than Katharina Linden had been. Not only was she not in my year at school—she was in the third grade—but she lived out in the village of Iversheim, a few kilometers north of Bad Münstereifel. I must have passed her in the school corridors or seen her in the playground, but I have no memory of it.

She was a very ordinary-looking little girl, with her long hair usually done up in two braids, as on the day she disappeared; she wore glasses with thin silver-colored rims, and studs in her ears; she had nondescript but pleasant features and a dark mole on her left cheek close to her mouth.

All this I learned from the photographs that appeared in the local and regional newspapers—front-page news, the second girl to disappear in the Town of Terror. My parents kept the papers out of my way at home, but still, whenever I passed a tobacconist's shop, Marion Voss's face would be staring out from the newsstand, repeated endlessly in grainy detail. So I knew what she looked like.

I also discovered that she was an only child, although she had a big circle of grieving cousins. She had a dog, a Labrador cross called Barky, and two rabbits (the newspapers did not say what the rabbits were called). She liked to dance, to sing; she was learning to play the recorder. She had a scar on one knee from an accident with her bicycle two years before. She had had meningitis when she was at kindergarten but had recovered. Her parents couldn't believe how lucky she had been at the time; now they couldn't believe what had happened to her. Her grandmother had promised to light a candle in Sts. Chrysostom and Daria every day until Marion was found.

All this the newspapers told us, and more. What they could not tell us was what had become of her.

No one could decide, in fact, exactly when and where Marion Voss had disappeared. Her mother, who worked in the mornings as a receptionist in a doctor's office, had not been expecting her daughter to come straight home after school; she thought Marion was going home with a schoolfriend who lived in the town.

The schoolfriend's mother, however, had not been expecting Marion, or so she said; she had an appointment herself that afternoon and couldn't entertain extra children.

The schoolfriend, when questioned, lost her head completely, thinking that she was being blamed for the disappearance, and became quite unable to give a coherent account of the situation. It was eventually surmised that she had invited Marion over without telling her mother, and then the two of them had quarreled and she had told Marion not to bother coming after all. It was never established at what point the quarrel had occurred, but Marion did not get on her usual school bus with her classmates, nor did she get on the later bus for Iversheim.

Since her mother was not expecting to see Marion until she picked her up that evening, the girl's disappearance would have been undiscovered for at least six hours, were it not for the fact that Frau Voss had suddenly remembered that Marion had a dentist's appointment at three. She had telephoned the schoolfriend's mother, and suddenly the two of them had realized that they did not know where Marion was at all.

There were more meetings, and this time when Frau Redemann called the school together to announce tighter security measures and remind us all not to go with strangers, she was flanked by Herr Wachtmeister Tondorf and another policeman we did not know, with knife-edge creases in his trousers and a face that looked as though it had been carved out of granite.

"If anyone knows anything about Marion Voss, or if any of you saw her on Wednesday afternoon, you must come and tell me," Frau Redemann announced, her voice sounding higher and less steadfast than usual. She was fidgeting, her long hands fiddling with the pendant on her bosom; there was an air of badly suppressed desperation about her. She was used to dealing with difficult parents, children who brought their family problems into the classroom and disrupted everyone else, fourth-grade boys trading cigarettes in the bathrooms. But this was something that was most definitely not in the job description.

You could see it on her face every time she looked around the crowded hall at the hundreds of children entrusted to her care, or glanced at the grim faces of the policemen. *This is not fair,* said her expression. *I didn't sign up for this.*

"Or you can tell the police," she added nervously, as though she could shovel the entire situation onto their plate. Herr Wachtmeister Tondorf shuffled his feet and raised his chin; the other policeman continued to look over our heads, his expression so neutral that it was impossible to tell whether he was bored or simply saving his energy for pouncing upon criminals.

The assembly was dismissed. Back in the classroom Frau Eichen was distracted, and kept popping out of the room to hold whispered conversations in the corridor, presumably with other teachers. The gaps in our educational program were enthusiastically filled by Thilo Koch, who expounded his lurid theories of what had happened to Marion Voss and Katharina Linden.

"My brother Jörg," he would begin, "my brother Jörg says they were eaten by a cannibal. That's why they haven't found the bodies. He's *eaten* them."

Repulsive though this was, it was better than Thilo's other line of argument, that both girls had exploded.

"Don't sit next to Pia Kolvenbach; you'll be next."

It was during one of these sallies that he revealed another unpleasant rumor of which I had previously been blissfully ignorant.

"My grandmother says that it was a sign." *It* was Oma Kristel's death.

"A sign of what?" I asked indignantly.

"A sign that Evil is at work in the town," announced Thilo, clearly quoting his grandmother; Good and Evil as concepts were not foremost in his perception of the world, which mostly revolved around getting his own way as often as possible.

I could almost hear Frau Kessel's words ringing in my ears: *it was Evil in Action again.* It did not seem to occur to anyone that Oma Kristel, who went to Mass faithfully every single week, was unlikely to be selected as the instrument of announcing all our Dooms.

"What absolute *Quatsch,*" declared Stefan loyally, but it was too late: the others were already staring at me as though I had personally set off my own grandmother like a Roman candle and then abducted two children as an encore.

Frau Eichen's tardy return and terse injunction to open our math books at page 157 was almost a relief. Twenty-three heads, some sleekly braided, some aggressively bristly like Thilo Koch's, were suddenly bent studiously over their books.

I sneaked a look at Thilo; at precisely the same moment he looked up and caught my eye. He shot me a look of mock horror, and made a swift cross sign out of his two nail-bitten thumbs, as though warding off a vampire. But before Frau Eichen had time to notice what he was doing, he had whisked his hands back into his lap and was perusing page 157 with apparent absorption.

I did the same, but the figures didn't make any sense to me; I might as well have been trying to read Mandarin Chinese. My whole body seemed to be seething. When was the teasing going to stop? Was anyone in the town *ever* going to forget that I was the girl whose grandmother had exploded?

Chapter Twenty

When I got home that day and let myself into the house, my father was already there. Very occasionally, if he had a meeting out of the office, he would make it home for lunch on his way back. But just at that precise moment it did not sound as though he was eating lunch, nor was my mother busying herself in the kitchen making anything. In fact, they were both carrying on an argument at the tops of their voices, my father in stentorian German, my mother mostly in German but with snatches of English thrown in whenever words failed her. As I closed the door, she was just finishing a sentence with ". . . this complete *arse* of a bloody town!"

My heart sank. I hated hearing my parents arguing; and arguing about whether to continue living in Germany was not only unsettling, it was pointless. Where did my mother think we would go? In the heat of the moment she sometimes said she wanted us all to move to England, but she might as well have suggested moving to the moon.

My father would counter, as he always did, by pointing out the difficulties of his finding a comparable job in Britain, the impossibility of buying a house anything like the one we had in Bad Münstereifel. It didn't make sense, anyway; when my mother wasn't having what she called one of her *Down with Deutschland* moods, she used to complain about Britain, the ludicrously high cost of living, the traffic that congested the whole of the south of England, the poor state of the schools, the hospitals . . . the only things she missed, she said, were British tea and Tesco. German supermarkets were never properly organized; whoever thought of putting the Christmas *Stollen* next to the soap powder aisle?

As for me, I knew quite firmly that I *didn't* want to go and live in England. Even the things that my mother spoke about with affection, such as British tea—with *milk* in it!—sounded awful. And then, as I well knew from hearing her describe it a hundred times, the school system was totally different; children started school at the age of five, and had to stay there *all day.* They had lunch in the school, and it always tasted terrible, according to my mother, who seemed to find this very amusing. Puréed potatoes and chunks of meat, without any cream sauce or anything.

I remember once we had to do a school project about where our families came from. I drew a wobbly map of Britain with my mother's hometown on it. We had to include some information about the major products of the area, so I asked my mother what Middlesex had lots of, and she said, "Roads."

I put my *Ranzen* carefully down on the floor of the hallway and was preparing to escape up the stairs without interrupting my parents, when the kitchen door opened and my mother stomped out. She was twisting a dishcloth between her hands as though she were wringing a chicken's neck.

"Pia, I'm glad you're home."

Uh-oh, I thought. My father appeared in the doorway behind my mother; he had composed his features into a mask of placidity, but the florid hue of his complexion gave him away.

"Kate . . ." he said in a warning tone.

"Shut up, Wolfgang," was my mother's conciliatory reply. She bent toward me, strands of dark hair flopping untidily over her eyes. "How would you like to go and visit Oma Warner, Pia?"

"She's not going," cut in my father over her shoulder.

"Yes, she is." My mother's voice was steely.

"She cannot go," announced my father. "She has things booked already for the summer holidays. The summer camp in the Schleidtal, the art course."

"I'll unbook them," said my mother.

"Thomas and Britta are also coming," persisted my father. "Pia should spend some time with her cousins."

I shot him a mutinous glance at this; spending time with Michel and Simon was akin to falling into a snake pit.

"What about *my* family?" demanded my mother, shaking the hair out of her eyes. "She hardly ever sees them. She should spend some time with *them* for once."

"We invited your mother for the summer, but she would not come," my father pointed out. This was perfectly true; Oma Warner could rarely be lured over the Channel to visit us in Bad Münstereifel. She claimed that both flying and sailing brought on her "funny turns," and she couldn't stand either German sausages or German bread, which she said tasted soggy.

"That's beside the point," snapped my mother.

"What *is* the point, then?" barked my father back at her.

"The point is . . ." began my mother, and stopped. "The point is . . ." She put her hands up as though to clutch her brow. "I don't want Pia staying here all summer. It's not . . ."

"Yes?" said my father in a loaded voice.

"It's not *safe*," said my mother eventually.

"*Ach,* this again!" said my father, throwing his hands up.

"Yes, this again!" my mother snapped back. "If you want the honest truth, Wolfgang, I'd like to pack up *right now* and move somewhere else, somewhere you can let your kids out of the house in the morning and know that they'll come home again in one piece, not bloody vanish like that poor Voss kid." She turned to me. "Pia, Oma Warner would love to have you when the holidays start. Would you like that?"

I looked at her dubiously. "Ye-es . . . but what about the summer camp?"

"You can do that next year."

"I really wanted to go."

"You heard her," cut in my father. "She wants to go."

"I know," said my mother. "I'm not deaf. But"—turning to me

again—"I think this time it would be better if you went to Oma Warner's, Pia. Maybe your English cousins can visit. It will be fun."

"Mmmm," I said noncommittally.

"And you can practice your English," she went on. She shot a look at my father; this was her trump card. "She can practice her English," she told him. "It will give her a really good start when she goes to the *Gymnasium* in the autumn."

If I had dared, I would have rolled my eyes at this. In my opinion, my English was perfectly acceptable, and it was certainly ten times better than the English of any of my classmates, since my mother spoke so much English at home. But it was sort of uncomfortable speaking it when I could be speaking German—a bit like putting your tights on the wrong way around; you could still walk about but it felt funny.

Unwillingly, I allowed myself to be dragged to the telephone while my mother dialed Oma Warner's number; perhaps she thought my father might manage to talk her out of the idea if she did not settle everything right away.

"Mum? It's Kate." The voice at the other end of the line said something tinnily, and my mother held lightly on to my shoulder as though to prevent me from running away. "Yes, I've spoken to Wolfgang"—*spoken* seemed an understatement considering the haranguing she had been giving my father when I came home—"and she's definitely coming." There was another explosion of crackling at the other end. "Would you like to speak to her?"

Now I stood in my mother's clutches in resigned dejection; she was going to make me talk English to Oma Warner on the telephone. There was no escape.

"Pia?" My mother handed me the receiver and I put it gingerly to my ear.

"Hallo, Oma."

"Oma?" said my grandmother. "Who's Oma? Omar Sharif?" She always said this, and I was never sure whether I was supposed to laugh or not.

"Ich meine . . . Grossmutter," I managed uncertainly.

"Granny," prompted my mother, poking me in the shoulder with a finger.

"Granny," I repeated dutifully.

"That's better, darling," said Oma Warner, chuckling. She clucked with her tongue. "Ooh, you do sound German, Pia."

"Yes," I said seriously. "I am German."

"Dear me," said my grandmother. "So you're coming to see your old granny?"

I tried very hard not to heave the sigh I could feel coming.

"Yes," I said.

Chapter Twenty-one

After lunch, which was a decidedly stiff affair, I dashed through my homework and then announced that I was going to visit Herr Schiller. I was looking forward to seeing my old friend, although I was still not sure whether I should tell him about what Stefan and I had seen on the Quecken hill. One moment I was full of an icy excitement, believing that we had found a clue to the strangeness that seemed to be overwhelming the town; the next I was convinced that it was nothing, just kids' imagination: the world was still the reassuring one of homework and my mother's cooking and Sebastian under my feet all day long.

I was not sure I even wanted to know what Herr Schiller would make of the affair; if he laughed, it would be awful, we would feel like idiots—but if he took it seriously, wouldn't that be *worse*? I was still cogitating the matter when I literally bumped into someone. It was Frau Kessel.

"*Vor-sicht!*" she screeched, then saw it was me. "Pia Kolvenbach." She studied me disapprovingly over the glinting moons of her spectacles.

"*Tut mir Leid,* Frau Kessel," I said, doing my best to sound contrite.

"You shouldn't be running in the street like that," she informed me severely.

"Um." I looked at my shoes.

"Where were you going in such a hurry, anyway?"

"Nowhere," I said mendaciously.

"Hmm," sniffed Frau Kessel. She regarded me speculatively. "Well, if you *really* have nothing to do, you can help me carry my shopping."

"*Aber . . .*" I began, but then stopped. Why not? I could never get to Herr Schiller's undetected now anyway, and besides, there were dozens of questions I had been dying to ask her the day she came over to tell my parents about Herr Düster. In her way, Frau Kessel was just as much of an expert on local folklore as Herr Schiller, although all her stories definitely emanated from the Dark Side. If the story of any of the subjects of her much-retailed gossip had appeared to be coming to a happy end, she would have disapproved it out of existence for sure.

I took the basket that Frau Kessel offered me with one beringed claw; it was packed with brown-paper parcels that appeared to be filled with stones, judging by the weight. Frau Kessel herself, who was a head taller than me and considerably heftier, loaded herself down with a folded copy of the *Kölner Stadtanzeiger* and a very small handbag.

Having accomplished this, she lifted her chin a little and proceeded in a majestic fashion across the cobblestones. I think she could only have been more pleased with herself had I been a little Moorish boy in satin knickerbockers and a jeweled turban, following her with a peacock-feather fan. We called in at the baker's on the Salzmarkt, where Frau Kessel purchased a small loaf of gray bread, and then to the grocery store on the opposite corner for a half liter of full-cream Eifel milk.

After that, Frau Kessel had finished her shopping, and she headed for home, with me staggering along behind her. When we arrived at her home, a very narrow traditional half-timbered house jammed between two others in a corner of the Orchheimer Strasse, she favored me with another of those looks over her spectacles.

"You'd better come in," she informed me, and when I hesitated she said rather tartly, "Don't just stand there. I won't eat you." I followed her inside with slight trepidation; the idea of being eaten had not occurred to me, but now I found myself wondering whether Frau Kessel had had anything to do with the disappearance of the two girls. Perhaps she lured them home by asking them to carry her shopping, and then kept them locked up indoors, slaving away forever, like some sort of evil Frau Holle.

"You can put the basket on the table," said Frau Kessel, leading me into the kitchen, which was excruciatingly neat and decorated in unrelenting shades of brown. A crucifix hung over the countertop; even the Jesus on it looked unnaturally clean-cut.

"I expect you would like a glass of milk and a cookie?"

I dared not say no, and the milk and the cookie were produced. I sat at the table trying very hard not to make crumbs or drip milk on anything. The cookie was soft and seemed to expand to fill my mouth; I tried to smile but it was difficult, like trying to grin with a mouthful of cotton wool. Eventually I managed to wash the cookie down with the milk.

"Frau Kessel?" I said as politely as I could.

"There aren't any more cookies," was the instant reply.

"I didn't want another cookie," I said hastily, then: "It was very nice, though." I cleared my throat. "I just thought . . . it was very interesting what you were telling Mama and Papa when you visited us."

"Hmm, and what was that?" inquired Frau Kessel. She was poised with the jug from the coffeemaker in one gnarly hand.

"About the town . . . after the war. And Fräulein Schiller."

"Hmph," said Frau Kessel. "Well, she was actually Gertrud Düster, of course. Herr Schiller changed his name afterward, after it all happened."

"What was she like? Can you remember her?" I asked.

"*Meine Gute,* I'm not senile," snapped Frau Kessel. "Of course I remember her." She sniffed. "She was about your age when she disappeared." She eyed me thoughtfully. "She was not unlike you, Pia Kolvenbach; she had the same brown hair, although she always wore it in *Zöpfe,* little braids, which she had fastened on top. It's such a shame these things went out of fashion. Why, there's that little Meyer girl who has her hair cut short, like a boy's! What her mother was thinking of, I can't say."

"And Gertrud Düster . . . ?" I prompted.

"Tsk!" clucked Frau Kessel in irritation. "I was just getting to that. She was a very pretty little girl, the image of her mother. Hannelore— that was the mother's name—well, she was a very beautiful woman.

There were a few hearts broken when Hannelore married Heinrich, or so my mother used to say.

"She also told me that Herr Düster, and I mean the current Herr Düster, not poor Heinrich, was one of the ones whose hearts were broken. Both brothers were mad about the girl, but she chose Heinrich." She sniffed again. "Who can blame her? By all accounts, he's always been the best of the two of them. Cain and Abel, that's what those two are, and I don't need to tell you which one Cain is."

Frau Kessel lifted her chin. "They say that's why he did it. He was bitter with jealousy, never got over it."

"Really?" I said, in a fascinated tone of voice, hoping that she would go on. She did.

"Of course, he couldn't get at Hannelore, because she died."

"Mama said she died in the war," I offered. Frau Kessel gave me a sideways look, a look that said *Just who is telling this story?* I shut up.

"She died in the war," Frau Kessel went on, as though I had never interrupted. "Not *from* the war; she got sick. I don't know what it was she had, though of course they didn't have all these modern medicines then, no antibiotics, so it could have been anything. I saw her a few times in the street and I remember thinking she was very beautiful but terribly thin; I even noticed that as a child, though a lot of children"—here she eyed me balefully—"never notice anything outside themselves." She shook her head. "It was dreadfully sad. Gertrud had to come to school anyway, even after her mother had died; there was nowhere else for her to go. It was wartime, and even her grandmother had to work."

She fell silent, and I pondered the story of poor Gertrud, wondering whether she had endured the same prurient interest and probing questions about her mother's death as I had about Oma Kristel's. I pictured her sitting at her desk with her head crowned with its brown *Zöpfe* bent forward as though to shut everyone else out. Had some contemporary Thilo Koch in white shirt and lederhosen made her life a misery too? Poor Gertrud.

"What happened to her?" I asked at last.

Frau Kessel looked at me. "No one knows exactly."

"Was it the war too?"

"It was after the war *ended*," said Frau Kessel, with irritation, as though I had not been listening. "And," she added with asperity, "when you children make such a fuss about what you will and won't eat, you should think of what it was like in those days. Bread, eggs, meat—all of it rationed. Chocolate—we never ever *saw* chocolate for years, even after the war. What do you think of that?"

"*Furchtbar,*" I said dutifully.

"*Doch,*" agreed Frau Kessel. "And the town . . . parts of it practically in ruins from the bombs. There used to be some lovely old houses right where the Rathaus Café stands, did you know that? Bombed flat. And men coming back from the war, and finding their homes completely gone."

"Maybe Gertrud got hit by a bomb," I offered.

"It was after the war ended," Frau Kessel reminded me again. "If things had been better, more might have been done to find her, to catch the person who did it—as though we didn't all know who it was! But with things in the state they were, and some soldiers coming back, and others passing through, and the Americans coming in with tanks—everything was such a mess for ages, for years afterward in fact . . . they never even caught all the war criminals, let alone anyone else, and by the winter of the next year we were all starving and nobody cared anymore." She shook her head. "Perhaps now people will start to think back to that time, and wonder whether it was such a good idea to let *him* carry on living here just as though he was as innocent as a lamb."

"Maybe he *didn't* do it," I suggested tentatively; in my imagination any number of ghouls might have come creeping up out of the darkness of the forest to snatch a child, in those long-ago times when war had devastated the land like one of the horsemen of the Apocalypse and all the adults' efforts were concentrated elsewhere.

"Maybe, *maybe,*" sneered Frau Kessel. She put her hands on her hips. "Listen to me, Pia Kolvenbach. The day Gertrud vanished, she was supposed to be going for a walk with someone. Do you know who that someone was? It was her loving uncle, Herr Düster. He was going to take her for a stroll in the Eschweiler Tal. Only she never came back, did she?"

"Well . . . then didn't everyone *see* that it was him?" I asked doubtfully.

"He denied it, of course," said Frau Kessel indignantly. "He said he never took her out at all. And Herr Schiller—Heinrich Düster as he was then—well, my mother told me you could see what a blow it was for him, his own brother doing that, but he never lost control for an instant. Some men would have gone for him with their fists if they had nothing else to hand, but Herr Schiller remained the gentleman to the last. My mother said he looked sad more than angry. He even defended Herr Düster, though I think that was beyond what most Christians could bring themselves to do." She frowned, pursing her lips. "I'm sure the poor man thought he was doing the right thing—it wouldn't bring Gertrud back, whatever he did, and he didn't want to be the one to condemn his own brother, but perhaps if he *had,* none of the other girls would have disappeared. It makes you think, doesn't it? Turning the other cheek is all very well . . ."

"The other girls?" I repeated. "Katharina Linden, and Marion Voss . . . ?"

"Oh, no." Frau Kessel turned the unwinking eyes of her spectacles on me. "Not those two. I mean the *other* ones."

Chapter Twenty-two

The other ones?" I repeated slowly.

Frau Kessel looked at me sharply, as though I were being purposely obtuse. "Yes, of course. There was the little Schmitz girl, I don't remember what her first name was. And Caroline Hack. Not," she added, "that it was a surprise when *she* disappeared. Always running around the town on her own at all hours, and her stepmother never doing a thing about it—though I suppose perhaps she was pleased to have Caroline out of the way." Frau Kessel's sniff of disapproval implied that she could barely begin to imagine the depths of depravity into which other inhabitants of the town might fall.

"I've never heard of anyone called Caroline Hack," I said doubtfully. "I don't think there's anyone in the *Grundschule* called that."

"Silly girl, of course there isn't," said Frau Kessel. "This was years ago. If Caroline Hack were still alive, she'd be nearly your mother's age."

"Oh." I thought about this. "The Schmitz girl, is she also the same age?"

"No, younger—well, she was younger at the *time*," said Frau Kessel. "Though I suppose she would be older than Caroline Hack now." She brushed her hands together, removing invisible dirt. "You do ask a lot of questions, Pia Kolvenbach. Do you ask as many questions in class?"

"Um . . ." There was no answer to such questions posed by Frau Kessel, none at any rate that would not merit another lecture.

"Well, I suppose you think I have nothing better to do than stand here gossiping," said Frau Kessel. "Come along, Pia; I'll show you out." I was dismissed. She led me back down the brown hallway and let me out the front door.

"Bianca, that was her name," she said suddenly, poised with one hand on the doorknob.

"Wie, bitte?" I looked at her in confusion.

"The little Schmitz girl."

"Oh," I said, and then: *"Tschüss,* Frau Kessel," as I stepped thankfully into the sunlight.

"Auf Wiedersehen," said Frau Kessel emphatically, managing to inject disapproval of my informal language into her tone. Then she shut the door.

It was too late to visit Herr Schiller now, I decided; and though I wanted to find out a little more about Caroline Hack and Bianca Schmitz, Herr Schiller was the last person I could ask, considering the furor caused by my inquiry about Katharina Linden. Instead I went home, scuffing my shoes along the cobblestones and mulling over what I had just heard.

Was it true? My mother always said you had to take what Frau Kessel said with a pinch of salt. She was prone to take a very small seed of rumor and grow it into a veritable aspidistra of supposed fact, like the time that Frau Nett's teenage daughter had gastric flu and threw up at school one morning, and Frau Kessel told at least six different acquaintances that she had it on good authority that Magdalena Nett was four months pregnant. Frau Nett had not spoken to Frau Kessel for months after that enormity. All the same, it was hard to imagine her *making up* someone's disappearance. Either a person was there, or they weren't. I wondered whom I could ask.

Chapter Twenty-three

"Papa?"

My father looked up from his habitual refuge behind the outspread pages of the *Stadtanzeiger.*

"Yes, Pia?"

"When you were at school here, did you know anyone called Bianca Schmitz?"

"No, I don't think so." My father glanced back at the page he had been reading, clearly eager to get back to some exciting account of local news.

"Well, did you know someone called Caroline Hack?"

Reluctantly, my father lowered the paper. "I don't think so, Pia."

"Are you sure, Papa?"

"Pia, I am *trying* to read the newspaper. What's so important about Caroline . . . what did you say her name was?"

"Caroline Hack. Papa, Frau Kessel says she—"

"Frau Kessel?" My father sighed. He was about to say something along the lines of what my mother had said about not listening to Frau Kessel's stories. Then light dawned. "She was the girl who ran away."

"She ran away? Frau Kessel said she disappeared."

"Well, she did, I suppose. She just took herself off without a warning. But how did you come to be discussing it with Frau Kessel?"

"She asked me to carry her shopping for her," I said truthfully.

"She did? *Unverschämt,*" grunted my father.

At another time I might have been tempted into a digression at this point, agreeing how disgraceful it was that Frau Kessel had made me carry all her things home, hamming it up a bit: my back had never stopped aching since, you wouldn't believe how many things she made me carry . . . however, for the time being the question of Caroline Hack was still more interesting than the possibility of dropping Frau Kessel in it.

"She says Caroline Hack just vanished, like—like Katharina Linden did."

"Hmph." My father straightened in his armchair, and looked at me rather severely. "Pia, I am not happy about this. Frau Kessel has no business frightening children with such stories."

"I wasn't frightened, I—"

"If she asks you to carry her shopping again, you tell her your papa told you to come straight home, *verstanden?*"

"OK . . . but Papa?"

"Yes, Pia?" My father sounded a little weary.

"Can you just tell me about Caroline Hack—please? I'm not frightened," I added hastily. "I'm just . . . interested."

"*Ach,* Pia! There really is nothing to tell. She was at the *Grundschule* at the same time as I was, but I really didn't know her; she was in the fourth grade and I was in the second or third, I don't remember which. She just didn't come into school one morning, and eventually it got around that she had run away. She didn't get on with her mother, I think."

"Her stepmother, Frau Kessel said."

"Frau Kessel said! Frau Kessel should mind her own business. Pia, I mean it quite seriously, I do not want you listening to such tales."

"Yes, Papa." Even I could see that any further questions were going to rouse my father's ire; reluctantly, I retired from the field.

·   ·   ·

The following morning I cornered Stefan at the break. We loitered in a corner of the playground, away from the jungle gym where the first-graders were flinging themselves around like monkeys, and a safe distance from the corner where Thilo Koch and some other fourth-grade boys were standing in a huddle.

"What's up?" said Stefan.

"It's not just Katharina Linden and Marion Voss," I told him without preamble. "Other girls have disappeared."

Stefan glanced about him, as though he might notice who had vanished from among our number.

"Who?"

"Not now," I said. "It was years ago, when my papa was at school."

Stefan's shoulders relaxed when I said this: *years ago, when my papa was at school*—that was a time so remote as to be meaningless.

"Really?" he said, without excitement.

"Yes, really. There was a girl called Bianca Schmitz, that was before Papa was at school, I think, but there was another one called Caroline Hack, who was here at the same time as he was."

"And what happened to them?"

"They just vanished. Frau Kessel told me."

"*Frau Kessel told you?* Pia, you can't believe a word that old *Hexe* says." Stefan sounded quite irritated; no doubt the Breuer family had suffered from Frau Kessel's hyperactive tongue in the past.

"No, really. It's not just her—my papa knows about it too. He says she just didn't turn up for school one morning, and everyone thought she had run away."

"Why would she do that?"

"She didn't like her stepmother."

"Well, maybe she *did* run away."

"Frau Kessel doesn't think so. She thinks someone took her."

"Someone?"

"Well . . ." I lowered my voice, glancing around me. "Frau Kessel thinks Herr Düster did it."

"Old Düster?" Now Stefan's interest was piqued.

"Yes. She says he took Gertrud out for a walk the day she disappeared—"

"Hang on, hang on . . . !" Stefan looked bewildered. "Who's Gertrud?"

"Herr Schiller's daughter," I said impatiently. "The one who also disappeared. Herr Düster took her for a walk in the Eschweiler Tal and she never came back."

"Well, if it was so obvious, why didn't anyone do anything?"

"Frau Kessel says Herr Schiller stood up for him."

"Why would he do that?"

"I don't know." I thought about it. "Frau Kessel says he took Gertrud to get at Herr Schiller, because he wanted to marry Herr Schiller's wife, before she got married to Herr Schiller, I mean."

"So why did he take the other ones?"

"Maybe it was like a man-eating tiger," I suggested. "Once he tasted blood, he had to do it again."

"Or a vampire," said Stefan. "You know, like Dracula. I saw a film about him once. He could turn himself into a bat, and fly into people's bedrooms through the window."

"I don't think Herr Düster turns into a bat," I protested. "And anyway, none of the kids has disappeared from their *bedroom*."

"Maybe he turns into a wolf."

"And nobody notices a wolf in the middle of the street?" I asked sarcastically.

"Or a cat. A big black cat with glowing eyes."

"Like Pluto, you mean?" I suggested.

Stefan gasped. "Of course."

"Oh, come *on*."

"No, really." Stefan looked at me, his face alight with the advent of a new idea. "Listen, has anyone ever seen Herr Düster and Pluto at *the same time*?"

"How should I know?"

"I bet they *haven't*." Stefan considered. "You remember that time we were at Herr Schiller's, and Pluto got in, and Herr Schiller just went mad? Like the cat was a devil or something."

I thought back; Stefan was perfectly right. A sliver of cold slid through me.

"That's crazy," I said, shaking my head. Pluto was just a cat. A very large, very mean-tempered cat, but just a cat all the same. He had made Herr Schiller jump, that was all. . . .

The bell rang for the end of break and as we went inside I dismissed the idea from my mind altogether; it is only in retrospect that I believe that was the point when the germ of an idea began to sprout, the idea of somehow getting into Herr Düster's house and searching for the lost girls, searching for the truth.

Chapter Twenty-four

At last the school term had finished, my time at the *Grundschule* had come to an end, and now the glorious vista of *Gymnasium* without Thilo Koch was opening before me. But first there were six weeks of vacation to get through, four of which were to be spent in the exotic environment of Oma Warner's semidetached house in Middlesex. My mother loaded me up with gifts for Oma Warner, and then put me on an airplane at Köln-Bonn airport. Oma Warner picked me up at the airport at the other end, and that was that. I was caught, with no prospect of parole for four whole weeks. Once we were in the taxi, I handed over the little parcels for Oma Warner like a prisoner giving up his personal possessions before being incarcerated.

"Ooh," said Oma Warner, peering into one of the little bags. "What's this then, Pia?"

"I think it is to eat," I said.

"Dear me, I hope it isn't one of those smoked sausages," she said doubtfully.

"Mmm," I said noncommittally.

I hazarded a glance out the taxi window. England seemed very much the same as last time we had visited: an endless vista of gray streets, slick with rain. Even though it was summer, it was still drizzling.

Everyone seemed to be scuttling along leaning slightly forward as though trying to push their way through the wind and wet. My mother claimed there were parts of England that made Bad Münstereifel look like the Ruhrgebiet, an area of Germany legendary for its factories and coal mines; she described villages with chocolate-box thatched cottages and old Norman churches, and rolling hills and meadows with cows dozing under trees. Looking out at Middlesex, I wondered whether she had got it mixed up with some other place.

Added to my woes was the fact that I was divorced from everything going on at home in Germany. Supposing they found one of the missing girls? Or they caught someone—Herr Düster, for example—disposing of evidence of the crime? Deprived of facts, my imagination ran riot, and I imagined the police bursting into his house on the Orchheimer Strasse and finding him crunching up the bones between his teeth. They would drag him away screaming, and when they searched him in the police station they would find that his body—the bits hidden by his clothes—was all covered in black fur. No one would ever see Pluto again, of course. And when they looked in his fridge, it would be full of bottles of blood—

"What are you thinking about?" asked Oma Warner.

"Nothing," I said.

A week passed, and then another, and I resigned myself to captivity. Oma Warner's house was a prison, but it was quite an interesting one; there were three bedrooms and a box room to explore, as well as the dining room with its cabinets full of curious ornaments and old photographs in frames. In the living room there was a dark wood bookcase crammed full of novels by Barbara Cartland and Georgette Heyer; Oma Warner was a fiend for romance.

"You can read one if you like," she said, coming up behind me suddenly as I was perusing a cover depicting a flame-haired woman in a green velvet dress repulsing three lovers at once. I almost jumped out of my skin, and slid the book back onto the shelf as quickly as I could.

"No, thank you," I said.

Oma Warner cocked her head and stared at me with her bright old eyes, like an intelligent bird. "Suit yourself." She held something out to me. "There's a letter for you from Germany." She turned the envelope over in her hands. "From Stefan Breuer, it says." She chuckled, handing the letter to me. "Got yourself a swain?"

"A what?"

"A boyfriend," said Oma Warner, raising her eyebrows meaningfully.

"No," I said shortly. Mentally, I added another imprecation to the long list of curses I had heaped on Stefan's head since our unwilling partnership began. *StinkStefan;* trust him to embarrass me again. Only he could drop me in it from a distance of five hundred kilometers.

I went upstairs to the bedroom Oma Warner had given me, and closed the door. Before I opened the letter I turned it over as Oma Warner had done, and examined it as though for clues. Stefan had dire taste in stationery, or perhaps he had purloined it from his mother; it was decorated with simpering mice, prancing along a graduated background of pink and yellow. With all that dripping sentimentality, it was no wonder Oma Warner had taken it for a love letter. Stefan had addressed it to *Mrs. Pia Kolvenbach.*

I opened the letter and read as follows:

Liebe Pia,

Are you having a good time at your grandmother's? I went to the summer camp last week but it was not as good as last year. They wouldn't let us go anywhere out of sight. Something happened on Wednesday. A group of people went to Herr Düster's house and shouted at him. The police came and told them to go home. Boris says Herr Düster is going to die. I wanted to tell you about it. It's a shame you're not here. I asked if I could telephone you but my mother said No.

Dein, Stefan

I read the letter through again. A thousand questions came seething up in my brain. Who had gone to Herr Düster's house, and why? I wondered whether Frau Kessel's accusations against the old man had finally become common currency, and whether she had been among those who gathered on his doorstep. Somehow I thought not; at ten I was years off understanding adult behavior, but even I could see that Frau Kessel's favored modus operandi was the behind-the-hand remark, the whisper behind closed doors. I could not see her as the leader of a torch-bearing lynch mob.

Stefan's letter was infuriating in the details it left out. The police had come—but what had they done, apart from telling everyone to go home? Had they arrested anyone—Herr Düster himself, for example? And what did it mean, Boris said Herr Düster was going to die? Was it a threat? I read the letter again, but there was nothing else to be gleaned from it. I went downstairs.

"Oma? *Ich meine* . . . Granny?"

"Yes, dear?" Oma Warner was enthusiastically scrubbing out the oven but she stood up when I came into the kitchen.

"Can I telephone?"

"Well, your mother's going to call you this evening, Pia. Can't it wait?"

"Mmm." I looked at Oma Warner, then away at the cluttered countertop. "I wanted to telephone . . ." I thought about it. "A friend." I hoped she would assume it was a female friend. But Oma Warner was not that slow.

"Your boyfriend, eh?" Before I could say anything, she was shaking her head. "I'm sorry, dear. It's much too expensive." She gave me a conciliatory smile. "You'll have to write back to him. That's what your Grandpa Warner and I always did, you know."

"Um." I shrugged. Nowadays, of course, I might have e-mailed him. But in 1999 the technology in Oma Warner's house did not even extend to a dishwasher. A public call box was no good either: a single international call would have taken more than the entire contents of my purse. That left only one option.

Chapter Twenty-five

*S*tefan?"

"Who is this?"

"It's me, Pia."

"Pia? Are you back?"

"No, I'm calling from my *Oma*'s house."

"In *England*?"

"Yes . . ." I paused. "She doesn't know. I can't stay on the phone for very long in case she comes back."

Stefan whistled. "What's she going to—"

"Never mind that," I snapped back in an urgent whisper; even though I had seen Oma Warner depart with my own eyes, I still felt as though I had to keep my voice down. "I got your letter. What's been going on? What's this stuff about Herr Düster?"

"Oh, that was *crazy*. There've been rumors going around about Herr Düster for ages, ever since he got picked up in that police car. It seems like someone has been stirring them up again—"

Frau Kessel, I thought sourly.

"—and, anyway, a whole group of people went to his house and were shouting at him to come out and explain himself."

"Did you see it?"

"*Nee.* Boris was there, though."

"Boris thinks Herr Düster did it too?"

"No, Boris just thought it was cool to be there, and see what they did." That made sense; terrorizing an old man who was outnumbered ten to one sounded just Boris's style.

"Did he come out? Herr Düster, I mean."

"No. I mean, would you? But he was definitely in there, Boris said; they saw him looking out the window."

"Who was there?"

"Well, apart from Boris . . . Jörg Koch was there, and he said Herr Linden, you know, Katharina's father, he was there as well. But I don't know who else. He said Herr Linden was knocking on the door and shouting at Herr Düster to come out. Herr Linden said if he had nothing to do with it, he had nothing to be afraid of." Stefan paused, thinking. "Then I think the police came."

"Who called them?"

"I don't know. Maybe Herr Düster did. But he still didn't come out, even when they arrived. It was Herr Wachtmeister Tondorf, and the other one, the younger one."

"What did they do?" I had visions of Herr Wachtmeister Tondorf laying into Boris with a club, and Herr Linden shouting about his daughter, and trying to beat down the door . . .

"Just talked to them."

"What did they say?" I couldn't make this out at all.

"I don't really know . . . Boris heard it, but he was mostly just annoyed that they didn't make Herr Düster come out or anything." That I could imagine; Boris would have loved the ensuing row. "I think they said it wasn't him." Stefan paused. "Then Jörg Koch shouted why did they arrest him before, if it wasn't him?"

"And?"

"Herr Wachtmeister Tondorf said they didn't arrest him, but it was confidential, you know, they can't say anything."

"They *did* arrest him, though, didn't they?" I said. "Frau Koch *saw* it."

"Yeah, I know it doesn't make sense," agreed Stefan. "I'm just telling you what Boris said. Anyway, then Herr Wachtmeister Tondorf said they had to go home and stop bothering Herr Düster because he was ill. He said they should leave it to the police."

"Did they just go?" I asked. It was hard to imagine the bereaved father and the local bullyboys departing like lambs when they had heard about Herr Düster's supposed ill health.

"Well, Boris said they gave Herr Wachtmeister Tondorf a hard time back, told him what could he expect if the police didn't catch the person who was taking all these kids, and a load of stuff like that. But you know Boris."

"*Doch,*" I agreed. I thought for a moment. "Has anything else happened?"

"What, you mean, has anyone else disappeared? No. I wish Thilo Koch would, but no such luck."

We both laughed. "They haven't found Marion Voss?"

"No."

"Have you seen Herr Schiller?" I asked, hoping a little jealously that he would say no.

"Yeah, I saw him a couple of days ago. He told me this really cool story about some treasure. He said when the town got attacked the nuns hid all the treasure, and so far nobody's found it. It could still be somewhere in the town, millions of marks' worth of it—well, thousands, anyway. Herr Schiller says—"

"Stefan, I have to go." I dared not stay any longer on the phone; every minute racked up a further enormity on Oma Warner's telephone bill, and a greater risk of discovery. "Can you call me if anything else happens?"

"I'll try," said Stefan, and I had to be content with that.

Chapter Twenty-six

The summer vacation, seemingly interminable, finally came to
an end. My much-loathed cousins Chloe and Charles came
to Oma Warner's house for the afternoon, ostensibly to bid me a fond
farewell, though there was no affection wasted between us. Oma
Warner sent us into the garden to play so that she could drink tea with
Aunt Liz. As usual, we went down to the bottom of the garden to
climb up the railings and watch the trains speeding by on their way
to London.

There was just enough room on the one stretch of railings not ob-
scured by bushes for us all to squeeze in if we squashed up together.
Charles and Chloe, first to climb up, did not want to squash together
with me. I tried to climb up anyway, just to annoy them; there was a
short struggle and Chloe fell off, with an affected shriek.

"You did that on purpose," said Charles, and gave me an almighty
shove with his meaty hand, intending to push me into the dust, quan-
tities of which his sister was now brushing off her pink sweater with
disgust. I hung on for grim death, and then I kicked him in the shins.

"Fuck, fuck," he squealed, then he flung himself upon me and began
prizing my fingers off the railings.

I tried to kick him again, missed, let go of the railings, and slid down to the ground. Undeterred, I gave him some of his own medicine. *"Fuck away!"* I hissed, taking a swipe at him with my open hand.

"Fuck *away?*" Charles laughed contemptuously. "What's that supposed to mean?"

"She means fuck off," supplied Chloe. They looked at each other and laughed theatrically.

"Can't she speak English?"

"No, she can't."

"Ner-errr . . ." They both flopped up and down in displays of simulated imbecility. "Fuck away!"

"No, you fuck away!"

"Scheissköpfe," I told them; having reached the borders of my knowledge of English there was no option but to relapse into German. *"Ich hasse euch beide, ihr seid total blöd."*

"That's German, is it?"

"Fuck away back to Germany, you . . . German."

"You *Kraut,*" added Charles, dredging up a word he could only have learned from Uncle Mark. "Fuck off with the other Krauts."

"Go back where you came from."

"Gerne," I told them. "England is *Scheisse,* Middlesex is *Scheisse, und ihr beide seid auch Scheisse."*

"Kraut, she's talking Kraut," said Charles delightedly. "Hey, Chlo', I can't wait until she tries that at school." He pulled a face. "Hey, Mrs. Vilson, I don't vont to do zis homeverk."

"God, she's not going to be in *my* class," said Chloe in disgust. "They'll put her in Batty's." She glared at me. "With all the other dummies who can't speak English."

"Good, I am not going to your school," I said disdainfully.

Chloe shrieked with malicious delight. "Oh, yes, you are."

"No, I am not going."

"Yes, you are."

They looked at me expectantly. Then Charles elbowed his sister in the ribs. "She doesn't know."

"I don't know what?" I demanded.

They both burst into laughter. "Look," said Charles eventually, in the voice of someone speaking to the terminally stupid, "where do you think you are going to school?"

"Sankt Michael Gymnasium," I answered suspiciously.

"And where's that, then?"

"Bad Münstereifel."

"You're going to need a plane to get there," Charles taunted me.

"I don't understand," I said resentfully.

"You want me to spell it out, dummy?" asked Chloe, hands on her almost nonexistent hips. "You're coming to live in England."

"No," I said, shaking my head.

"Yes, yes, yes," chanted Charles.

"Quatsch," I told him.

"Quack? What's that?"

"German for 'duck,'" supplied Chloe. They guffawed at me. I stood there in silence and looked at them. "I am not living in England."

"Oh, yes, you are. Hasn't Aunt Kate told you yet?"

Impulsively, I turned on my heel. "I will ask Oma Warner." I started up the garden path toward the house. Behind my back I heard Chloe and Charles hissing at each other. "Idiot—she doesn't know."

"Mum didn't say not to tell. Anyway, you started it."

"Stop her. Mum'll go mad."

"You stop her."

By the time they had finished arguing and started after me, I had reached the back door. They piled into the house after me, and were so close on my heels that when I pushed open the living-room door the three of us almost fell into the room.

"Oma Warner," I blurted out, "I don't want to live in England."

Aunt Liz and Oma Warner turned startled faces toward me. Aunt Liz put her cup down on its saucer with a rattle and looked furiously toward Chloe and Charles.

"Chloe? Charles?" There was a silence. "What have you been saying to Pia?"

"Nothing," said Chloe quickly.

I glared at her mutinously. "She says I am going to school in England, not in the Sankt Michael Gymnasium."

"Oh, Chloe." Aunt Liz made a sound like a long sigh. She looked at Oma Warner and rolled her eyes. "Where do they pick these things up? I haven't discussed it in front of them, not even with Mark."

"Little pitchers have big ears," said Oma Warner grimly.

"It's not true," I said. It was a question, not a statement. Oma Warner looked at Aunt Liz.

"Chloe and Charles shouldn't have said anything to you, Pia," said Aunt Liz eventually in the soulful listen-to-me-little-girl tone that I sometimes heard from my mother when she had something serious to impart. "Your mother and I were really just discussing what it would be like if you ever *did* come back to England to live. You know, the idea. Maybe your family won't always want to stay in Germany. People move, you know."

I pursed my lips and shook my head as emphatically as I could.

"Bad Münstereifel is very pretty, but it's just a small town, you know, and besides . . ." Her voice trailed off.

"Yes, Aunt Liz?" I said. Out of the corner of my eye I saw Oma Warner shaking her head. Aunt Liz saw it too and a frown flitted across her face.

"There are other nice places to live," she finished.

"Not like Bad Münstereifel," I said.

Chapter Twenty-seven

I flew back to Germany a few days before the autumn term at my new school started, my English much improved and my bags laden with British delicacies that Oma Warner had insisted on packing for my mother—unpalatably strong tea and pots of gravy powder. My head was still full of the twitterings of Aunt Liz, who had impressed upon me not to say anything about moving to England to anyone; she had not actually come out and forbidden me, but she had gone on and on in such a wheedling tone that I had got the message. Somehow it did not make me feel any better. If it was just an idea, why the secrecy? But soon I had other problems to deal with, more immediate ones.

"Are you Pia Kolvenbach?"

I turned around and found myself looking at the front of a battered black leather cycle jacket; looking up, I saw a face upon which the adult features were already sketched: the big jaw, the heavy-lipped mouth, the beginnings of stubble. I didn't know him, but he looked old enough to be in the upper end of the school, maybe the *Abitur* year. A faded gray backpack was slung over one shoulder by a fraying strap.

A cigarette—strictly forbidden in the school yard—dangled from thick fingers.

"Sorry?"

"Are you the Kolvenbach kid?"

I looked at him dumbly, and he shook his head impatiently. "You deaf?"

"No." I shook my head.

"Well, *are* you?" He flicked ash from the cigarette onto the ground between us. "Are you Pia Kolvenbach?"

"Yes."

"The one whose grandmother exploded?"

"She didn't—" I started, then stopped short. What was the use? If I said she had just burned herself by accident, or if I said she had spontaneously combusted, or even gone off like a Roman candle in a shower of multicolored sparks, what was the difference? I stood still and silent and waited for the inevitable.

"So what happened?"

I looked away, searching for a friendly face in the milling crowd of schoolchildren. Where was Stefan? He should be here. I risked a look back at the boy's face; he was still looking at me, waiting to hear what I would say; you could see the avid spark of prurient interest behind those heavy features like a tea light burning in a jack-o'-lantern. I threw caution to the winds.

"It was a hand grenade."

"A *what*?"

"A hand grenade." Now I had recovered my courage. *Um Gottes Willen,* I thought; it couldn't make things any worse, whatever I said. "My Opa kept it from the war."

"Really?"

"Yes, really." I warmed to my theme. "He kept it in a box under the bed. When he died, Oma Kristel started carrying it around with her as—as a reminder of him."

"Unbelievable," said the boy incredulously. He looked as though he were about to start dribbling with excitement. The cigarette was burning down unnoticed in his fingers. "How did it go off?"

"Well . . ." I thought about it for a moment. "It was in her handbag. She *always* carried it around in there. She put her hand in to get her keys out, and instead of the key ring she put her finger in the ring on the hand grenade, and pulled the pin out." I put my head on one side. "And then it went off. Boom! Just like that."

"*Scheisse.*" I had succeeded in impressing a teenager. "Was there anything left of her?"

"Only her shoes and her left hand. That's how they could tell who it was afterward, by her rings."

"How could . . ." He shook his head. "That's incredible. Wasn't anyone else hurt?"

"My cousin Michel had his nose blown off." How I wished *that* were true. "They had to make him a new one in the hospital." I put a hand gently to my lips as though feeling the words as they came out, checking them for truth. "It looks as good as new, you wouldn't know."

"Did they find the nose?"

I shook my head. "A cat ate it."

There was a long silence. The boy looked down at me, and I up at him. He flicked the long column of gray ash from the cigarette, took a last deep drag, and then dropped the butt on the ground, where he extinguished it under the sole of one grubby sneaker.

"*Du bist pervers,*" he said at last: *you're sick.* He turned and shambled off, leaving me standing there alone, with the sound of the school bell ringing in my ears.

That was my first day at the big school.

Chapter Twenty-eight

ia," said Herr Schiller, peering around the door. "How kind of you." He stepped back to let me into the house. Herr Schiller had been unwell; that was why he had declined my mother's invitation to come and share coffee and cakes with us to celebrate my transition into the big school. Instead I had brought him a slice of cheesecake in a box.

"I'm sorry you had to miss the party," I said shyly.

"I am sorry too, Pia," said Herr Schiller. He raised his hands in a gesture of regret. "What can I say? The years are catching up with me." Certainly he did look as though every one of his eighty-odd years was weighing him down today. Although his clothes were as dapper as ever, they seemed to hang off his broad shoulders; even the flesh of his face seemed to hang loosely, as though he lacked the energy to smile.

I looked up at him doubtfully.

"I brought you some of the cake."

"*Danke,* Pia." He held out a hand to indicate that I should go into the living room.

"Do you want the cake now?" I asked, plumping myself down in one of his armchairs.

"No, thank you." Herr Schiller subsided into his favorite chair with a seismic effect on the springs. We regarded each other for a moment. He did look pale, I noticed.

"Herr Schiller . . . ?" I said uncertainly.

"Yes, Pia?"

"You're . . . I'm sorry you're sick. You're not . . . ?"

"Dying?" supplied Herr Schiller in a dry voice. He chuckled slightly; in my imagination I saw puffs of dust coming out with each wheezing breath. "My dear Pia, we are *all* dying." He must have seen my face, because his tone softened as he added, "I'm sorry, Pia. But when you are my age, you will see that everything comes to an end. There's nothing wrong with that. It's nature."

He patted the arm of his chair with a gnarled hand. His eyes were focused elsewhere, not on me; he was thinking. "The important thing to do," he said eventually, "is to live every day as though it were your last one." He looked at me. "I expect they tell you that at the children's Mass, don't they?"

I nodded, not liking to say that I never went to the children's Mass.

"Live every day as though it were your last one," he repeated. "You know what that means? It means if there is something you want to do, something you *have* to do, you should do it now, before the chance has gone away forever."

"Mmmm," I concurred uneasily. I could not think what else to say.

There was a long pause, and then at last Herr Schiller said in a brighter tone, "And how are you finding the *Gymnasium,* Pia?"

I stopped myself from saying *Scheisse* just in time. "It's all right," I said noncommittally.

"Just all right?" Herr Schiller raised his eyebrows.

"Well . . ." I hesitated. "*School* is all right. But some of the other kids . . . they're mean."

"Oh?"

I heaved a great sigh that sent strands of hair floating about my face. "They want to know about Oma Kristel. About . . . you know. Why can't people just forget it? Why does everyone have to keep going on about it? Well—not you," I added hastily.

"People have trouble letting the past go," remarked Herr Schiller. He leaned over to the coffee table that stood between us and pushed the box with the cheesecake in it toward me. "Perhaps you should eat this, Pia. I think it will do you more good than me."

"Aren't you hungry?"

"No."

I opened the box and extracted the plastic fork that my mother had laid neatly alongside the slice of cake. Licking smears of cheesecake off the handle, I said, "Herr Schiller, would you tell me another story . . . please?"

"Well . . ." Herr Schiller seemed to consider. "What sort of story would you like?"

"Something *really* scary," I announced. "Something . . ." I pondered, then with a sudden burst of petulant inspiration: "Something with a boy who says something stupid, and then something horrible happens to him." I thought of cigarette ash drifting to the ground at my feet, grubby sneakers grinding out a butt on the stones. "Something *really* horrible."

"Something really horrible . . ." repeated Herr Schiller. He leaned his head back against his chair for a moment and looked upward as though seeking inspiration. Then he looked at me, and his eyes were bright. "Did I ever tell you about the Fiery Man of the Hirnberg?"

"No," I said. "Is it horrible?" I felt in the mood for a really terrifying story today: one with lots of rending and screaming. The fact was, I felt like doing some rending and screaming of my own.

"Pretty horrible," said Herr Schiller drily, and I had to be content with that. Settling himself more comfortably in the chair, he began:

"You know where the Hirnberg is, don't you?"

I did; it was a thickly wooded hill adjoining the Eschweiler Tal and crisscrossed with woodsman's tracks.

"The Fiery Man dwells in the woods on the Hirnberg, in a cave lit by fires that burn deep within the hill, night and day."

Herr Schiller reached slowly for his pipe and began stuffing it with tobacco. "He burns eternally and is never consumed by the flames, and if he embraces you with his fiery arms you will be burned to cinders in an instant."

Herr Schiller struck a match, and for a second his craggy features were lit up by the spurting flame. He puffed at the pipe, keeping his eyes on me. Then he continued, "Now, what I am about to tell you happened in the village of Eschweiler, to the north of Bad Münstereifel. One summer evening, many years ago—"

"When?" I interrupted.

"Many years ago," repeated Herr Schiller, lifting his bushy eyebrows. "A *great* many years ago. One evening, the young people of the village were sitting out on the grassy hillside telling stories and eventually the discussion turned into something of a contest, with increasingly gruesome tales of ghosts, witches, and monsters. They spoke of treasure guarded by a specter on a glowing horse, and of the Fiery Man who is supposed to live in the Teufelsloch—the Devil's Cave—on the Hirnberg.

"The contest went on until one lad stood up and announced recklessly, 'Well, I would give the Fiery Man of the Hirnberg a *Fettmännchen* if he would come here and fetch it himself.' A *Fettmännchen,* you know, was a small coin that they had in those days.

"The moment the words were out of the lad's mouth he knew his mistake by the expressions on the others' faces. The argument was forgotten; the merry chattering was finished, and the girls gathered their shawls around them and scurried away home like frightened mice, in spite of all that the young men said to try to make them stay.

"Well, it was coming into twilight now and the shadows were deepening, so it was not long before one of the young men noticed a light that was burning at some distance in the woods. Faint at first, it burned slowly more brightly, until it became clear that the light was not gaining in size but coming nearer.

"The young men watched it with growing dismay until it came out from under cover of the trees, and they could clearly see what manner of thing it was. It was a man—at least, it was something in the shape of a man—but it was all over molten fire, which blazed and spurted from every part of its body; and its eyes were two dark pits, like sunspots in the glaring sun of its face. Slowly it came on, wading through fire like a fisherman wades through flowing water, until the horrified young men could hear the sizzle of the burning feet as they charred the grass black.

" 'The Fiery Man! The Fiery Man!' screamed one of the lads at last, and they took to their heels and ran for their lives. At length they crowded into a barn and with shaking hands barricaded the door, then flung themselves down in the darkness, trembling and sweating like horses that had been driven too hard.

"For a little while all was black and silent, and then their eyes began to distinguish thin lines of white light in the darkness. It was the light of the Fiery Man, showing through the cracks between the door planks. Closer and closer he came, until the thin white lines were surrounded by a corona of dazzling light and the crackling of the fire could be heard right outside the door.

"Then a great voice called out, 'The *Fettmännchen,* the *Fettmännchen* you promised me!' and there was a mighty blow upon the door. No one dared move, much less open up. They lay on the floor of the barn, petrified and shivering, cursing the lad who had made the stupid boast, and praying to the holy saints for rescue.

"Then the Fiery Man gave a roar of fury, and laid both of his blazing palms on the door, intending to burn right through it. The door began to smoke and blacken, and the smell of charred wood pervaded the barn, the flames licking around the planks throwing an ugly orange light. Seeing this, the young men became desperate and told the lad who had made the boast that he must open the door and give the Fiery Man the coin he had promised.

"White with fear, he refused to go, so they laid hands on him and prepared to drag him to the door, but he fought them tooth and nail.

" 'Don't put me outside!' he screamed. 'I don't have the *Fettmännchen,* I have no money at all, and he will kill me!'

" 'You fool,' said one of the others. 'You offered him a coin, and you didn't even have it?' He would have struck the lad, but another youth stopped him.

" 'That's no use,' he said. 'Turn out your pockets and find a coin, or we are all done for.'

"So they went through their pockets in desperation, and at last someone found a coin. Now there was no escape for the foolish young man who had made the boast in the first place; the others pushed the coin into his hand and then they stood behind him and thrust him toward the door with a strength born of terror.

" 'Here is your *Fettmännchen!*' shouted one of them, and opened the door. Instantly the barn was lit up so brightly that they had to close their eyes—but they could still feel the heat on their faces; it was like leaning into a baker's oven. The young man with the coin stood trembling like a rabbit, the *Fettmännchen* in his outstretched palm.

"'The *Fettmännchen* you promised me,' said the great voice that crackled as though the lips and the larynx and the lungs forming the words were themselves on fire.

"Then the young man felt a terrible heat and a searing pain in his hand, as though he had thrust it into the hottest part of the blacksmith's furnace. He made a choking sound in his throat, and then he fell senseless to the floor, so that he did not see the Fiery Man striding away and the darkness closing in. They carried him home to his mother and put him to bed, where he lay like the dead until the next morning.

"Perhaps it was as well for him. The hand the Fiery Man had touched was charred right down to the bones, the crumbling and blackened ends of which protruded through the stumps of incinerated flesh. And that," concluded Herr Schiller, "is the tale of the Fiery Man of the Hirnberg, and the consequences of speaking without thinking first." He looked at me, unblinking.

"That," I said, not without admiration, "was *very* horrible."

"*Bitte schön,*" said Herr Schiller drily, inclining his head.

Chapter Twenty-nine

They found a shoe," said Stefan.

We were standing on the cobblestones outside the *Gymnasium* savoring the autumn sunshine. Winter is bitter in the Eifel; you have to enjoy the warmer months while you can.

"A shoe?" I repeated, uncomprehending.

"Marion Voss's shoe," said Stefan with a trace of impatience.

I gaped at him. *"Marion Voss's shoe?"*

He nodded.

"Where?"

"Somewhere in the woods. I'm not sure where. Maybe up near the chapel at Decke Tönnes. It was somewhere like that."

"Who found it?"

"Some kids out walking with their mom, that's what I heard."

"Oh." I could not help feeling disappointed. Why did other people have to make the discoveries? Why couldn't it have been *me* who fell over Marion Voss's shoe while out walking? "Who told you?"

"Nobody told me," said Stefan. "I overheard Boris and his *Dummkopf* friends talking about it." He didn't say *where* he had been when he overheard the conversation, and I didn't ask. "You know what?" he added. "They sounded shit scared."

"What've they got to be scared of?" I asked. "So far, whoever it is has only taken girls."

"So far," said Stefan meaningfully. He scuffed the toe of his sneaker along the ground, thinking. "Next time it might not be."

"Yes, but . . ." I frowned. "Who's going to attack Boris and his friends? They'd have to be crazy."

"Maybe he is, whoever's doing it," said Stefan.

I was not convinced. Even a maniac (and here I imagined the cannibal Thilo Koch had described, crunching bloody bones between his discolored fangs) would hardly choose Boris as a victim when there were so many smaller kids who would be much easier targets. Not to mention the repulsive idea of eating Boris, who had the unhealthy look of someone marinating in the effluent of his own sebaceous glands.

Still, I reflected uneasily, it was worrying when even the likes of Boris were afraid.

"Shall we go and see Herr Schiller after school?" asked Stefan, breaking in on my thoughts.

"I can't just *go*, I have to check it with my mother first," I pointed out. The curfew had relaxed a little since the summer vacation had passed without any more disappearances, but all the same my mother insisted on knowing where I was virtually every minute of the day, much to my disgust.

"I can," Stefan said. He brushed dirty blond strands of hair back from his forehead. "Sure you can't?"

"Yes," I replied gloomily. "But I'll walk as far as the door with you. I can just go home that way."

"OK."

The school bell rang. We went into the courtyard together, but then I stopped on the pretext of doing up my shoelace. I wanted to wait until the crowds of children were inside before I went in. I would rather be late than risk the nudges and whispers that meant someone had noticed it was *Pia Kolvenbach—wasn't she the girl who—? Didn't her grandmother—?*

I watched Stefan run up the steps and sighed. Me and StinkStefan. It was always me and StinkStefan. Together forever, like Batman and Robin, only not so cool.

·　　·　　·

"It's Pluto," said Stefan in astonishment. He leaned closer to the window, peering into the gloom beyond. Then he glanced at me. "It's Pluto. It is. It's definitely him."

"Let me see." I pushed Stefan's shoulder, trying to get him out of the way so that I could look. Then I pressed my nose to the glass.

Herr Schiller's house was dark inside; there was not a single light on anywhere. It took my eyes awhile to get used to the dimness within, then gradually I was able to pick out the pieces of furniture, the bulk of Herr Schiller's old-fashioned radio squatting on the sideboard, the outlines of the pictures on the walls.

"I don't see Pluto."

"On Herr Schiller's chair."

I strained my eyes, then caught my breath. Stefan was perfectly right: there, on Herr Schiller's favorite armchair, was the sleek and muscular form of Pluto, curled into a comfortable ball. As I looked, his head suddenly came up, as though he had sensed that he was being watched, and I saw the twin gleam of his yellow eyes, then the flash of white fangs as he gave a languorous yawn.

"What's he doing in there?"

"I don't know," said Stefan. "But Herr Schiller's going to go mad if he comes back and finds him there."

We looked at each other. I was not much concerned for Pluto's welfare; he could look after himself, as a number of small dogs in Bad Münstereifel could have testified. But I wondered how Herr Schiller would cope with the discovery. I envisioned him having a heart attack, theatrically, like they did in the movies, clutching his chest and then plummeting to the floor taking small tables and china ornaments with him.

"Where is Herr Schiller, anyway?" said Stefan suddenly.

I peered into the room again. "I can't see—"

"*Ha-llo!*" bawled someone behind us. I almost jumped out of my skin. I turned to see Hilde Koch, grandmother of the repulsive Thilo, waving at us energetically from her doorstep farther up the street. I looked at Stefan, but he didn't look as though he knew what was going on any more than I did. We didn't move.

Frau Koch lumbered down off her doorstep and began to stump along the street toward us. The effect was somewhat like a bull walrus flopping over an ice floe. Her flabby dewlaps undulated alarmingly as she approached.

"*Ha-llo!*" she bawled again, this time waving a mottled finger at us. She wiped her hands on the immense floral overall that shrouded her bulky figure, then put them on her hips.

"Get away from there, you *Quälgeister*! What do you think you're doing?"

Neither of us said anything. We stood in silence and watched Frau Koch's elephantine approach.

"What do you think you're doing?" she demanded again when she was within a few meters of us.

"We came to visit Herr Schiller," answered Stefan in an amazingly calm voice.

It was one of those things that always made me wonder about Stefan; he could be so good with adults, but he was such a disaster with kids his own age. Now he was looking at Frau Koch as though she was not the nearest thing we had seen to a fat and bewhiskered walrus in this town, almost smiling at her in fact, and she was looking back at him, already slightly mollified.

"Hmph," she said skeptically. "You kids." She eyed us narrowly. "Who pulled all the flowers out of my window box, that's what I'd like to know? Don't think I don't know these things."

"That's . . ." I began, intending to say, *that's terrible,* but one glance from those basilisk eyes and I was struck dumb.

"What are you doing bothering poor Herr Schiller, anyway?" demanded the relentless Frau Koch.

"We weren't bothering him, Frau Koch," said Stefan politely. "We visit him quite often."

"He's our friend," I tried daringly, and was rewarded with another terrifyingly disapproving glance.

"If he's your friend, Fräulein," retorted Frau Koch with withering irony, "you should know that he isn't there, shouldn't you? And don't think this is your opportunity for some *Blödsinn,* because I'm watching you."

"Of course not," said Stefan.

"You kids," grumbled Frau Koch again. "It's bad enough, all that's happened with Herr Düster, though who cares about him, *um Gottes*

Willen, but you don't need to start on Herr Schiller. No sense of respect these days, none at all."

Stefan looked at me. He was as transparent as a fish tank; you could almost see the thoughts swimming back and forth.

"Frau Koch?" he said. The look he got in return would have scorched paint but he didn't flinch. "What *has* happened to Herr Düster?"

"As if you don't know," she grunted back at him. All the same, she could not resist the temptation to retail a bit of interesting gossip. "Someone's been leaving things on his doorstep, haven't they?"

"Things?" I stared at her, my imagination running riot, conjuring up poison-pen letters, giblets from the butcher's, a fat dog turd . . . "What sort of things?"

Frau Koch was never one to admit there was something she didn't know. "Never you mind," she said brusquely. "I don't want you getting ideas." She glanced at Herr Schiller's house. "And you get away from that window before I call the police."

"Yes, Frau Koch," said Stefan, pulling me away. I let him drag me a few paces up the street and then I stopped and turned to see whether Frau Koch was still watching us. She was, standing with arms akimbo and her hands on her massive floral hips. Hastily, I turned away and followed Stefan.

It was not until we had rounded the corner by the bookshop that I realized we had gone the wrong way; at any rate, we had taken the long way around from Herr Schiller's. I looked at my watch, wondering whether I would be late home.

"She's made us late," I complained to Stefan. "My mother's going to be mad."

He didn't answer. I glanced at him and saw that he was staring down the Marktstrasse. I followed his gaze and saw the familiar green-and-white livery of a police car; it was parked directly outside the *Grundschule.* While we watched, the driver's door opened and Herr Wachtmeister Tondorf climbed out. A moment later someone got out on the passenger side: I recognized the stony-faced policeman who had been at the school after Marion Voss had vanished.

Herr Wachtmeister Tondorf glanced around him quickly and almost furtively; the other policeman stared up at the facade of the school without apparent emotion. Then they circled around the end of the chained fence that ran along the front of the building and disappeared through the archway leading to the school.

"Did you see that?" breathed Stefan, turning to me. "Police."

I nodded.

"They must have found something," he went on. We both stared up the street toward the spot where the police car was parked, as though it could somehow tell us something. "I wonder what they've found," said Stefan, almost to himself. "I wonder what they've found."

Chapter Thirty

"Mama, are we going to stay in Germany forever?"

The question had been simmering in my mind ever since I returned from England. For three whole weeks I had resisted the temptation to ask my parents about it, but finally the desire to know the answer had overcome my anxiety about somehow getting into trouble with Aunt Liz. I was sitting at the table with a plate of spaghetti Bolognese cooling in front of me when the question just tumbled out. To my surprise my mother didn't react at all. I gathered my courage and asked again, a little more loudly.

"Mama, are we going to stay in Germany forever?"

This time my father's head came up, and he shot my mother a glance that was heavy with meaning. My mother didn't see it, or chose not to; she was looking at Sebastian, and busying herself wiping his chin, which was liberally smeared with sauce. When she had cleaned him up so thoroughly that not one atom of the sauce was perceptible, she put down the napkin she had been using and picked up her glass of water. I was just about to ask the question a third time when she forestalled me.

"That's an odd question, Pia."

She sipped the water, then put the glass slowly down. Then she said, "Why do you ask?"

"Well . . . I just wondered," I said in the end. "I mean, you were born in England, and then you came here."

"Yes, I did, didn't I," said my mother. She sounded as though she were talking to herself, not to me. Then she looked at me and this time she gave me a broad smile. "You never know," she said. "People do move. One day you might live in England."

"You mean, when I'm grown up?" I asked.

"Yes," cut in my father. He was looking at my mother again, with a significant expression on his face. She shrugged.

"Well," she said. She picked up her fork and made a tentative stab at the spaghetti.

"We have been through this before," said my father in an ominous tone.

"I didn't say anything," said my mother. She sketched a quick bright smile on her face. "Eat up, Sebastian."

"You didn't need to say anything," pursued my father. "I can see it in your face."

"Oh, so now I have to watch how I look?" The smile dropped from my mother's features. "What are you, the bloody Thought Police?" she said in English.

"We are not moving," said my father; he had been holding a glass of beer and now he put it down on the table a little too hard.

"So you say," said my mother. She rotated the fork, gathering swirls of spaghetti. "But people do move." She looked at him evenly. "The Petersons are moving. I saw Sandra in the supermarket. They're going after Christmas. Tom's got a new job in London."

My father looked shocked. "But they are happy here."

"Seems not," said my mother.

"They said they would never go back to England." My father sounded as though they had personally let him down. "And they have children in the school here."

"Ah, that's just it," said my mother. "Children in the school here." She took a mouthful of spaghetti and chewed it, her eyes still on him.

My father sat back in his chair, as though he had just received a shocking piece of news. Then suddenly he sat forward again.

"Of course, Tom is British."

"So?"

"So it is quite natural for him to take a new job in England."

"Sandra works too," my mother pointed out. "And she'll have to give up her job when they move."

"Well . . ." said my father dismissively.

My mother pounced like a hawk. "Well what?"

"Well, she has the children."

There was a clatter as my mother's fork dropped to the edge of her plate. "I don't believe I'm hearing this." She put the palms of her hands on the tabletop in front of her, as though she were going to push away the table and all of us with it. "Look," she said, "apart from the unbelievable chauvinism of what you just said, you've totally missed the point."

"Which was?" My father was now sounding as angry as she did.

"That it isn't an easy decision for them to leave." My mother brushed a strand of dark hair out of her eyes with an impatient flick of her hand. "They both loved it here. But Tom was offered this job and, well, with everything that's been going on, they thought maybe this was the time to leave."

"Well, I think you have missed *my* point," responded my father stiffly. "Tom is British. He trained in England and he works for a British company. He can move back to England at any time he likes. It's different for us."

"Why?" demanded my mother. "Your English is good enough, we could manage."

"I would have to retrain."

"So, retrain."

This time my father's hand hit the table so hard that we all jumped. "It's not as easy as that, and you know it." My father saw Sebastian's face crumpling as though he was about to burst into tears, and with an effort he lowered his voice. "Be realistic, Kate. We have to live on something."

"I could go back to work."

"No."

"Don't be so—"

He cut over her. "And we couldn't afford to buy a house in England. Not like this one."

My mother shot a poisonous glance around the room as though to say, *what's so great about this one,* but she didn't say anything. She picked up her fork again and turned it idly in the mess of spaghetti on her plate. There was a long silence. Then she got to her feet with a great scraping of the chair legs against the floor.

"Ah, fuck it," said my mother, and stalked out of the room.

Sebastian and I looked at each other round-eyed.

"Children," said my father portentously, "your mother is upset. But I never wish to hear that sort of language in the house again."

"Yes, Papa," I said.

Chapter Thirty-one

Winter came early that year. I always used to think of St. Martin's Day, November 11, as a high point in the approach to Christmas. That year, the year when Katharina Linden and Marion Voss vanished from the streets of the town, it was a cold St. Martin's.

My mother dressed us in layers and layers of warm clothing: sweaters, down jackets, thermal boots, scarves, and mittens. I had a pink fluffy hat with a bobble on the top and Sebastian had a little navy-blue fleece hat with earflaps. We looked like a pair of fat gnomes. All the same, it was necessary; during the short walk to the Klosterplatz we could feel the biting cold on any centimeter of exposed skin. Even through the thick insulation of my mittens, the cold was seeping into the hand that held the lantern.

As a grown-up *Gymnasium* pupil, I would normally have dispensed with a lantern as being seriously uncool, but at the last minute my mother had bought me one and I hadn't the heart to refuse it. It was a round yellow sun face made of crimped paper. Sebastian had a much grander lantern, constructed by my mother along with the other parents at his playgroup. It was a green caterpillar with pink and purple spots, made of tissue paper on a skeleton of black cardboard. The caterpillar had an insane leer on its face because my mother had cut the pink mouth out as a wiggly line. She said it was "a blow against uniformity"; my mother never could stand the German fad for sitting in a group and all making exactly the same item. In fact she hated arts and crafts. Sebastian should probably have been grateful that my mother had made a lantern for him at all, considering the agonies she had to go through to do it.

When we got to the Klosterplatz it was already full of people milling around, stamping their feet and blowing on their hands. The fire brigade was there as usual, the firemen hanging around the gleaming fire engine parked at one side, and doing their best to look nonchalant. An enormous bonfire had been built in the middle of the square. It would be lit by the firemen when the procession was under way around the town, so that it would be burning merrily when we all got back.

As well as the firemen, there was an unusually high number of policemen. Normally Herr Wachtmeister Tondorf and perhaps one of the other local policemen would be in attendance, just in case anything went awry, like the time Thilo Koch's brother Jörg set off a fire alarm and the firemen had to abandon their posts by the bonfire and dash off to the rescue. This year, however, the police seemed to have dragged every spare officer from here to Euskirchen into the town for the evening, including the granite-faced one from outside. They were being discreet, but they were everywhere.

I noticed Herr Wachtmeister Tondorf talking quietly to one of the schoolteachers who was supervising the *Grundschule* children. All the teachers and the police officers had a grim look to their faces, as though about to undertake a military maneuver; only the children were as unconcerned as usual, waving their glowing lanterns about and jumping up and down with excitement. I saw Frau Eichen, who was now in charge of a new class of first-graders, counting her charges, her finger stabbing through the air as she did so. She counted them once, and two minutes later she was counting them again.

Now the penny dropped. The adults were all so twitchy because they were afraid something might happen again, like it had at Karneval. Nobody wanted to be the one who was in charge of a child who vanished.

"Is anyone from your class here?" my mother asked suddenly. I guessed she was wondering whether things were going any better in the new school than they had in the previous one. Dutifully, I scanned the square for familiar faces.

"No," I said. It was a relief in a way; Stefan was the only one who would have spoken to me, and I knew he wasn't coming.

"There's someone waving," said my mother, pointing. She sounded pleased. I followed her gaze. It was Lena Schmitz from the fourth grade, the year that had been below mine in the *Grundschule.* The Schmitzes lived only a few doors away from us and Lena's mother worked in the hairdresser's where my mother periodically had her gray roots covered, so we knew each other slightly. I waved back enthusiastically, conscious of my parents' eyes on me.

It was almost time for the procession to begin. The local brass band, resplendent in hunter-green uniforms and peaked caps, was assembling at the corner, hoisting trombones and trumpets and horns, which glittered in the light of the lanterns and torches. Someone tried out the opening notes of one of the songs, a song so familiar that the words formed themselves inside my head as I listened: *Sankt Martin, Sankt Martin, Sankt Martin ritt durch Schnee und Wind . . .* It finished with a squeak that sent a ripple of laughter through the crowd.

Someone from the town council had climbed the steps at the side of the square and was talking inaudibly into a bullhorn. Then we heard a clatter of hooves on the cobblestones and St. Martin rode into the square.

Of course, all the spectators except the very youngest knew that St. Martin was really someone from the town, dressed up in a red velvet cloak and Roman helmet; in fact my parents even knew the family who lent the horse. But there was always something magical about St. Martin; he was real in a way that St. Nikolaus and the Easter Bunny weren't. For one thing, he was undeniably solid, and so was the horse: if you followed too closely behind it you had to look where you stepped.

As we watched, St. Martin wheeled the horse around and began to ride slowly out of the south side of the square, the crimson cloak undulating on the horse's hindquarters as it moved, the torchlight making the great golden helmet glitter. The band fell in behind him, and struck up with the first bars of "Ich gehe mit meiner Laterne," the signal for the schoolchildren to follow. As the rest of us surged forward, I could see Frau Eichen counting the children again.

"Can I go on ahead?" I asked my mother hopefully, seeing that she was making woefully slow progress with Sebastian in his buggy. I was afraid we would be stuck right at the back, where we could hardly hear the band, and we would be last back into the square to see the bonfire.

She shook her head. "I don't think that's a good idea, Pia." I didn't bother to ask why.

"I'll go with her," said my father, turning up his collar. He looked at me sternly. "And stay where I can see you, Pia. No running off."

"Yes, Papa."

I fell into step beside him; with his long legs we made good progress, and were soon pushing our way further up the procession. First it wound up the Heisterbacher Strasse and past our front door, then it followed the line of the medieval defensive walls west toward the great gate, the Orchheimer Tor. I looked about me at the excited faces, the flickering torches and glowing lanterns, and the ancient stones of the walls, interspersed with arrow slits. We could have been back in the Middle Ages, on our way to a coronation—or a witch-burning.

Trotting along beside my father, I found that we were overtaking the fourth-grade children, who were swarming along with their three teachers running around them distractedly like sheepdogs. I picked out Lena Schmitz from the sea of faces. At the same moment she saw me. "Hallo" was all she said, but it was enough. It was such a relief to be treated even with that courtesy after nearly a year of being the class pariah. I slowed my pace a little to keep level with her.

"Hallo, can I see your lantern?"

She showed it to me. It was made of papier mâché, and I think it was supposed to be an apple, but somewhere along the way it had been dented or crushed. Now it looked more like a plum tomato.

"Schön," I said anyway.

She peered at my lantern. "My mother bought it," I said hastily.

"Oh. What has your brother got?"

"A caterpillar."

Up ahead, the band had finished "Ich gehe mit meiner Laterne" and started on "Sankt Martin, Sankt Martin." Dutifully, I glanced behind me to check that my father was still there, and then I fell into step with

Lena's class. The procession was reaching the little intersection where King Zwentibold stood atop his fountain, now drained for winter in case the pipes froze and cracked.

"Do you like it at the new school?" asked Lena, who would be moving up herself next year.

"It's great," I lied. Actually, the school was all right; it was the past that kept hanging around me like a bad smell, but I didn't want to raise that with Lena. "Are you coming to Sankt Michael next year?"

"Probably Sankt Angela."

"Oh."

We passed out of the town walls through the Werther Tor and back in again by the Protestant church, its starkly modern design strident against the traditional form of the buildings that flanked it. A couple of minutes and we would be back in the Klosterplatz, warming ourselves around the bonfire and watching St. Martin reenact his good deed with the beggarman.

"Mein licht ist aus, ich geh' nach Haus," we sang. *"Rabimmel rabummel rabumm bumm bumm!"*

"Hurry up," called Frau Diederichs, Lena's class teacher; she was no doubt keen to get back into the Klosterplatz and unload her charges back into the care of their parents. She moved up and down the line of children, patting a shoulder here and there or stooping to peer into a well-muffled face. She jabbed me in the upper arm as she went past but did not see my look of indignation; she had already moved on.

As we turned into the square the bonfire was revealed in all its glory. The piled wood and kindling must have been three meters high, and the flames shot into the air above it in a great flaring corona, with sparks peeling off in all directions. I would have made a beeline for it and warmed my hands, which were aching with cold, but Frau Diederichs was shepherding her class determinedly toward the side of the square, where the drama of St. Martin was to take place.

"Do you want to come?" Lena asked me, and I nodded, glad to be included for once; who cared if it was with a class from the baby school? I glanced behind me. The substantial form of my father was still in tow, shadowing me like a bodyguard.

I crowded into the ranks of waiting children. St. Martin was before

us, astride the chestnut horse, which was becoming a little restless surrounded by flaming torches and the shrill voices of several hundred
children. As it moved, the sound of its iron-shod feet rang out on the
cobblestones. St. Martin leaned forward and patted its neck.

The man who had used the bullhorn earlier in the evening addressed
us again, not much more audibly than before, though we all knew the
story so well that we hardly needed his commentary. St. Martin wheeled
his horse about and rode it a little way, ascending the ramp at the side
of the square so that we could all see him. He made a big deal of adjust-
ing his fine crimson cloak for warmth; his golden helmet glittered as he
moved. We all waited expectantly for the beggarman to appear.

Someone was pushing through the ranks of children; Lena was
shoved into me, and trod on my toes.

"Ow." I grimaced, then smiled at her sheepishly, not wanting to
spoil the friendly atmosphere that had bloomed between us. Whoever
it was who was shoving had created a ripple through the crowd of assembled children, like a Mexican wave. It caught Frau Diederichs's eye,
and she looked up disapprovingly.

A stout woman with a crop of henna-red hair, teased so that it stood
upright like the spines of a hedgehog, was forcing her way through
the crowd. I did not recognize her, but Frau Diederichs did. "Frau
Mahlberg," she said in a tone that balanced friendly recognition with
mild disapproval; the woman was disrupting the class and blocking the
view of St. Martin.

Frau Mahlberg's head turned, and she began to wade toward Frau
Diederichs through the ranks of schoolchildren as though through waist-
deep water; indeed her brawny arms moved vigorously as though she
would sweep them out of her way. When she reached Frau Diederichs
she did not bother with any niceties.

"Where is Julia?" she demanded. Her voice was sufficiently strident
that several of the children looked around and someone behind us
hissed *"Shhhh!"*

I could not hear Frau Diederichs's reply, but she seemed to be saying
something placatory, and she made a small gesture, a sweep of her hand
taking in the crowd of children.

I turned my gaze back to St. Martin for a moment; the beggarman had appeared, suitably dressed in rags, and was pantomiming cold and hunger, stooping and rubbing his hands up and down his upper arms. This was the part of the play that we all looked forward to: St. Martin would unsheathe his sword and cut his magnificent cloak in half. I saw him reach to his side and begin to slide the gleaming blade out of the sheath—and then suddenly I couldn't see him at all, because someone had bumped into me again and I had staggered down on one knee, dropping my lantern in the melee. I snatched it up again as quickly as I could, but it was too late; it had already been trampled and the broadly smiling sun face had acquired an oddly sunken look.

"Wo ist meine Tochter?" someone was yelling. It was Frau Mahlberg. It was she who was responsible for shoving several of us over; she was wading around among the assembled children like a farmer at a shambles, grasping shoulders and pushing at backs, all the time peering fiercely into the upturned faces, some of them now wearing uncertain expressions, others indignant.

"Frau Mahlberg, Frau Mahlberg!" That was Frau Diederichs, the teacher, now following behind and wringing her hands ineffectually. Behind us, more voices were raised in protest at the interruption to the play.

"Shhhh!"

"Julia!" Frau Mahlberg was bellowing, oblivious to them. I glanced back at the ramp where St. Martin and the beggarman were posed in a tableau, looking rather nonplussed at the racket. I had missed the critical moment when the cloak was divided; half of it was now draped over St. Martin's hands, which were frozen in the act of handing it down to the beggar. The other half, truncated, hung from his shoulders.

The man with the bullhorn said something, and then repeated it in a slightly irritated voice. Still St. Martin did not react, and eventually in a departure from tradition the beggar reached up and helped himself to the cloak. There was a crackle of interference from the loudspeaker, but the narrator was lost for words for once, perhaps stunned by the beggar's rapacious behavior. Someone was approaching us; it was the granite-faced policeman I had seen with Herr Wachtmeister Tondorf.

"Hallo."

It was a command, not a greeting. Frau Mahlberg whirled around and caught sight of him. She pounced like a vulture. For a moment I thought she was going to physically catch hold of him, but at the last moment he put up a hand and stopped her in her tracks.

"My daughter!" She gestured wildly at Frau Diederichs, flailing a brawny arm. "She's supposed to be in charge of my daughter!"

"Well, I am, I . . ." Frau Diederichs was flustered; she could see that most of the people within earshot were no longer watching St. Martin and the beggarman, but were all listening to the exchange between herself and Frau Mahlberg.

"And you are . . . ?" said the policeman.

"Frau Diederichs. I'm Julia's class teacher."

"Julia is my daughter," said Frau Mahlberg.

"Verstanden," said the policeman.

"And she's not here." Frau Mahlberg's voice was beginning to rise, hysterically. "This woman was in charge of her, and now she's not here, and God only knows what's happened to her." She made a wild gesture in Frau Diederichs's direction, as though to strike her. "After all that's happened! How could she let my daughter wander off?"

"I didn't let her wander off," protested Frau Diederichs. "I've been with the children every single moment of the procession. I've counted them at least six times."

"Where is she, then?" demanded Frau Mahlberg.

"Are you sure Julia isn't here?" cut in the policeman. He glanced at Frau Diederichs, who was the less hysterical-looking of the pair.

"Well . . ." She pulled her coat closer around her body, as though she wished she could disappear down into it, and then she began to count the children again, stabbing the air with her finger as she did so. "One . . . two . . ."

"What was Julia wearing?" cut in the policeman as Frau Diederichs continued to count.

"A dark-blue jacket, a pink hat . . ." Frau Mahlberg screwed her face up as if the effort of staying calm was almost killing her. ". . . white woolen mittens . . ."

I turned to Lena, to say something about Julia, to ask her whether she had seen her, so for a moment I didn't notice that Frau Diederichs had stopped counting. "Isn't that her?" she said suddenly in a voice made tremulous with excitement. I looked up and saw that she was pointing at me. I looked at Lena and then half turned to look behind me. There were no children behind me, only the dark bulk of my father in his winter coat. I swiveled back to look at Frau Diederichs. She was still staring at me, and her hand was still outstretched.

"The pink hat," she said.

Suddenly all eyes were upon me. The next second, Frau Mahlberg had stepped forward and with a sharp jerk of her hand had pulled the pink hat from my head, almost taking a handful of hair with it.

"Ow," I said, but nobody heard me. Frau Mahlberg was screaming at the top of her voice, screaming like a stuck pig. She grabbed me by the shoulders and shook me until my teeth chattered. "She's not Julia! *She's not Julia!*" she was shrieking, centimeters away from my face.

I froze in her grip like an animal caught in the lights of an express train, unable to move as doom bore down upon me. My head snapped back; as the hurricane of Frau Mahlberg's fury swept across me, I imagined my eyes popping from their sockets and bouncing across the cobblestones like marbles.

"*Hör auf!*" boomed my father's voice. For a moment, insanely, I thought it was *me* he was telling to stop it, whatever it was that I had done to outrage Frau Mahlberg. Then he was pulling me away from her, and the granite-faced policeman was holding on to her while she struggled in his grasp like a madwoman. His face still looked impassive.

Frau Diederichs was standing beside this tableau, looking white-faced and shocked. She kept looking from me to Frau Mahlberg and back again, as though she could not really believe what she saw.

"I counted them," she kept saying. "I counted them."

"You counted this child," the policeman said, nodding at me. "Is she from the class, or isn't she?"

"No," said Frau Diederichs. "I don't know . . ." She approached me tentatively, as though she suspected me of some criminal act, of having spirited Julia Mahlberg away in order to take her place. Then she said, "It's Pia Kolvenbach. The girl whose grandmother . . ." She faltered.

"The girl whose grandmother what?" said the policeman, but I didn't hear any more.

My father was pulling me into his embrace, as though I were a kindergarten child and not a great big girl of eleven. I buried my head in the front of his coat; I could still feel the vibration of his chest as he spoke determinedly to the policeman, but mercifully the words were muffled. I thought I would go mad if I had to listen to Oma Kristel's accident being dragged up all over again. I clung to my father until finally he stopped speaking and prized me off.

"Pia, you can go home now."

My mother had surfaced from somewhere in the crowd, with Sebastian in his stroller.

I didn't bother to listen to the brittle exchange between her and my father, nor did I bother to look around for my lantern, which I had dropped while in Frau Mahlberg's tempestuous grip, and which was almost certainly trampled beyond repair. I let my mother lead me away from the row that was still continuing, her arm around my shoulders while with her free hand she negotiated the stroller over the cobblestones.

My father remained with the policeman and Frau Mahlberg; I glanced at him over my shoulder as my mother walked me away from them, my chest tight with the horrible conviction that I had somehow got us all in trouble, that my father was having to face the music for me.

"What's happening?" I asked my mother.

She looked at me, and her face was grim in the low light, but she only shook her head. People were milling all about us; the man with the bullhorn was standing on the steps with it in his hand, looking startled. No one seemed disposed to leave the square, but the usual buzz of excited voices was replaced with curious looks and whispers. The policemen who had been stationed at intervals along the procession route were all coming back into the square; I had never seen so many policemen in Bad Münstereifel before; it looked as though they were expecting a riot. Some of them were speaking into walkie-talkies.

My mother increased her pace, pulling me along. When we reached the corner, I looked back to see whether St. Martin was still there. But the ramp at the side of the square was empty. He had gone.

Chapter Thirty-two

That was not the end of it for me, of course; later in the evening Herr Wachtmeister Tondorf called at the house and spent a long time going over what had happened during the procession. I was glad it was him and not the granite-faced policeman whose impassive gaze made me feel as though I were guilty of absolutely everything you could name.

Herr Wachtmeister Tondorf was his usual kindly self, but unimaginably meticulous; he went over everything again and again, asking questions in an unvaryingly gentle voice, until I was too tired to answer them properly. Why had I decided to walk with Frau Diederichs's class? Had someone suggested it? How did I know Lena Schmitz? Did I know Julia Mahlberg? Had I noticed her at any time during the procession?

My mother put Sebastian to bed and then she came down and sat next to me, stony-faced, silently holding my hand. At half past ten she simply said, "Enough." She got to her feet.

"Herr Wachtmeister Tondorf, Pia has to sleep."

"Frau Kolvenbach—" He didn't get any further.

"Don't tell me it's important. I *know* it's important. But she's only a child and she's exhausted. Look."

I tried to look alert, but I could barely keep my eyes open. "I'm not tired," I started to say, and ruined it with a massive yawn. My eyelids felt as though they would slide shut under their own momentum like the roller shutters we had on our windows.

"She can't possibly tell you anything else. You've asked her the same things at least twice, anyway."

"Frau Kolvenbach," began Herr Wachtmeister Tondorf doggedly, "I am sorry that your daughter is tired, but you must understand, the Mahlbergs have a daughter too. We must do everything possible to find her."

"I know that," snapped my mother. "So why don't you get out onto the street and help look for her?"

At this piece of rudeness I was suddenly wide awake again. I was used to my mother's occasional volcanic outbursts, but still I was stunned at her daring, telling the police their business. I looked at her; her face had a drawn-in look to it, with deep furrows between the brows and at the corners of the mouth. She looked suddenly older, witchlike.

Herr Wachtmeister Tondorf's avuncular expression froze over in an instant. When he stood up, his movements were stiffly formal. "I will have to come again tomorrow," he informed my mother coldly. She merely nodded, making no move to show him out. Herr Wachtmeister Tondorf looked at her for a moment, then picked up his cap and made his own way to the door, closing it softly behind him.

My mother took me upstairs in silence and helped me to get ready for bed. Her face still had that oddly puckered look, as though she was keeping something tightly under control. Still, she was gentle with me, brushing my teeth for me as I stood before her swaying a little with tiredness, and helping me into my nightdress. She even let me leave the bedside lamp in my room on, as though trying to keep off the night monsters that very small children fear. She sat by my bed for a while, and I think she was still there when I fell asleep.

Chapter Thirty-three

I don't know exactly what time it was when I woke. I was lying on my back on the bed, with my comforter half on, half off my body, and my head flung back so that the light from the bedside lamp was shining directly on my face. I was dreaming of a wailing sound like a siren, rhythmic pulses of sound, and the light was so bright that it seemed to pulsate too, in time to the rising and falling of the wailing.

I opened my eyes, then shut them again instantly, dazzled. The siren sound was still going on, and for a moment I thought it was still part of a dream, that I was not properly awake. But it was real. As I sat up, blinking, I could hear my parents moving about outside on the landing, speaking in low voices.

"Mama?"

I felt strangely disoriented. Was there a house on fire or something? I slid my legs off the side of the bed, intending to get up and go to my parents. My mother forestalled me by opening the bedroom door; she was in her dressing gown, her hair spread over her shoulders in a dark mass.

"Pia, what are you doing awake?" she said, but her voice sounded vague rather than annoyed.

"I heard a noise." My bare feet touched the floor; the boards were cold.

"It's nothing."

My mother came right into the room and picked up my comforter, intending that I should lie down and she should cover me up with it. But now I was wide awake. I glanced at the doorway and saw my father standing there. Unlike my mother, he was fully dressed in outdoor clothes—dark cord trousers, boots, and a down jacket.

"It sounded like the fire brigade—or the police," I said.

"It's nothing to worry about," said my mother. She shook the comforter a little as though to encourage me back underneath it. "Get back into bed."

"Do they want to ask me some more questions?" I wanted to know.

"No." My mother glanced at my father. She plumped up my pillow, thumping it savagely. "Not tonight. Get in," she added. I did so, reluctantly.

"Why is Papa dressed? Is it nearly morning?"

"He had to go out," said my mother, then added tartly, "He thinks I don't have enough to do, so he thought he'd tread mud right through the house."

"I will clean it up," said my father in an irritable voice.

"Good intentions," snapped my mother. She pushed her hair back behind her ears, but it wouldn't stay; unruly strands immediately fell forward over her eyes again. She looked different from the daytime Mama with her habitual ponytail: this mother looked younger, but somehow slightly wild.

"Did you find that girl, Papa?" I asked.

My father shook his head. "No, Pia. But the police are still looking."

"So where did you go?" I was starting to feel sleepy again, but this was too interesting to miss: all three of us up in the middle of the night. I hoped Sebastian would not spoil it by waking up and howling.

"Castle Dracula," snapped my mother. "That's where he went."

"Castle *Dracula*?"

"Kate—" started my father, but my mother interrupted him.

"Well, he might just as well have been there. That's where crowds of screaming peasants carrying pitchforks usually go when they want to lynch someone, isn't it?"

She clawed her hair back from her face again and regarded my father mutinously.

"We didn't want to lynch anybody, and they are not *peasants,*" he said in an ominous voice.

"Did I say—" started my mother sarcastically, and then stopped short, shaking her head in frustration. "Why do you always take everything so bloody literally?"

"And why do you say things if you don't really mean them?" he countered.

"Well, that's what it was, wasn't it?" she demanded resentfully. "A lynch mob? Or did you knock on his door and try to sell him encyclopedias?"

"Whose door?" I asked, but the question was lost somewhere in the atmosphere crackling between my parents like electricity arcing between two points.

"If you want to know the truth," said my father portentously, "we went there to make sure he *didn't* get lynched."

"That's very good," said my mother, nodding vigorously. My father looked at her suspiciously. "No, do go on," she added. "I'm interested."

"There are some people in this town who make very quick judgments," began my father doggedly.

"You don't say?"

"Kate, this is why you find it difficult here, if you always think the worst of people." My father had become rather flushed in the face. He shook his head. "All I am saying is, there are some people who might jump to conclusions before they know the truth. We cannot just take the law into our own hands."

"So you went there to make sure nobody *did* try to take the law into their own hands?"

My father nodded.

"And the thirty or so other concerned fathers, they were just some sort of UN peacekeeping force?" said my mother.

"You have to make fun," said my father.

"I'm not making fun. I just can't believe it. What, did you think he'd look out his front window and see you lot arriving and think, *Hey, I'm safe now?*"

"Kate, that boy Koch, the one who had a brother in Pia's class, he had already broken a window."

"And where were the police?"

"Looking for the little Mahlberg girl. But they are there now, you know that."

"Are you sure they didn't take their time on purpose?"

"What do you mean?" asked my father.

"Breaking windows . . . it seems to me that some people in this town have been having their own little Kristallnacht," said my mother.

There was a very long silence. The two of them were motionless, my father filling the doorway, my mother standing by my bed, one palm resting on the surface of my little dressing table as though for support. The silence was broken by the sound of her fingers rubbing back and forth across the painted wood.

"Sorry," she said eventually.

My father looked at her, but his face was so still that I could not tell whether he was angry, or upset, or indifferent.

"There are good people in this town," he said quietly.

"I know—"

"They don't deserve insults like that—comparing them to Nazis."

"I said I'm sorry, isn't that enough?"

"No," said my father. He turned away. "I will go and get a broom, and clean up this floor."

"I can do it."

"Not necessary," said my father.

For a minute or so after he had disappeared downstairs, my mother continued to stand by my bed looking toward the doorway, like a person on a quay watching a ship disappearing into the distance. Her fingers brushed the surface of my dressing table again, making a whispering sound. When she spoke, it was from the corner of her mouth, her voice soft, her eyes never leaving the door.

"Go to sleep, Pia. Go to sleep."

Chapter Thirty-four

The following morning when I came downstairs my father had already left for work. My mother was in the kitchen making waffles, a rare treat for breakfast. Sebastian was chomping happily, a heart-shaped waffle with a crescent bitten out of it clutched in his chubby fingers. My mother closed the waffle iron with a hiss and a little puff of steam.

"Yours will be ready any second," she said, and smiled at me. She sounded bright this morning, like a mother in a TV commercial, the sort who smiles cheerfully when her son gives her the whole team's muddy football uniforms to wash.

I slid into my habitual place behind the table.

"Where's Papa?"

"He had to leave early." She opened the waffle iron and slid a frying fork under the waffle to lever it out.

"Oh." I was disappointed; I had wanted to ask him about the night before. "Why did he have to go so early?"

"Oh, you know." She put the waffle on a plate and set it on the table in front of me. "Work."

"Hmmm." I tried the waffle; it was warm and delicious. For a while I gave myself up to the enjoyment of it. Eventually, however, when the edge of my hunger had been dulled and I was starting to think that perhaps waffles were not so wonderful after all, in fact more than six of them was positively off-putting, I said, "Mama? Where did Papa go last night?"

"Oh, Pia." She yanked the plug of the waffle iron from the outlet before answering the question. "If you must know, and I suppose you'll soon find out, considering what a hotbed of gossip this town is, your father went round to Herr Düster's."

"Herr Düster's? Was it his windows that were broken?"

"Not *windows*," said my mother. "One window. And yes, it was his. It was Jörg Koch who did it. Why am I not surprised?" she added with heavy irony.

"Why did Jörg Koch break his window? Was it an accident?"

"No."

My mother picked up a cloth and began to wipe down the countertop, which was splattered with waffle batter. With her back to me, and her elbow working like a piston, she did not look very approachable. All the same, I persisted.

"Why did he break it?"

"Because he . . ." She paused, turned around, and looked at me. "Because some of the kind citizens of this delightful town have decided that Herr Düster is a criminal."

"Hmmm." I thought about it. "Frau Kessel says it was probably Herr Düster who took Katharina Linden and the other girls. She said some girls disappeared in Bad Münstereifel when Papa was at school too, and it was Herr Düster then as well."

"Pia." Now my mother's gaze had acquired a laserlike intensity. "Frau Kessel is a poisonous old—well, never mind. I don't want you listening to her stories about who has done what in this town, and I *particularly* don't want to find out you've been passing them on to anyone else. If it wasn't for her and her cronies, we probably wouldn't have had a bloody lynch mob on the streets last night. She's a witch."

The literal-minded side of my personality, inherited from my father, struggled to digest this last nugget of information.

"Didn't Herr Düster do it? Take the girls, I mean?"

"Oh, *Pia*. I don't know. Nobody knows. And even if he did, it still wouldn't be right for people to just go round there and attack him. In civilized places," she added more to herself than to me, "people are innocent until proved guilty."

"But if he *did* do it . . . ?"

"Then it has to be handled properly. The police have to question him, and if it looks as though there is enough evidence that he did it, then it has to go to court. Do you know what that means?"

I nodded.

"And a court can't decide to punish anyone unless there's proof that they did something wrong. You can't just decide that someone *looks* guilty, or that you *think* they did it. You have to be sure. And being sure means you have to have proof."

"Like what?"

"Pia, I hardly think the breakfast table is the place to be discussing forensic science," said my mother drily. I was used to her occasional digressions into Baroque vocabulary, so I simply waited for her to explain.

"In this case we don't even know exactly what happened to Katharina or those other girls. It's always possible that they went with someone quite happily and that they are still . . ." My mother stopped herself. "That they will eventually show up safe and well. And then how would everyone feel if they had turned up on Herr Düster's doorstep and beaten him up?" She sighed. "Isn't it about time you were off to school? Another five minutes and you won't be in before the bell rings."

I slipped out from behind the table. "But, Mama, what would be proof?" I persisted, reluctant to leave without closing the conversation to my satisfaction.

"Well, it's things like someone actually seeing the person committing a crime . . . or maybe finding stolen goods in someone's house," said my mother.

"Or a body?" I asked.

"Or a . . . ? Pia, I don't think anyone is going to find dead bodies in anyone's house in Bad Münstereifel. Can we drop the subject? It's gruesome. And some little people"—she nodded meaningfully toward Sebastian—"are starting to understand more and more these days."

"Mmm-hmm."

Reluctantly, I went into the hallway to find my coat and the backpack that had replaced the now-babyish *Ranzen*. It was raining outside and I had three minutes to get to school before the bell rang. With a sigh I stepped out into the rain.

Chapter Thirty-five

*B*oris says he's definitely the one."

"How does he know?"

Stefan and I were sitting on a wall in the *Gymnasium* courtyard. The stone felt glacial even through the thick jeans I was wearing. Stefan seemed unconcerned by the cold, even though his jacket was too thin for the time of year.

"He says it's obvious." Stefan shrugged. "Everyone's heard the rumors going around, about Herr Schiller's daughter. Where there's smoke there's fire, he says."

"That doesn't sound much like Boris—it sounds more like Frau Kessel," I said.

"*Doch,* well, I guess that's where it started," agreed Stefan. He kicked the heels of his sneakers against the wall, thinking.

"My mother says there has to be proof before you can say somebody did something, like a crime or something," I said.

"If he took Herr Schiller's daughter . . ." said Stefan.

"But they didn't ever get him for that, did they?" I pointed out. "He didn't go to prison or anything. And Herr Schiller's supposed to have stuck up for him. Surely he wouldn't do that if he thought his own brother had taken his daughter away?"

"Who knows? Grown-ups, sometimes I think they're all crazy," said Stefan with feeling. "If we were both grown-up, twenty or something, and you went off and married someone else, like maybe Thilo Koch—" Here he broke off, laughing at my disgusted expression. "Well, I wouldn't kidnap your kids and murder them."

"If they were Thilo Koch's kids maybe you should," I said, shuddering at the thought. "Anyway, it's still just a rumor. Nobody ever even found the body."

"Maybe she just ran away," suggested Stefan.

"*Nee.*" I shook my head emphatically. "Would *you*? It would be too cool having Herr Schiller as a father, if he were younger, I mean. Imagine all the stuff he could tell you. That one about the fiery man, that was *really* horrible. It was a shame you didn't hear it."

"Hmmm." Stefan raked a hand through his dirty blond hair. "Pity we can't ask *him* about what happened."

"No way," I said regretfully. "If *he* didn't get angry, my mother would when she found out."

There was a silence as we both pondered this. Finally, Stefan said, "Well, someone needs to find proof."

"I suppose the police are doing that," I said dubiously.

"They haven't come up with anything so far, or they would've arrested him."

"They did arrest him once," I pointed out.

"Yes, but they had to let him go, didn't they? If they'd found something they wouldn't have done that." He paused, then added, "In fact, according to Boris, that time at Herr Düster's house Herr Wachtmeister Tondorf said they *didn't* arrest him, he was just helping them or whatever. You remember, when you were in England?"

A hot flame of guilt spurted up inside me at the memory of the telephone calls I had made from Oma Warner's house. That was months ago and still I hadn't heard a thing about them, but it was too much to hope that the crime could be concealed forever. Oma Warner was old but she was definitely *not* senile. There was no way she could miss those calls when the bill came in, which it must do any day now.

Worse, the defense I had so blithely imagined at the time, that the deceit was for the greater cause of solving the mystery blighting the town, was patently *not* going to hold up.

The stray bits of information we had gathered had singularly failed to coalesce into anything solid; instead it was like trying to do a jigsaw, not realizing that you actually had two or three different jigsaws at the same time with all the pieces muddled up together. Here there was a section with a sleek black cat curled up in someone's armchair; here there was one depicting a ruined castle by moonlight, and a boy running white-faced down the hill from it. Here was a single piece with a child's shoe on it. None of them seemed to fit together to make a recognizable scene.

I shook my head despondently. "So maybe he didn't do it."

"Or maybe they just don't have proof," said Stefan.

I slid off the wall. "This is stupid. We're just going around in circles."

There was a gentle thump as Stefan's sneakers also hit the ground. He hauled his bag off the wall and slung it over his shoulder.

"So let's *get* some proof."

I stared at him. "Very funny."

"No, I mean it."

I put my hands on my hips. "What are you going to do? Break into Herr Düster's house while he's out, and search it?" A hot little prickle of excitement ran through me even as the words left my lips. It was the thing to do, of course; it was the thing all this had been leading up to. The question was whether we would really, *really* try to do it. This was in a whole different league from using Oma Warner's telephone when she was out at bingo. This was like climbing to the highest platform at the swimming pool and deciding whether to dive off—no: this was like climbing up to the top of a *cliff* and deciding whether to dive off. Just contemplating the idea was like anticipating that sickening plunge.

Now it was Stefan's turn to stare. "I was going to suggest we *follow* him," he said. "But you're right, we should try to search the house."

"Stefan—" Hearing the idea on someone else's lips, suddenly it sounded real and also completely crazy.

"What?"

"We can't just break in. . . . What if we get caught?"

"We won't get caught. And, anyway, who says we have to *break* anything?"

I hugged my schoolbag to my chest. "Well, what else are we going to do? Knock on his door and ask if we can search the house?"

"We could get in through the cellar."

"No way." Now Stefan had me seriously concerned. We were discussing this as though we were really and truly about to get into Herr Düster's house and turn it upside down looking for dead girls. I shivered.

I knew exactly what he was proposing about the cellar. Most of the old houses in the town had a grille or even a little trapdoor somewhere at ground level, leading into the cellar. In times gone by it would have been used to deliver fuel. Nowadays most of them were rusted up, covered with cobwebs—but still there. Now that I thought about it, I was pretty sure Herr Düster's house had the trapdoor sort, two little doors set at an angle to the wall and fastened with a padlock. If we could find some way of removing the padlock it would be easy to just open the doors, hold on to the top of the frame, and slide one's body down into the darkness below . . .

"We'd never get in that way," I said as firmly as I could.

"Yes, we would." Stefan's voice was earnest. "Look, Frau Weiss is off sick today, anyway, so who's going to notice if we're not in class?"

I looked at him in horror. "You think we should do it *now?*"

"No, I just think we should go and *look.*" Stefan rolled his eyes. "I'm not *that* stupid. We'd never get in there in broad daylight, not with Thilo Koch's *Oma* watching the whole street. When we get in there, it has to be at nighttime. After dark."

Chapter Thirty-six

Walking up the Orchheimer Strasse I felt as though every eye in the street must be upon me. I dared not think what would happen if we ran into anyone we knew—such as Frau Kessel, for example. What a field day *she* would have if she found out the pair of us were playing truant.

"This is a crap idea," I hissed under my breath.

"Stop worrying," said Stefan. He smiled beatifically at a passerby. *"Guten Morgen."* He sounded disarmingly polite and as innocent as a lamb.

Herr Düster's house was almost opposite Hilde Koch's. There was no sign of the old lady, but still I felt uncomfortable, as though the small windows of her house concealed piggish little eyes that were watching our every move. Even the drooping remains of flowers in the window boxes seemed to be craning forward to listen.

"Look." Stefan nudged me in the ribs, then gave a low whistle of wonderment.

Someone had indeed broken one of Herr Düster's front windows; it had been hastily boarded up with what looked like a piece of white Formica. Never the tidiest house in the street, now it looked positively disreputable, like an old seaman with a dirty patch over one eye.

Stefan wandered over to the house, with me following, trying desperately to restrain the urge to shoot furtive glances around me.

The cellar trapdoor was more or less as I remembered it: two small doors that had once been painted crimson but were now the color of dried blood. There was a small metal handle on each; fastening them together was a heavy padlock. Looking at it, I felt relief.

"We'll never get that open."

Stefan squatted on the cobblestones and fingered the padlock. "We won't have to." He hooked a finger under one of the metal handles and pulled. "Look." The handle was coming away from the door, flakes of rust crumbling off it.

"*Stefan!*"

"Shhhh . . ." He got to his feet, brushing the brown flakes from his fingers. I opened my mouth to tell him exactly how crazy I thought he was, but before I managed to get a single word out, someone interrupted me.

"Pia *Kolvenbach*."

For a moment I really felt as though my knees would buckle under me.

"Frau Kessel."

I turned with a horrible sensation of inevitability and found myself staring at a familiar Edelweiss brooch of quite stunning ugliness pinned firmly to a brown woolen bosom. With reluctance I raised my eyes to Frau Kessel's face. Under the towering confection of white hair, the twin lenses of her glasses flashed as she tilted back her head, the better to look down her nose at me.

"What *are* you doing?" She regarded me with distaste, but the glance she shot Stefan was pure poison. "Shouldn't you be in school?"

It was Stefan who saved us both from a fate worse than death, namely, being hauled back to the school in public by Frau Kessel, probably by the ears.

"We're doing a project."

Frau Kessel swiveled toward him with the oiled precision of a machine-gun post rotating to face its target.

"Indeed. Didn't your mother teach you any manners, young man?" When Stefan looked at her blankly, she added tartly, "I have a name."

"We're doing a project . . . Frau Kessel," said Stefan with a sangfroid that took my breath away. How he could remain unmoved under that basilisk glare was beyond me. He flourished a slim ring binder that he had managed by some sleight of hand to remove from his schoolbag. "Old buildings in Bad Münstereifel." Frau Kessel looked as though she might take the binder from him, but he was too quick for her; it had already disappeared back into his bag.

"And what precisely does this project have to do with *this* house?" demanded Frau Kessel, nodding toward Herr Düster's house; I had the impression she avoided saying *Herr Düster's house* on purpose, the same way she would have avoided greeting him by name.

"We have to write down the words on the front," said Stefan without missing a beat.

Automatically we all looked upward. Sure enough there was an inscription carved into one of the horizontal timbers, though it had weathered badly; all that could be read now were the words *In Gottes Namen:* in God's name.

"Hmmph," said Frau Kessel disapprovingly. She eyed us suspiciously over her spectacles. "Couldn't you have found a better example?"

"They've already been done," said Stefan.

"Is that so?" said Frau Kessel. She sniffed. "I don't believe anyone has written down the inscription on *my* house. I am sure," she added, "that I would have noticed if any young people had been hanging around outside."

"Your house has one too?" asked Stefan in tones of intense interest. I shot him an evil glance: *Don't go overboard, or the old* Schrulle *will make us go and look at it.* It was too late.

"Of course it has. I'm surprised you didn't know, especially if you are supposed to be doing a project about it," Frau Kessel informed him. She patted her monstrous coiffure. "It is considered significant, I believe."

"Fascinating," said Stefan in such an enthusiastic voice that even Frau Kessel was suspicious; her eyes narrowed. "No, really," he went on earnestly. "I would love to see it."

"Hmmm." Frau Kessel eyed us both doubtfully. "Well," she said eventually in a grudging voice, "I suppose you can come and look at it. But you can make yourselves useful and carry these." She handed us each a bulging cloth bag.

"Yes, Frau Kessel," we chorused obediently. I adjusted my grip on

Frau Kessel's shopping bag, as ever apparently stuffed to the brim with bricks and lumps of iron. She wheeled about and set off up the street with the pair of us trotting behind her.

"Stefan—" I hissed under my breath.

"Yes?" he answered from the side of his mouth, without turning to look at me.

"What are you *doing?*"

He kept his eyes fixed on Frau Kessel's brown woolen back. "I want to find out what she knows."

"What, you think *she* did it?"

"No, *Dummkopf.* But she knows every single thing that happens in this street."

"You're nuts." I shook my head.

With relief we dumped Frau Kessel's shopping bags on her doorstep. She unlocked the door and carried the bags inside; for a moment I thought she was going to shut the door on us and Stefan's efforts would be wasted, but her vanity got the better of her. She could not resist coming back outside again to point out the most interesting features of her house. We duly admired the inscription, which simply read, *God protect this house from evil.* Evidently a previous inhabitant of the building had shared Frau Kessel's obsession with Evil in Action.

"Well?" said Frau Kessel, hands on hips. We gaped at her. "Aren't you going to write it down?" Dutifully we pulled out pens and notebooks and copied down the words. I hoped Frau Kessel would not notice that I was writing across the top of my English homework.

"Hmm," she said grudgingly, "it's nice to see the school encouraging an interest in local history for once." She sniffed. "There are few enough people around here who take an interest in their own town."

"Yes, Frau Weiss—she's one of our teachers—she says a lot of important stuff is being forgotten," said Stefan. "She says once the old people of the town have died, it will all be lost forever."

I observed signs of an internal struggle on Frau Kessel's face at this point; the desire to prove that she, too, was a repository of invaluable information about the town was fighting with the reluctance to be styled one of the *old people* of the town.

If Stefan noticed this, he gave no visible sign of it, but went on innocently: "We're going to interview some of them if we can. Frau Koch, well, everyone says she knows *everything* about the town."

"Do they?" said Frau Kessel grimly.

We both nodded enthusiastically as though our heads were on springs.

"Hilde Koch may *look* old," said Frau Kessel severely, "but it may surprise you to know that she is actually seven months younger than I am. I am sure there is *nothing* she could tell you about the town that *I* couldn't."

"We didn't think of that," said Stefan. "We thought you were a lot younger than that."

I shot him a sideways glance: *Don't overdo it.* Surely even Frau Kessel wouldn't swallow a blatant piece of flattery like that? But she did.

"Well," she said, favoring Stefan with a grisly smile, "the years have been kind."

Privately I wondered what she would have looked like had they been *unkind,* but I stifled the thought before it could creep into my expression.

"Of course, I can't spare more than half an hour," she went on. "And don't think I won't be watching you every second you're in my house."

"Of course, Frau Kessel," said Stefan politely.

"We promise not to touch anything," I added.

Frau Kessel regarded me with disfavor. "I should think not, Pia Kolvenbach." She turned on her heel, and we trooped after her into the house.

Frau Kessel's kitchen proved to be just as intimidatingly tidy as it had the first time I had been inside it. Stefan and I sat together on one side of her table, pens dutifully poised to take down whatever pronouncements she cared to make: these poured forth in such abundance that I could barely record a third of what she told us.

She began with the history of her house, which as far as I could see was almost phenomenally boring. It had never been inhabited by the town alchemist, it had never had treasure hidden in it during the French invasion or been burned down during any of the wars that had touched the town during its long history. Ghosts sensibly chose somewhere else to haunt. It had experienced a brief moment of excitement in the 1920s when Frau Kessel's Great-Aunt Martha's pet dog had fallen in the well in the cellar and drowned, but disappointingly the well had been capped in the 1940s when running water was installed.

"What about the other houses in the street?" asked Stefan, which earned him a disapproving look; Frau Kessel hated to be interrupted once she was in full flow.

"The wells in those were capped too," she said shortly.

"No, I don't mean about the wells. Can you tell us anything about the people?" asked Stefan. "How about the house we were looking at before?"

"Which house?" said Frau Kessel sharply. Stefan glanced at me.

"Herr Düster's house."

There was a pause that stretched out uncomfortably while I looked up at the crucifix hanging over the countertop, at the brown wallpaper, out the tiny window, anywhere in fact but at Frau Kessel.

"What do you want to know?" said Frau Kessel. Her voice was hard.

"Well . . ." Now that he had the opportunity, Stefan seemed lost for words. "How long has he lived . . . I mean . . . has the same person been in it . . ."

"Since before the war, yes."

Stefan looked down at the scrawl on his notebook as though consulting a list of interview questions. "And did anyone else live in it . . . ?" I think Stefan meant, *Who lived in it before Herr Düster?* but Frau Kessel replied, "No, he's always lived on his own. No family." She laid a curious emphasis on these last words, as though they explained everything.

Stefan said nothing; he seemed uncertain how to proceed. I guessed he had assumed that once we were sitting cozily around Frau Kessel's kitchen table she would let fly with a torrent of local gossip, out of which deluge we would pick some critical nuggets of information, like miners panning for gold. Instead the conversation seemed to be grinding to a halt. Frau Kessel looked at each of our faces in turn, her eyes bird-bright behind her spectacles, her arms folded ominously across her brown woolen bosom.

"Suppose you show me that file," she said eventually.

"Which file?" said Stefan.

"The one with your school project in it."

Instinctively Stefan clutched the top of his schoolbag, holding it closed. "Umm . . . it's not finished."

"I know it's not finished," said Frau Kessel acidly. "Nevertheless, give it to me, please."

For a moment I almost thought Stefan might reach into his bag and extract a ring binder full of notes about the old buildings in Bad Münstereifel; up until now he had seemed so confident, so in control, that I could imagine him having prepared the whole thing as backup. Instead he just sat there gaping at her.

"I thought so," said Frau Kessel. She leaned toward us like an ancient eagle craning forward on its perch. "There is no project, is there?" Her voice was steely. "I may seem old to you, but I'm not stupid. What did you think you were going to get out of me?"

"Nothing," stammered Stefan. "I mean . . . we just wanted to ask you some things, that's all."

"About my house?"

"Well . . ."

"I don't think so." The lenses of Frau Kessel's glasses glittered; I could not see her eyes behind them. "You wanted to know about Herr Düster, didn't you?"

Reluctantly, Stefan nodded.

"Well, I'll tell you all I know about him." Frau Kessel squeezed her bony hands together, as though crushing something between her palms. "But first *I* want to know something. I want to know why you were trying to break into his house."

Chapter Thirty-seven

❦

*S*tefan was the first to recover. When he spoke, his voice was unexpectedly clear and strong.

"We weren't trying to break in, Frau Kessel."

"So what were you doing, trying to open the lock on the cellar doors?" she cast back at him tartly. "Don't think I didn't see that, young man. You wanted to get in, didn't you?"

"We wouldn't really do that, Frau Kessel," I butted in. The basilisk eyes were instantly upon me, but with an effort I kept my cool. "We were just . . . thinking about it. We wouldn't really *do* it. It was just . . . a game."

"*Quatsch,*" she snapped back. "You know," she added, and her voice was low and poisonous, "I really should report you to the school. Or perhaps the police."

"Please, Frau Kessel—"

"But I'm not going to," she went on, without acknowledging me. "And do you know why? Because someone *ought* to break into that house. It's about time that old"—(and here she used a word that actually shocked me; I had heard it from Stefan's cousin Boris but had never expected to hear it from someone of her age)—"had his comeuppance."

She tilted her head back self-righteously. "So if you want to know

about *that man,* I'll tell you. I'll tell anyone who asks me. And then, finally, maybe someone will do something." Abruptly she fell silent.

Neither Stefan nor I spoke; what was there to say? I was not about to
admit that we had really been thinking of trying to get into Herr
Düster's house, but still I wanted to know what Frau Kessel could tell
us. Underlying my curiosity was the uncomfortable knowledge that my
mother had expressly forbidden me to listen to any more of the old
lady's gossip. If she knew we were sitting in Frau Kessel's kitchen listening to the old woman's venomous outpourings I would be grounded
for weeks. I could just imagine her telling me how *disappointed* she was
that I had disobeyed; the thought made me squirm.

"He was in love with Hannelore," said Frau Kessel, plunging without prelude into her story.

Hannelore? Stefan shot me a puzzled glance.

"Hannelore Kurth," said Frau Kessel. "Beautiful girl, the beauty of
the town. She was the May Queen two years before she married Heinrich Schiller." Stefan still looked confused; she gave him an impatient
look. "Even then, that *other one* was making trouble. Two May trees outside the house! He should have stood back and let the better man win."
She pursed her lips, her shoulders stiff. "As though she would look at
him."

"Was he ugly?" I asked.

"Oh, I suppose he had looks in a superficial sort of way," replied Frau
Kessel derisively. "I imagine that is why he fancied Hannelore would
look at him. But she had better sense."

She spoke with authority, as though she had been privy to Herr
Düster's every unwelcome move. But when she had told me about
Herr Düster and Hannelore that first time, when I had carried her shopping home for her, hadn't she said her mother told her all about it? I
found myself staring at her. Was she older than she made out? Or had
she started out very early on her prurient quest for information about
other people's lives? I rather thought it was the latter. It was not difficult to imagine that face as a pale spiteful moon framed by brown hair
yanked into plaits, eyes narrowed to slits as she inhaled the heady and
poisonous incense of gossip. A whisperer in the back row of the classroom, a peeper around corners.

"When she married his brother, he was supposed to have been

heartbroken. *Some* people in this town think that's when he went to the bad." She did not say *what* people. "But he was bad long before Hannelore Kurth turned him down. She was right to do it, but he wouldn't leave it alone. There were dozens of young women in the town, but it had to be *her.*"

Something flickered in Frau Kessel's wrinkled face like a lizard looking out from a hole in a stone and whisking back inside again. I saw it, but at the time I could not think what it meant. Now I think of the clawlike hands with every finger encrusted with rings except one, and I think perhaps I know.

"I saw them together," she hissed.

"Saw who?" I was confused.

"Hannelore and *that man.* You'd think when it was his own brother's wife . . . and she had the child by then. Gertrud."

"What were they doing?" asked Stefan.

"Doing? Hannelore wasn't doing *anything.* You don't think she'd meet him on purpose? But him . . . he was ranting away like a mad thing. Taking her hand, and trying to kiss it . . ." Frau Kessel sounded as though she had just bitten into something disgusting. "She wanted to get away, but he wouldn't let her. Oh, he was sly, cornering her there. He thought no one would see them, but *I did.*"

The venom in Frau Kessel's voice was making me feel queasy. She did not say *where* she had seen Hannelore with Herr Düster, but the picture was plain enough in my head: the two of them altercating in some secluded spot, and the teenaged Frau Kessel watching them unseen, her eyes glinting with malice. *Had she followed them?* I wondered. *Had she hidden on purpose?*

"I've never told anyone that before." Frau Kessel's hand strayed to her bosom and the bony fingers clasped the spiked Edelweiss brooch. Her eyes were impenetrable behind the reflective lenses of her glasses. "But it always comes out. Everything comes out in the end."

"Yes," said Stefan politely; it was impossible to do anything but agree with her. She was hardly even talking to us anymore; she was lost in the plot of a story that had been told more than half a century before.

"Then Hannelore died," said Frau Kessel. "And he couldn't get at her anymore. There was only Gertrud. His brother's daughter—his own niece. When she disappeared, it was all equal, don't you see? Herr

Schiller lost the only person he cared about, the same as that Düster lost the woman he wanted. I wonder if he was happy then." Her voice was hard.

"Didn't anyone suspect?" asked Stefan incredulously.

"Suspect? Of course they suspected. But there was no proof, that was the thing. No body; they never found her. And after the war everything was in ruins. Rubble everywhere, every second building a deathtrap, people struggling just to survive. There was no one with time to investigate it."

"Didn't Herr Schiller try to find out?" asked Stefan.

"Herr Schiller is a true Christian," said Frau Kessel. "He said that if Herr Düster had taken Gertrud, the knowledge that he was responsible would be punishment enough."

"Frau Kessel?"

"Yes?" She turned and looked at Stefan.

"Does everybody think Herr . . . does everybody think it was *him*? Who took Katharina Linden, I mean, and the other girls?"

"Not everybody." The old lady's voice was cold. "Your father, for example, Pia Kolvenbach. He and his friends actually *protected* him."

So my father's side of the story was true; he really had tried to prevent anyone from taking the law into their own hands that night.

"Papa thinks . . ." I began, and ground to a halt under Frau Kessel's icy glare. I tried again. "He thinks the police should do it."

"Does he?" Frau Kessel pursed her lips. "It's easy to say the police should handle it, if you're not involved. If you've never lost anyone."

"My mother says there has to be proof," I protested, stung at the criticism of my father.

"Proof? Of course there's proof," snapped Frau Kessel. "How much more proof do they want?"

Stefan and I looked at each other. "What proof?"

Frau Kessel looked at us as though we were terminally stupid. "The shoe, the shoe they found in the woods on the Quecken hill. From the little Voss girl."

"They found it on the Quecken hill? Where the old castle is?" This was news. I had heard that it was found in the woods, but most people seemed vague about exactly where it had been discovered. I wondered by what arcane route Frau Kessel had come by this nugget of information.

"How do they know it was hers?" asked Stefan. He was rewarded with a withering glance.

"Because the other one was still in the school," said Frau Kessel, as though this were self-evident. "They both had her name in them. Though," she added, "they say you could hardly make it out on the one they found in the woods, it was so badly burned."

"How do you know it was burned?" Stefan asked.

Frau Kessel stared at him. "I—" She started, then stopped. "Someone told me." Her expression forbade further inquiry. I wondered who the someone was: the daughter or niece of one of her cronies, working in the police station, or the wife of one of the officers. It was hard to believe that anyone could be so indiscreet as to share the information with Frau Kessel; they might as well have printed it in the local paper, or announced it on Radio Euskirchen.

"It's horrible," I blurted out before I could stop myself.

"*Doch,*" agreed Frau Kessel in a brittle tone. "To think that *he* is living here in the town, right among us, as free as a bird."

I nodded sickly, but that was not what I had meant. I had had a sudden vision of Marion Voss's shoe, charred and blackened, lying on its side in a tangle of undergrowth, and I was thinking about the Fiery Man of the Hirnberg, and how the very touch of his hand would crisp your skin up instantly, and make the flesh sizzle. How he could take you into his fiery embrace, and wrap himself right around you until every inch of your skin was a mass of fire. I wondered how anyone could stand such pain.

"Pia?" Stefan's voice seemed to be coming from a long way off. "Are you sick?"

I shook my head, but I felt as though my head were a child's snowdome, roughly shaken so that the liquid slopped from side to side and the snowflakes flew everywhere in a wild blizzard. My mouth was full of saliva; I thought I might vomit, right there on Frau Kessel's kitchen table.

There was a scraping sound as Frau Kessel hauled the table away from me, and the next moment her clawlike hand was on the back of my skull, pushing my head down between my knees. She was surprisingly strong, and her rings dug into my scalp. Suddenly I was looking at a patch of spotlessly clean tiled floor framed between my thighs.

"Stay there," she ordered, although to my relief she removed the hand. A few moments later I heard the tap running; Frau Kessel was getting me that time-honored cure-all, a glass of water.

"Pia?" Stefan's anxious face moved into my line of vision; he must have been contorting himself on the floor to do it. "What happened?"

"I don't know," I said to the upside-down face. I couldn't dredge up the words to describe what I had been thinking about—the fiery man, the charred shoe. "I felt sick."

"Are you OK?"

"What an idiotic question," said Frau Kessel's acid voice. I heard a click as she put the glass of water on the table. "Stand up," she added. "You needn't roll around on my floor like a badly behaved dog."

As Stefan scrambled to his feet, one of Frau Kessel's hands came down on my shoulder, with all the finesse of a vulture landing on its prey. "Do you still feel faint?" she asked me.

"I don't think so."

"Then sit up and sip this." She handed me the glass. I looked at it dubiously. It was an *old lady* glass, decorated with a faded design of tit-mice perched on a blossomy branch. I took a sip. She hadn't let the tap run for long enough and the water was unpleasantly tepid. I didn't want it but I couldn't think of any reason to refuse it, so with a grimace I drained the glass.

"Well?" said Frau Kessel. Her tone was brusque: she might have been Frau Eichen, inquiring about the answer to a math problem, rather than someone asking about my current state of health.

"A bit better," I hazarded.

"Hmm." A claw swooped down and removed the glass. "I can't say I'm surprised it happened. The idea makes me feel sick too."

I didn't bother to contradict her.

"And I think that *you* had better take Pia home in a few minutes' time when she's recovered," Frau Kessel observed to Stefan in a disapproving tone, as though he were personally responsible for my state.

I risked an upward glance at her face; her lips were pursed and her eyes hard. Any other person might have suffered pangs of guilt if a child had fainted in their home as a result of listening to their gruesome insinuations. Not Frau Kessel. I expect that if she had lived to be a hundred and twenty, then in all those twelve decades she would never have apologized once, for anything. In Frau Kessel's eyes she was totally blameless; it was other people who did all the reprehensible things.

"All right, Frau Kessel." Stefan sounded resigned. He offered me his arm, as though we were two old-age pensioners out for a stroll.

"I *shan't* mention this visit," said Frau Kessel in the same high tone.

"Thank you, Frau Kessel."

"All the same, I don't expect to see you hanging around in the street during school hours again, otherwise I might *have* to say something."

"*Verstanden.*"

Stefan and I shuffled toward the front door. Frau Kessel had her hand on the doorknob, ready to usher us out into the street, when Stefan said, "Frau Kessel, why is it so important to you?"

Why is what *so important?* I thought. *Getting us out of the house? Not seeing us in the street again?* But Frau Kessel knew exactly what he was asking.

"Because Caroline Hack was my niece," she said crisply. We stepped out into the street, and I turned to say goodbye, but she had already closed the door.

The following day after school Stefan and I went surreptitiously back to Herr Düster's house to reexamine the cellar doors. The aim was to wander nonchalantly past them, and if we were sure no one was watching, to try the loose handle again. But the visit proved futile. In the intervening time, someone had removed the old handles completely and replaced them with gleaming new ones, firmly screwed onto the doors and fastened with a padlock even bigger than the old one.

Chapter Thirty-eight

$\mathcal{P}$ ia?" said Herr Schiller. He was holding a small cup of coffee out to me.

"Sorry."

I shook my head as though to clear it, wondering how long he had been holding the cup out, then carefully took it from him.

"You have a lot on your mind today, *Fräulein,*" said Herr Schiller drily.

"Mmm." I sipped the coffee gingerly; I was anxious to consume it without visibly choking, but it was about as thick and pungent as I could bear.

"And how is life in the big school?"

"Umm . . ." I hesitated, wondering whether to give the standard answer, *fine,* or to tell the truth, which was: *about the same—I'm still the girl whose grandmother exploded.*

While I was pondering, Stefan sprang in with, "It's good, but we have a lot of work."

"Ah." Herr Schiller looked at us both over his coffee cup, his bushy eyebrows raised. "A lot of fieldwork, *oder?*" Looking at our blank faces, he broke into a smile which creased his craggy face in a hundred places. "I have seen you farther up the street, examining the houses."

I shot Stefan a glance. Had everyone in the entire street seen us outside Herr Düster's house? I should have known it, of course—Bad Münstereifel is one of those towns where closed-circuit television cameras would be totally redundant. Hours of videotape could tell you nothing that the neighbors couldn't.

"Oh," said Stefan offhandedly. He shrugged. "We were thinking of doing a project about old houses . . . but it didn't work out."

"A pity," said Herr Schiller, but he didn't pursue it. That was another thing I liked about him—he didn't harp on about things like other adults did. If we had told my mother the same thing she would have wanted to know why we were abandoning a project we had already started, and what the deadline was, and whether we had a suitable new project, and what the others in our class were doing for theirs . . .

"Herr Schiller?"

"Yes, Pia?"

"Have you told us *all* the stories there are about Bad Münstereifel? The ones with ghosts and things, I mean?"

"Why, are you going to do a project about those?" asked Herr Schiller.

"No," I said. "I'm just interested."

"Hmmm." Herr Schiller leaned back in his armchair and felt about for his pipe. Fascinated, I watched him stuffing tobacco into the bowl of it. It looked disgusting, but he kept on smoking, so I supposed he must like it.

My gaze moved from the pipe up Herr Schiller's face and I realized that his eyes were upon me. Between puffs, he said, "I haven't told you all the stories there are about the town. I don't suppose anyone can. But," he added, perhaps seeing my face fall, "I can tell you *one* of the stories you haven't heard already. If you have time, that is, between your studies." There was an almost imperceptible twang of humor in his voice.

"Of course." I was not eager to pursue the topic of my studies any further. I shuffled a little farther back into my chair and looked at him expectantly.

"This," said Herr Schiller slowly, "is a story about our old friend Unshockable Hans.

"One evening, Hans was standing outside the mill with his pipe in his mouth watching the sun setting behind the hill, when he saw from a long way off a figure coming toward him. Oddly enough, it carried over its head a large basket, the sort they used to put fruit in.

"There was something about the figure that made Hans narrow his eyes and take a longer look. Perhaps it was the way that it seemed to glide through the wet grass without once sticking fast in the muddy earth or stumbling over a clump of weeds. Or more likely it was the way that basket sat so low upon the shoulders of the figure— unnaturally low, one might think, considering that the person's head must fit underneath.

"Hans took his pipe out of his mouth and knocked out the ashes on the stone wall of the mill. Then he put it away, and stood there with his hands on his hips, waiting for the approaching figure to reach him. It was dressed in a curiously old-fashioned costume for that date. The fabric, indeed, had a rusty look about it, as though it had discolored from age and hard wear.

" *'Guten Abend,'* said Hans to his visitor.

"The stranger said not a word in return, but reached up with his hands and lifted off the basket that covered him. Now Hans saw the reason for the curious appearance of the basket, so low upon the man's shoulders. He had *no head.* Where his shirt collar rose out of his rusty-looking jacket there was a nub of skin and flesh, like the stump of a chicken's neck when its head has been cut off, and protruding from the middle there was a little nub of bone. But as to chin, face, or cranium, he had none. There was simply nothing there.

"Another man would have taken one look and fled shrieking back into the mill to bar the door. But Hans, as you know, was made of stronger stuff. He had heard his grandmother speak of the headless ghost of Münstereifel when she was a wrinkled crone of eighty and he a fresh-faced little boy of six or seven. Where another man might have died of fright, Hans was filled with simple curiosity. He determined to address the ghost and ask it its business.

" 'Who are you, and what do you want?' he asked boldly.

"Then the ghost gave a great sigh, and it was a strange sound, because it came from the stump of his neck, and it seemed to echo deep within his torso.

" 'Dear Hans,' he said in an oddly resonant tone, 'for the sins of my lifetime I was condemned to wander Münstereifel, a fearful thing with no head, until some soul braver than the rest dared to ask me who I am and what I seek. Long have I wandered, knowing no rest. When I began to walk here, there was an ancient town and a castle high upon a hill with the flag of a feudal lord flying over it and soldiers marching along its battlements. The castle fell and the town dwindled, and the woods covered the ruins. Still I walked among the broken stones and the grass and weeds. At last a new town sprang up in place of the old one, and still I walked, and no one dared to speak to me.'

" *'Lieber Gott,'* said Hans. 'What can you have done to deserve such a fate?'

"Then the ghost came closer to him, and told Hans his sins, and Hans, who feared neither man nor spirit, grew pale and silent to hear such a catalog of evildoing.

" 'I thought,' said Hans at last in a low voice, 'that no one could have done so much evil as to deserve such a punishment, but I see that I was wrong.' And he crossed himself like the good Catholic he was. 'I am sorry for you,' he said.

" 'Do not pity me,' said the voice of the ghost. 'By speaking to me, and asking me who I am, you have freed me.'

"And then Hans saw that in his hands the ghost was holding a head, the head of a man of fifty winters, seamed with wrinkles, the features bearing the stamp of a long and wicked life. The ghost's fingers were entwined in the grizzled hair. As Hans watched, the ghost lifted the head onto his shoulders and settled it there, and when he seemed quite satisfied that it had stuck fast, he made a low bow to Hans and vanished.

"And," added Herr Schiller, "since that day he has never been seen again, so it seems that Hans really did free him."

Stefan shifted restlessly in his chair. "He just vanished?"

"Doch."

"And what were the sins that he told Hans?"

"Nobody knows," said Herr Schiller. "Hans never told a soul what he had heard. The story goes that the ghost's crimes were so terrible that they were better left between him and God."

"Hmmm." Stefan sounded disappointed.

"I know," said Herr Schiller drily. "It is rather unsatisfactory, is it not?"

"I wish I knew what the ghost had done," said Stefan.

"Better not to know, that was the idea," said Herr Schiller.

"It can't have been *that* bad," said Stefan. "Nothing's *that* bad."

"It's good to believe that, when you're ten," said Herr Schiller gently to Stefan.

"I'm eleven—"

"But I'm afraid that when you get older, you will discover some things *are* that bad." Herr Schiller sounded sad.

With a hot feeling akin to guilt I wondered whether he was thinking about his daughter, Gertrud, about what might have happened to her, and whether the person who did it would ever be punished.

"Some things are better left untold," he added, as though he had read my mind.

I tried to catch Stefan's eye, to somehow telegraph to him that he should shut up before we upset the old man and got ourselves thrown out again, but he was deep in thought and not prepared to notice my significant looks. That was one of the things that always irritated me about him, and continued to relegate him back to the position of *StinkStefan:* he never knew when to let something drop.

"If it was that bad," he persisted, "then how come the ghost would be freed the minute anyone asked him who he was? Supposing the first person who ever saw him did it? Then he wouldn't have been punished at all."

"But they didn't," I pointed out. "He spent years and years, probably *hundreds* of years, wandering about before Hans asked him."

"Yes, but *if*," said Stefan stubbornly.

"Then his sins would have caught up with him some other way," said Herr Schiller softly. "They always do." He shook his head. "But I fear you are missing the point of the story."

"I don't understand."

"The ghost was freed only because someone dared to speak to him. That is the point of the story. Hans dared to address the ghost. Most people would have run for their lives." Up went Herr Schiller's bushy eyebrows. His eyes were bright. "Hans was the only one who could put aside his own fears, and *act*."

"So the story means you shouldn't be frightened of anything?"

"The story means that if something needs to be done, then you should do it. Even if it is something that most people would find difficult. Even if you are afraid."

Walking back to my house in the Heisterbacher Strasse with Stefan, I could still taste Herr Schiller's coffee in my mouth, a dark and acrid taste that made me think of ashtrays and bonfires. Neither Stefan nor I said anything for a long time. Stefan had his hands jammed deep into the pockets of his coat and his breath showed in little clouds. It reminded me of Boris smoking, the way the white wisps of breath drifted out from between his lips. I was thinking about Herr Schiller, and about Unshockable Hans, and about the ghost with no head.

If something needs to be done, then you should do it.

We had decided to go back to my house via the Salzmarkt and the bridge, passing King Zwentibold on his fountain. So we did not pass Herr Düster's house, but still I was aware of its location in relation to myself, just as though we had been two gigantic red-points on a map of the town: *you are here* and *here* it *is.*

"Pia?"

I glanced at Stefan, but he was looking at the cobblestones, not at me.

"Yes?"

"What did you think of the story?"

I sighed. "I don't know." I realized that Stefan had stopped walking, so I stopped too.

Stefan looked up at the sky. A first tiny flake of snow drifted down and settled on his upturned face, melting instantly. He looked at me. "Don't you think Herr Schiller was trying to make a point? Like the moral of the story or something?"

"I suppose."

I didn't feel ready to commit myself. The thought that perhaps *we,* perhaps *I* should be the one to do the thing that *needed to be done* was still too uncomfortable to be examined closely.

"He was," said Stefan. "I know he was. He thinks we should do something."

"About what?" But I already knew the answer.

"About Katharina Linden, and the other girls," said Stefan with a trace of impatience in his tone. He lowered his voice. "About *him*. Herr Düster."

"He can't really want us to do anything about Herr Düster," I protested. "He's cool, but he's still a grown-up. He's not going to tell us to break into someone's house or anything."

"Why not?"

"Because there would be a huge row if we got caught, and he'd get in trouble too."

"Maybe he thinks it's worth risking it."

Now I was really uneasy. "But it's not him who's got to do it. And, anyway," I added, "*he* didn't do anything about it when his daughter disappeared, did he? Frau Kessel said he was too much of a Christian. So how come he's now telling us to do it?"

"I don't know," said Stefan. He raised an arm and then let it drop in a gesture of frustration. "Look, even if he wasn't trying to tell us to do it, it's still—it's still a good idea, isn't it?"

"A *good* idea?"

"Well, a *right* idea, anyway." Stefan's mouth set in an obstinate line.

"Stefan, we're two *kids*, we're not Batman and Robin." I shifted uneasily from foot to foot. "If we get caught, he'll *kill* us."

"Well then," said Stefan. "We won't get caught."

Chapter Thirty-nine

*C*hristmas was coming, and the shops were suddenly full of Advent crowns again.

"Nearly a year," said my father lugubriously.

My mother was more pragmatic. "We won't be wanting one of *those.*"

Inevitably, the appearance of the Advent crowns signaled a renaissance in interest about Oma Kristel's untimely death. Suddenly I was the object of unwanted attention again. Stefan was irritating me a lot—he was forever harping on about Herr Düster and what we should do about him. I remembered why the name StinkStefan had seemed so appropriate—he had a habit of hanging around like a bad smell. And now I was forcibly reminded of the reason why he was the only person I could consider a friend at school.

My former friends, such as Marla Frisch—who had dropped me so rapidly for fear of being contaminated by the Incredible Exploding Family—were now the chief broadcasters of Oma Kristel's grim story. Children from the grades above, who had not been at the same school as I was when Oma Kristel died, were now eager to hear the sorry tale from the lips of those who had been.

In a way I could not blame them; it was too grotesque to be taken seriously—it was more like a made-up horror story. All the same, this did not alleviate the distress caused whenever I walked into a classroom or into the girls' toilets and heard whispered conversations stopping dead at the sight of me. It could only be a matter of time before they all started to refuse to sit next to me again.

My parents, meanwhile, were involved in planning the first year's memorial Mass for Oma Kristel. My mother, who was Protestant, and lapsed at that, was somewhat removed from the planning of the church service, but the burden of the catering was to fall upon her shoulders, much to her disgust.

The great debate was when exactly the service should be held. Oma Kristel had died on the last Sunday in Advent, but to hold the service over Christmas was a depressing idea. My mother said that it was a good thing really; we could hold the memorial Mass in January. It would be just what we needed to cheer us up when Christmas was over. My father, who never could understand my mother's gallows humor, was offended; but he couldn't suggest a better time.

One afternoon I came home early and found my father's car wedged into the paltry cobbled rectangle that served as a parking space for our house. When I saw the car I assumed my parents were embroiled in yet another summit meeting about which music to have, and whether to have white roses or lilies. Discussions could become surprisingly heated on such topics, but even so I was taken aback when I opened the front door and heard my father bellowing like an enraged bull.

I put down my schoolbag very carefully, wondering whether I should simply sneak back out again. The next second a gust of icy wind sucked the door shut, and it slammed with a sound like a gunshot. I was still standing there half stooping with the strap in my hand and a guilty expression on my face when the kitchen door opened and out came my mother. Her cheeks were rather blotchy and her dark hair was very rumpled, as though she had been raking her hands through it.

"What are you doing home at this time?" she snapped.

"Frau Wasser was off sick," I stammered. My father's bulk filled the kitchen doorway behind my mother.

"Don't shout at her."

"I wasn't bloody shouting." Now she almost was.

"You've done enough already."

"I haven't *touched* her," said my mother, as though he had accused her of beating me.

"I'm not talking about touching." My father was as literal-minded as ever, even in the heat of an argument. "You think it won't have an effect on the children, when you—"

"Wolfgang!" My mother's voice cut across his, a clear note of warning in it.

I glanced at the staircase, weighing up my chances of escaping.

"Pia." My mother sounded calmer but her voice had steel in it. "Come into the living room with me."

"Pia, stay where you are." That was my father. He glared at my mother. "I'm not having you telling her *your* side of the story."

My mother put her hands on her hips. "Well, I'm not letting *you* do it."

"Do what?" I asked, bewildered.

"Go into the living room please, Pia," said my father. Reluctantly I did so, picking up my schoolbag as I went; if they were going to insist I shut myself up in there while they argued, I might at least get on with my homework. I started to spread the files out on the coffee table, but it was difficult to concentrate; the muffled sound of raised voices was too clearly audible from the hallway outside. I selected the English exercise to do first. Opening my exercise book at a clean page, I carefully wrote "A VISIT TO ENGLAND." Then I stuck the end of the pen into my mouth and stared at the page.

". . . you owe me that . . . !" boomed my father's voice from the hallway.

My grandmother, I wrote, and stopped again. I had been going to write *My grandmother lives in Middlesex,* but the raised voices from the hallway had reminded me of the major row that was surely heading my way when Oma Warner got her phone bill. My flesh prickled uncomfortably at the thought. The bill *must* have come in by now; I had stayed with her in the long summer vacation, and now it was nearly Christmas.

The door opened. It was my mother. "Can I come in?" she said, as though it were my bedroom she were entering, and not the living room. She slid into the room and closed the door very carefully. Then she came over to the couch and sat down beside me.

"Where's Papa?" I asked.

"Upstairs," said my mother. "He'll come down later. Then you can talk to him."

She looked at me, flashed me a tight smile, and then glanced out the window. An old woman was walking along the street; she kept turning and stooping, and I guessed she was dragging an unwilling dog along with her.

I shuffled in my seat. "I've got English," I said eventually, touching the open exercise book.

"Hmmm," said my mother, and then: "That's sort of what I want to talk to you about, Pia."

"My English homework?"

"No, not that." She folded her arms across her chest. "Pia, your English is really good, even though I know we don't speak English at home as often as we should."

"Charles and Chloe make fun of me when I speak English," I said.

"Well . . ." said my mother, "try not to take any notice of your cousins. Your English *is* good."

"They can't speak German," I pointed out, but my mother was not to be diverted down that route.

"You could manage—in England, I mean," she said. "You did really well with Oma Warner in the summer."

"Ye-es," I said warily, wondering whether in some roundabout way this was leading up to a showdown about the telephone bill. But my mother didn't seem angry with me; if anything she seemed nervous, as though she was afraid I would be angry with *her*.

"If you . . . I mean, if you lived there, you'd soon be speaking it perfectly. At your age, you'd be able to lose the accent. Then people wouldn't laugh, they probably wouldn't even notice."

I picked up my exercise book and stared at the empty page with "A VISIT TO ENGLAND" emblazoned across the top. "Are we going to visit Oma Warner again?"

"Well, no, not exactly."

"Mama?"

"Yes?"

"I don't really like going to England. I really like Oma Warner, but . . ."

My mother sighed. "Pia, we can't always choose."

"What do you mean?" I said. An unpleasant realization was surfacing in my mind like some ghastly waterlogged thing that refused to sink however hard you pushed it under. When Aunt Liz and my mother had discussed our moving to England, the idea had not been hypothetical at all.

"You're half English," said my mother, as though that explained everything. "We've lived in Germany for years, but there was always a chance . . . you need to get to know the English side of yourself." Her tone was pleading.

"I don't know what you mean," I said stubbornly.

"We'd see lots more of Oma Warner. She *is* my mother, you know, and I'd like to spend more time with her. It would be nice for you, too, now that Oma Kristel isn't . . ." She paused, and rubbed her palms together as though suddenly embarrassed. "You might even find you like your cousins."

I won't ever like my cousins, I thought, but I did not say anything out loud. I just looked at my mother fidgeting and smiling nervously. I felt cold, as though she had been a complete stranger offering me stupid lies, lies designed to hurt.

"You know what I'm saying, don't you, *Mäuselein?*" I registered the endearment with a faint stab of irritation; it was years since she had called me her *little mouse*—why was she doing it now? "We're . . . well, we're probably going to live in England."

"Probably?"

"Well, we *are* going, but there are a few things to sort out first, and—"

"What about Papa's job?"

"Papa . . ." My mother paused, and once again she was rubbing her hands together, rubbing and rubbing as though she were trying to brush something off them. "Papa probably isn't coming." She realized she had said *probably* again, and amended it to: "Papa *isn't* coming with us."

"But he can't stay here without us," I protested. "And, anyway, I don't want to go to England."

"Pia." My mother sighed. "I know you think you don't want to go there. But we really can't stay here."

"Why not?" I demanded.

"Because . . . well, because I need Oma Warner and Aunt Liz nearby. Sebastian's still very little and I'm going to need help, otherwise I don't see how I can go back to work." She sketched a quick smile on her features, and reached out to touch my shoulder. I drew back, still trying to assess whether my mother was in earnest or making some horrible joke. "Why don't you go back to work here?"

The smile vanished in a twitch. *"Why?"* She exhaled heavily through her nostrils. "Pia, this isn't easy, you know. Do you have to keep picking me up on everything I say?" She glared at me, and then her face relaxed again into a defeated expression. "If we're going to be on our own, I need to be near the family. *My* family."

"We've got lots of family here," I pointed out. "Onkel Thomas and Tante Britta and—"

"They're Papa's family."

"But . . ." My voice trailed off. I was not sure how to put into words the feeling I suddenly had that the family was splitting into two halves, like medieval armies arranging themselves at either end of a battlefield. My mother seemed to be telling me that I had to be on one particular side, the one flying the English flag, but she might as well have told me I was fighting for Outer Mongolia.

"I could stay here with Papa," I said with a sudden flash of inspiration.

"Pia, you can't—"

"Oh, yes, I can." I could feel my mouth thinning into a hard line.

"You can't." My mother's voice was harsh. The ugly truth was coming out: like a hare breaking cover it streaked across the landscape of my mind. My mother had done with *Mäuselein* and *getting to know the English side of yourself.* "You have to come to England, Pia. End of story. I'm sorry." She didn't sound sorry, she sounded furious. "That's just the way it is."

I stared at the words on the crumpled page before me. "A VISIT TO ENGLAND." A hot feeling was welling up inside me. It felt like dough in a pan, rising and rising until it burst out over the top. My face, my shoulders, my fingers were rigid, but I could not stop the scalding tears from leaking out of my eyes. A drop fell onto the page, blurring the letters ENG. I could not prevent it now; a sob like a roar was breaking out of me. My mother tried to put her arms around me, but I fought my way out of her embrace, arms flailing. The exercise book ripped and fell to the floor, leaving me with half a page in my fist.

"Pia—"

"I hate you!" I shouted at the top of my voice, the words scouring my throat. "I hate you, I hate you, I hate you!"

"Pia, calm down, *Schätzchen,* it's going to be all right, it *will* be all right, you'll see . . ."

My mother's voice was now gentle and reassuring, but even through my rage I was aware that she was just trying to soothe me. She was not saying, *All right, we won't go to England, we'll stay here.* She was just trying to get me to calm down sufficiently to accept the unpalatable truth, just the same as a person might try to calm an animal down before administering an unpleasant medical treatment.

I broke away from her and actually *ran* to the door. She followed me to the threshold, still offering broken blandishments, but I was determined not to hear, and when I ran up the stairs she did not try to follow me. I went into my room, locked the door and put my bedside chair up against it as an extra barricade, and then I threw myself on the bed and howled like a baby.

Chapter Forty

Much later my father came up and knocked. At first I didn't answer, but when he spoke and I knew it was him, I got up and opened the door.

"Can I come in?" he asked. I nodded. He came into the room, dragged the chair out from behind the door, and sat down heavily on it. I sat on the bed and looked at him, through eyes that felt like puffy slits from crying.

"*Ach,* Pia." My father sounded tired. "I'm so sorry."

I trembled. "Papa, we're not *really* going to England, are we?"

He sighed. "*Doch.* I wish I could tell you otherwise."

"I don't want to go."

"And I don't want you to go, *Schätzchen.*"

"Then can't I stay here—with you?"

"I don't think so." My father's words were uncertain but they had the ring of doom in them.

"Why not?"

"It's not settled yet, but your mother wants you to go with her."

"She can't make me."

"Well, maybe she can't, but the courts can. She wants—Pia, do you know what *custody* is?"

I shook my head.

"It means that one of the parents is allowed to take the children with them . . . after a divorce."

"A divorce?"

My father nodded; he did not need to explain that one.

"Why . . . ?" I began, but I couldn't get any further than that. The question wouldn't shape itself.

"It's grown-ups' stuff," said my father sadly. He opened his arms and I got to my feet and went to be hugged. The feel of the hardness of his shoulder through his shirt as I laid my head on it was somehow reassuring. I sniffed noisily into the thick fabric.

"Papa, Charles and Chloe laugh at me."

My father said nothing, but his arms tightened around me.

"And I don't want to go to school in England." I ground my forehead into his shoulder. "And I hate English food, even Oma Warner's."

I felt my father's shoulders heaving and for a moment I wondered what I had said that was so funny. Then I pulled back and looked at his face. And that was only the second time in my life that I had seen my father cry; the first was when Oma Kristel died.

Chapter Forty-one

After that, the house took on the appearance of a vast military camp in the process of packing up and moving on, my mother playing the grim general who strode about among the crates and boxes, overseeing everything. We were not actually to move until the new year; a family with school-age children cannot be transferred from one country to another in a day or two, and furthermore my mother had agreed to stay in Germany for Christmas.

"That much she has agreed," said my father dolefully.

At school, the news that Pia Kolvenbach was moving to England and that her parents were divorcing had circulated with lightning speed. Suddenly I was no longer ostracized for being the Potentially Exploding Girl, but the new attention was worse. I could tell that the girls who sidled up to me and asked with faux-sympathetic smiles whether it was true were doing it on the basis of discussions they had heard between their own parents, to whom they would report back like scouts. Soon there would be nothing left of me at all, nothing real: I would be a walking piece of gossip, alternatively *tragic* and *appalling* and, worst of all, *a poor thing*.

"Why's your mother doing it?" Stefan asked me one morning. We were the last to leave the classroom after a hefty session of algebra. The winter sunlight streaking through the windows was white and cold. "Has she got someone else?"

I looked at him stupidly for a moment, momentarily wondering what he meant; did he mean my mother had got other *children*?

"Someone else?"

"You know," said Stefan offhandedly. "Another man."

"No," I said emphatically, although I had never even considered the idea up until that moment.

"Well, why's she going?"

"I don't know. Can you shut up about it?"

"Sorry."

I shoved my math books into my schoolbag. "She says she hates Germany and she hates Bad Münstereifel."

"*Na,* I hate it too sometimes."

"Well, she *really* hates it," I said, straightening up. "But I hate England, and I can't see why I have to go and live there, just because she . . ." I bit my lip, willing myself not to burst into humiliating tears.

"It's *Scheisse,*" agreed Stefan sympathetically. He hefted his bag onto his shoulder, and cocked his head toward the door. I trailed out after him, disconsolately. As we walked across the courtyard, he said, "Have you told Herr Schiller yet?"

I shook my head. "He probably knows." Resentfully, I added, "Everybody in the entire town seems to." It was true. Even though the adults were not quite as shameless as my schoolmates in approaching me with questions, I could tell that they were thinking about it when they looked at me. The attention was almost unbearable. When Frau Nett in the bakery gave me a free ice cream, an unprecedented piece of kindness, I knew it was just because she was thinking *Poor Pia Kolvenbach.* I would rather have dispensed with both the ice cream and the sympathy.

Walking up the Orchheimer Strasse, Stefan said, "We have to do something about . . . you know." He threw a significant glance toward Herr Düster's house.

"Stefan." I felt exhausted. "I'm going. Don't you understand? I'm going to stupid *verflixten* England."

"That's exactly why we have to do something." Stefan sounded excited.

Without even looking at him, I knew he would have that eager expression that I found exciting and infuriating by turns, his eyes alight with enthusiasm. "We have to do something *now,* otherwise you'll never know what happened."

"I am never going to know," I said bitterly.

"We have to find out before you go," said Stefan.

"Oh, what does it matter?"

I looked up at the leaden skies, rolling my eyes in frustration. Our futile investigation, which now seemed like a child's game in comparison to the fresh woes descending upon me, was just one more item on the long list of things I was never going to finish in the town where I had always lived. I was never going to sing at the school concert in the spring, I was never going to start a new school year at the *Gymnasium,* I was never going to take part in another St. Martin's procession.

All the things that seemed so reassuringly solid around me were going to vanish like a dream, be rolled up like a map and stuffed into the storage space of my mind. When I was far away and in my unimaginable new life I could take the map out and unroll it and pore over the marks on it, the shapes, the figures, the landmarks, but they would all be theoretical, like something in a book about dead cultures. I would come back at some time in the future and visit the town, but my friends would be grown up, and I—I would be like Dornröschen, the sleeping beauty, who had slumbered for a hundred years while everyone outside the castle grew old and died, and the hedge of thorns grew higher and thicker until there was no way through it anymore. When at last I came back to the world I had known before there would be nothing to recognize.

"Pia?"

I realized I was crying and hurriedly began to search through my pockets for a tissue.

"I'm all right," I said crossly. I blew my nose and we resumed walking.

For a while Stefan said nothing, then: "Pia, if you don't want to come, I'm going on my own."

I did not reply.

"We have to do *something.*"

"Why is it always *we?*" I retorted. "Why don't the police sort it out, or someone else?"

"They aren't getting anywhere with it," Stefan pointed out.

"And what makes you think we're going to get anywhere with it?" I realized I had said *we,* as though I were still involved with the whole idea, and winced.

"We have to try."

"We don't have to try," I snapped. I rounded on him. "The whole idea is *Scheisse.* Supposing he did do it? Then it's crazy to even think of going in his house. We might be next."

"Not if you come with me. The kids who've disappeared, they were all on their own."

"Look," I said irritably, "it's absolutely crazy to even think about it. He's put a new lock on the cellar door, anyway. So what are we going to do—walk up to his door, knock on it, and ask if we can come in?"

"Of course not." Stefan sounded offended.

"Well, what?"

"We wait until after dark when everyone's gone to sleep, and then we—"

"No," I said emphatically, shaking my head. "No way." I glared at him. "You really are stupid. I can see why—"

I was going to say *I can see why they call you StinkStefan,* but in spite of my anger something held me back, the muffled voice of conscience telling me that none of this fury I felt was really Stefan's fault at all. My voice trailed off for a moment, and then I rallied. "Anyway, maybe *your* mother lets you wander all over town at night, but *mine* certainly doesn't."

I saw a shadow cross Stefan's face and realized that I had hit a nerve with my gibe about his mother's lack of interest, but I was feeling too raw myself to apologize.

Stefan looked at me for a long moment. When at last he spoke, his voice was low and urgent and not angry at all.

"Why do you care what your mother thinks anymore?" he said.

Chapter Forty-two

The plan was simple: we would wait until it was late in the evening and the white Christmas lights that were strung across the Orchheimer Strasse had been switched off. At a prearranged time we would slip out of our houses and meet in the narrow alleyway that ran between two of the old buildings on the east side of the street. If either of us arrived much earlier than the other, the alleyway would provide cover from any prying eyes, and we could also hide our bicycles in it.

"Bicycles? What do we need bicycles for?" I asked.

"In case we need to get away in a hurry," said Stefan. "Like a getaway car."

I felt a familiar twinge of disquiet; Stefan always seemed to talk about the venture as though it were a scene in an action movie.

"Are we going to have walkie-talkies too?"

He gave me a look of disdain. "Don't be silly."

I was going to bring a flashlight, and Stefan was going to raid his father's toolbox to get a hammer and chisel to open the cellar doors.

"How do you know what to do?" I asked dubiously. "You haven't ever done that before, have you?"

"No, but . . ." Stefan's voice trailed off. I was relieved; I really did not want to hear him say *they do it all the time in the movies.* I feared if I heard him say that I would lose my nerve altogether.

Once Stefan had opened the doors we would climb inside and pull them shut behind us, in case anyone should pass by or look out of their window; it was unlikely, since Bad Münstereifel was generally pretty dead by nightfall, but you could never tell. It would be just our luck if Hilde Koch were to get out of bed at midnight to ease her ancient bladder and couldn't resist a peep out her front window.

"And once we're inside?"

"We search," said Stefan simply.

"What about Herr Düster?"

"Well, obviously we can't search *upstairs,*" said Stefan impatiently. "But he's not going to have hidden anything up there, anyway, is he?"

"Why not?"

"Serial killers never do," said Stefan with authority. "He's probably put the bodies in the cellar."

"Yeuch," I commented, shuddering. "And if we find something, what do we . . . ?"

"We get proof." Stefan said it firmly.

"Proof? You mean . . . ?"

"We have to get something, and bring it out with us."

"Stefan, if we find a dead body I am *not* touching it."

"Who said you have to, silly? We can get a bit of the clothes or something."

I gazed at him hopelessly. There really was no escape this time. We really *were* going to do it.

"All right," I said.

I still thought I might put the expedition off. When Stefan brought the topic up again I prevaricated: there was no point attempting it with the weekend coming up—the Christmas market was open until late from Friday to Sunday, so the town center would be packed with people. There was a cold snap and snow was expected—we would freeze if we went out of doors at midnight, and we would leave tracks in the snow if we did. I had a couple of long days at school coming up and needed the sleep. I thought I had a cold coming on . . .

"*Pech gehabt,*" said Stefan with a supreme lack of sympathy.

"It's not just tough luck—I'm really sick . . ." I sniffed theatrically.

"Look, Pia." He sounded excited. "Herr Düster has gone away. We have to do it *now.*"

"Now?" I looked about me wildly.

"I mean tonight."

"How do you know he's gone away?"

"I heard that old *Schrulle* Frau Koch telling someone in the bakery at lunchtime. She said he left this morning and good riddance." Stefan looked at me, his eyes shining with the fervor of a fanatic. "Don't you see? This is our chance! We have to do it tonight."

"OK," I said. I felt sick.

The rest of the day passed in an agony of suspense. When school finished I deliberately walked home via the Marktstrasse, avoiding the Orchheimer Strasse, where Herr Düster's house lurked like a trap. I wouldn't let Stefan walk me home.

When I arrived at the house, both my parents were there, but were occupying spaces as far as possible from each other. My mother was energetically cleaning out one of the kitchen cupboards, perhaps deciding who was to have custody of her extensive Tupperware collection, and my father was enthroned in the wickerwork armchair in their bedroom with a file on his lap and the telephone within reach. Sebastian was sitting in front of the television with his thumb in his mouth and a heap of toy cars lying neglected around him, his round eyes glued to the screen, where the Teletubbies were cavorting among gigantic rabbits and futuristic windmills.

No one seemed to notice my arrival; we had all become like individual planets traveling on their lonely orbits around a pitiless sun, our paths concentric, never meeting. I fetched myself a glass of apple juice, then sat at the kitchen table and tried to do my homework, but it was impossible to concentrate.

In the end I closed the files and went outside to find my bicycle. It was icy cold outdoors, and already beginning to get dark; the streetlamps made little impression on the gloom. I would have to leave the bike out in the street and trust that neither of my parents noticed it and made me put it away again. I wheeled it into the space between my father's car and the wall in the hope that it would not be seen. I lingered for a while in the street, hunched against the cold, and hacked aimlessly at the ice in the gutter with my heel, but after Frau Kessel had passed and said, "Hallo, Pia Kolvenbach," in a disapproving tone, I realized that I had better go indoors; I was simply drawing attention to myself.

At suppertime I tried to break the silence by asking my mother, "Is it true that Herr Düster has gone away?" but she merely said, "Mmmm," and continued to gaze out the window at the darkened street with a distracted expression on her face. Her fingers were forever working at her dark ponytail; the ends were becoming lank.

My father was reading, or pretending to read, the *Kölner Stadtanzeiger.* Every so often he would put the paper down in order to reach for something—the plate of cold *Wurst* or the butter—but he never asked anyone to pass him anything. He preferred to stand up and reach over the table, looming oppressively over the rest of us.

When the telephone rang it was a relief. I was sliding out of my place to go answer it when my father got to his feet, raising one large hand to indicate that I should sit down again, he would do it.

"Kolvenbach."

I stared listlessly at my plate, wondering whether Sebastian could be fed the last piece of salami, like a dog waiting under the table.

"What?"

My father's voice rose as though he were shocked. My mother turned her head for an instant but then resumed her vague surveillance of the window. Her lips were pursed slightly as though in irritation, and I guessed she thought my father was trying to get attention that she was determined not to give.

"When?"

This time my mother did not even move her head. My father listened for a long time. *"Mein Gott,"* he said at last, and then, "Do you want me to—?"

There was a further silence as he listened to someone speaking at the other end, then he said, *"Bis gleich,"* and put down the receiver. He came back into the kitchen.

"Kate." It was almost a shock hearing him speak my mother's name out loud. The silence from my mother was ominous. "I have to go out. I have to—"

He got no further. "Just go," said my mother.

"Don't you want—?"

"Just go," she said again.

My father's brows knit together but he said nothing. He went back into the hallway and removed his winter jacket from its hanger; a moment later the front door banged shut and he was gone. I looked at my mother.

"I wonder what—"

"Eat your supper, Pia."

I did eat my supper, though without relish. Something was going on outside, I knew. I could hear voices at regular intervals as people passed our front windows. It was not one of the days for the Christmas market, so there was no particular reason for so many people to be out on the street.

I saw my mother glance at the window herself and guessed that she was regretting her refusal to hear what was going on. Still, she was determined not to advertise her interest. She finished her own supper in silence and then cleared up with a lot of clattering of plates and slamming of drawers.

"Pia, go and get ready for bed" was about the only remark she addressed to me in the entire evening; she had closed up like an oyster shell. I went upstairs and changed into my nightdress. When I was ready for bed I went down and kissed my mother, but it was like kissing a waxwork. She hardly seemed aware that I was there.

I went back upstairs and put my head around Sebastian's door. He was fast asleep already, curled into a ball with the covers wrapped around him so that he looked like a spring roll. My father was still out. It seemed that no one had the slightest interest in me or in what I was doing.

I climbed into bed and lay there for a very long time, my eyes tracing the familiar outlines of my room as they adjusted to the dark. Sleep seemed unimaginable. I had set my alarm clock for half past midnight; after some thought I hopped out of bed again and went to close the door, in the hope of preventing the alarm from waking anyone else.

Eventually I heard the creaking of my mother coming up the stairs, and shortly afterward the groaning and clanking from the pipework that meant she was running a bath. A house as old as ours is as garrulous as an old lady: it can tell you everything that is going on. I slipped into an uneasy doze from which I awoke, disoriented, as my mother's bedroom door closed.

I groped for my alarm clock and pressed the little button that illuminated the dial. It was nearly eleven o'clock, and I had not heard my father come in. If he were not home before twelve thirty, I dared not try to leave the house: he would surely look in on me before he went to bed and, besides, there was the actual risk of meeting him on the stairs.

In the event, however, he came home a little after half past eleven; I heard the front door close with a bang and then the sound of him stumping heavily up the stairs. I curled into a ball facing away from the door and closed my eyes, feigning sleep. I heard the door open but my father did not come in as he normally did, to straighten my covers or kiss my forehead. I simply heard him give a very heavy sigh, and then the door clicked shut again.

A little later the toilet flushed to the accompaniment of more percussion from the plumbing, a door closed, and there was silence, or as much of it as our aged house could manage.

Perversely, after my father came home I really did fall asleep at last, so deeply that it took me some time to surface after the alarm went off. For what seemed like a long while I was dimly conscious of its relentless beeping nagging at me, then suddenly I snapped into wakefulness. I almost fell out of bed in my eagerness to push the button down and silence the racket.

My heart was thumping so hard that it felt as if it might leap into my throat and choke me. My fingers still around the alarm clock, I listened. There was no sound of anyone else stirring; the two closed doors between me and my parents had done the trick, or perhaps they were both too worn out by the constant tension between them to wake.

I put the bedside light on, and listened again; still nothing. I was really going to have to get up and go out. As quietly as I could, I slipped out of bed and dressed myself in jeans and a dark sweater. Just as I was about to open the door, I had a sudden afterthought: plucking my largest teddy bear from the chair in the corner of the room, I stuffed him into the bed and arranged the quilt over him. To a critical eye it was not a very convincing effect, but if one of my parents were simply to look into the room without putting the light on, it might just fool them. Then I opened the door.

Now that I was committed to action, I really hoped that my parents would *not* wake up. I couldn't imagine how I would explain what I was doing fully dressed on the landing in the middle of the night. Going down the stairs was agony; every creak and groan from the ancient boards threatened to give the game away.

In the darkened hallway I fumbled for my down jacket and my outdoor boots. When I had finished lacing the boots I went to the door and discovered one thing that had worked in my favor; my father had forgotten to bolt and chain the door when he came in, being perhaps too exhausted to remember.

Carefully I opened the door. Instantly, icy midnight air hit my face. Snowflakes were whirling down from the leaden darkness above the rooftops. I slid out the door and pulled it gently shut behind me. Then I waited for a moment, but there was no sound from the house, no light suddenly coming on. The street was very dark. The white Christmas lights that festooned every building in the town from October to January had been switched off, leaving only one feeble old-fashioned lamp at the other end of the street casting a faint circle of light.

I retrieved my bicycle from its slot between my father's car and the wall, and wiped snow from the seat with my sleeve. I would have to take care; the cobbles were slick with snow too. After one last glance about me, I got onto the bicycle and cycled off into the night.

Chapter Forty-three

※

*Y*ou're late" was the first thing Stefan said to me as I dismounted from the bicycle.

"I nearly didn't come at all," I told him. "My father didn't come home until really late."

"Oh." Stefan sounded uninterested. "Get the bike in here, quick."

I wheeled the bicycle into the alley. Stefan followed me in, glancing about to make sure that no one was around. He need not have worried: the street was deserted. The snow was starting to settle; if I had arrived five minutes later I would have left telltale tracks in it.

"Have you got the tools—the chisel and stuff?" I whispered.

"Yes." We looked at each other.

"We'd better get on with it," said Stefan. "I'm freezing."

It'll be warmer indoors, I thought, with a sudden frisson as I realized that once we were *indoors* we would be inside someone else's house—we would have broken in. I followed Stefan out of the alley. He moved quickly and silently over the cobblestones, keeping close to the wall in a way that I strongly suspected was copied from the movies.

We crouched down close to the cellar doors. Stefan unwrapped the hammer and chisel from the rag he had used to carry them in. He shot me a glance.

"Go on," I said. I was not going to touch the tools myself; I had no idea what to do.

"Have you got a flashlight?"

I nodded, slipping my little light out of my pocket. I switched it on and attempted to train the beam on the cellar doors. Carefully, Stefan positioned the chisel against the padlock, then took a swing with the hammer. The resultant *clank* sounded horrifically loud. I winced, screwing my eyes shut, but when I opened them I was disappointed to see that the padlock was still as tightly fixed to the doors as before.

"What are you doing?" I hissed.

"I can't help it," Stefan hissed back crossly. He shook his head, trying to get his snow-dampened hair out of his eyes. "Hold the light straight."

"I'm trying to."

Stefan took another swing. Again there was the appallingly loud *clank* followed by *"Scheisse"* in muffled tones.

"Did you hit your fingers?"

"No." Stefan sounded agonized. "I jarred my hand." He nursed his hand. "You try."

"I don't know what to do."

"Just *try.*"

Reluctantly, I took the tools from him. I made a few experimental chips with the chisel but the sound seemed enormous, a neon sign announcing our presence, and I could see I was not making the slightest impression on the padlock.

"It's not going to work," I whispered.

"Scheisse, Scheisse, Scheisse."

"Well, what do you expect me to do?" I said fiercely. I stood up. "You have another go."

I handed the hammer and chisel to him; I could not face even holding the flashlight for him anymore. I slid it into my pocket. Inside me emotions were washing back and forth like a tide. When Stefan had failed to break open the padlock, my first feeling was one of relief: honor had been satisfied, we would not have to go into Herr Düster's house, I could cycle home and creep back into my bed before anyone knew I was gone. We had done everything that anyone could.

Then came the inevitable reaction, like a persistent undertow dragging me back out to sea: *Katharina Linden, Marion Voss, Julia Mahlberg . . . if something needs to be done you should do it.* I closed my eyes, but still I could feel the cold creeping into my flesh in spite of my down jacket—a damp insinuating chill, the cold of a night that no one should put a dog out in, let alone a child. It was impossible not to think of those girls, Katharina and the others—were they lying out there somewhere, far from the warmth of their beds, pale faces lapped in wet black leaves, the snow in their hair gathering but never melting?

It was not possible simply to stand there and peer at Stefan through the darkness. Disheartened, I went to stand on Herr Düster's doorstep, where the slight recess offered some meager protection from the snow. I glanced up and down the street; all was still and silent. I couldn't help but wince at the *clink* of the chisel on the padlock. Even if Stefan managed to get the padlock open, it was going to be blatantly obvious what we had done.

Hugging myself, I leaned against the door. Like the rest of the house, it was old and uncared for. The wood felt rough and weathered under my touch. As well as a newish metal lock there was still a brass doorknob, tarnished with age, and underneath it the old keyhole, the worn edges giving it the appearance of a toothless old mouth. Without really thinking about what I was doing, I slid my freezing fingers around the doorknob and gently turned it. With an audible *click* the door opened.

For a moment I stood there dumbfounded, with my fingers still gripping the knob. Herr Düster's house yawned in front of me, the interior a black pit.

"Stefan."

"What?" came the reply, in an irritable stage whisper.

"Stefan, the door's open."

"What?"

"The door's open." I heard him get to his feet and a moment later he was by my side.

"What did you do?"

"I didn't do anything. It just opened. He can't have locked it."

"Mensch." Stefan sounded impressed.

"Stefan—maybe he's at home."

"No way. Frau Koch said he'd gone."

"So? Maybe she's as big a storyteller as her grandson."

"Come on—does it *look* like anyone's at home?"

"No-o-o," I said doubtfully, but looking around the street none of the houses looked any livelier than Herr Düster's; all were utterly dark.

He gave me a little push. "Go on."

"You go first," I said, not moving.

I heard an impatient little sigh, and then Stefan had brushed past me and entered the house. It was inky black inside, and almost immediately I heard a *bump* followed by a smothered exclamation.

"I'm going to put my flashlight on," whispered Stefan, fumbling for it.

"Someone might see us."

"Someone will definitely *hear* us if I don't."

There was a tiny *click* and a small circle of light appeared, traveling slowly over a heavy oak cupboard, its front panels carved with twining leaves and prancing stags, a section of faded wallpaper with an indistinct design of foliage, an old-fashioned clock whose metal face was spotted with tiny patches of rust. There was a smell on the air of dust and old furniture polish.

"What's that?" I whispered as softly as I could. Stefan let the light move up the wall until it illuminated the thing I had glimpsed; it was a wooden crucifix, the metal Jesus on it contorted in pain.

Stefan said nothing, but let out a little sound like a sigh. He swung the flashlight around and the yellow beam drifted through the musty air like a phantom, touching without touching. We were in a narrow hallway, the wooden floor overlaid with a shabby-looking runner, the walls lined with dark blocks of furniture. Directly ahead of us the wooden staircase began. The treads were worn, and the newel post, carved into the shape of a face peeping out from a nest of leaves, had a dull shine that I suspected came more from the touch of many hands over the years than from polish. The beam of light moved on and the peeping face was swallowed in the darkness once more.

To the left of the staircase the hallway continued farther back, but from where we stood the light was insufficient to do more than suggest a doorway at the end. As Stefan completed the sweep with the flashlight, I saw there was also a door to our immediate left, a stout wooden door, firmly closed. Just the living room, of course—it could hardly be some kind of Bluebeard's chamber, facing onto the street as it did.

All the same I was losing my taste for investigation. In the pervasive gloom it was difficult not to imagine the absent Herr Düster still lurking within, perhaps hunched in a high-backed armchair in the dark, like a lobster concealed within its cave in the rocks deep under the black water, nothing visible but the dull gleam of a carapace and the two shining beads of eyes.

Stefan reached for the handle, and with infinite care opened the door. We slid cautiously into the darkened room. Inside, it was an obstacle course of standard lamps and cabinets and chairs. The same depressing smell of dust and old polish permeated everything. From the little detail that I could pick out by flashlight—the fringed edge of a lampshade, the claw foot of a chair, the dull gleam of a pewter plate—it looked as though the room hadn't been redecorated for many years. The reflective glint of glass showed that the walls were crowded with framed pictures, though it was possible to see what they were only by training the light directly on them.

I wondered what the friendless Herr Düster used to decorate his house. Fumbling for my own flashlight, I switched it on and examined some of the nearest pictures. They were all photographs, but old ones: some of them were sepia, and had the soft-focus effect at the edges that some very old photographs have.

A portrait shot of a young woman in old-fashioned clothes caught my eye; hers was the only genuinely pretty face among the collection of stolidly respectable subjects with long upper lips and indignant eyes. I stared at her for a moment, wondering whether this was perhaps the Hannelore about whom Frau Kessel had gone on at such length, but looking at the style of her high-necked dress and her upswept hair, I was doubtful. Wasn't this picture too old to be her?

I was still contemplating the photograph when I heard a *thump!* somewhere behind me. I whirled around as though I had been stung.

"Stefan, can't you—?"

He didn't let me complete the sentence.

"*Shhhhh.*" He stretched a hand out toward me, as though warding something off.

The next moment he switched off his flashlight. "Switch yours off too," he hissed at me.

I hesitated. The thought of being plunged into darkness was not a pleasant one. Stefan had no such qualms; he took a couple of steps nearer, plucked the light out of my hands, and switched it off.

"What—?"

"*Shut up.*" His voice was so emphatic that I did shut up, and for a few moments the pair of us stood there in the darkness, listening.

"Stefan?" I whispered eventually. "That was you, wasn't it?"

"Shhhhh," came the reply, then: "No. It came from upstairs."

"Up—?"

Realization trickled through me, momentarily robbing my limbs of the power to move. *Scheisse, Scheisse,* boomed my thoughts incoherently. I almost staggered, then grabbed Stefan's arm, trying to pull him with me toward the door, knowing even as I did so that if someone—or *something*—was to come down the stairs at that moment, we could never get out of the house without passing within an arm's reach of it.

Stefan stood his ground, and the fingers of his free hand closed around my wrist with surprising strength.

"Stay still," came the whispered words out of the darkness.

"No—" I twisted like a landed fish in his grasp.

"He'll hear you."

That was enough. I froze. Then from somewhere above us came another muffled sound, as though someone had dropped something on the floor. I could not help myself; I struggled to break away from Stefan.

"Keep still," hissed an agonized voice. "Your jacket—"

He was right; with every movement the fat arms and body of my down jacket rubbed together with an audible rustle. I clutched Stefan in panic. "What are we going to do?" I whispered.

"Get down. He might not come in here."

It was a slim hope, but I couldn't think of a better plan. We squatted down on the worn carpet, so that a heavy armchair flanked by a little table with a lamp on it shielded us from the doorway. I felt for Stefan's hand. His fingers closed around mine gratefully. We waited.

For a brief moment I had entertained the hope that all we had heard was Pluto, springing down from some favorite sleeping spot onto the floor above. But now I could quite clearly hear footsteps moving across the room above our heads. There was a scraping sound, as though someone had moved a piece of furniture slightly, and then the sound of the footsteps changed and I realized that whoever it was must have moved out onto the upstairs landing.

I put my lips close to Stefan's ear. "He's going to come downstairs." I was near to tears.

I felt Stefan's breath on my cheek, and then his voice said very softly, "Stay here."

No. The moment I realized that Stefan meant to move I was flooded with panic. Suppose he managed to make a break for it and left me here, trapped in the house with the monster? I made a grab for him, with an alarming hiss of fabric rubbing fabric, but I was too late. As swiftly and silently as a cat, he had risen and slipped toward the door. Now that my eyes had adjusted to the dark he seemed painfully visible.

A moment later I heard the first creak as someone put a heavy foot on the topmost stair. Smoothly as a dancer, Stefan slipped behind the door, which stood ajar. His head turned and I guessed that he was looking through the vertical crack by the hinges.

Inexorably, the footsteps came on down the stairs, each one as heavy and final as a prison door closing, the wooden treads protesting under the weight. Kneeling on the floor, I curled my hands around the claw feet of the armchair, clenching them into fists as though trying to anchor myself against a storm.

I squeezed my eyes shut in an agony of suspense, but it wasn't possible to close them against the series of images that seemed to be running in my head on an eternally repeating loop: a girl of my own age, light brown plaits bobbing as she ran down the street with her *Ranzen* on her back, running into nowhere; Frau Mahlberg screaming hysterically for Julia; Herr Düster hiding out after the war in the ruins on the Quecken hill, coming back to his lair at daybreak with the blood of slaughtered chickens on his lips. I was really afraid that I might wet myself, so intense was my terror; I squeezed my thighs together, the muscles rigid under the fabric of my jeans.

There was a final creak and then a more muffled *thump* as whoever it was stepped onto the worn runner in the hallway. There was a pause, and then the footsteps moved slowly down the hall. At any moment they must pass the door.

I opened my eyes again, and could clearly see Stefan still poised behind it, absolutely motionless. Whoever had come downstairs was carrying a light of some kind: the crack between the door and the frame showed as a dim yellow streak. I saw Stefan lean back toward the wall slightly, trying to make himself invisible.

The door, I thought suddenly: the door had not been open when we entered the house, and now it was ajar. Too late to do anything about it now; I ducked my head, trying to compress myself into as small a space as possible, in case the unseen person in the hallway looked into the room.

The footsteps passed the door. There was a slight hitch to them, as though whoever it was had hesitated, perhaps seeing that the door was ajar. But the next moment they had passed it, and I heard the front door open, then softly close.

I sagged forward, my body loose with relief, and let my forehead rest upon the shabby seat of the armchair. *Thank you, thank you* was all I could think. I heard Stefan's light footsteps approaching and the next moment I felt his hand on my shoulder. His flashlight clicked on too close to my face, making me wince.

"Are you OK?" said his voice close to my ear.

"I think so."

With an effort I sat back on my heels. I felt peculiar; my lower jaw seemed to have taken on a life of its own and was quivering as though I were about to burst out crying. "Stefan?" Even my voice sounded strange, vibrating as though I were trying to speak while being driven over rough ground.

"It's OK."

"I want to go home."

There was a silence. Finally, Stefan said, "Pia, I think he's locked the door."

"What?" My voice rose wildly. Careless now of being heard, I began to succumb to panic.

"Calm down," said Stefan quietly. He put an arm around my shoulders.

"He can't have locked the door," I babbled. "I didn't hear him lock it."

"Pia," said Stefan in the same low voice, "I don't think he had a key."

"That's *Quatsch.*" I said eagerly. "He can't have locked it." I tried to push Stefan away. All I could think of was getting to my feet and getting out of the house.

"He *did* lock it," said Stefan.

Shaking my head, I got up and went to the door as quickly as my cramped legs would allow. I looked into the hallway; the door certainly was closed. I ran to it and tried the handle. Stefan was right. It was locked. I tried it again, rattling the handle violently, putting my shoulder against the door and shoving as hard as I could.

Intransigent as a barricade, it refused to budge an inch. In desperation I kicked the bottom panel, then fell back, panting. Silently Stefan came to stand by me.

"I can't open it," I gasped.

"I know."

Before I could stop myself, I had struck him on the shoulder with the flat of my hand. I could not understand how he could be so infuriatingly calm.

"We can't get out!" My chest was heaving. Fear and frustration were buzzing through my body like toxins. "He's locked us in. He's locked us in. Herr Düster—"

"Pia." Stefan put out a hand to ward off another blow. "It wasn't Herr Düster."

"What do you mean, it wasn't Herr Düster?" I was beside myself. "Who was it then? *Verdammter* Dracula—?"

"It was Boris," said Stefan.

Chapter Forty-four

oris?" The information stopped me in my tracks. "It was *Boris?*"

"*Doch.* I saw him through the crack in the door."

"But—but—" I was floundering, trying to make sense of it. "How could it be Boris?"

"I don't know. But that's why the door was open. He must have un-locked it."

"How?" I demanded. "He can't have a key, can he?"

"Of course not. But that wouldn't stop him."

Stefan's voice was matter-of-fact; closer to the epicenter of Boris's questionable pursuits than I was, he found the idea of his cousin pick-ing the lock of someone's house quite unremarkable. "It's a good thing he didn't hear us come in. He'd have gone nuts."

"But—if that was Boris, where's Herr Düster?"

Stefan shrugged. "Gone away. Like Frau Koch said." He clicked his flashlight back on, then leaned past me almost casually and tried the door handle, but of course the door did not budge.

"Why did he lock it?" I asked, sullen with the unfairness of it.

"So Herr Düster wouldn't know he'd been in here—I suppose."

"Can you unlock it?"

Stefan shook his head. "I don't think so." He glanced at me swiftly and took in the hunched shoulders, the fists held out in front of me like claws. Gently, he reached out with his free hand and grasped my wrist. "Hey. Don't panic."

"We're locked in." My voice sounded unnaturally high.

"We'll get out."

"How?"

"I don't know . . . we just will."

"But we're locked in!"

"You said that." Stefan's voice was mild. He cocked his head. "We're in here already, so why don't we finish looking?"

The sudden realization that if there *were* any corpses in the house we were now locked in with them was almost too much for me; it felt nothing short of miraculous that I was still on my feet and not writhing in paroxysms of terror on the threadbare runner. I kept staring at Stefan as though concentrating on him rather than the house around me would stave off the thought.

"Come on," I managed in a weak voice.

He shook his head. "Take your jacket off first."

"Why?" I was reluctant to emerge from the warm shell of down and expose myself to the house's atmosphere.

"Because whenever you move it makes that stupid noise."

I sighed, but he was right. I undid the zip and shrugged out of the jacket.

"Put it in there," said Stefan, indicating the living room. He didn't need to add *in case anyone sees it.* I was already spooked enough. I stuffed the jacket underneath one of Herr Düster's ancient sideboards.

"Now what?"

"We can go upstairs first, or down into the cellar."

"You said we didn't need to go upstairs," I pointed out. "You said serial killers never leave dead bodies up there."

"Well, they probably don't." Stefan made a face. "I mean, could *you* go to sleep at night if you knew there was a dead person stuffed in your wardrobe?" He saw my expression and added hurriedly, "Look, we couldn't have gone up there if Herr Düster had been here, but we can now he's away. We might as well."

I looked at the black space at the top of the stairs and then down at the floor under my feet.

"I don't know," I said feebly.

"Toss for it, then," said Stefan briskly, fumbling in his pocket and eventually producing a single ten-pfennig coin. "Which side do you want?"

"The oak leaves."

Solemnly Stefan tossed the coin into the air, made as if to catch it, fumbled, and dropped it on the floor. We both squatted down. In the flashlight's beam we could just make out the coin, glinting dully: *10,* we both read. I stood up and leaned against the wall. I felt a strange lack of interest in which option Stefan would choose; the whole affair seemed out of my hands.

"The cellar," he said decisively. He set off down the dark hallway, then turned, his flashlight winking at me. "Come on."

I trailed unwillingly behind him. The hallway narrowed slightly as it passed the stairs; in the dark it felt oppressively like entering a tunnel. Outside the sickly yellow of the flashlight beam, everything was draped in velvety shadow. Anything could have been lurking in the corners of the hallway and the angles where the walls joined the ceiling: great spiders, snub-nosed bats, chittering rodents. I shuddered.

"Here," said Stefan.

There was a narrow door under the stairs, the wood worn and battered. There was no lock, only a black metal latch, which Stefan carefully lifted. The door opened easily. "I bet he oils the hinges," said Stefan. "So nobody hears him going in and out—you know, with the bodies."

"Shut up."

"Come right inside," he said, unabashed, as he stepped into the rectangle of darkness. "Come on," he added, seeing me hesitate. "I want to shut the door."

"What?" I could not imagine anything worse than being shut inside that unfamiliar dark space, with the smell of dust and decay and the weak light from the flashlight picking out little night creatures as they scurried away across the walls, their many legs working furiously.

"I want to put the light on." Stefan sounded impatient. "No one will see it, as long as we shut the door."

"Oh."

Reluctantly, I squeezed in beside him, peering down and feeling about with the toe of my boot, afraid of taking a tumble down the stairs. A moment later there was a firm-sounding *click* and the light came on. Suddenly Stefan was no longer a dim shape highlighted with the yellow flashlight, but a solid figure standing close to me with his fingertips still grasping the old-fashioned switch. I was grateful for the light; a half turn showed me that we were both perilously close to the top of the cellar stairs. A fall down those in the dark would have been disastrous. The little space we were standing in seemed to double as a closet; a row of Herr Düster's battered-looking jackets hung from pegs.

I nudged Stefan. "Look." There was an ancient-looking rifle propped up against the wall under the coats.

Stefan shrugged. "Everyone has those. I bet even Hilde Koch has one, to keep off burglars."

He started down the stairs and I followed him, not without an involuntary glance back at the firmly closed door. It was hard not to think of the cellar as a trap. If we had not been able to break the padlock from the outside, it had to be completely impossible to burst through the cellar hatch from underneath. With no other way out, it felt very uncomfortable to be moving farther and farther from the door. Worse, my entire skin seemed to be one enormous itch, crawling with imaginary spiders and insects. I rubbed my palms together and shivered.

As we descended the stairs we found ourselves in a room a little larger than my bedroom. I supposed it must be directly under the living room. The walls had been thickly coated with whitewash, now a dirty ivory color. I guessed the cellar was very old, older perhaps than the main house. It was clear that Herr Düster did not use it very much. Most of what was in it was lumber. There were broken sticks of furniture, and a few dirty sacks containing salt for wintertime gritting and what looked like very old and very dried-out peat.

Stefan went scuffing his way through the accumulated dust on the floor, peering into the sagging sacks and poking at the broken furniture with the toe of his boot. Under the yellow light of the bare bulb that illuminated the cellar he looked unhealthily sallow. The whole place smelled damp and musty, and I was reluctant to touch anything with my bare hands, as though the filth were somehow infectious.

Trying not to brush against any of the gray-looking furniture, I wandered about the cellar. I supposed I was looking for clues, but nothing suggested itself. Most of the things looked as though they had not been moved or touched for years.

Eventually my meandering path brought me to the far corner, where Herr Düster had abandoned an ugly carved cupboard so large that I could have climbed inside it. There was nothing in it now; one of the front doors was hanging by one hinge, giving a view of an interior inhabited by nothing other than mouse droppings.

I frowned; how had people ever lived with such ugly things? I went to the side of it; it was just as ugly seen end-on. I noticed that it wasn't actually flush against the wall. There was a gap of perhaps eighty centimeters between its ramrod back and the rough surface of the wall. Enough for a person to pass between them without difficulty, unless it were Hilde Koch with her barrel figure.

I heard a sigh close by my right shoulder; Stefan was standing there.

"Found something?"

"Not really." I shrugged.

"Let's look." He shouldered past me and into the gap.

I stayed where I was; I didn't relish the idea of gathering black dust and cobwebs on the shoulder of my sweater if I brushed the wall.

"Pia?" came Stefan's muffled voice. "There's a sort of door."

Chapter Forty-five

*S*ort of?" I repeated slowly. "What do you mean a *sort of* door?"

"Well, it's not really a door." Stefan's voice was suddenly clearer—I guessed he had turned to face me. "There's no actual door, but there's a gap. You can get through into the next room."

I examined my reaction to this information as calmly and carefully as a surgeon examining a limb for broken bones. I felt neither frightened nor alarmed. There was an inevitability about it. I pictured a hidden room tucked away behind the monstrous cupboard, a secret place with vaulted ceiling and stone floor, the missing girls laid out like a repeating series of Snow Whites, red lips and white, white skin, eyes shut tight as though sleeping.

"Pia? Are you coming?"

"Yes."

"Look out, there's no light in there."

I followed Stefan into the space between the cupboard and the wall. He was standing in the very corner, shining his flashlight into the darkness. Now I could see what he meant about a doorway. With the cupboard masking the corner you would naturally assume that it was just that, a corner, no doubt full of lurking spiders and beetles. In fact, the far wall of the cellar did not quite meet the other wall in the corner; there was a gap wide enough for a person to pass through.

Together we peered inside. With the cupboard blocking out most of the light, it was pitch dark in there. The flashlight beam could illuminate only a little at a time, settling hesitantly here and there like a moth. We could not see to the back of the room. The floor appeared to be made of flagstones, worn smooth with age. Several of them, levered up from some spot outside the weak circle of yellow light, were stacked against the stone wall.

As I leaned into the room I could smell a difference in the air. It was subtle but noticeable, a smell I could not identify but that I thought of as an *outside* smell, a cool smell.

"I don't know," I said doubtfully.

"Don't know what?" Stefan sounded impatient. "We might as well look now."

He stepped into the room. Unwillingly, I followed. I found I was shivering a little in my sweater. I wished I had not left my down jacket upstairs. At any rate my dark imaginings of dead girls laid out like medieval ladies on their sarcophagi were not realized; a sweep of the beam showed nothing at all on the stone flags, not a stick of furniture, not so much as a lump of coal.

"What's that?" I said, touching Stefan's arm. He swung the flashlight around. Almost in the dead center of the floor was a black patch, a circle like a dark pool.

"Cool," said Stefan loudly. His voice echoed, giving it a strangely disembodied effect. "I think it's a well."

"A well?"

"Yeah. Don't you remember what Herr Schiller said about it? *Ach, Quatsch,* you weren't there that day, were you? He said all the houses in Bad Münstereifel used to have one."

"I don't think ours does."

"No, they sealed them all up after the war, remember?"

Dimly, I recollected something of the sort. I remembered Frau Kessel's tale about her Great-Aunt Martha's dog falling into the well in her house and drowning, before the well was capped in the 1940s.

We approached the hole, Stefan brandishing the flashlight like a weapon. I circled it with caution, not wanting to meet the same end as

Great-Aunt Martha's dog. We stood on each side, gazing down. Stefan was right: it *was* a well. About two meters below us I could see the dark glint of subterranean water. That was what I had sensed when we had entered the room: the cool smell of water flowing.

"Phew," said Stefan with exaggerated relief.

I looked at him. "What?"

"That's what the stones were taken up for. I was thinking . . ." His voice trailed off and he looked at me, his face ghostly in the light. He gave a false-sounding little laugh. "Stupid or what?" He cocked his head. "Don't look like that. It's OK. It's just a well." He leaned over it, gazing down into the dark waters. "It's deep, too."

"Stefan?"

"Hmm . . . ?"

"Can we go?" I could not keep the pleading tone out of my voice. I had tired of playing detective. I was desperate to get out of the house. "I really want to go home."

"Shut up."

"Wie, bitte?" I was instantly enraged at his rudeness.

"Shut *up*."

"You shut—" But my indignant tirade was cut off short as the flashlight suddenly went off with a click.

"What are you—?" I began, but this time when Stefan's sharp *"Shhhh!"* came out of the darkness there was no mistaking the urgency in its tone.

"What are you doing? Put the light back on!" I hissed in a loud whisper. I fumbled for my own, but realized with a sinking feeling that it must be in the pocket of my jacket.

"Shhhh. I can't." There was a pause during which I frantically tried to make Stefan out in the darkness. "Be quiet," ordered his disembodied voice.

"What—?"

"I think there's somebody there."

Fright and anger flared up inside me like twin gas jets. "You *Blödmann*, don't try to scare me!"

"I'm not trying to scare you. *Listen*."

Fear seemed to have solidified in my chest like a stone, shot through with veins of disbelief. I simply could not *believe* that someone else was in the house with us, not after the narrow escape with Boris. The very idea made me sick with injustice. The whole universe seemed to be conspiring against us, firing off volleys at our every move. I strained to listen, willing there to be nothing.

"I don't hear anything," I whispered. "Put the light back on."

"No. Just wait."

The darkness was not quite absolute; a dim rectangle of dark gray showed the gap between the room we were in and the next, but most of the light from the other room was cut off by the cupboard in its corner. On all other sides the dark was absolute. My eyes strained to make out anything in a blackness so complete that it seemed to have a texture of its own. I imagined it as black velvety fur like Pluto's, black fur that my outstretched fingers could almost have touched as they groped uselessly in the air. It pressed in softly and insistently from all sides, enveloping and choking me.

"Stefan—" I started, and then I heard it. A muffled but very definite *thump.* It sounded as though someone had tried to bounce one of the heavy balls they had in the school gym. I flailed with my hands in the air, trying to catch hold of Stefan's shoulder, his sleeve, anything, just as long as I didn't have to be in the dark all on my own. A moment later I heard a second *thump,* then a dragging pause, and then the sound was repeated. *Thump.* My heart seemed to pound in time with it, a sledgehammer threatening to shatter its cage of ribs.

"*O Gott.* What are we going to do?" I quavered. The sound had to be coming from the cellar we had just passed through—hadn't it? It must be disorientation from the darkness that made me think it came from somewhere behind me, somewhere in the black depths of the unlit room. Since we could not escape through the cellar we must try to hide ourselves here. But how?

"Stay still," whispered Stefan.

Stupidly I nodded, forgetting that he could not see me. I swallowed, and it was like swallowing a mouthful of dust. I did my best to stay absolutely motionless, but it was not like playing some sort of children's game, trying not to blink while someone walked around you looking for involuntary movements. Now my pose felt more like the painful rigidity of a muscle spasm. My right leg was trembling so violently that the sole of my boot made soft sounds on the stone floor. Out of the darkness came a rasping sound like someone clearing their throat. The next second something brushed past my calf with muscular intent. Hot panic seethed through me like acid. With a scream that scoured my throat I lunged away from the unseen thing, and suddenly found myself plunging forward into space. I had stepped over the edge of the well.

Instinctively, I raised my arms to protect myself from the impact against the opposite side. My right forearm hit the stone with such force that pain ricocheted up to my shoulder in a blazing trail, then I felt myself falling backward for what seemed like an interminable time. At last I hit the water.

It was shockingly cold. I went right under, and then struggled my way to the surface, my clothes soaked and heavy, my right arm throbbing with pain. I put my hands out to find the sides of the well and touched nothing. With a titanic effort I lifted my waterlogged arms out of the water, treading water frantically, but I couldn't feel anything above me either.

A sudden horrible vision streaked across my mind—I had fallen into an enormous subterranean lake, limitless in all directions. I would flail about in it until exhaustion and the weight of my sodden clothes dragged me under. I screamed, took in half a mouthful of water, and choked. The water tasted foul, tainted. For a second I went under again. Even when I was fully submerged my feet did not touch the bottom. I surfaced again, gasping.

At last one of my groping hands brushed against something solid. My fingertips scraped along what felt like stones, slick with wet. My relief was short-lived; there was nothing to hang on to. My fingers trailed uselessly along the smooth surface. I struck out, mindless of the pain in my forearm, fighting to stay afloat. The cold was seeping through every inch of clothing. Struggling to keep my face out of the water, I shouted, *"Stefan!"*

There was no reply.

"Ste—!" I swallowed another mouthful of water and the shout turned into a choking cough. I threshed about with my arms, beating at the stone wall with the flat of my hands as though trying to break a door down. Then finally my fingers closed upon something, something I could grasp with both hands.

At first I thought it was some sort of debris, a piece of tree branch wrapped in a tangle of rubbish, carried along from some part of the river that was open to the air and now jammed against the side of the well. It was not pleasant to touch the sodden surface of it, something that felt like sacking, slimy to the touch.

I hung on with my left hand and let my right roam over the thing, my mind trying to make sense of what I felt, blinded by the dark. There was something suggestive about the shape of whatever I was clutching, something from which my imagination shied.

Dimly I was aware that it was no longer fully dark in the well. Someone had put on a light in the room above, or else carried in a powerful lantern. I should call for help. Regardless of who was up there, and of the consequences of the enormities Stefan and I had committed, it was too late to recover the situation ourselves. Still something kept me dumb, some dawning realization that closed my throat with horror. My fingers were moving over something appallingly familiar, but from the shape only; the texture was all wrong.

Wax, I thought, *or soap.* For a split second a spurt of hope so strong it was like joy flared up inside me. I was touching a doll. Or a dummy. My fingers moved over the curve of a cheek, the unmistakable whorl of an ear. A doll. Crudely made, but . . .

The light was growing stronger. Someone was letting a lamp down the well; I heard a brittle *clink* as it swung into the stonework, then it cleared the bottom of the walls and yellow light flooded the space below. Suddenly I could see what it was that I was holding and screamed. In blind animal panic I let go and tried to flail my way backward through the water, anything to get away from it, the thing that had somehow jammed itself against the wall, a thing I recognized but in a form I had never seen before, a *wrong* form. *"O Gott, O Gott,"* I howled. All I could think was, *It has teeth.*

Chapter Forty-six

⁂

*S*tefan! Stefan!" I had literally screamed myself hoarse. With a supernatural energy born of sheer terror, I lunged upward, trying to grab the lantern that swung overhead in a desperate attempt to pull myself out of the well with its appalling occupant.

Instantly the lantern moved up with one swift jerk, out of range of my flailing hands. Whoever was holding the cord it was attached to was reeling it in. The light was receding, and the shadows were racing in from all sides.

"*Noooooo!*" Threshing and kicking, I felt my boot come into contact with something in the water, a thing that bobbed and spun away from me in the darkness. Something seemed to implode inside me. I could not even scream anymore. A tiny croak, a squeak, forced its way out, and then all I could hear was the sound of my own ragged breathing sawing painfully through the air. I would go mad; I *was* going mad.

I could no longer feel the thing that had bobbed away from me in the dark, but I knew it was there, spinning around in the black water an arm's reach away from me. How many of the things were there in the well with me? *Katharina Linden. Marion Voss . . .* but even if I had been lucid enough to count, it would have been meaningless. These things floating like sodden logs in the inky water with me had nothing to do with the missing girls—they had become something else altogether.

Far above me, where a dim circle of yellow light was still faintly discernible, there came a curious grinding sound. Grinding—or scraping. Someone was lugging something heavy across the stone floor.

"Hilfe." I tried to yell for help but the sound came out flat and tiny, as though the darkness had muffled it. *"Hilfe."*

There was no answering call, but I heard someone make a grunt, as though with exertion. The next second there was a dull thump as a flagstone fell into place over the top of the well, cutting off the last of the light and sealing me in the darkness.

Chapter Forty-seven

❧

I don't remember very much about the time after the light went out. I had no sense of time passing. It might have been five minutes or it might have been an hour that I spent suspended in the cold and dark, with nothing but the rasp of my own breathing, vibrating with the shivers that racked my body.

I dared not try to swim back to the wall, but in the absolute blackness I became disoriented and eventually bumped right into it. My hands closed over a stone that jutted out a little and at last I was able to hang on and gain some respite from the exhausting effort to swim in waterlogged clothing.

My thoughts, which had been racing around my brain like trapped insects, seemed to have run themselves down in ever-decreasing circles, until I was conscious of nothing but the pain of my freezing fingers clamped over the cold stone.

There were no last-minute visions of my life flashing before my eyes, no last prayers for my parents and my little brother. There was no past, no future, only the cold and the dark, and the implacable stone. The water seemed to be rising; it was no longer merely at my shoulders, it was lapping my chin. Was it really rising, or was I sinking? It no longer seemed important.

When the sounds started above me I was hardly even interested any-more. My brain registered them without understanding. Metal on stone, scraping, muffled voices. None of it seemed to add up to any-thing that had any relevance to me. The pain in my right arm had set-tled into a nagging ache and I couldn't even feel my fingers. I wondered if they were still clamped over the jutting stone. Perhaps I had let go and drowned already, and this black limbo was all that awaited me afterward.

"Pia?" Stefan's disembodied voice drifted down the well shaft. I didn't reply. *"Pia?"* There was a note of panic in it this time. Voices murmured at the top of the well. Then I heard something whisper down the shaft and hit the water with a soft splash. Someone had thrown down a rope.

"Pia! Pia, are you all right?"

"Yes," I croaked faintly.

More conferring at the top of the well. Then light pierced the dark-ness. It would have been comical in other circumstances; Stefan had let down his flashlight on a string. It hung there like a visitor from another world, the light of a submarine deep in a black ocean. I concentrated on the light, not wanting to look at anything else in the well. My neck felt stiff from turning. With one hand I let go of the stone. Hesitantly, I reached for the rope.

"Can you hold on?" shouted Stefan.

"No," I said. I wasn't sure I had spoken loudly enough for him to hear me. I felt too tired to care. I watched with little interest as the rope vanished upward and there were more voices. It sounded as though Ste-fan were arguing with someone.

I closed my eyes. It was like listening to a radio playing in another room. I tried to imagine that I was in Oma Kristel's kitchen, sitting at the table waiting for her to finish making me a mug of cocoa, the radio playing in the background. There were scuffling noises, and then an-other splash as something hit the water, somewhat louder than the first time.

"Pia," said Stefan's voice, very close by. I felt something touch my shoulder. Then: "Oh, *Scheisse.*" I guessed Stefan had seen the other things that were in the well. I squeezed my eyes more tightly shut. "Oh, *Scheisse,* Pia. Oh—"

I wished he would shut up. I didn't want to be reminded of what was in the water. But the feeling of his arms around me, his hands gripping me, felt reassuring. Rope slid around me and then I was going upward. I let myself be lifted like a rag doll. There was light above me and I was moving toward it in painful jerks. I thought, *Perhaps I have died.* I had not expected it to hurt so much afterward. Then I was at the top of the well, lying like an enormous fish on a fishmonger's slab, my mouth opening and closing wetly. Water was streaming down the side of my face from my hair. Someone was turning me over. I looked up and in the lamplight I saw who it was and screamed.

Chapter Forty-eight

hut up, Pia!" shouted Stefan. He was standing over me, water dripping from the bottom half of his jeans and his boots. As I paused to
draw breath, I heard him say, "Shall I slap her?"

With a superhuman effort I stifled my screams. My lips worked uselessly; no coherent words came out. Still I pointed with a shaking hand
at the person who stood next to Stefan, watching me silently: Herr
Düster, his starved features even craggier than usual in the lantern
light. If his thin upper lip had drawn back to reveal the long, gleaming
canines of a vampire I couldn't have been more hysterically terrified.

Uppermost in the boiling cataract of my brain was the conviction
that at any moment Herr Düster would throw *both* of us back into the
well. Without a rescuer we would both drown there in the dark, with
the atrocious things that wallowed in the black waters.

Stefan kneeled by me and took my shoulders in his two hands. "Calm
down, Pia. You're OK now. You're out of the well."

"He—" I gibbered, trying to point at Herr Düster again. Stefan had
his back to him—couldn't he see what danger he was in?

"It's OK," Stefan said, as though talking to a kindergarten child.
"Herr Düster *helped* us. I couldn't have got the stone off the top of the
well without him."

Doggedly, I shook my head. *Didn't you see what was in the well?* I wanted to scream. I struggled to get up from the floor but my limbs were stiff with cold and damp and I simply succeeded in floundering about like a pig in mud.

"She will get hypothermia," said someone. With a shock I realized it was Herr Düster. I had so rarely heard him speak before. His voice sounded calm and measured. This was a surprise too; somehow I had imagined him having a wild, insane voice like an animal, or being like the girl in the fairy tale who dropped a toad out of her mouth every time she opened it to speak. On the contrary, he actually sounded quite sane.

"Put this around her," said Herr Düster. He was holding out my down jacket. Either he or Stefan had retrieved it from underneath the sideboard.

Stefan pulled me toward him and for a sickening moment I thought they were both in league; he was going to roll me over the edge of the well again and the pair of them would listen to me drown. But I realized that he was pulling off my sodden sweater. Icy water ran down my back. The T-shirt he left on for modesty's sake; the down jacket went over it.

While Stefan was struggling with the zip at the front, I stared mistrustfully at Herr Düster over his shoulder. Why was he helping us?

"What did you see in the well, Pia?" he asked. His eyes were sunk in pools of shadow. I could not tell what he was thinking.

"Nothing," I stuttered.

Stefan pulled back from me and shot me a look of astonishment. "Pia, tell him."

"Nothing," I managed again. I was not about to let Herr Düster know that I had seen the bodies of his victims down there in the inky waters. I had a vague conviction that if he did not know that we knew what he had done, we might still get away. But before I could stop him, Stefan had blurted it out.

"Herr Düster—there are *dead people.*"

Herr Düster must have seen my face.

"Do you think that *I* put them in the well, Fräulein Pia?" he asked.

Frantically, I shook my head. Stefan had finished zipping up the jacket. I made another attempt to get up, and this time I was more successful. I managed to rise until I was on one knee, as though I were about to propose to someone. I wondered if my cramped legs could carry me if I tried to make a run for it.

"You told him," I accused Stefan through cold lips.

"Of course I did," he answered impatiently. For a sickening moment Stefan strode through my imagination in the role of murderer's accomplice. Perhaps he felt me stiffen. He said, "Pia, he didn't do it. Someone else did."

Involuntarily I glanced upward. This was Herr Düster's house. Somewhere above our heads was the living room where he sat among the fading photographs of friends and family long dead. How could the well under his house be full of—those things—and it wasn't him who had put them there?

"What did you see, Pia? How many?"

"Nothing."

There was a pregnant silence during which we regarded each other in the yellow lantern light. Herr Düster opened his mouth to say something else, and in that moment we all heard it. A muffled sound, but very definite. The sound of a door closing.

Herr Düster raised a bony finger to his lips. In the silence, the shuddering of my breath sounded enormous. With a great effort I made myself breathe more deeply and quietly, pressing my hands to my face as though to stop my teeth chattering.

Herr Düster picked up the lantern, and mimed a twisting motion: *I'm going to turn it off. Don't panic.* A moment later we were in darkness. I hunched forward, trying to curl myself into a protective ball. The arms and body of the jacket whispered together and instantly I froze.

Thump. Thump-thump.

My body cringed at every muffled sound as though it were a blow. *Run!* screamed the most primitive part of my brain, howling and ranting like a caged animal. The only thing that prevented me from trying it was the knowledge that the well was still uncovered, waiting for the unwary to plunge into its black waters.

As my eyes adjusted to the darkness I stared with horrid fascination at the long gray oblong that was the door to the first room of the cellar. Again I had the dizzying feeling that the sounds were not coming from

there at all. I felt a light touch on my shoulder: Stefan. I turned, gazing
into the dark.

To my astonishment, I realized that where there had been absolute
blackness at the other side of the room, now there was a jagged patch of
faint gray-yellow light. As I struggled to make sense of what I was seeing—could it be some sort of reflection of the doorway?—it became
stronger and brighter, and I realized that the light patch was another
entrance to the room, a narrow ragged-edged hole, just large enough for
a man to step through. Where it led to I could not imagine. Thoughts
seethed in my brain like a swarm of darting fish. Terror and cold had
banished rational thought, but even an animal, unable to reason, knows
when it is in danger. Someone with a light had come through that entrance once before and shut me in the well to die; that someone was
coming back.

In blind panic I scrabbled at the flagstones, struggling to get to my
feet, and my boot struck something on the floor: the lantern. With a
clatter that sounded alarmingly loud in the chill darkness, it rolled over
the edge of the well. There was a loud *clank* followed by a splash.

A split second later the approaching light went out. There was a silence so pregnant that involuntarily I held my breath. Then we heard
the sound of someone stumbling in the hole, turning around in a lim-
ited space with difficulty, moving heavily, perhaps burdened with something that made it hard to move easily. We heard ragged footsteps, the
sound of someone moving as fast as possible over uneven ground in the
dark.

There was a muffled exclamation from Herr Düster, and a click. As
light bloomed I saw that he had Stefan's flashlight in his hand. He nodded at Stefan. "Come." He glanced at me. "Stay here, Pia."

"No!" I couldn't think of anything worse than being left there alone
in the dark.

Staggering to my feet, I tottered stiffly as a scarecrow. Herr Düster
had not waited to see whether I had obeyed his injunction: he was already at the mouth of the hole, Stefan close behind him. In savage
determination I limped across the flagstones, although every movement
seemed to jar painfully through my whole body, and stumbled after
them into the hole.

Chapter Forty-nine

*E*ntering the jagged hole in the wall, I could see little more than the black shapes of Stefan and Herr Düster, backlit by the flashlight. Still, I could make out a little of the tunnel we were in, from the weak yellow light and the feel of the walls under my hands. They felt surprisingly regular: I thought I could feel the shape of bricks, as neatly fitted together as a garden path.

Somehow I had imagined the hole as an organic thing, a tunnel burrowed crudely through the earth as though by a monstrous mole. It had no right to be there, after all. But this tunnel was *meant.* Someone had taken the trouble to build a secret pathway underneath the Orchheimer Strasse, though what their motive might be I could not begin to guess.

It was long: we must be out from under Herr Düster's house by now. The movement was bringing some sort of life back into my frozen limbs, though my legs felt as cold as a butcher's slab, my sodden trousers sticking uncomfortably to my skin. I felt as though I had returned to myself; fear and excitement had sobered me up as smartly as a slap to the face.

Abruptly, Stefan stopped and I suddenly found myself pressed up against his back.

"What?" I asked excitedly. I could see absolutely nothing apart from the halo of the flashlight around his head.

"It is a room." Herr Düster's voice sounded oddly flat. I shoved at Stefan's back.

"Go on."

Stefan stepped forward, moving warily: I guessed that he was thinking of my fall into the well. Now that he was out of the way I could see a little of the room we were in.

"It's someone's cellar." I could not keep the disappointment out of my voice. I had been expecting something more dramatic: a vampire's crypt, or a mad scientist's laboratory. Not this smugly dull room with its contents so neatly stored away.

Shelves filled one side of the cellar, stacked with boxes and crates. On the other side old furniture stood in a prim line, backs to the wall like old maids at a tea dance. A selection of garden tools had been hung up on hooks, spaced at exactly equal intervals, like a display in a museum. The only thing that was at all out of place was right at my feet: a pile of bricks, still with ragged chunks of mortar attached.

Herr Düster was standing in the center of the room, moving the beam of the flashlight slowly over the stacked shelves. He did not seem disposed to continue his pursuit of whomever or whatever it was we had heard escaping through the tunnel.

"Herr Düster, we have to go," said Stefan, urgently.

The old man raised his head and looked at him.

"He's getting away!" Stefan sounded beside himself. "We have to move."

Herr Düster moved his head. I think he meant to shake it, but the movement was so slight that it looked as though he had simply turned his neck, as if there were something he didn't wish to hear. The beam of light wavered along the line of shelves.

"We have to—" began Stefan.

"I think," said Herr Düster, and his voice sounded curiously sad, "I think that we must call the police."

"No," said Stefan instantly. He gave a great sigh of exasperation. "If—if we go back now and call them, he'll get *away*."

Herr Düster said something in such a low voice that neither of us could hear what it was. Then he said, more loudly, "It is for the police. Not for—children."

"*Verdammt!*" snapped Stefan. He actually stamped his foot, like a small child. His hands clutched the air in frustration, as though trying to tear something down. "We're not *babies.*" He glared at Herr Düster. "*We'll go.* Give me my flashlight back."

Herr Düster didn't move. Stefan took a step toward him, and Herr Düster involuntarily stepped back. The beam swung in a wide arc. Perhaps they would actually have come to a hand-to-hand struggle for the flashlight. However, as the beam swept across the cellar floor, I saw something.

"Look."

They both followed the direction of my outstretched finger. Something lay on the stone floor, close by the claw feet of an ugly escritoire. A single boot. A girl's boot made of pale pink suede with a fussy-looking fake-fur trim. The side zip was undone and the boot yawned open, exposing its furry throat.

"What is that?" said Herr Düster in a voice rimed with dread.

"It's a boot," said Stefan in the tone of someone stating an obvious fact. The real import of Herr Düster's question, *What in God's name is that doing here?* had passed him by. He stooped and picked it up. As he turned back to us, Herr Düster flinched. He looked at the boot as though it were some repulsive thing, a great spider or a decomposing rat. In the sickly light his seamed face looked more wrinkled than ever. The myriad lines on his ancient features seemed to shiver and reform under the influence of a powerful emotion, but what it was I could not tell.

"It's probably from one of the girls, the ones—" I began, and stopped. I had been about to say *the ones who went missing.* But those girls were no longer missing; we knew where they were.

"Maybe," murmured Stefan, turning the boot over in his hands. He looked at me. "Or maybe it's a new one."

I stared at him, my mouth open. Suddenly an image flashed across my mind: my father standing in the kitchen with the telephone in his hand, saying, "Kolvenbach" and "*Mein Gott.*" If my mother had not told him to *just go,* he would have said, "Another girl is missing."

"*Lieber Gott,*" said Herr Düster quietly.

"Herr Düster—?" started Stefan.

The old man regarded him, an unfathomable expression on his face.

Then, slowly, he nodded. "We will go. But," he added somberly, before Stefan could take off like a greyhound, "as soon as it is possible, we will call the police. *Verstanden?*"

"Yes," agreed Stefan instantly. He held the boot out to Herr Düster, but the old man shuddered and declined to touch it, so he stuffed it inside his own jacket.

Cautiously, we picked our way to the other end of the cellar. In the far right corner was an opening the size of a doorway but with no door across it. Stone stairs spiraled up out of sight. Stefan found a light switch on the wall by the staircase and tried it, but nothing happened. Either the bulb had blown or the power had been switched off.

Stefan made as if to start up the stairs, but Herr Düster laid a restraining hand on his shoulder.

"*I* will go first," he said firmly. There was a challenging note in his voice that made me think of Oma Kristel's reaction whenever my father or Onkel Thomas had told her to take things easy and think of her age. He began to climb the stone stairs, Stefan and I following as closely as we could.

Inevitably the stairs, having curled back on themselves, reached an abrupt end at a narrow and very firmly locked door. Herr Düster applied his shoulder to it and it jumped a little but did not open. However, the very fact that it had moved was encouraging; if it had been bolted in place from the other side I doubted it would have moved at all.

Stefan pushed past Herr Düster and hurled himself at the door, thumping it with his shoulder like an American football player so that it rattled in the frame. But still nothing happened. Herr Düster and I crowded onto the lower steps to give him more room.

This time Stefan aimed a mighty kick at the lock. I listened in frank amazement to wood splintering. More and more I had the impression that Stefan lived his life in some sort of imaginative action movie. He launched another kick and with a mighty *crack!* the door gave way and swung open, almost precipitating him on the other side. He steadied himself and would have started through the doorframe, but Herr raised a finger to his lips to indicate that we should stay silent and listen first.

I could see very little of what was on the other side of the door, since both Stefan and Herr Düster were now crowded into the frame. I could make out a wall papered with a rather old-fashioned design, and the side of a light-brown lampshade lit from within by a low-wattage bulb. The lamp was nondescript but the wallpaper pattern gave me pause: it was somehow familiar. Wreaths of stylized foliage, faded green and brown against an ivory background. Every so often there was a curling leaf shape faintly reminiscent of a fish.

Gently, I pushed at Stefan's back. "Let me out." As he moved forward I stepped out into the room behind him. We stood, side by side, Herr Düster's presence forgotten. I could hear Stefan panting from the exertion of kicking in the door; he sounded as though he had been running. He was staring about him like a tourist in a cathedral, as though he couldn't quite take in everything he was seeing. At last he turned to me, with the words on his lips, but I got there first.

"I know this house."

Chapter Fifty

⁂

*H*ow can it *be?*" said Stefan. He looked dazed. "How can we be . . .
here?"

I glanced at Herr Düster, as though being the only adult he might
produce a rational explanation. Herr Düster was the only one of us who
didn't look as though he were overwhelmed with surprise. He looked
grave and incalculably sorrowful, like a doctor at a deathbed.

"My brother . . ." He pronounced the words strangely, as though
rolling an unfamiliar and bitter taste around his mouth. "My brother's
house," he said eventually.

"But it can't be," I said, as if I were pointing out an obvious fact to
the very stupid. "It can't be Herr Schiller's house. I mean . . ."

My voice trailed off. I looked around me again. We were in a narrow
hallway, one that I knew. I had stood very close to this spot a hundred times,
perhaps more, shrugging my coat off my shoulders so that Herr Schiller
could hang it on one of the pegs. I put out a hand and touched the shining dark surface of the hall table. It felt hard and cool under my fingers.

"Did he—you know—" I didn't want to say *the murderer* "—I mean,
how did he get in here? How could he go through the cellar without
Herr Schiller—" I looked from Herr Düster to Stefan, not understanding their expressions "—without Herr Schiller knowing?" I finished.

There was a long silence. The two of them, old man and boy, were staring at each other. Something was passing between them that I didn't understand.

"He's gone," said Stefan in a tight voice.

"Yes," said Herr Düster, but his lips barely moved, and his voice was very low.

"I'll look . . ." said Stefan, and he went to the front door and tried the handle. It opened easily and the door swung open. Stefan leaned out. I could see that a considerable amount of snow had fallen since we entered Herr Düster's house; everything outside was blanketed with pure white. It was still falling; when Stefan pulled his head back inside, his hair was covered with melting white flakes. He came up to Herr Düster like a foot soldier reporting to his sergeant.

"I couldn't see him—but there're tracks."

Herr Düster nodded, almost absently.

"I'm not sure, but I think they went around the side of the house."

"The car, yes," said Herr Düster, almost inaudibly. He seemed sunk in thought.

"What car?" I asked, but no one answered me.

"Do you know where—?" asked Stefan, and I shot him a look of frustration; everyone seemed to be talking in code.

Herr Düster nodded. "I think so. Yes, I think so."

"What are you going on about?" I was almost hopping with annoyance. "Look, why don't we wake Herr Schiller up?"

"Pia—"

"We're in his house, after all."

"Yes, his house," said Herr Düster with gentle emphasis. Still I didn't get it.

"Pia," said Stefan in a tired voice, "it's Herr Schiller. Don't you see?"

"What do you mean?" I stared at him. "What do you mean, it's Herr Schiller?"

"It's Herr Schiller who . . ." Stefan changed tack at the last moment, as though swerving to avoid an obstacle. "It's him we have to follow," he said. "He's the one who's gone."

"I don't understand—" I began, but suddenly I did. A wave of nausea swept over me. I sagged back against the wall with the pattern of foliage on it. "No," I said in a strangled voice.

Stefan looked at me helplessly. Then he turned back to Herr Düster. "We have to go. We have to go right *now*." I was being dismissed.

"Stefan, this is a joke, right?" I said. My voice sounded unconvincing even to my own ears. "Where are we going? Shouldn't we call the police—if someone—?"

"We don't have time." His voice was cool, but he was not trying to be unpleasant. He was stating a fact: if there were even the remotest chance of finding the owner of the boot before it was too late we had to leave *now*. If we waited we would lose any chance of catching—*him*. The one who had taken all those girls. The one who had left me in the well to drown among the wallowing horrors. I could only think of him as *the one*, not as Herr Schiller. It was impossible.

"Pia, you stay here."

"No! No way, no . . ." I was stuttering in outrage. "No, you're not leaving me here! I'm coming with you."

"Pia." Herr Düster sounded remarkably calm, although he must have been as aware as Stefan was of the seconds ticking by, the minutes trickling away, snowflakes twirling lazily down from the black sky and blanketing the tracks in snow. "You are soaked through. You can't go out in the snow. You'll freeze to death."

"You said a car," I pointed out sulkily.

"*His* car," said Stefan.

"Yes, but you can't follow him unless you go in one too," I retorted. I glared at Stefan. He regarded me for a moment and then turned to Herr Düster.

"We have to go."

Herr Düster looked at me for a long moment. If he were any other adult in the world I think he would have insisted that I stay inside in the warm. But either Herr Düster had been out of the company of other adults so long that he had forgotten the way things were supposed to be done, or he was one of those rare people who do not treat children as though they are completely incapable. He nodded sharply to me and said, "Pia, you may come with us, but you *must* stay in the car. *Verstanden?*"

"Yes." I was breathless in my gratitude.

"Stay here, both of you, while I fetch the car."

"But—" I started, but he cut me off.

"He's not coming back. Not for a while, anyway. You're quite safe here."

I shut my mouth but I felt uneasy. My objection to staying in the house was not that I was afraid of Herr Schiller coming back, but that it gave Herr Düster the opportunity to go off without us. All the same, I could see the logic of his plan when he opened Herr Schiller's front door: the icy draft on my wet jeans was so glacially cold that the skin of my legs felt as though it were burning off. I hugged the down jacket around me. My teeth were chattering.

"This is crazy," said Stefan, not unkindly. "You should stay here, Pia. You're going to freeze to death."

"No way," I said, clamping my mouth shut to try to stop the chattering.

"I wonder how he knows where—you know, where *he* went?" said Stefan.

"Um." I couldn't think of any reply. That Herr Schiller should have had any involvement at all in the disappearances of my schoolmates was terrifying enough; to try to imagine where he might have gone to and for what reason was completely beyond me. I still had the feeling that I might wake up and discover the whole thing was some kind of out-landish dream.

For what seemed like ages Stefan and I stood in the hallway of our friend's home and waited for Herr Düster to arrive with the car. There was a feeling of subdued expectancy about the situation, as though we were the survivors of some bloody accident, waiting for the ambulance to arrive. I could not think of anything to say and it seemed that nei-ther could Stefan, so for a long time we stood there in silence.

I was starting to wonder whether Herr Düster *had* gone off without us, when I suddenly heard a slight sound behind me. It was a soft sound, the sound of a velvet curtain brushing the floor, but it struck me cold. I do not know whether it is true that at such times the hair on the back of one's neck stands up, but I felt as though an icy hand had been placed there. Before I could turn around or say anything, the soft slith-ering was followed by a sound like someone clearing their throat.

"Ste-fan . . ." I thought I might faint or be sick.

"What?"

"There's something . . ." I forced myself to turn around.

There in the cellar doorway sat Pluto, regarding us balefully with his great yellow eyes. As I watched, his mouth yawned open, revealing a pink tongue and needle-sharp teeth, and he spat again. Then he turned with sinuous swiftness and disappeared down the spiral stairs.

Stefan exhaled slowly at my shoulder. "*Verdammter* cat."

I nodded, swallowing.

"Are you all right? Did he scare you?"

"Not really. I just thought . . ." But I was not sure what I had thought. Useless to try to describe the grotesque ideas that had flitted through my brain when I heard that soft whispering noise and the rasping sound. I had stepped into trolldom that night, and now nothing was too horrible to be true. *The monsters are loose,* I thought, and my mind skidded neatly around the memory of what I had seen in the well.

"That's how he got into Herr Schiller's house," said Stefan suddenly. He touched my arm. "You remember, that time he made us jump?" He had conveniently forgotten that it was *he* who had jumped, *he* who had screamed the place down. Still, I couldn't be bothered to correct him. I nodded. Stefan was still looking at the doorway where the cat had been. At last he gave a low whistle.

"No wonder Herr Schiller went mad when he saw him. He must have known Pluto came through the cellar. He probably didn't shut the door properly." He shook his head disbelievingly. "I bet he thought Pluto had given the whole game away."

I wasn't listening. I was thinking of the moment before I fell into the well, of the sounds I had heard and the thing that had brushed against my leg and made me panic so that I sprang forward into nothingness. Pluto. I was thinking that if I ever got hold of him I would like to put my hands around that furry throat and strangle him.

Chapter Fifty-one

ights outside the front door and the low purr of an engine announced the arrival of Herr Düster and the car. I yanked on the zip
of my down jacket, trying to ensure maximum protection from the
cold, and then Stefan and I stepped outside. It was dark in the street
and snowflakes were still falling, whirling down so thickly that it was
difficult to make anything out, but still we were impressed when we
saw the car.

"Wow," said Stefan.

Herr Düster leaned over and pushed open the passenger side door a
little. "Get in," he shouted. Stefan slid into the front passenger seat; I
had to make do with the backseat. Herr Düster did not wait for Stefan
to finish doing up his seat belt; he had already started moving forward.

"We need to get the car warm," he said, glancing back over his
shoulder at me.

"I'm all right," I said, hugging myself.

"This is an amazing car." Stefan was looking at the interior as though
studying the ceiling of the Sistine Chapel. "What is it?"

"A Mercedes 230 *Heckflosse,*" said Herr Düster without turning his
head. He was peering at the street ahead through a screen of swirling
snowflakes.

"Is it really *yours?*"

Now Herr Düster did give him a look. "*Natürlich.* I am not in the habit of stealing cars."

"It's just . . . I've never seen it before."

"I don't take it out very often," said Herr Düster. He patted the steering wheel. "That is why it took me a little time to fetch it. I had to move a few things, and get the cover off."

"If I had a car like this," said Stefan, "I would drive it everywhere."

"Then you would need a very large bank balance," said Herr Düster drily.

I stared out of the window at the darkened street. We were turning right, toward the Klosterplatz, where the bonfire had been on St. Martin's Eve, and where Frau Mahlberg had shaken me until my teeth chattered, screaming for her lost daughter. The muffled white shapes of a few snow-covered cars were visible, snowflakes tumbling down around them. I leaned too close to the glass and the window was suddenly opaque.

"Where are we going?" I asked.

"The Eschweiler Tal," said Herr Düster. His voice was cool and precise.

I sat up. "Why the Eschweiler Tal? How do you know he's going there?"

Herr Düster did not reply. We had crossed the Klosterplatz and were traveling down the street toward the Protestant church. In a few moments we would have passed underneath the arch in the town walls. Herr Düster was driving as fast as he dared, but the road surface was treacherous. I could feel the old Mercedes gliding on the snow and ice.

"Herr Düster?" I had the uncomfortable feeling that I was being rude, but I couldn't bear not to ask the question. "How do you *know* he's going to the Eschweiler Tal?"

"I don't," said Herr Düster grimly.

"Then why—?"

"He is my brother," said Herr Düster, "and I know him."

I recognized the uncompromising tone in his voice and sat back, not daring to ask any more questions, though my brain was seething with them. How could he say he knew Herr Schiller when he never spoke to him? How could he be so sure where Herr Schiller was going?

Once out of the town walls, Herr Düster turned toward the railway station and the north end of the town. There was no one about. Small Eifel towns like Bad Münstereifel are always pretty dead by midnight, but tonight the cold and snow had driven even the taxi drivers and the bored street-corner youths back indoors.

I saw a police car parked outside the station: at first I thought there was no one in it but then the windshield wipers lurched into life and cleared an arc of snow away. Herr Düster hesitated and I felt the car slow, but then he suddenly accelerated and the car lurched forward. Before I could see who was inside the police car, we had passed it and were heading out of town. The interior of the car was warming up; soon my wet clothes would be steaming.

"Can we get into the Eschweiler Tal in the snow?" asked Stefan.

Herr Düster said nothing.

It took another five minutes to reach the track leading into the Esch-weiler Tal, during which time we saw not one other car. On the last stretch of asphalt road the tracks of another vehicle stood out like ruts in the deepening snow. There was a factory there at the end of the road, with a parking lot in front of it and a security gate at the side, but the tracks went straight past it and into the Tal. My skin prickled as I saw them, leaning over Stefan's shoulder to peer through the windshield.

There are a couple of houses in the Eschweiler Tal, but I knew whoever had driven through here before us was not an honest householder on his way home. It was far too dark, too cold, and too late for that.

The road rose very slightly where the asphalt ran out and the track began. For a moment I thought the old Mercedes wouldn't manage the slope, but Herr Düster knew what he was doing. He accelerated just enough to get the right momentum without skidding. Whoever had been before us had not been so lucky, judging by the wild sweeps of the tracks in the snow ahead of us.

"Where *is* he?" hissed Stefan.

Herr Düster said nothing. We traveled in silence along the valley. He dropped a gear and the car successfully crested the slight rise by the old quarry. There is a right turn there uphill toward the village of Esch-weiler, where the young men were supposed to have been sitting when they saw the unholy light of the Fiery Man of the Hirnberg coming toward them, but it must have been impassable in the snow. In any event, the fishtailing tracks ahead of us went right past it and deeper into the Tal.

"He can't have got away," said Stefan, but it was a question, not a statement. Still we had not seen any sign of the vehicle ahead, only the tracks. If we failed to catch up with the car ahead, they were about as much use to us as archaeological relics. I racked my brains to think where the track ended. I had been in the Tal dozens of times, either with the school or with my parents, but we had always entered it from the end by the factory or from the footpath leading down from the Hirnberg. I wasn't sure where the main track itself ended. If it came out on a main road somewhere, then the car we were following would have vanished untraceably by the time we reached the end of the Tal.

"There," said Stefan suddenly, and Herr Düster must have jumped, because the car lurched and I bumped my forehead painfully on the window.

"Where?" I said.

He pointed. Herr Düster brought the car to a careful standstill as we all gazed out through windshield. Less than a hundred meters ahead of us was an intersection where the track went straight ahead up the Tal or sharply left over a stone bridge toward the tree-covered hillside. Parked by the bridge was a dark-colored car with the driver's door open. I say parked, but it looked as though the tail end of the car had slewed around and struck the stone wall of the bridge. The yawning door gave the car an abandoned look. There was no sign of anyone near it.

There was a creak as Herr Düster applied the hand brake. He turned the ignition off and as the purr of the engine died he leaned forward as though he were praying, until his forehead was almost touching the steering wheel. He was motionless for a few moments, thinking. Stefan began fumbling at the passenger door, but a gnarled hand reached out and grasped him firmly but gently by the shoulder.

"No," said Herr Düster, turning his face to him. There was a weariness about the gesture that made me think of Sebastian when he had cried himself out. "Stay here. I'll go."

"I want to come too," said Stefan stubbornly.

"No." Herr Düster shook his head. "This is for me." He paused. "You have to stay here and take care of Pia."

I was outraged by that, and started to say that I wasn't a baby, and didn't need taking care of by anyone, but Herr Düster simply said, "If anyone comes . . . it's safer with two." He opened the door of the Mercedes and climbed out. The sound of the car door shutting was immediately echoed by the thump of Stefan's clenched fist on the upholstery.

"*Scheisse—Mist—!*" His rage filled the inside of the car like a fly buzzing inside a bottle.

"Calm down." I watched through the window as the dark shape of Herr Düster went to the back of the Mercedes and opened the trunk. He retrieved something, a coat, I thought, and closed it again. As he moved away from the car I said in a low voice, "Wait till he's gone."

We watched Herr Düster trudging off into the snow, lifting the coat so that he could thread his arms into it and pull it tightly around himself.

"Stefan?"

"Yes?" Stefan sounded distracted.

"What's going on? With Herr Düster, I mean. What's he helping us for?" *Helping* was not exactly the right word; *taking over* was more like it, but I couldn't think of a better way to put the question. "Wasn't he furious when he found you in the house?"

Now that I started to think about it, questions were sprouting up everywhere like weeds. "Wasn't he supposed to be away, anyway?"

"*Mensch,* Pia! I don't know." Stefan's voice was irritable. "Look, he just came home. I don't know where he was and I didn't get time to ask him. When you and I heard someone coming in the cellar, I just ran and hid. I heard you fall into the well but I couldn't do anything about it until he—whoever it was—had gone. Then I couldn't get the stone off the well so I *had* to get help. I went upstairs and Herr Düster was just coming in."

"Was he angry when he saw you?"

"No—yes—I mean, he was shocked, but he wasn't angry. He was cool. But he did say we'd have a lot of explaining to do later."

"*Scheisse.*"

"What was I supposed to do? I couldn't get the stone up by myself."

"Weren't you scared? Supposing it really was him who put the stone on?"

"But it couldn't have been," Stefan pointed out. "He was upstairs. He couldn't have been up there and down in the cellar at the same time."

"Hmmmm." I wondered at Stefan's composure. If it had been me, I doubted I could have thought things through so clearly. "Stefan?"

"Yes?"

"Did you see those—things—in the well?" I knew that he had.

"Mmm-hmm." He seemed reluctant to say more.

"Well . . . how do you know it wasn't him who put them there?"

"It *couldn't* have been him, Pia. He wouldn't have helped me get you out of the well. He would probably have . . ." His voice trailed off.

I guessed that he was thinking the same as I was, that if it had been Herr Düster who had put those things in the well, there would have been nothing easier in the whole world than to just go down to the cellar, with Stefan unsuspecting, and tip him in after me. I felt cold thinking of the risk he had run. With an effort I tried to wrench myself back to the business at hand.

"Do you think he knew about the tunnel?"

"No . . ." Stefan shook his head. "I think he hardly even knew about the room with the well in it. I mean, he must have known it was there, but he'd practically forgotten about it. I don't think he goes into the cellar much."

I thought of the disarray, the dusty sticks of furniture, the half-hearted attempts to hang a few things from the walls. "I guess not."

"He wouldn't have gone in there if I hadn't gone in first," said Stefan. "He said something funny, you know, like 'I see you have been busy, young man' or something like that."

I raised my eyebrows, forgetting that Stefan could hardly make out my face in the dark. It was almost impossible to imagine Herr Düster saying anything like that. Before tonight he had seemed the most taciturn man on the planet. Discovering that he owned an enormous Mercedes with chrome fenders and tail fins had been enough of a surprise. If he had ripped open his shabby old checked shirt to reveal a superhero's costume underneath I could not have been more amazed.

"He hates kids," I pointed out dazedly.

Stefan shrugged. For a moment he was silent, then: "He's gone. Look." We both peered out through the windshield. The whirling snowflakes seemed to have stopped, and we had a clear view of the dark form of the other car standing out against the luminous white of the snow. There was no sign of Herr Düster or anyone else near it.

"So?" I realized my teeth were starting to chatter again. Now that the engine was no longer running the temperature in the car was dropping and in my wet clothes I was starting to feel seriously chilled.

"So, we get out and look. Or—no." Stefan broke off suddenly. "You stay here. *I'll* go. I'll come back and tell you if I see anything."

"Why you?"

"Because it's freezing out there." He reached out and touched the back of my hand. "*Mensch,* Pia, you're like a block of ice."

"It's the wet," I said miserably.

"Look, I'll get out and see if I can find Herr Düster. I'll shut the door as quickly as I can. You keep the doors and windows shut, OK?"

I nodded unhappily.

"Maybe . . . maybe you should lock the doors as well."

I didn't allow myself to think too carefully about that. "All right."

"I'll try to be quick." Stefan opened the door and instantly there was an influx of glacially cold air. I shrank back like a plant wilting under a late frost. The next second the door had closed again, then Stefan moved past the window. A moment later he had gone and I was alone.

Chapter Fifty-two

⚜

After what seemed like half an hour but was probably only ten minutes, I looked at my watch, but it could tell me nothing: water had seeped into the casing and the second hand had stuck at six.

I hugged myself and tried to breathe life into my frozen fingers. The car windows were slowly becoming opaque. I rubbed at them, wincing at the damp cold, but there was no sign of life outside the portholes that I made. I leaned into the front to see whether Herr Düster had left the keys in the ignition, wondering whether I would have the confidence to try starting the engine, but they were gone.

"Hurry up," I muttered through clenched teeth, shivering. Even assuming that it was Herr Schiller's car at the bridge, it seemed highly unlikely that Herr Düster and Stefan would bring him back between them, hog-tied and bloody-handed. I was starting to think that we might have done better to take up Herr Düster's original suggestion and call the police instead. If I had to stay much longer in the car I would actually freeze to death, and add my name to the roll of victims. Immobility was definitely making things worse. If I had been able to stamp my feet or really wheel my arms about, I might have brought life back to my extremities. I looked at my watch again, pointlessly.

Why not get out of the car? The thought kept hovering around. The idea had its attractions: the temperature was falling inside the car and very soon there would be little advantage in being there. If I climbed out, I could stamp my feet, wave my arms, run up and down if I wanted to. The snow was no longer falling and as far as I could tell there was no wind to flay my freezing legs. If I saw Herr Düster or Stefan I could call to them and tell them that we had to go for help before I died of cold.

There was also a sly thought burgeoning at the back of my mind, that perhaps it might be *me* who played the leading role in the drama; it might be *me* who saw where Herr Schiller had gone, or found a clue in the snow, another furry boot or a dropped hair ribbon. The thought persisted until it was more strident than the fear urging me to stay where I was, in the safety of the car. It was infuriating to be told to sit there while the menfolk went off and performed all the heroics, as though I were not quite as old as Stefan or just as brave. I bit my lip, considering. Then with resolution I slid along the seat and opened the door.

Stepping out into the cold was like hitting a wall. The sheer physical impact of it made me stagger. I stood for a moment with my hand on the door, then I pushed it shut. I must keep moving. I stamped furiously in the snow, trying to bring life back to my feet. My boots were no longer actually sloshing with water, but the lining was all sodden. My jeans felt like cardboard.

I knew this was a bad idea, even without Oma Kristel's memory hovering at my shoulder like a guardian angel, telling me to get back indoors and drink something hot before I caught my death. I kicked at the snow as though to push the thought away. Frau Kessel, Hilde Koch, my parents, even poor Oma Kristel: they were always telling me what was good for me. Just for once I wanted to strike out, to do something audacious. In truth I wanted it to be *me* who was surrounded by admiring faces back at the school, with everyone begging me to tell them how I'd done it.

Hugging myself against the cold, I followed the others' footsteps to the other car: Herr Düster's long narrow ones and Stefan's short rugged ones. Sometimes Stefan had walked in Herr Düster's tracks and it was no longer possible to distinguish between them, but when they came to the parked car they parted. Herr Düster seemed to have walked almost

258 · HELEN GRANT

the whole way around it, and to have backtracked several times; I guessed he had been checking the vehicle thoroughly in case anyone was still inside. Afterward he had struck off up the Tal. Stefan appeared to have peeled off Herr Düster's tracks just before he got to the car, and to have headed uphill toward the woods.

I looked for other tracks. At first I saw nothing, but then I realized I could pick out a third set leading away from the car. These must be Herr Schiller's, assuming that it really *was* him, and not some innocent person just trying to reach home in the dark. I soon saw why the others had not been able simply to follow them: they curved around and went down toward the river, its waters flowing black and sluggish between slabs of ice.

It was not difficult to understand the reasoning behind it: the fugitive would have some minutes of severe discomfort from his freezing feet and ankles, but the water was not very deep, and it would cover his tracks completely. He might have gone up or down river, and he could have come out on either side.

I looked left and right, but there was no sign of either Herr Düster or Stefan. I looked back at the car. The cold on my damp legs was so intense it felt as though the skin were peeling off. I hugged myself and tried to tuck my chin into the collar of my down jacket. A stifled sob choked its way out of me, but I realized with a mounting sense of desolation that there was no one to hear it. There was nothing for it but to keep moving.

I decided to follow the river, taking a little-used path on the opposite side from the main track. In the summer months the path was overgrown with grass and weeds, but now it was blank and white with snow like everything else.

I set off at the briskest pace I could manage, desperate to pound some warmth back into my limbs. With the snow clouds gone and the pale winter moon shining down, I could see quite well. The wet trunks of the trees that lined the riverbank stood out like dark stripes against the white of the snow. I counted five trees, and then ten. When I had passed twenty I would turn around.

The night was absolutely silent apart from the huffing of my own breath and the crunching of snow underfoot. The woods around Mün-

stereifel are full of game—deer, hares, foxes—but now there was nothing moving among the bare trees. Glancing behind me I thought the
car seemed unimaginably far away. I counted the twentieth tree and
stood still, listening.

Somehow the silence was worse than any sound could have been,
however threatening. There was an air of expectancy about it. I thought
of Unshockable Hans, the intrepid miller, waiting and watching for the
spectral cats. The headless ghost of the evildoer, doomed to roam the
valley until someone dared speak to him.

Abruptly I stopped short, sucking in a painful breath of glacial air.
There were footprints in front of me, footprints that came from the
middle of nowhere and started in the middle of the path. The footprints
of a man: I could see the marks of heel and toe sharply defined in the
crisp snow.

For a moment I held my breath. Then with a surge of relief I exhaled.
Of course, the footprints did not *really* start in the middle of nowhere.
When I looked properly I could see brown tufts of foliage sticking up
through the kicked-over snow where he had come up the riverbank before he stepped onto the path. *Herr Schiller.*

I looked at the path ahead, looked back behind me at the bridge and
the cars, then back at the path again.

About fifty meters ahead of me there was a rocky outcrop where the
hillside met the level ground, slightly obscuring my view of the path.
The black skeletons of shrubs stuck out on it like bristles. As I watched,
a yellow glow suddenly bloomed behind the bristles, backlighting
them with a pulsing corona of dazzling brightness. I was as shocked as
if the world had tilted sideways and sent me sliding about like dice in
a cup. My brain simply refused to process what my eyes were seeing.
Dumbfounded and rooted to the spot, I watched that eerie light flame
upward, gilding the snow with its golden radiance, and then I knew: it
was the *Fiery Man of the Hirnberg.*

I think I took a step back, staggering, but I was still unable to run.
Wide-eyed and openmouthed, I saw a figure clothed in blinding flame
step from behind the outcrop, into the middle of the path, arms outspread as though crucified by the fire that streamed from every limb.

Distantly, I could hear someone screaming. *Stefan?* I dared not turn my head, as though the blazing thing would swoop upon me with those flaming talons outstretched if I took my horrified eyes off it for an instant. I took another step backward.

The fiery form was coming toward me, it was coming *nearer,* although each step was halting, as though wading through the inferno that surrounded it. I could not feel the heat yet, but I saw the incandescent figure brush against a broken branch and a bundle of desiccated leaves instantly ignited, shriveling and sparking.

Panic forced its way up inside me. I was aware that I was babbling nonsense, but I seemed to have no control over my own voice. *No, no, go away, I didn't call you, I didn't, I didn't.* Terror was expanding inside me, but still I could not run.

Paralyzed with dread, I watched Death close in on me with feet that scorched the bare earth under the snow. I thought I could feel the deadly heat of the blazing hands that were held out to me, as though in supplication. I closed my eyes against the searing brilliance of the fire, fists drawn in tight to my body as though I could somehow shrink into myself and escape the branding heat of that fiery touch. Even through closed eyelids I could see the yellow glare. A sound like a creak escaped from a throat too constricted with fear to scream. I could hear it now, the roaring and crackling.

"Go away," I whispered, and waited, my eyes still screwed tight shut, my whole body trembling. I waited. Nothing happened. Then suddenly I heard a sound that was ponderous but somehow soft, the muffled sound of a burning bonfire falling in on itself. There was warmth on my legs.

I opened my eyes. The burning figure lay outstretched on the melting snow in front of me, the clawlike left hand almost touching my boot. Flames were still licking over something horribly black and charred. I took a step backward, and then another, and then all of a sudden my paralysis had broken and I was turning to run, run for my life. My breath was painful and ragged. The glacial night air seemed to stab my frozen limbs with a thousand tiny knives. My boots skidded on snow and I almost fell, but righted myself like a galloping colt, my heart pounding as though it would burst. Anything to get away, to put as much distance as possible between myself and the thing I had seen.

I turned to look back, staggered, taking in nothing but a dizzying slice of starry sky and black branches against snow, and ran slap into something in my path. For several seconds I clawed at it, desperate to get past, shrieking in frustration, and then suddenly I realized I had run into a person. My flailing arms were being held gently but firmly by gloved hands. I felt the rasp of woolen fabric against my cheek. Words were being spoken; in the confusion born of panic I could not take them in, but the effect was calming, as though I were a terrified animal.

I pulled back a little and took in a jacket of the traditional sort, with a stand-up collar and polished horn buttons. It was probably hunter-green but in the moonlight it looked almost black. My eyes traveled upward: the face was deep in shadow underneath a jaunty Tyrolean hat. I sucked in a deep breath.

"Hans," I said, and my heart swelled with recognition. "Hans—it's you."

"Yes," he said, and his voice sounded surprised.

I flung my arms around him and clung on. Safe at last. "Unshockable Hans," I murmured over and over again into the rough wool of his jacket, as though the name itself were a talisman. "Unshockable Hans. At last."

Chapter Fifty-three

❈

W hatever else one might say about Stefan's cousin Boris, whose dubious career has probably by now culminated in a custodial sentence somewhere, he did commit at least one public-spirited action in his life. It was Boris who, having let himself out of Herr Düster's house as easily as he had let himself in, slipped into the little alley, intending to make his exit unseen, and had literally fallen over our bicycles, ripping his jeans and laying open the skin of his calf in the process.

Shielded by the alley, he had taken out his flashlight to inspect the damage. He didn't recognize my bike, but he knew Stefan's. It had a stupid hooter on it, a rubber thing shaped like the head of Dracula, with fangs agape. It was quite distinctive—I've never seen another like it. Stefan had been given it when he was a lot younger and had become attached to it, although it was so goofy-looking that it probably took his cool rating down another notch every time he took the bike out.

Boris was no Sherlock Holmes, but still he was puzzled about the bike. Perhaps another person, having found it, would have assumed that Stefan had simply left it there for reasons of his own, or that it had been stolen for a prank and dumped. But Boris had just been in Herr Düster's house, and the reason was this: he thought it was Herr Düster who was plucking girls from the streets like an elderly vampire, and he was determined to find out. Discovering the bicycles only confirmed his worst fears.

He made his way home thoughtfully, mulling the thing over while smoking a series of cigarettes, presumably for their intellect-enhancing qualities. I am still not convinced that he would have gone so far as to notify the police, but when his aunt, Stefan's mother, called the house an hour later to accuse Boris of harboring her errant son, he put two and two together and for once in his life made four.

Boris, obeying the instincts that would no doubt serve him well in his future encounters with the law, denied any knowledge of Stefan's whereabouts. Eventually, however, the matter weighed on his mind to the extent that he actually decided to do something about it. Perhaps he could no longer enjoy the bottle of Jägermeister he had filched from his father's drinks cabinet, or perhaps it was the Jägermeister that did the talking when he rang the police (anonymously, of course) and told them what he had seen.

The police had other things on their minds that evening, but all the same an officer was dispatched to check the scene. As he stood prodding the front wheel of my bicycle (sadly bent under the weight of Boris's trampling feet) with the toe of his boot, he was summoned by Hilde Koch, who was hovering on her doorstep, terrifying in a hairnet and re-volting old Birkenstocks, her nightdress hastily covered by an outdoor coat.

Frau Koch was not interested in abandoned bicycles; she wanted to know what the police were going to do about the noise and nuisance suffered by God-fearing people who were awakened in the middle of the night by a bunch of kids driving a monstrous car with tail fins up and down the street.

The mention of *kids* might have been the thing that caught some-one's attention. It turned out that two policemen sitting in their patrol car down by the station had also seen a large car with tail fins going past, with passengers both in the front and back, but it was definitely being driven by an elderly man. It was probably nothing (such was the prevailing opinion), but a patrol car was sent to check it out. In the deep snow there were virtually no other cars on the road, so it was rela-tively easy to track Herr Düster's Mercedes to the Eschweiler Tal.

The two cops in the patrol car were the genial Herr Wachtmeister

Tondorf and a younger man whom I didn't know; I think his name was Schumacher, like the race driver. Herr Wachtmeister Tondorf wasn't feeling as genial as usual, being forced to abandon his thermos of coffee to drive up a track in the snow. When they reached Herr Düster's car, he assumed the "kids" mentioned by Frau Koch had been joyriding, and had abandoned it there. He told Schumacher to get out of the car and take a look.

The younger man started to ask why it had to be *him,* but he saw Herr Wachtmeister Tondorf's expression, brows drawn together and mustache bristling, and decided to take the line of least resistance. He got out and went to look at the Mercedes. The windows were patchy with condensation so he opened the back door and looked inside.

There was no one in the car. He closed the door, and was wandering around to the rear to look at the license plate when Stefan came running up. He had an odd feverish look about him, two spots of high color standing out on his cheekbones, his face otherwise waxy and pallid.

"You've got to come," he panted.

It took a while for him to persuade the two policemen that he was not an underage joyrider. Sitting in the back of the patrol car with melted snow dripping from his clothes and boots and his voice ragged with excitement, almost bouncing on the seat in his desperation to get away, he did not make a very convincing witness, especially once Herr Wachtmeister Tondorf had recognized him.

"You're the Breuer boy, aren't you?" Herr Wachtmeister Tondorf glanced at Schumacher. "The same family as Boris Breuer," he added significantly.

"He's my cousin," said Stefan impatiently.

"Are you sure *he* wasn't driving this car, young man?" asked Herr Wachtmeister Tondorf sternly.

"Yes!" said Stefan frantically. He was squirming in anguish on the seat.

"Then who was driving the car?" Herr Wachtmeister Tondorf wanted to know.

"Herr Düster," said Stefan. The two policemen looked at each other.

"Düster? From the Orchheimer Strasse?"

"Yes." Stefan nodded.

"And you say he has this girl—Pia Kolvenbach?" Herr Wachtmeister Tondorf's voice was stern.

"Yes." Stefan realized what Herr Wachtmeister Tondorf was getting at, and suddenly he was confused. "No. I mean . . ."

But Herr Wachtmeister Tondorf was already reaching for the door handle. "You stay here, young man," said Herr Wachtmeister Tondorf severely.

"But I want to come with you," said Stefan instantly. He was rewarded with a very uncompromising stare from Herr Wachtmeister Tondorf.

"You stay in the car. Do I have to lock you in?"

"No," said Stefan unhappily, subsiding back onto the seat.

The two policemen got out of the car and walked toward Herr Schiller's car. The door was still yawning open and there was a dusting of snow on the driver's seat, but no sign of Herr Schiller or anyone else. Herr Wachtmeister Tondorf was still not sure whether he was dealing with juvenile joyriders, a couple of senile old men who had taken it into their heads to go walking in the snowy woods in the middle of the night, or an actual criminal: the person responsible for the disappearances. He thought Stefan was saying anything that came into his head in hopes of staying out of trouble, and of me he had seen no sign; he was not even convinced I was out there. He decided to take a brief look around.

And thus it was that the two policemen found me there in the Eschweiler Tal, not a stone's throw from the site of the haunted mill, almost catatonic with hypothermia, and hanging on for dear life to—Herr Düster.

Herr Düster was clasping me to the front of his green woolen hunting jacket, crushing me to him so that afterward I had the mark of one of the polished horn buttons on my cheek. He was preventing me from turning around again to look at the charred and loathsome thing lying there on a scorched patch of earth from which all the snow had melted, its blackened claws outstretched as though making one last attempt to grab me. When the policemen reached him, Herr Düster turned his head and looked at them quite levelly.

"Johannes Düster?" said Herr Wachtmeister Tondorf, and Herr Düster inclined his head.

Herr Wachtmeister Tondorf looked at his partner, Schumacher, but Schumacher was not looking at him or at Herr Düster. He had stepped forward to look at what was on the ground, the shriveled and blackened form, and he was vomiting noisily into the snowy bushes.

It was some time after we had gone, Herr Düster and Stefan to the police station and myself to the hospital in Mechernich, that the police discovered the body of Daniella Brandt. Herr Schiller, whom I had thought was my friend, kindly Herr Schiller, who let me have coffee and told me that if something needs to be done you should do it, even if you are afraid—Herr Schiller had carried her in his arms when his car could go no farther in the snow, and placed her body in the low cave that the local people call the Teufelsloch, the Devil's Hole. I had hated Daniella the day she came to our house and I screamed at her. She had revolted me with her blatant desire to get close to the epicenter of my family's pain. Now she herself would be the center of attention, her name spoken on every street corner, her family's anguish unraveled for everyone to examine.

People said afterward that it was unbelievable that a man of his age could carry a child of that size. But great emotions can give us great power, and Herr Schiller was carrying a lot of hate in his heart. They think he meant to burn the body, so that there would be nothing to link him to the crime, just as there was nothing recognizable about those things that bobbed and wallowed in the well under Herr Düster's house. He had intended that Herr Düster should be blamed for the existence of *those*, were they ever discovered.

No one knows exactly what happened out there in the snow, not even me, and I was the closest to him when the gasoline he had brought for Daniella's funeral pyre ignited like a bomb and sent him screaming and staggering into my path, a human inferno. Did he lift the gas can to pour its contents onto the corpse on its pall of pure snow, and accidentally drench himself? Did he know he had soaked himself in gasoline, and if so, why did he light a match? No one knows the answers to these questions.

Daniella did not burn; her body was spared that indignity. The policeman who peered into the Teufelsloch, scanning it with his flashlight, found her on her back with her hands folded across her stomach, as though lying in state. A poisonous scent of gasoline hung over her. Still, she looked as though she were sleeping, but for the deathly pallor of her face: a perfect snow princess, with ice crystals sparkling on her white skin and her light hair. The policeman who found her thought that perhaps some spark of life might still lurk within the coldly beautiful form. It was not until he had pulled aside the collar of her jacket to try for a pulse that he saw it was no use.

Chapter Fifty-four

I was drifting in and out of an uncomfortable sleep when my parents arrived at the hospital. My mother burst into the room, closely followed by my father and a harassed-looking doctor in a blue smock.

"Can I please ask you—" the doctor was saying plaintively, but my mother ignored her.

"Pia? Oh my God, Pia!" My mother was all over me like a maternal whirlwind, kissing my forehead and cheeks, touching my hair. "Are you all right, *Schätzchen?*"

"I'm fine," I started to say, but it came out as a croak. Even smiling felt like too much of an effort; my mother's anxiety was exhausting.

Abruptly she burst into tears. My father laid a tentative hand on her shoulder.

"Kate? She's all right."

"She's *not* all right," sobbed my mother. "Look at her. Just look what that—that—"

She let out a wail and the doctor's hands came up in a gesture of protest; there were other patients to think of; if she would just—

I think she would have told my mother to leave, except that a bell was ringing somewhere else, and she had to leave the room herself.

Silently, my father enfolded my mother in his arms. I saw him hug her to him, rubbing her back, kissing her hair. She was *letting* him, I realized, and even in my exhausted state I felt the first spurt of hope.

"She's all right, Kate, she's all right," my father was murmuring over and over again, and my mother was clinging to him. She cried for what seemed like a long time, until the last sob turned into a cough and she started trying to wipe her nose with her fingers. She raised her head at last, and her face was only inches from my father's. For a moment they stared at each other.

Then my mother said, softly, "I'm sorry, Wolfgang," and putting up her hands she very gently pushed him away.

I could hardly bear to look at my father's face.

"Kate," he said, and there was a question in his voice.

Slowly my mother shook her head. She stood there for a moment, not looking at him, her head turned to one side. Then she said rather too loudly, "One of us should stay here. Why don't you get the bag from the car?" The last few words were tremulous.

My father came up to the bed and took my hand for a moment, pressing it with his strong fingers. Then he turned and went out of the room. He must have come back sometime later with my mother's bag, but by then I was asleep.

I was in Mechernich Hospital for two days, and it would have been longer had my mother not broken me out of there. If you are admitted to a hospital in Germany you can expect to be there for a full seven days—or, at least, you could when I was a child and the health insurance was still paying for anything you cared to have. My mother, however, was having none of it. She packed up my things and buttoned me into a new fur-lined jacket. Then she dragged me downstairs to the car.

"Oma Warner's arriving this afternoon," she informed me as she reversed out of the parking space, so rapidly that I feared for the cars parked on the other side.

"Are we going to get her?" I asked.

"No." My mother rammed the car into gear and gunned the engine. "She's taking a taxi from the airport this time. I said we'd pay."

"Oh." I supposed this was for my benefit; the invalid had to be rushed home and kept there.

The mention of Oma Warner made me uncomfortable: there was still the matter of the telephone bill, though I hoped it might somehow have been forgotten among the recent dramas. I looked out of the window at Mechernich speeding past. It was as bad as Middlesex: gray streets and rain-slicked pavements. The weather was never so severe here as it was in Bad Münstereifel for some reason, and the snow that had fallen had quickly thawed. Brown mush clogged the gutters. I leaned my forehead on the cool glass and sighed.

Chapter Fifty-five

I saw Herr Düster only once more in my life. I wouldn't have seen him at all, but for my father's insistence. My mother was adamant that I should not have anything more to do with him. Even when it was clear that he was completely innocent of any kidnapping or killing, now or ever, she was still furious with him for taking me to the Eschweiler Tal, where I might have died of hypothermia—or worse.

In fact, in her mind the entire town was guilty by association. It was typical, she said, that every person in the whole place could spend all their spare time discussing other people's business and still miss what was really going on under their very noses. The sooner she, Sebastian, and I were out of the place forever, the better.

Oma Warner didn't add anything to this, but she pursed her lips and went about the place silently, folding things and shelving things and packing things up for the move. She and my father behaved as though they were ambassadors from hostile countries, too polite to indulge in open warfare, yet unable to be warm to each other, even at Christmas. Unexpectedly, however, she came out on my father's side when I raised the question of whether I might see Herr Düster.

My mother said I was visiting him over her dead body, but both my father and Oma Warner thought it would be a good idea. Nowadays people like to use that American word *closure,* but Oma Warner just said she thought it would help me to put the whole thing behind me for good.

I wasn't allowed to go to Herr Düster's house. Instead he was permitted to come to our house, where my mother (who opened the door) eyed him suspiciously. She let him stand on the doorstep for a few seconds too long before she stepped back to let him in. Herr Düster doffed his hat and stepped somewhat gingerly into the hallway.

"*Guten Tag,* Herr Düster," said my mother; she was unable to keep the chill out of her voice.

"*Guten Tag,* Frau Kolvenbach," said Herr Düster politely. He didn't try to win her over with smiles and compliments; charm was never his strong point, and anyway, my mother was distinctly unreceptive. She hardly said another word to him before she ushered him into the living room, where I was waiting.

"Pia? If you want anything, just . . . *yell,*" she said with heavy emphasis as she closed the door. I didn't reply. I imagine if Herr Düster had lived in the town for much longer he would have had to become inured to innuendo—since Herr Schiller was not there, he was the only possible target for gossip and speculation. *Where there's smoke, there's fire* is the town motto: they should have engraved it on a crest and stuck it on the front of the *Rathaus.* I doubt Herr Düster's reputation as town reprobate would have improved even if it had become known that he had grappled with half a dozen murderers single-handed and brought the lot of them to justice.

Herr Düster put his hat on the coffee table and sat on an armchair a little distance from me. He did not seem inclined to say anything.

"Herr Düster—thank you," I blurted out in a rush.

A faint smile sketched itself on his gaunt features. "I hope you have fully recovered?"

"Yes—thank you." I fell silent for a moment. There were so many things I wanted to ask him, but I could not think of any way to introduce the topics. If I had been a little older, as I am now, I might have known the way to do it. But at that time the tremendous age gap yawned between us.

"I'm very sorry," said Herr Düster at last. I looked at him, wondering why *he* was sorry.

"Herr Düster?" I couldn't help it; my voice was trembling. "Why do you think he did it?"

"My brother, Heinrich, was sick," he replied gently. "I think he had been sick for a long time."

"Yes, but *why* did he do it?"

Herr Düster sighed. "I don't really think it is a suitable topic for a young lady . . ."

My heart sank; he was going to pull that favorite stunt of adults on me, and tell me that I was too young to understand.

"But I think all the same you have a right to know," he finished. He gazed past me for a moment at a blank spot on the wall. I knew he was seeing things that had happened a long time ago.

"Did you know that Heinrich was married?" he asked.

I nodded. "Yes, and he had a daughter. Frau Kessel said I looked a bit like her," I added, and saw a shadow pass across Herr Düster's face.

"A little, yes," he said. "Gertrud was perhaps slightly thinner than you are. But that was the war, of course . . ." He paused, remembering. "Heinrich was never an easy person, not as a young man. He had a hardness in his heart somehow. Once he made up his mind to do something . . . he could be very hard on other people, too, if he made a judgment."

I said nothing to this; none of it sounded like *my* Herr Schiller. But on the other hand *my* Herr Schiller would not have been in the Eschweiler Tal on a freezing night, trying to splash gasoline on the corpse of a young girl. I shivered.

"Hannelore—Heinrich's wife—she was very beautiful, you know," went on Herr Düster.

I thought of Frau Kessel, spitting venom in her kitchen: *Both brothers were mad about the girl, but she chose Heinrich. Who can blame her?*

"Is that a picture of her in your house?" I blurted without thinking.

Herr Düster looked at me. "No. I don't believe there is a photograph of her anywhere in existence." He did not say, *Why should I have a photograph of her?* I noticed. I thought there was a slight undercurrent of wistfulness in his voice, as though he should like to have had one.

"Heinrich—well, he made a mistake about Hannelore," continued Herr Düster. He paused, and his gnarled fingers rubbed the arm of the chair, making little circles. "He thought she really wanted to leave him. He used to get—very angry with her. He had some idea that Gertrud wasn't—that she was . . ." His voice trailed off. He was old, after all, incredibly ancient in my eyes, and I was only a child. He was of a different generation, one that thought unpleasantness was better not discussed in front of children. All the same, I thought I heard him say one single word in a very low voice: *Meine. He thought she was mine.* I said nothing.

"They say," went on Herr Düster almost to himself, "that they might have to exhume Hannelore. They think perhaps it wasn't natural causes."

I remembered what Frau Kessel had said about the scene she had witnessed between Herr Düster and his brother's wife. The ranting, the pulling away, Herr Düster trying to kiss Hannelore's hand. *He thought no one would see them, but I did.* Had Herr Düster really cornered his unwilling sister-in-law and tried to kiss her? Or had the argument been about something else? About protecting Hannelore from her husband? *I don't know what it was she had . . . it could have been anything.*

"And Gertrud?" I prompted tentatively.

"In the well," said Herr Düster. He sounded weary, as though he would like to get the story told and over with. "They say it has to be verified, but yes, they think it is her. She was the first one, they think, the oldest . . ." He looked at me with bloodshot eyes. "How could he do it, that's what everyone wants to know. How could he do it?"

"His own daughter," I said, and the idea was horrible, nasty, framed in words I wanted to spit out as soon as possible, like the girl in the story from whose mouth toads dropped every time she spoke. *His own daughter.*

"Yes, but that was it, you see," said Herr Düster softly. "He didn't think she *was* his own daughter. He thought when she disappeared it would hurt *me.* He thought he was taking away any chance I had of ever . . ." He was silent for a few moments, then he went on: "Heinrich was not the man to support a child who was not his own, you know. Not to love a child, even if she called him Papa."

"That's horrible," I exclaimed, and drew Herr Düster's grave gaze to me.

"He was her father," he said. His voice was helpless. "She was his daughter—and he killed her." His eyes seemed to blur and brim over, and at last a single tear ran down one gaunt cheek.

We sat in silence for a while. It was late in the afternoon and the light was fading. It was becoming gloomy in the room, with its small windows. If I did not get up soon and put the lights on, we would be sitting in the dark.

"I don't see what Katharina Linden had ever done to him," I said eventually. "Or Julia Mahlberg, or anyone else."

"They did nothing," replied Herr Düster sadly.

"Then why—?"

"I think he was trying to get at me," said Herr Düster. "I think he thought that every time another girl went missing, I would think of Gertrud. He—Heinrich—was very sick, you know. And of course he would have known what everyone was saying, about who was taking these girls."

I *did* know what everyone had said, at least everyone as personified by Frau Kessel. Everyone thought Herr Düster had done it. He would have been lynched if a few more levelheaded people hadn't insisted on letting the law take its course instead—people like my father. And then, when he had been driven out of the town, or even arrested for something he hadn't done, someone would have searched his house, and there in the cellar they would have found all the evidence they needed. Herr Schiller had only to brick up the tunnel again and no one would have been any the wiser.

I heard later that the tunnel had been there for hundreds of years. Older residents of the town said it was not the only tunnel; the ancient streets were riddled with them, a rotten honeycomb underlying the neat rows of houses. There used to be a synagogue on the Orchheimer Strasse, where now there is nothing but a memorial to the Jewish community who vanished in the war. They think the tunnels enabled the Jews to go about on the Sabbath, when they were forbidden by their faith to go out into the street. How and when Herr Schiller came upon the one under his house, it is now impossible to say.

I was dazed by the enormity of what Herr Schiller had done. People did things I didn't like, things I *hated*, every day. If I had heard that Thilo Koch had been trampled by wild horses or had fallen into the big cats' enclosure at Köln Zoo and been rent limb from limb while screaming for mercy, I would not have been sorry. But I wouldn't have pushed him in there. "I still don't understand," I said. "*Why* did he do it?"

Herr Düster was silent for so long that I thought perhaps he had not heard the question. Then he uttered just one word in a low voice. *Hass.* Hate.

Chapter Fifty-six

※

We stayed in Bad Münstereifel a few weeks more, long enough to see the new year in: the year 2000, although the millennium celebrations mostly passed us by. I did not see Herr Düster again, and I heard later that he had outlived his brother by only a few months. When Boris had told Stefan that Herr Düster was sick, he was right: the old man had cancer, and at the end it carried him off very quickly. I'm thankful for that.

I have often wondered about him and his brother, how the hatred between them could have led to what happened, and why it seemed to accelerate toward the end: four girls taken in one year. I think perhaps Herr Schiller knew that they were both dying, and he was determined to wreak his revenge before it was forever beyond his power to hurt his brother, Johannes.

I wonder if the fact that Herr Düster never reacted infuriated him, and drove him on? Even though Herr Düster was cast as the town villain, he never indulged in any unseemly displays of emotion. Not when the woman he had loved faded away and died. Not when his brother changed his name as a sly means of accusation. Not even on the day when (as later publicized by that inexhaustible supply of local information, Frau Kessel) he opened his front door to find a little packet on the doorstep, a packet containing a child's hair ribbon. Or the time it was a single glove, a little girl's glove.

If his brother had hoped to provoke him, he failed, or at any rate he failed to taunt him into any public signs of grief or anger. Herr Düster had simply called the police, as any good citizen might, and had been taken off in a patrol car, stony-faced, seemingly unmoved, to help them with their inquiries. The fact that this had been interpreted by Herr Düster's neighbors as an arrest for abduction and murder can only have gladdened the icy splinter that was all that was left of Heinrich Schiller's heart. He would have liked to see his brother, Johannes, torn to pieces by the citizens of Bad Münstereifel, their fists and nails and teeth the instruments of his vengeance. It must have eaten him up inside, the fact that his brother never reacted. That he never succeeded in shocking him.

The police traced the call placed by Boris on the night of our adventure; Stefan's cousin, in spite of his almost professional burglary skills, had failed to take the simple precaution of calling from a public phone. Or perhaps the Jägermeister was responsible for this oversight. Boris made some attempt to conceal the reasons for his presence in the Orchheimer Strasse that night, but dissembling was not his strong point. He made one unfortunate remark, tried to backtrack, and tripped himself up again.

Eventually the whole story came out. It was Boris who had acquired one of Marion Voss's shoes, by the simple expedient of paying Thilo Koch to steal one for him from the rack at the *Grundschule*. It was Boris and his friends who were responsible for burning it, late one night on the Quecken hill, and it was in an attempt to obtain further items belonging to the dead girls that Boris had broken into Herr Düster's house that night.

Shamefacedly, he was forced to admit that he and his cronies had been attempting a kind of black mass, inspired more by popular television programs than any actual arcane knowledge. Hunched around the stone circle they had built in the ruined castle, they had done a little chanting and drumming, and a lot of smoking (not all of it tobacco), and attempted to raise the spirit of Marion Voss.

Did he do this sort of thing on a regular basis? the police had asked him incredulously, and Boris had had to admit that yes, he had tried it after Katharina Linden had disappeared; when nothing happened he had hit upon the idea of using possessions in the ritual belonging to the missing girls. When the police had discovered the burned remains of a shoe and connected it with the disappearances, Boris had been struck with terror, foreseeing that his involvement would propel him to the head of the list of suspects.

Unfortunately he was not even able to offer any psychic clues to the murders since the spirits of the dead girls had refused to appear at all. Who could blame them? If the dead come back to tell us anything, they are unlikely to say it to a group of scruffy strangers smoking pot at midnight in a wood, one of whom, it seems, was also too drunk to stand up. Boris claimed that he had been trying to find out where the bodies were by asking the girls themselves, but later it went around that he had been trying to get them to tell him the following week's lottery numbers. I have no idea which of these is true, but the latter story stuck to Boris and will probably pursue him for life.

As for me, I spent a long time secretly worrying about Oma Warner's telephone bill. Up until Christmas Eve she had still not said anything, but I did not like the way that she glanced at me, eyebrows raised, whenever the phone rang and my mother said, "It's for you, Pia." I had visions of her waiting until we were all assembled for Christmas dinner and then announcing it in front of the entire family: *Did you know that Pia ran up* a thousand pounds *on my telephone bill, and me a pensioner?* I tried to avoid her, as though she were a walking time bomb. If we spent too much time together, she might say something.

In Germany everyone opens their Christmas presents on Christmas Eve, not Christmas Day, a fact that my mother had long bemoaned: she said it was ludicrous letting the children open their presents at eight o'clock at night and then expecting them to go straight to bed like lambs. But then my mother was not one to give her wholehearted approval to German customs.

When we assembled for the annual exchange of gifts, Oma Warner had still not said anything. I purposely sat as far away from her as possible. Still, it was not likely that I would get away without any contact with her at all. I had to get up and hand her the little parcel of scented soap that was purportedly from me and Sebastian, and she had to hand me her gift in return.

We didn't often see Oma Warner at Christmas, so she usually sent me an envelope with a cheery card and a twenty-Deutschmark note inside it; she got the Deutschmarks from the travel agent in Hayes. I was not surprised therefore when she handed me a little envelope, slightly fat as though something were folded inside.

"Say thank you, Pia," said my mother, and dutifully I parroted, "Thank you."

Oma Warner waited until my mother was looking elsewhere and mimed *stop* at me, putting up one ring-encrusted hand. *Stop, don't open it.* I tucked the envelope into the little pile of presents I had already opened. Later, when my mother was in the kitchen swearing at the turkey in two languages, I slipped upstairs to my bedroom.

Sitting on my bed, I tore open the envelope Oma Warner had given me. Out fell what I first thought was confetti, but then realized were the pieces of a red telephone bill, torn to tiny shreds. I sat on my bed with a lapful of ripped-up telephone bill, reading the card, which read, *Happy Christmas to a favourite granddaughter,* and really I did not know whether to laugh or cry.

That part of my life is closed now. After more than seven years in England, German words are becoming like an unfamiliar taste in my mouth. When I think of my conversations with Stefan, with my classmates, with Herr Schiller, sometimes I remember them in English. It's strange to think that if I have children myself one day, then whenever they visit their grandfather they will speak to him in English and he will reply to them in English too, his accent strange in their ears. We will open our Christmas presents on December 25. We won't celebrate St. Martin's Day at all.

Thinking about my friends in Germany is always a little painful because I can't help but remember the goodbyes, just as you can't watch a sad film a second time without thinking about the ending. So I don't often think about Bad Münstereifel, about Stefan, and Herr Schiller, and Oma Kristel. Or about Herr Düster, the last time I saw him, standing on the doorstep of our house in the Heisterbacher Strasse, with his Tyrolean hat in his gnarled old hand.

"*Auf Wiedersehen,* Herr Düster," I had said, very politely, before he stepped out of my life forever. And he had looked at me very solemnly and said:

"Hans. Please, call me Hans."

Glossary of German Words and Phrases

aber	but
Abitur	high school graduation examination
Ach, Kind	Oh, child!
Alte Burg	The Old Castle
Ach so!	Aha! I see!
Angsthasen	"Scaredy-rabbits"—the German equivalent of "scaredy-cats"
Apfelstreusel	apple cobbler
auch	also
Auf Wiedersehen	Goodbye (formal)
Bis gleich!	See you in a minute!
bitte	please
Bitte schön	You're welcome
Blödmann	stupid fool
Blödsinn	stupid tricks, messing about
böse	bad, angry
Bürgermeister	mayor
Danke	Thank you
dein	yours
doch	yes, indeed

Dornröschen	Briar Rose, the sleeping beauty
Du bist pervers	You're sick
Dummkopf	blockhead, idiot
etwas seltsam	something strange
Fachwerk	half-timbering
Fettmännchen	small coin (now obsolete)
Fettsack	Fatso
Frau	Mrs., Ms.
Fräulein	Miss
furchtbar	terrible
Gänsebraten	roast goose
gerne	willingly, gladly
Gott	God
Grossmutter	Grandmother
Grundschule	Elementary school
Guten Abend	Good evening
Guten Morgen	Good morning
Guten Tag	Good day
Gymnasium	the most academic type of high school, offering the university entrance exam
Hasse	hate
Hauptschule	less academic type of high school, often leading to vocational training
Heckflosse	tail fin
Herr	Mr.
Herr Wachtmeister	Constable
Hexe	witch
Hilfe!	Help!
Himmel!	Heavens!
Hör auf!	Stop it!
Ich gehe mit meiner Laterne	I'm going along with my lantern
Ich hasse euch beide	I hate you both
Ich kenn' dich nicht, ich geh' nicht mit	I don't know you, so I won't go with you
Ich meine	I mean
Ihr beide seid auch Scheisse	You're both shit too
Ihr seid total blöd	You (pl.) are totally stupid

In Gottes Namen	In God's name
Jägermeister	a German liqueur made with herbs and spices
Kaufhof	a well-known German department store
Kind	child
Klasse	great, fantastic
Köln	Cologne
Kölner Stadtanzeiger	a regional newspaper
Komisch	funny
Leberwurst	liver sausage
Liebe	Dear
Lieber Gott	Dear God
Maibaum	a May tree
Mäuselein	"Little mouse"; a term of endearment
meine	my, mine
Mein Gott	My God
Meine Gute!	My goodness!
Mein Licht ist aus, ich geh' nach Haus	My light is out, I'm going home
Mensch!	Wow! Oh boy!
Mist	crap
natürlich	Of course
Na, und?	So what?
Nee	No, nope (informal)
Nun	Now, well
Oberlothringen	Upper Lorraine
Oder?	Right? OK?
O Gott	Oh God
Oma	grandma
Onkel	uncle
Opa	grandpa
Pause	break time
Pech gehabt!	Hard luck!
Pfarrer	Father (i.e., a priest)
Quälgeister	pests
Quatsch	nonsense
Ranzen	school satchel
Rathaus	town hall

Rosenmontag	Karneval Monday
Sankt	saint
Sankt Martin ritt durch Schnee und Wind	St. Martin rode through snow and wind
Schätzchen	"My treasure"; a term of endearment
Scheisse	shit
Scheissköpfe	idiots (rude)
schön	good, lovely
Schrulle	hag or crone
seltsam	strange
sicher	certainly
Stollen	fruit loaf made at Christmastime
Strasse	street
Tal	valley
Tante	aunt
Teufelsloch	Devil's Hole
Tor	gate or archway; in Bad Münstereifel each *tor* is a tower with an archway underneath it
Tschüss!	Bye! (informal)
Tut mir Leid	I'm sorry
Um Gottes Willen!	For Heaven's sake!
und	and
unverschämt	shameless, brazen
Verdammt!	Damn!
Verdammter	bloody (rude)
verflixten	blasted, damned
verstanden	understood
Vorsicht!	Look out!
weggezaubert	made to disappear by magic
Werkbrücke	Works Bridge—a Bad Münstereifel landmark
Wie, bitte?	I beg your pardon?
Wo ist meine Tochter?	Where is my daughter?
Wurst	sausage
Zöpfe	pigtails or braids

Baron Münchhausen (Chapter One) was an eighteenth-century German baron renowned for his extravagant tall tales.

Frau Holle (Chapter Twenty-one) is a character from a German fairy tale. She is an old woman who lives down a well; she rewards her hardworking servant girl with a shower of gold and her lazy servant with a shower of pitch.

Decke Tönnes (Chapter Twenty-nine) is a shrine to St. Anthony, located high on a hill in the woods near Bad Münstereifel.

Karneval (Chapter Six) is the carnival season, which starts on November 11 but reaches its climax on Rosenmontag, the Monday before Ash Wednesday. Karneval is celebrated by *Sitzungen,* which are shows incorporating dancing, singing, and comedy turns, and also by Karneval processions, which take place on or around Rosenmontag.

Kristallnacht (Chapter Thirty-three), November 9–10, 1938, was the infamous night during which the Nazis murdered and deported Jewish people living in Germany, and ransacked thousands of Jewish businesses and synagogues. The name Kristallnacht ("Crystal Night") refers to the huge amount of broken glass from shopwindows.

The **Ruhrgebiet** (Chapter Twenty-four) is a heavily industrialized area associated with coal mining and steel production. It belongs to the same German state as Bad Münstereifel (North Rheinland Westphalia) but lies north of the Eifel.

Acknowledgments

I would like to thank Camilla Bolton of the Darley Anderson Agency for her support, encouragement, and honesty. I would also like to thank Kate Burke Miciak, vice president, editorial director of Bantam Books/Delacorte Press, for her unbounded enthusiasm and vision. Thanks are due to my husband, Gordon, for his unflagging support and for believing in *The Vanishing of Katharina Linden* right from the beginning. Last but not least I would like to thank all my friends in Bad Münstereifel, for helping me to learn so much about the history, legends, and culture of the Eifel.

ABOUT THE AUTHOR

HELEN GRANT was born in London. She read classics at St. Hugh's College, Oxford, and then worked in marketing for ten years in order to fund her love of traveling. In 2001 she and her family moved to Bad Münstereifel in Germany, and while exploring the legends of this beautiful town she was inspired to write her first novel. She now lives in Brussels with her husband, her two children, and a small German cat. Delacorte will publish her second novel, *The Glass Demon*.

ABOUT THE TYPE

This book was set in Garamond No. 3, a variation of the classic Garamond typeface originally designed by the Parisian type cutter Claude Garamond (1480–1561).

Claude Garamond's distinguished romans and italics first appeared in *Opera Ciceronis* in 1543–44. The Garamond types are clear, open, and elegant.